About the author

Tony Kaplan, when not immersed in his writing, paints portraits of characterful people, leads a long-established drum circle, and finds time to travel the world with his camera. He was, for thirty years in the NHS, a pioneering consultant child and adolescent psychiatrist and family therapist. He grew up in an activist family in South Africa, leaving his homeland in his twenties having refused, after medical school, to serve in apartheid's army. He now lives in London.

SIGNS OF A STRUGGLE

Tony Kaplan

SIGNS OF A STRUGGLE

Vanguard Press

VANGUARD PAPERBACK

© Copyright 2020
Tony Kaplan

A CIP catalogue record for this title is
available from the British Library.

ISBN 978 1 784656 00 3

*Vanguard Press is an imprint of
Pegasus Elliot MacKenzie Publishers Ltd.*
www.pegasuspublishers.com

First Published in 2020

**Vanguard Press
Sheraton House Castle Park
Cambridge England**

Printed & Bound in Great Britain

Dedication

For those who have suffered and for those who have
died in their struggles for freedom and justice.

Acknowledgements

I am grateful to the many people who helped and inspired me in getting this book written. I thank especially Malcolm Kohll and Mariel Kaplan for reading the first draft of this novel and giving me incisive feedback; Colin Moss for his suggestions about pacing after reading the second draft; Faye Zachariadis for checking my rendition of Greek phrases and forms; Barbara Trapido for her enthusiasm for my writing which gave me the confidence to persist; Costa Gavras whose movie, *Z*, started my fascination with Greek political history; my cousins who married Greek men; my wife and children who share my love of Greece; and Julian Morris, whose wide-eyed credulity and wonderment in response to my riffing on some of the characters in the Greek village our families stayed in all those years ago, convinced me I had a story worth telling.

Prologue

"He knew he would die long before they killed him. After they'd burned the soles off his feet and gouged out his eyes, all he could see were his sons' faces when they told them their father was dead; his youngest not understanding why his father had gone forever, his wife moaning and trembling, her hands over her face. He gave no names – he would never give up his comrades to them – I could have told them that. But once the torture started, it would only finish when the torturers had had enough, when they'd shown the American how ruthless Greeks could be in eradicating the filth of communism. Once the torture had gone that far, then it was certain the man would die. He knew that. But when they took him from the car, his mouth was numb. He wet himself, the stain spreading, and with it his shame, which he vainly tried to hide from the men he knew were watching and judging. I don't know for certain whether he knew that I was there, but I believe he did. His legs could not bear his weight and his shoes, loose without the laces they'd taken from him so he would not hang himself in his cell, made a trail in the dust as they dragged him to his place of execution on the wasteland behind the town's dump, beyond the first ridge of hills. As they pushed him to the ground, he tried to scramble away, slithering on his belly, his fingers clawing at the sand. He knew it was no use, but I understood his wish to go to his death resisting them, not giving in. A boot on his back forced him down. All of this in silence. The American grinned, his eyes under his dark glasses, hidden, his trousers sharply creased. The man, his face pressed to the earth, would have felt the metal of the gun in his neck. The air went out of him. I thought I heard him groan, *'Eleftheria',* but this may have been what I wished, my prayer for him. Then the explosion, brief, discreet. His body went tense… *ena lepto…* and then he relaxed.

"The American shook a packet of cigarettes loose, placed one on his thin lips and offered the pack around. The executioner unrolled the tension from his neck and shoulders and took one. His men murmured and each accepted the gift. The American flicked his lighter open and a flame sprang up, and the faces of the defenders of Greek purity were lit, as they leaned forward, like a Caravaggio, proud and mean. Then the American, exhaling a thick cloud of fragrant tobacco in my face, offered the pack to me. I am ashamed of it now as I tell you this, but although my hand was shaking, I took a cigarette and allowed him to light it for me.

"I have carried the ghost of that man on my back for nearly 40 years. He never leaves me, and I must not desert him. To do this, I must be a wandering spirit. This is how my debt is paid.

"Greeks in all their wars have said *Eleftheria i Thanatos*. Freedom or Death. There have been many wars. Many people died. Who is free? Am I free? You tell me."

****

1

The day I arrive on the island, I hear about the body in the bridge.

"Un-be-*lieve*-able!" Yiannis sets down the tiny white cup of dark coffee and a glass of water on my table facing the sea, the pale blue water in the bay glistening in the still fierce heat. The table is in the shade of an ancient tamarisk tree, its trunk twisted and deeply lined, its bark whitened with lime to keep away the ants. "Unbelievable!" he says again, "A hand - sticking out the cement - like this!" He shows me, his arm outstretched into a balled fist, his face contorted in disgust.

"Yianni! *Ela!*" His wife calls him. Yiannis, sighing his protest, goes back into the tiny kitchen where all the food for the *taverna* is prepared on a two-plate electric cooker and a charcoal burner to see what she wants.

When I'd arrived at the island's airport earlier, I'd expected to see Lucy waiting for me. The terminal building was a low-roofed single room with a glass partition to separate the newly arrived from the already there. Nauseous and bone-jangled from the ride on the single prop island-hopper which had brought me to Mythos from Athens, I'd managed to retain a hope that, against the odds, she'd be there. I'd searched for her face amongst the bored faces waiting for their relatives to appear. I don't know how I'd managed to convince myself, to believe, she'd actually come to fetch me. She hadn't replied to any of my messages. My forefingers-to-temples eyes-tightly-shut visualising a positive outcome hadn't seemed to work.

Striding out from the conditioned air of the terminal building, I slammed into the dry heat, like something solid, like a fist in the chest, the blazing sunlight dazzling white. I fumbled in my pocket and extracted my shades, and looked around. The lenses polarised the vast dome of cloudless sky a cartoon blue, like it had been photoshopped with

13

'saturation' on max. Greece. Blue and white. My feet on the ground for the first time in the land of my father's birth.

In front of me, a row of taxis pretended indifference – Mercs, none less than ten years old, clones of white with silver trim. The driver of the saloon at the front of the queue leaned against his car, his meaty arms folded over his prodigious belly, a cigarette hanging off his lower lip. The briefest of eye contact from me, immediately but without haste, he ambled to the back of his car and opened the trunk. I passed the scrap of paper with Lucy's address in Agia Anna scrawled on it to him. He scowled at it, then nodded faintly. *"Endaxi,"* he growled and signalled for me to get in the back seat.

No traffic to speak of on the freshly-laid tar road to the village, as I'd taken in my first views of the island – scrubland and white rock all the way to the coast, and then suddenly the turquoise sea, jewel-like and immaculate. The taciturn taxi-driver liked the glide in his driving, and sped us smoothly and silently around the coast road's gentle bends.
And then we'd been held up at the bridge. The taxi driver had cloaked his frustration in long-suffering forbearance. In a gully several feet below us, the old bridge, back broken, leaned unsteadily on concrete legs poking out of a scribble of brush and weeds. Construction vehicles stood idle; demolition workers in hi-vis jackets sat on rubble, smoking. A section of the bridge had been demarcated with crime-scene tape and off to the side two figures in white forensic suits contemplated the edifice, hands on hips. A muscular young cop sat on his motorbike shouting into a phone. My driver wound down his window and let in the hot air, acrid with new tar, and called over one of the workers, his cousin, as it turned out. A body had been found in the concrete of the old bridge two weeks before, the laconic taxi driver relayed to me in an offhand way as we drove off. The body in the bridge. Was *this* the story Lucy wanted me to come to Greece for? I'd soon find out, or so I'd hoped.

I angled the air-con onto my face, closed my eyes and imagined what would be my first encounter with Lucy for more than two months. She'd be there, reading a book, her legs tucked up under her, frowning at the text earnestly, a wisp of hair to tuck back behind her ear. I'd knock on her door, a slight mocking smile playing on my lips. She'd look up slowly, irritated to be interrupted, then her kitten eyes would widen in amazement and then melt into *joy* as she'd take in that it was me. That I'd come.

This being real life, my knocking had remained unanswered. Eventually, I'd accepted that she wasn't there and let myself in. The key was under a flowerpot, the same hiding place she'd used at her flat in Amsterdam. Not very original. Then again, I'd surmised, there probably wasn't much crime in Agia Anna. Not right then, but later, I wondered who the key was meant for.

The house Lucy was renting had only enough space for a smaller version of itself. I put my suitcase against a wall so as not to intrude and poured myself a glass of cold water from the half-empty bottle of *Nero* in the fridge. The fridge was well stocked, but some of the vegetables looked senescent and a piece of cooked lamb had gone a mournful grey. The water in the bottle tasted vaguely of ammonia.

Once I'd got used to the idea that Lucy wasn't home, I thought there was no point in waiting for her, so I went down to the beach to get something to drink and maybe something to eat. There were two *tavernas* to choose from, conveniently placed side by side – a modern-European one, with clean lines and rattan furniture, condescending like an entitled, rich kid, hands on fat hips, to the more down-at-heal 'traditional' *taverna* under an old tamarisk tree next door. I'd chosen the poor cousin.

****

So, here I am now, sitting, mesmerised by the gentle undulation of the patterns on the blue sea, when Yiannis ("Call me Johnny!" – I never do) reappears with a cloth to wipe down the tables from the dust of the tamarisk tree. I ask if he knows Lucy. "The Australian? *Fiisiika!* Of course. How many people there are in this village? - I know everybuddy!" he beams prodigiously. But Yiannis hasn't seen her for a while, he'd thought she'd maybe left and gone home. "But why she no come say goodbye?" he says, sounding hurt. He calls his wife, Soulla, to check. No, they've not seen her for two weeks. His wife comes out the kitchen wiping her hands on her apron.

"I keep for her bread. *Psomi.* Every day. She no collect," she says seriously, then, eyebrows lifting, lips tightened, *"Dhen peirazei,"* she shrugs, hands open. With no more to say on the matter, she goes back inside.

About two weeks ago, the phone on my desk at New World Order had rung. I was half way out the door. "Your phone, I think," said Eric, without looking up from the book he was reading. There are only three of us on the recently downsized office staff at New World Order, the small progressive journal I write for: Marsha Galpin, the Editor, Eric Listed, the Deputy-Editor and me - sub-editor, occasional on-the-spot investigative reporter and general dog's body, a tight little hierarchy in descending order of egos. Print journalism is in freefall, so now we gather stuff from our well-sourced network of freelance reporters, turn it into readable prose, publish a bit and sell on what we can to more well-to-do sibling papers for a commission. Nothing that would need me to answer a phone when I'm already leaving it late to get to the Barbican for the legendary Ornette Coleman, anxious as I was already that the dizzying free jazz would prove to be above and beyond the fresh-cheeked young woman whom I'd persuaded to join me for the concert (and maybe for the night). Fuck it, my phone can wait, I'd thought, as I'd walked out the door.

The next morning, emerging from the fug of all the overpriced lager I'd drunk later in Soho to try to redeem myself to the girl who had not liked my taste in music at all, I remembered I'd turned my phone off before the concert, found it under a pile of clothing (my own – she had declined to come back to my flat with me), and turned it on. I made myself a strong cup of coffee and checked my messages. Two text messages – one from my sister inviting me for dinner and one from the phone company offering me a new deal.

And a voice message. From Lucy. Lucy's excited voice: "I've got *such* a good story for you, Tom. I'm in Greece. On a small island. Why don't you come visit me? I miss you… Call me." That Australian accent! - the vowels stretched and bent out of shape. Lucy! I hadn't heard from her for months, five months to be precise; five months of waiting for her to call and getting used to pretending it didn't matter that she hadn't. And now this – "I miss you" – just that, and my breathing dysregulated. *God, Lucy!* I'd been so into her. Especially after our last weekend. All those months ago. When I had, by most conventional definitions, been seriously in love with her. Then, after an *amazing* weekend (to me only, apparently), she'd upped and left on the Monday morning without even waking me to say goodbye. And nothing from her until now. "I miss you." Really?

"Don't jump in," I counselled myself wisely. Not that I am known for accepting good advice. I waited until I got to my desk at the office before trying her number. Lucy had worked as a 'stringer' for us quite a bit, but it had been a while since she had called a story in. I wanted to be able to make notes, have my props around me. I would be professional, cool and analytic. Let her do the running. I made another cup of coffee and gave myself time to surface and ponder her invitation. Was she playing me, or was she thinking seriously of us being together?

I called. No reply. The invitation to leave a message was in what I took to be Greek. I didn't understand it, but a beep is a beep, so I left a message after it. She didn't get back to me, so I left another message later and then left it at that. I didn't think too much about Lucy not calling back straight away – Lucy was like that, or at least that was my image of her – racing from one far-flung country to another to get a story, the intrepid environmental activist – more adventurous (to me, her allure) than unreliable (her reputation with Marsha and Eric, and most of our colleagues). In my mind I prompted her to call back. But nothing. Maybe she didn't miss me that much after all. I'd been right not to jump in.

A few days later, my sister, Irini, called. Lucy had left her a voicemail – on the same day she'd called me. Irini said there was something about Lucy that wasn't right. She'd sounded *too* excited about some "serious shit" her research was uncovering.

"There's something not right, Tom. Her cheerfulness sounded *wrong*... forced," said Irini. "She went off on one - bird migration patterns, wild pigs, killer fish, the smoke of forest fires in the evening sky, and god knows what, then joked about not being able to trust 'The Authorities'. I tried to call back. No reply. Nothing. No e-mails or facebook postings. You think we should be worried?" Irini said, in a worried voice.

"This *is* Lucy we're talking about, Irini," I'd patiently reassured my neurotic sister. "She's probably gone off like a hound after some environmentally subversive squirrel. You know what she's like," I told her. "Lucy's wild." I had tried to hold from my voice the pang of disappointment that Lucy hadn't called back.

I thought I was over her, but apparently *not entirely*. Straight after Irini had rung off ("Ooh, I don't know, Tom, I don't know. Something's not right." Click.), I tried to call Lucy's number again, but this time, not even voicemail. I sent an e-mail and messaged her on facebook. I didn't want my desperation to show, so kept it professional. "What's the story?" I'd written coolly. But then couldn't resist writing, "I miss you too" – and then I deleted it. I wanted her to make the moves this time. I wanted to be sure.

A week later, still no return calls from Lucy, no e-mails and no facebook activity, and Irini's view was that *not* worrying was definitely *over*-relying on a sometimes-useful psychological defence. "Tom, I know you probably don't want to get involved. But we're the only proper friends of hers I know of. She's never not been in touch with me for this long before," Irini said apologetically, her voice catching. "The only proper friends…" this was my little sister being manipulative. That kind of language made me back off instinctively. I'd been hurt before. How much did I want this? For the purposes of *this* crisis, Lucy was first and foremost Irini's *friend*.

"Of course I am worried too," I said. I wasn't really. Disappointed maybe. But worried? Not really. Not yet. What she'd told me hadn't contradicted my notions of what Lucy-being-Lucy was like. What I *did* feel, in spite of my caution, was a half-suspended excitement for the romantic possibilities of time with Lucy. Also I *was* genuinely curious about the "great" story Lucy was onto, virtuously and *professionally* curious. Segue into pleasant day-dreams of Lucy and I, side by side, deep undercover, developing startling headlining copy, our heroic quest rewarded with a Pulitzer Prize and us in bed, with me on top of her, my nose in the fold of her neck, smelling her delicious warmth…

Fuck, you need to get a grip! I told myself censoriously – hold back. Slow down. Lucy was beautiful, but she was complicated. I'd been so into her. I'd thought that weekend, maybe, we had a future together. And the outcome? - Like throwing my body onto a grenade. Get perspective - think two steps ahead.

Irini, I decided, was just being her usual melodramatic self – wanting to be at the centre of someone else's drama. Making herself indispensable to others. Especially to Lucy. There was a pattern there. I *had* wondered on occasion whether my sister was actually *in love* with Lucy.

But what if Lucy *was really* in trouble? With Lucy that was not improbable. I could see her locked up in a jail somewhere. Wouldn't be the first time that had happened. She'd been locked up in Lagos for two weeks for covering the oil drilling in the delta and then bad-mouthing a Minister. She'd handled that. So, Lucy could handle *this*, whatever 'this' was. She didn't need me to rescue her. She'd get out, get in touch with the Australian Ambassador, or at least get a lawyer.

Maybe she's just lost her Blackberry. She could be on a remote island without internet access.

"You still there?" Irini's voice brought me back.

"Maybe she's lost her phone and can't get online," I offered.

"This is 2005. There must be an internet cafe where she is surely," my sister said.

"Maybe not."

"Really?!"

"Maybe she's not bothered."

"Oh, come on, she'd know we would worry."

"You think so? She's that considerate?" I said, remembering the way she'd ditched me. No note. No explanation.

"Oh, Tom, don't be so sorry for yourself!" Irini snapped.

I sighed. She was probably right. "Have you tried to contact her family? Does she *have* family?" I said, in my problem-solving voice, almost surprised to find I didn't know this, feeling I should have, considering I'd asked her to move in with me.

"Lucy's mother has Alzheimer's and is in a home in Melbourne. She doesn't have contact with her father. Her brother is a hippy somewhere in South America."

"*Other* relatives...? Friends...? Colleagues...?" I offered.

"I don't think so, Tom." A hesitation. "And you know, Tom, she *is* very fond of you."

"Is she?" I said, hoping I sounded more hurt than hopeful.

"You know she is. She's just scared of getting in too deep. She's been hurt before."

And me? I almost said, but I didn't. Instead I said, "Is she working for anyone at the moment? Maybe they've had contact." If she was, Irini didn't know who they were. More likely to be freelancing. She'd told Irini that she was on a Greek island called Mythos. She'd texted Irini the address of the cottage she was renting. Sounded like she was working on the usual sort of stuff – environmentalist intrigue.

I could feel the weight of self-doubt and inertia dragging me down. "Let's wait," I said. I got Irini to agree to us both trying to call Lucy the next day.

But nothing. Neither of us could get hold of Lucy. Increasingly I was hearing that "I missed you" on a loop in my head. The sultriness of Lucy's voice, the depth of that phrase, almost whispered. Took me straight back to that last weekend we'd had together, when I imagined being married to her... Christ, I'm not old enough to imagine being married to *anybody* – and haven't since. Then she'd left on the Monday morning, without even saying goodbye... and I'd... fragmented, like a tearing out from inside. I don't trust easily - the legacy of a child who has lost a parent at too young an age for it to be remotely normal. I am naturally circumspect. I hedge my bets. How did I lose that with her? Fuck, I was so... *disappointed* - in her... in myself! I felt so foolish, like I'd seriously over-reached myself and had been slapped down. It had taken me time to surface.

Now Irini's 'damsel in distress' scenario and Lucy's voice-over: "I miss you".

"Can't you go out there?" Irini asked me finally. "See if she's in trouble? I'd go, but it's term time." (My sister, for her sins, is a teacher at a Comp.)

Maybe Lucy *did* need help. Maybe Irini wasn't just placating me – maybe Lucy did care for me after all. Maybe she was just as cautious as me. Was this a second chance? Could this be destiny? Or was this just me wanting my life to turn out like True Romance?

But what the fuck, I was between stories and I *deserved* a break after covering the Uzbekistani petro-chemical scandal, two weeks on a Greek island in late September was, I told Marsha, my boss, small reward for my relentless and ultimately productive enterprise. I don't think it's too much to claim that it was mainly down to the report I put out that the Uzbeki Minister of Energy had been arrested and was going down for a long time – so long, fuckhead! What I didn't tell Marsha was that Lucy was in Greece and there may even be a story in it for us – probably because by then I was stuck on imagining surprising Lucy, swimming in warm turquoise water, eating grilled fish, drinking the local wine, and then, when the heat of the day cooled down, leading Lucy back home, peeling off her clothes and making gentle love to her. That didn't sound like work.

****

So, a big disappointment now, not finding Lucy at home. And now that I'm here and she's evidently not been around for a while, I'm starting to worry that her not answering e-mails and phone messages is more than her being flighty and frightened of commitment. There is something unnerving about the stillness in her cottage and all her things left untidy, the foetid smell, as if she'd left in a hurry, or had intended to come back by now. Maybe something bad *has* happened to her, not just that she's in a prison somewhere (although that is still the most likely).

In spite of myself, I suddenly imagine her unconscious in a hospital bed – could she have had a motor-bike accident? – you hear of that all the time – fucking Greek truck drivers are infamously dangerous…! Oh, God, what if she is seriously injured, bones broken, her face cut and bruised? What... what... if she's *dead*? What if she's lying unclaimed in a morgue somewhere? Oh, God, no! Not that! No, it can't be, I reassure myself by magical thinking- Lucy isn't *the type*. She's too young and robust and lively. It's just Irini's neurosis talking. Fuck you, Irini. It's way too early to be thinking of all the possible *calamities*. I don't want to be melodramatic like my sister. I am *not* melodramatic like my sister. I am the rational one. Lucy will probably be home later. But if she *doesn't* turn up, should I at least contact the hospital, and the police, tomorrow? Or leave it another day? "Let's not worry about what hasn't happened yet," I tell myself.

The yellowing fronds of the tamarisk are moving gently in a faint breeze. Then the breeze dies and the fine-fibred fronds settle. The sea beyond is an impossible blue - a cerulean blue, shading to indigo where it gets deep. The smell of oregano from the aromatic grilled pork gets to me. A *souvlaki*, a chilled beer, and then my first slow luxurious swim in that beckoning water.

I order a beer from Yianni, who barks the order at a young man, sitting, smoking on a bar stool. The young man – he's about twenty, I guess - gets up slowly – he makes a show of not jumping to it – and pours my beer and brings it over. The beer is in a glass which has been frosted in a cabinet. I like that. He looks at me with enquiring amber eyes. He says nothing. He is very good looking, his strong features classically Greek, Adonis-like, but shy. (I wonder if people here can tell that I have Greek blood - that I am part-Greek. I will find out in time.)

Yiannis tells me, with a tone of quiet exasperation, that the waiter is his son, Dimitri, whom they call Bobby, for reasons he doesn't explain. Their daughter, two years younger, is Katerina, or Kat, she demurs from working in the restaurant – she prefers to sit upstairs – he points at the overhanging balcony - painting her toe-nails and watching married people fight on television.

"Know anything about the body in the bridge?" I ask Yianni. He bats his eyes modestly, like of course he knows. In his tortured tenses, he tells me that the body was found by construction workers demolishing the old bridge. The cops have had a look at it and called in archaeologists *("archaiologoi")* to advise on getting the body out. They will want it as intact as possible to try to identify it. It must have been there from when the bridge was built thirty-five years ago. "What they can find now?" he asks, shrugging, not once, but twice.

Suddenly Yiannis is distracted by a young man who is cleaning the floor of the next-door restaurant and swilling dirty water onto Yianni's side. Yiannis cusses explosively and abruptly cuts short our conversation and strides angrily over to the young man, his arms hacking his disapprobation in the air. The young man puts up no argument. He picks up his bucket and mop and goes inside. "What's the story with the restaurant next door?" I asked when the old man comes back to me, shaking his head and sighing loudly. "Why so close? Why right on top of you when he had the rest of the beach?"

"You speak *very* good English," Yiannis says without irony, "But me, I speak Greek. *Ellinika. Se parakalo*, you please speak more *zlow. Z-low. Pio arga."* And then an indulgent smile. "*Sigga-sigga.* Later. Come tonight. Soulla she is make stuff-ed to-*may*-toes and peppers. Special. Very good. You and me, we drink Metaxa. I tell you what's happen."

2

I've not been to Greece before. Even though I'm half-Greek by blood. My father was Greek. Petros Xanakis (although he always called himself Peter). He was a lovely guy – a lover of jazz and lost causes, warm, funny, although, it seemed to me, somewhat disabled by his baldness - he had, I imagine, in his youth cherished an image of himself as an older man with a full head of hair. In photos from his student days in Athens, his sumptuous black mane is tied back in a ponytail. By his middle-age, which is how I remember him, my father was handsome but no longer beautiful. His baldness introduced a diffidence, a shyness in a garrulous man, a man with a full heart, a man prone to moods – I now recognise these as episodes of depression. His baldness was just a symptom of all he had lost.

He left Greece in 1971 and came to London where he had friends, met my mother, who was Home Counties English, and cut his ties with the land of his birth. He never said why. Never spoke of it. Had me and Irini – and worked in some capacity at the TUC, the Trades Union Council, in Central London until he died when I was ten. A cerebral aneurysm, bursting in his brain. Other than our surname (and my middle name – Alexandros), I wouldn't have known I was part Greek. We never went to Greek school, we didn't have Greek friends or Greek family to visit and I'd never heard my father speak Greek. But I have some things in me which I know are not from my mother's family, ways of being and physical resemblances which are not exact copies. He never showed us any photographs of our Greek family. I sometimes caught him looking at me like he was seeing a familiarity. I think it must have saddened him, my phantom inheritance. Once he barbecued lamb, marinated in vinegar overnight and crusted in oregano, which he told us was a Greek delicacy. I remember the strange faraway look of pride and sadness he had as he ate the soft meat in silence.

When he died, his family claimed his body and took him back to Athens to be buried. My mother had no say – it turned out they'd never legally married, even though his name was on my birth certificate and my mother had gone by the name Xanakis. His family made no attempt to contact us. My mother was bereft - she changed our names to Pickering – her name – as soon as she could. Then she went to pieces. I was left to look after her and my sister. I wasn't very good at it. I was only ten.

I loved my father. But I was so angry with him. For years. For dying, for leaving me to look after my mother and my sister - *his* wife and *his* daughter – that was *his* job! Angry for leaving me without a father. For never introducing me to his parents, my grandparents in Athens, to his family – *my* family. Like I was something to be ashamed of. For leaving me with no story to account for the absence from my life of anything Greek. I missed him like a phantom limb.

I mused on this on the plane coming over, as I shuffled through the Greek phrasebook and scan-read the Brief History of Modern Greece I bought at the airport. What would I make of Greece? What would Greece make of me? Would I find an affinity, a familiarity, a recognition from dormant programmes hidden in my genes? Would I find my way back to loving my father?

****

Lucy's house is, I find, just one room with a bed, a set of drawers, a cupboard with doors that don't meet, a table and two chairs, and against one wall, a single-plate cooker and sink. A shower-cum-toilet is tucked into an airless room without any space to turn. An afterthought. I suppose there used to be an out-house. Out the back, there is a table and two chairs under a pergola, which supports an old vine and tangled jasmine. The chairs look out over wild grass to a grove of ancient olives, and beyond that, the bruised mountains, their tops shrouded in bulbous clouds.

I go back inside. I'm back from lunch. The place is a mess. Lucy's stuff is everywhere. I'm looking for somewhere to put some of my things (is it presumptuous of me to unpack?), when I find Lucy's laptop in the cupboard. A MacBook Pro. With a Greenpeace logo stuck on the lid. Nice bit of gear. Perhaps I could quickly find out where she is by discreetly checking her mail. Shit, I'd come all the way from London. I *did* have cause for concern. I wouldn't normally snoop. Okay, sometimes. But it's legit - I'm an investigative journalist - it's what I do! At least I can check if she'd received the e-mails I sent her. I want to know how worried to be. Maybe, if it's right there, I could also sneak a look at what she's been working on. Just a quick peak.

I find her charger under the sink, set it up and press POWER. The screen wakes up slowly, reluctantly it seems, offers me two spheres: Lucy and Guest. I click on Lucy. With a grumble, up pops a box for a password I don't have. Okay, okay. What would it be? LD (Lucy's initials) I try. Stutter, blink… no. 'LD 2005' I try. No. Shit, I don't even know her date of birth. But she wouldn't have used her date of birth. I consider which of my friends would know how to crack a password. Mmm. Fortunately, I don't have any friends like that. Maybe someone in the office has a contact. We've used geeks before. Or I'll have to message Irini – she may know, or at least have some ideas. I guess she'd be okay with me trying to open Lucy's computer.

Or maybe… *maybe* I should just be patient and wait for Lucy to show up. Patience is indubitably a virtue. Unfortunately, not one of mine. I want Lucy to be here *now*. I don't want this feeling of foreboding lurking in my abdomen to swell and form into alarm. I want this to be a momentous coming together of two souls destined to be together. Blah blah blah… Fuck, so prosaic! Basically, I don't want to be let down.

I suppose I could google her on *my* laptop and see if it showed up who she was last working for. I should have done that already. I don't know why I haven't. Maybe the colleagues she used to work with have heard from her or know what she is up to. I need to get online. Who in this fishing village on a small island in Greece would have internet connection? Anyone? I'll ask Yianni.

I put her computer back in the cupboard. On a lower shelf, next to a jumble of tee-shirts, there is an unruly stack of cards and photos. I don't expect Lucy would mind me having a gander. Not like they are very private - I mean, they are not locked away or anything. I take them over to the table. The postcard on top is from Agia Sofia, an elevated view of the harbour, with its pretty whitewashed houses rising on a hill, open restaurants under bright blue awnings along the quayside. She hasn't written on it yet. Who is it for, I wonder?

The second is a photo of a younger looking Lucy, bundled up in fleece, a snowy setting and in the background, penguins. That must be Antarctica. I remember her telling me how, in her gap year, she'd paid her way to Cape Town ("the scenic route", a thirty-seven-hour super-cheapo flight via Doha, Addis Ababa and Lusaka, or some such), and then, in Cape Town, she'd blagged a berth on a research ship to South Georgia as a galley-hand and companion to the First Mate, a fellow Aussie. "The skies were fantastic, and the penguins were so *serious*," she'd said. "At our infant's school in Canberra, the nuns had been given lessons in deportment by actual penguins, I swear to God. Our teacher, Sister Beatrice, would waddle down the corridor, stop, have a little poo, then waddle off again!" My credulity and horror had produced an explosion of glee. "Only jesting, you buttock!" she'd roared, "Come here! You're so *adorable!*" she'd laughed and hugged me to her like I was a little kid. I didn't mind being the sap when the reward was her affection. In the photo with the penguins, she is grinning madly, no doubt thinking of her portly teacher. "Just jesting!" I hear her chortle.

The next photo in the pile is an abrupt contrast - an artfully framed photo of a bombed out building in front of which stands a war-ravaged Somalian or Eritrean child, its hollow eyes begging the photographer to stop. On the back is scrawled, "Happy birthday. Be grateful for what you've got. Wim. 2004." That must be from the war photo-journalist she was with for a time. The photo must be one of his, the self-indulgent creep, I think, resenting that the prick actually knows when her birthday is! I put the photo to the bottom of the pile.

Next, some receipts - no doubt to be claimed later as expenses, and then - and for some reason, it startles me - a photo of Lucy and me next to the canal. I remember her asking a passing couple - Japanese tourists no less - to take the photo of us. I've not seen it before. I angle it to the light and stare into it, deciphering our expressions, inviting the wash of memory to surge in. Not a great picture of me. But she looks radiant... triumphant, clutching my arm - a woman who has got her man. I bask in the warmth of this remembered intimacy, then I wonder why this photo is not on top? Why is Wim's photo above it on the pile? Is Wim around?

Is that why she is avoiding me? Did he pitch up before me and persuade her to go off and do some photo-journalistic take on whatever this "great" story she is onto, and now she's embarrassed she'd contacted me? Maybe it would be prudent to check up on his whereabouts when I eventually get online. Has she gone Wimsical? Has the competition got there ahead of me?

3

Yiannis tells me that the only internet access in Agia Anna is at the other restaurant, "the new one" Yiannis spits out, like "new" is the worst curse word in the hood. Unless I want to go into the port town, Agia Sofia – they have the internet. Internet connection for the village had been held up, Yianni tells me - the communists on the municipal council have objected to the work being done by an Israeli company. The Mayor is a PASOK man who will do business with anybody it if means a favourable deal, especially if there are enticements.

"Nikos Angelopolis," Yianni pronounces with mocking grandeur, "Our Mayor. A big shot. PASOK. He is say no *rousfeti*," (Yiannis rubs his forefinger against his thumb to indicate money changing hands) "but is lots *rousfeti*, believe me. He control everything. Everybuddy here in Agia Anna they love him because he is bring for them the new road. So now the tourist busses can come with tourists from the Port, from Agia Sofia, for day trips, and everybuddy will get rich. Hmph!" he says dismissively. "Now everybuddy is fight. Look what that one has built next door. 'Modern', he says, the tourist will want 'modern'. Everything clean. The furniture from Sweden. The food – only what is quick to prepare it. No love. No tradition. No... in the *heart*." He beats his chest and shakes his head, gravely disappointed.

"So what you wunt to eat?" he asks grimly, his mood darkened by the thought of his neighbour. "You wunt try the stuff-ed vegetables? Stuff-ed with *riso - solo*. Soulla she put in her own spice. Is popular," he says, holding his pencil tip to his order pad. "You wunt?"

"Yeah, okay," I give in without a fight. He writes it down with a flourish. We settle on a bottle of *retsina* to drink – the taste of the pine goes well with the spices in Soulla's vegetables apparently (cumin and fennel, he tells me, after he's checked with Soulla and found the translation in his frayed Greek-English dictionary, which he displays to me proudly). I write this down in my notebook. I collect recipes from places I've visited. I love cooking. I suppose I picked up the habit from having to provide meals for my mother and sister after my dad died. My dad had done most of the cooking before and took pride in the meals he produced for his family. I suppose I am like him in that way. My mum was rubbish at cooking, and once she had succumbed to the bottle, she had no interest in eating, and an only sporadic inclination to look after Irini and me. Cooking for me was survival. Irini was little; she was always hungry. That she had hot meals was mainly down to me. Not that Irini ever thanked me. Our mother remained as thin as a child until she died.

"So why are people fighting?" I ask, as he puts down the bottle of *retsina*, a glass, a basket of cut bread and my knife and fork wrapped in a red paper serviette.

"The people who will make money are those with land next to the sea. The *kapitalistes* will want the land for hotels, restaurant, fancy apartments. You will see. Once the new road gets to here, lots of peoples will come, Germans, Dutch, from Norway. They will want to buy places, make hotels. Those with land near the sea will get the top prices."

"Do you own this land?"

"Yes," he said and grins. "I own. On this island most of the land is own-ed by the womens." He sees my surprise and is amused. "We have to be nice to our womens here," he says and chuckles. "They are the rich ones. Us poor men have nothing other than what we have got in our trouser! This piece of land Soulla's father gave it me to marry his daughter. He thought it was worth nothing. That is also what he thought of his daughter's husband!" he laughs as one who has had the last laugh. "Soulla has farmland in the valley. Before was worth a fortune. Now is worth nothing. *I'm* now got the good property. Soulla! Soulla!" he shouts and gets up suddenly, to tell her to do something urgently it seems, but maybe just to lord it over her.

Yianni's and Soulla's *tavern, To Meltemi,* is empty. Yianni and Soulla will stay open anyway. I think of all the food Soulla must have prepared for the evening customers that will go to waste. Their business is probably mainly lunches I surmise, but I feel a sadness for these two hard-working old people. Maybe it's the *rebetika* music, mournful, muted and indistinct, coming from a worn cassette tape player – they haven't even graduated to cds yet – that is getting to me. So much tragedy in the voice of the female singer, those sinuous Middle Eastern minor scales… My father never played Greek music at home. Yet, this music touches my soul. Is it in my blood? Or is it the *retsina*? I *am* on my second glass.

Beyond the *rebetika*, the music from the *taverna* next door, insinuates itself onto the still, warm night air - smooth jazz, discreet background music for discerning Northern Europeans. Yianni's neighbours, I notice, are doing good business. Their clientele on the neat balcony are all smart-casual and mostly blonde. Greek holiday makers have long since gone back to work and taken their children back to school; it is already too cold for the Italians, Yiannis tells me, as he returns and sees me looking over at his neighbour. "It is only the Germans who stay in late September," he says, "but is the best time now – the wind, the *meltemi,* has die down, the sea is still warm and the nights they are cool so zleep with no mosquitoes," he chuckles. He puts down my plate, with an enthusiastic "*Kali orexi!* Good appetite please!" He backs off and then hovers, beaming, waiting for my response to his wife's cooking. I do not have to dissemble. The stuffed peppers, especially, are fantastic, and he is right about the *retsina*. The pine complements the aniseed beautifully. He is delighted and goes to tell Soulla I am enjoying my meal. He comes back with Soulla in tow. She looks at me hopefully. "You like?" she says. I am effusive in my praise. Soulla smiles modestly and then she puts a motherly hand on my shoulder. "Is good you eat," she says tenderly. I miss my mother who died six years ago. Soulla has a warm maternal glow that melts me. Soulla must be the same age as the sister my father infrequently spoke about and who is still in Athens, as far as I know. Is she small like Soulla, I wonder, kind like her? I have never met this aunt of mine.

Yiannis is pleased to have me as his only customer and wants to make it worth my while. He wants my regular custom. He senses in me an ally against his competitor next door. Already he is worried I will go next door for the internet connection and I won't support him. But he doesn't like being upstaged by his wife, "Go" he tells her, and ushers her back to the kitchen.

31

He comes back with a pack of cigarettes, and two glasses of Metaxa brandy – "On the home," he pronounces generously. Yiannis is knowledgeable and garrulous in equal measure, and is happy to… no, he is *obliged to* explain the intricacies of land rights on the island, and how come "womens is pull the string". Not that he agreed with this – but that is the way it is. He is philosophical. He has, since he was a boy, had an interest in the history of the island, he tells me. He wishes he had been a scholar, but he had to leave school at thirteen to help his family. But he tells me proudly that he has read many books. Mostly, however, he gets his knowledge from listening to the old people, to the stories they tell. He will tell me about land-ownership on the island to prove to me, he says, that "History is walk like a man drunk from bad wine." He gestures this, his hand a snake slithering through time.

Yiannis is a good story teller, and as he is talking, the brandy is going down and is being refilled without any prompting, I have the thought that I could file a series of stories for New World Order about life on the island. I resolved to talk Marsha into it the next day. Maybe she'd let me take extra leave days in lieu. The apricot brandy is mellifluous. The night is warm. The scent of the wild jasmine is enchanting. The sea gently laps onto the shore. I could spend more time here. I could *force* myself (ho-ho). Especially if things go well with Lucy. If Wim hasn't beaten me to it. The bastard! Lovely Lucy, who has brought me to this lovely island… I pour myself another shot… I am definitely drunk already… maybe I should have asked….

Yiannis waves for me to keep pouring. "On the home! Drink!" he says emphatically. His story gets on to his neighbour. "The mother of next door," he says, "It is her land. Stavroula. It was come to her from her father. He bought it when he was come with his little girl, with Stavroula, to the island - refugees from Smyrna. 1921. They killed all the Greeks. You know about Smyrna?"

I did, as it happens, read about Smyrna in my book on Modern Greek history. Smyrna, where the Turks routed the over-reaching Greeks in the early 20s – the last battle of the First World War. The King had dismissed Prime Minister Venizelos, the hero of independence, who had favoured compromise with the Turks and had offered land for peace. The King put his Generals in charge and went to war. The cosmopolitan Greek citizens of Smyrna, in their thousands, had to flee certain massacre at the hands of Ataturk. I had seen photographs of the insanely overcrowded boats, the dark hollow eyes of people who'd had to leave everything behind.

"Her father, he had a bit of money. His wife she die with her family – bloody Turks! But he got out with his baby daughter and they come to this island. All the land he could get was land next to the sea. He bought it from Soulla's father who did not wunt it. It was just a field - sand, stones, bushes. He pay too much for it – Soulla's father he was not a nice man. What they could grow? He paid out the last of his money to buy a fishing boat which was leak-leak, and then it sink. Finish." One hand slaps the other clean, one way then the other. "No boat. No money. They was living like poor people. He was ashame-ed. He died during the war, poor man, and left Stavroula, as a young girl, with nothing. Nobody wunted the land. She was not from here and she have nothing to give a husband's family for him, no *proika* - how you say, 'dairy?'"

"Dowry?"

"*Nai*, no dow-er-y," (he articulates the word torturously) "- so nobuddy want to marry her, even although she was hardworking woman. Boy-o-boy, she was work. Strong like a man. A nice-looking woman. But poor-poor. There were those that took advantage. There was, for a time… somebody… but no, that came to nothing." He pauses, thinking to digress, but then changes his mind, and goes straight on. "Everyone thought she would end up a women with no child.

"And then Mavros he come to the island – Gregorios, but everyone called him Mavros because he was have dark skin, like from Africa, but Greek. It was in the 60s, 1963 I think. '63 or '64. Stavroula, she was forty-two… maybe forty-three. He was a bit younger. A nice-looking man. She look after him for her cousin who was bring him here. They fell into love. Everyone was happy for her. Everyone, before, maybe they felt guilty, maybe they were sorry for her. So, when Mavros took her for his bride all the people in the village was happy. But she never forgive-ed the villagers who don' help her father, and she blame *Soulla* for the price Soulla's father had ask-ed for the land - she was find out later her father he paid much too much for such a piece of land where nothing would grow.

"They left in about 1970 – Michalis, he own the next door – was just zmall boy. They went to the mainland. Stavroula made a business, sewing, materials, then clothing... export, import. Stavroula is..." He taps his head and nods, his downturned lips denoting respect for her business nous. "Michalis he was have big business in Thessaloniki, factory, I don' know what. They come back a few years" (he shows me 'ago' with a gesture - behind, in the past) "when they found out the land was worth something now, with all the tourists. To revenge on Soulla, they build-ed their restaurant right on top of us, right onto the beach, so now you cannot even see the sand to other the end from here," he says, his indignation darkening the small veins in his cheeks. "Stavroula would be happy to see Soulla go out of business, for Soulla to be poor like she was be. Now her son, Michalis, he has got lots money, she make like she is queen. Like the old Queen, the King's mother, Frederika, the German bitch! Soulla she was used to be sorry for Stavroula. Not no more. Now they don' zpeak."

He knocks back the last of his brandy. "But what I was say… the ones who was have the best land, the ones who was used to be rich, now they are poor – and the ones with the land next to the sea where nothing will grow, they are the ones who now have the money. This is history, my friend. *Historia.* So is why the people in the village fight." He shrugs and smiles modestly at his own wisdom.

I look over at the tavern next door. I see the owner - at least, I think that must be him - a large man with waves of blonde hair, scurrying to and from the kitchen, peremptorily bossing the young waitresses, one of whom comes with her tray to the table nearest where I am.

She is looking down, a slight frown darkening her forehead, the ringlets of her lustrous copper hair falling across her face as she clears the table of its debris. Prominent polished cheekbones and a bold Greek nose, her hooded eyes downturned in thought. A strong face – a face with a story to tell. As she stands up straight to wipe her hair out of her vision, she notices me watching her. The tiniest of smiles arcs one corner of her full lips. She averts her eyes, loads her tray and walks away purposefully.

There is, on the warm night air, the smell of figs and jasmine.

4

The next morning, I go down to Yianni's for a morning coffee. I am stiff from sleeping on the couch at Lucy's. I had to sleep on my side with my legs bent. I thought it would be too presumptuous to sleep in her bed. Definitely embarrassing if Wim is around.

"Hey, Yianni!" I call in greeting when I see him laying tables, turning chairs the right way up.

"*Geia sou, Dhomas!*" he answers, pleased to see me. "You want coffee? *Loukoumades?*"

I agree to coffee and the doughnuts dipped in honey, which is what *loukoumades* turn out to be.

"The body in the bridge," he says seriously as he puts my coffee down, "The hand is opening a little. Now is black. Is maybe the sun. They found in..." (he shows me with his hand, the fist opening) "a ... badge, for how you say... for the jacket..." he taps his chest.

"A lapel-badge?" I guess.

"*Nai.* The flag of Cuba. The Communists think they know who it is," he says and wanders off. I sip my coffee and gaze at the mirror surface of the water which, at this time of the morning, is aquamarine and turquoise all the way out to the deep channel where it shifts into an Indian ink blue. The sheen is mesmerizing. What would Lucy's interest be in a body in a bridge? She is into environmental stuff, not murder mystery crime reporting. Intriguing.

Yiannis is gone a good ten minutes. He comes back with a mop and bucket, and begins cleaning the marble floor energetically. As he gets to me, he asks, "Lucy - she come back?"

"No," I tell him. "Listen, could you call the hospital for me? Maybe she is there? Is there more than one hospital on the island?"

"No, is only the one. Soulla!" he calls out, and I hear him speaking imperiously, *importantly,* to his wife in Greek. Soulla is evidently the one who is good on the telephone. As I sip my sweet coffee, I hear her shouting into the phone what I judge, by the intonation, are questions.

"Lucy!" she shouts. *"Lu-cy."* Then she turns to Yianni and asks him something. He comes to me urgently. "What her name is? Lucy what?"

"Discombe," I tell him, Lucy Discombe. D-i_s-c-o-m-b-e," I spell it out for him.

"Discom*ber*", he shouts out to his wife, who shouts it at the receptionist or nurse, or whoever is at the other end of the line.

There is a pause Soulla shrugs with her eyebrows, as in 'what can you do, you must wait'. Then she straightens. I straighten too. News? Soulla shakes her head at me, letting me see she is sadder about this than I am disappointed. She replaces the receiver. "Nothing," she says. Then a thought strikes her. "That is good," she says cheerily.

I suppose it is. I suppose I should try the police too. "Yianni, I'm sorry, but could you also call the police station? Ask them."

"What for you say 'sorry'? Of course I do this! But police? Mmph," he snorts, "they do nothing." But he sees the look in my eye and shouts for his wife again. She calls the police in the main town, then has to hold. She shakes her head. "What they do there all day? They got nothing to do." Then she speaks to someone. Her tone is sharp. She is insistent. But frustrated. She puts the phone down. "They can give no informations over the phone."

"So there *is* information?" I ask.

"They didn't say to me," she says. "Tickets for the parking. That's all they know how."

"You must go in to the police station," Yiannis says. "I am go into the port at eleven o'clock for shopping. You want to come in the van?"

"Yeah, sure. Great. Thanks," I say, as I count out the coins for the coffee and doughnuts. "Now I must go next door and see if I can get internet," I say.

"Don't say about the body in the bridge to Michalis," he says earnestly. He considers whether to tell me more. Then he decides. "The Communists are say it is his father."

****

The restaurant next door is, a bold sign in blue on white tells me, "The Sea View Restaurant, Bar and Coffee Shop." All in English. No Greek translation. I notice 'restaurant', not *'taverna'*. Michalis Epistemos, the owner, is talking earnestly to the waitress with the ringlets I saw last night. When her hair catches the sunlight, its copper hues turn to gold. She smiles gently as if humouring him, says, "*Nai,*" and goes off, a spring in her step. He turns and sees me. His face opens into a wide grin. "Welcome!" he says exuberantly, "Come in. Sit. What can I get you?" He ushers me to a table with a glorious, unimpeded view of the bay. The beach is still empty, although there are towels reserving the few beach chairs under umbrellas there are in front of the restaurant. When the tar road gets here, the beach will no doubt be colonised by Northern Europeans and their essential sun-tanning accessories.

Michalis is tall and broad-shouldered. The hand he offers me, by way of introduction, is large and meaty. His hair is golden and wavy, his lips are full, his nose flat and his eyes are sea-green and good humoured. He stands with his legs splayed, confident of his stature and his place in the world. "Where you from?" he asks. I tell him, and ask if he knows Lucy.

"Sure," he says, and looks furtively at a small dark woman sitting at a table at the back doing the accounts, waves at her, she grimaces and goes back to her work. Could that be his wife? He looks back at me smiling. Has he slept with Lucy? "She your friend? How is she? Still crazy?" he asks, grinning. "I have not seen her for a time."

I tell him I am trying to trace her – she is missing. I want to look on the internet to see if I can find out who she was working for. "I don't know *who* she was working for," he says, "but every day she was going to the new resort being constructed on the other side of the island. "The Poseidon". Christos Papademos is the Developer. I know him. You want me to ask if he has seen her?"

"Yes, please. Hey, gee, thanks," I say. What luck.

"The internet – you have to connect. Nitsa," he says to the dark woman, "Switch on the modem. Let him use. Okay?" The dark woman, sighs and nods, and gets up reluctantly. "My wife," he says with a look of ironic forbearance.

"Did Lucy ever use your internet connection?" I think to ask.

"Sometimes. Not a lot," he says.

At least now I know that Lucy could get online if she'd wanted to. So scratch that one off the reasons why she didn't get back in touch with me and Irini.

I follow Michali's wife into an office, and thank her as she switches on the modem, takes the connecting cable I offer her and plugs me in. "Wait," she says, "Is *zlow*." I thank her again. "You pay now?" she asks/tells me, "Five euros for one hour." I reach for my wallet and pay her. She examines me with brooding eyes, pockets the money and goes off. I hear Michalis shouting, and then he comes in. "You want breakfast? A frappe? A beer maybe?"

I look at my watch. It's only nine thirty. "Maybe orange juice? You have fresh?" I ask. My English is already simplifying to accommodate the locals. Somehow I think they will understand me better if I speak English like it's my second language.

"Sure," he says, and goes out. I switch my laptop on. The screen lights up.

I check my e-mails first. Nothing from Lucy. I check her facebook page. Nothing. I google 'Wim war photojournalist' and, after a brief pause, up pops his face, looking smug and world-weary. Wim Mueller. I find his facebook link and select. There is an entry from... yesterday - from the Congo - and the thread suggests he has been in Goma, embedded with the UNHCR for at least a month. Good. He hasn't been here. Sucker! I sit back, relieved and stupidly victorious.

The waitress with the ringlets comes in with my fresh orange juice. She bends down to put the glass carefully on the desk next to me. My entire view is taken up by her full breasts hanging perilously close to my face. I try not to look. I close my eyes. I breathe her scent in - orange rind and sandalwood. When I open my eyes, she is looking at me with an amused expression. Her eyes are a luminous green. Smiling to herself, she turns and leaves me to my work.

She is plump but shapely. No doubt she is regarded with lust by the local Greek men, and probably takes this attention with good humour but I don't expect she flirts back. She seems self-possessed. She is probably younger than she looks. She has, I suppose, a natural beauty... unaffected, unencumbered. She looks *healthy,* and handsome even. Not my type though. It's almost a sign that I am not actually Greek, not *properly* Greek that I do not feel a sexual attraction to her. I get an urge to tell her I'm half-Greek – the wrong half, I'd quip - almost as an apology for *not* feeling sexual desire. But by the time I work all that out she's already walking away and I think better of it. What would it matter to her?

Back to my research. I type 'Lucy Discombe' into the search engine. All that comes up is old stuff about her previous jobs and speeches she has given at conferences which have been reported. Nothing about what she's up to at the moment.

I send an e-mail to Marsha at New World Order, pitching my idea for a series of articles on "Life on a Greek island – politics and culture", as well as asking her for extended leave to do this work. I am pleased with the thrust of my proposal and hope she will interpret my enthusiasm as a sign of my indisputable instinct for a good story, and not as a decoy for a nice little paid holiday in the Greek sun. I don't tell her about Lucy. She's bound to be cynical. But I don't know how long it will take me to track Lucy down. I may need more time.

I send an e-mail to Irini, asking if she thinks it's okay for me to try get into Lucy's laptop (I shall disregard her innuendoes and her disapprobation if I have to) and does she have any idea of what the password might be.

I type into the search engine "Poseidon hotel resort", and after it does its pondering ('We are searching'… the wheel goes round and round for a good two minutes) up pops reams of offers of accommodation as far afield as Melbourne, Australia, reviews of at least three different Poseidon hotels, then eventually, on page three, a link to a news report of a failed appeal by an environmental NGO to the siting of the Poseidon Leisure Resort and Spa (Mythos) on what was previously designated protected land under something called the "Natura 2000" scheme. That's it. That's something which would have interested Lucy for sure. I download it as quickly as the internet speed will allow - that is to say, painfully slowly – and it freezes half way through and I have to start again, and only get it downloaded just before my hour is up. I'll read it later, I don't want to miss my lift into town.

5

We get into the port, the main town, Agia Sofia, by eleven thirty. It is busy with locals doing their shopping and tourists looking for souvenirs and beachwear. We park in the square. There are people, looking cross, chanting and waving placards in front of a squat, official-looking building. "What's that about?" I ask Yiannis.

"It's the Communists. They want a statue to commemorate their ELAS comrades who died in the Resistance and in the Civil War," Yiannis says. "It is the body in the bridge. It make them angry."

"They think the body is from then?"

"No, no, the bridge wasn't built then. But during the junta, the Colonels, in the late 1960s, the early 1970s, the Left suffered. People disappeared. The bridge was built then."

I study the protesters. Mostly old people, shabbily dressed. A few young people, mainly women. The young people are the ones making the most noise. The older people tend to be serious and silent. An older woman with her hair tied back raises a bull horn and shouts a slogan. The protesters chant a response in unison. The woman with the bullhorn, encouraged, yells her imprecation more stridently, now raising her fist into the air. The protesters shout back and pump the air with their fists.

"Calliope Gavras," Yianni says. "The leader of the Communist Party on Mythos. A strong woman!" He says admiringly. Then with a shift in tone, "I wouldn't want for her to be my wife. *Boy-o-boy!* She too *strong*," he laughs, "With muscles! *Boy-o-boy!* A wife, she must listen to the man. Calliope, she listen to no-one!"

I take a couple of pictures on my phone. Maybe I could write something about this.

"You come back …" (he looks at his watch) "… in two hours. The police is just there, around this building…" (he shows me with his hand cocked at a right-angle) "… next to the Town Hall – this one. Two hours I am back. I go to the bank – the crooks! They take all my money! – and to get for the *taverna* some things, to put a bet on Panathinaikos to win the Cup!" he grins. "Also, I will have a coffee with my friend. You get coffee too – around here lots of places," he says with a sweep of his arm. "*Endaxi?* Okay?"

He hurries away, shouting greetings to people as he goes. I head to the police station.

The police station is two rooms - a front room with a wooden counter, behind which sits a young and handsome cop, bored and dismissive, behind him, behind a glass door, his senior, balding, with a huge belly behind a chaotically disorganised desk, talking loudly on the phone with rising tones of indignation and exasperation.

"Yes?" says the young cop. He asks in English – he can tell I'm foreign.

"I'm trying to get information about Lucy Discombe. You said you couldn't give information over the phone?" I hand him my passport, which he examines disinterestedly, flicking the pages without making eye-contact with me.

"What informations?" he asks.

"That's what I'm trying to find out. Is there information you have about where she is?"

"What?" he says querulously.

"Lucy – do you know where she is?"

"Why I would know where she is?"

Maybe there isn't information after all. "Maybe you had a report? Maybe she came to report something to you? I don't know..."

"You her family?" he asks.

"No. A friend - a colleague," I tell him.

"We can't give informations to not-her-family," he says peremptorily. He is pleased with his retort.

"So there *is* information?" I press him.

He scowls and sucks his teeth. "What you want?"

"I want to report her missing," I say. That could be a better way to go. Fucking cops.

He looks behind him at the fat cop, still battling with the phone. "*Ena lepto.* You wait," he says, signals to some chairs against the wall and searches out some papers so he can pretend he is very busy.

There is a sudden swelling of people shouting, a man in a suit and an open-necked shirt leads the Communist Party leader, Calliope, into the room. He stops her at the door, signalling to her to keep the other protesters back. She turns and says something to the crowd. They shout back but stay where they are. She pulls an older man in with her. The man in the suit seems to accept this. The older man, who is not quite as tall as the Party boss, has a handsome face, with bushy white eyebrows and intelligent eyes. His hands are worker's hands.

The young cop gets up and is deferential to the Suit, who shouts at him, then shouts at Calliope and points for her to put on the counter the paper (is it a petition?) she has in her hand. She narrows her eyes at the Suit, he apologises and touches her arm reassuringly. She sets the paper down, with a look of withering contempt at the young cop.

The fat cop comes out of the back office and greets the Suit with friendly familiarity. "Mr. Mayor!" he says in heavily accented English and laughs. The Mayor (the guy in the suit is the Mayor it seems) has no time for conviviality, shakes the fat cop's hand in a business-like way and ushers Calliope out. She shouts something over her shoulder at the policemen, who both wave her away.

The young cop says something to his senior, hands him my passport and points at me. The fat cop looks at my passport quickly, then approaches me, his face widening slowly into a lugubrious smile. "Come into my office, Mister," he says.

The sign on his desk tells me that he is Chief of Police Panagiotis Valoudsakis. He shows me where to sit – there is not a choice – and squeezes himself into the chair behind the devastation of his desk. The office smells of stale sweat and nicotine. The leather on the armrest of his chair is worn. Behind him is a poster of a benevolent Prime Minister and a map of the island surrounded by advertisements.

"My friend," the Chief says, examining me, "you are looking for *dhespeneedha* Discom*ber?* Why?" He makes a show of reading my passport.

I explain that she tried to contact me three weeks before, but since then no word from her and I haven't been able to get in touch with her.

He looks at me coolly. He is disguising his suspiciousness, his mistrust. "Maybe she don' want you to find her?"

I am affronted that he thinks I'm some kind of stalker or abusive boyfriend. I swallow my indignation and tell myself to stay calm. He's only doing his job. I tell him Lucy's good friend, my sister, Irini, hasn't been able to reach her either and we're both worried. I've been to her house. Her things are still there. There was stuff in her fridge, as if she was expecting to be around for a while.

He appraises me as he considers his options. He settles for having a conversation with me. "Okay. She ever do this before? Maybe get an idea, and…?" He snaps his fingers.

I hesitate. Well, yes. But I don't want to tell *him* that.

The Police Chief sees that I have doubts, he identifies with what he takes to be my realisation that maybe she's just flaky and what can you do? Men suffer by the whims of women. I read all of this in his resignation. "Okay, I'll tell you this – it can do no harm." (To him or to Lucy? I wonder.) "Kosta!" he calls to the young cop. He says as an aside to me, "My son," and shakes his head, then in his authoritative voice, "Kosta, did Lucy say to you maybe she was going to the big island sometime to get something?"

Kosta shouts something back. His father, the chief, berates him in rapid-fire Greek.

Kosta answers his father in a surly juvenile tone.

Valoudsakis Senior turns to me with a long-suffering smile. "He agrees. Maybe she has gone to collect informations. Maybe she go on the ferry? You ask in the harbour," he says, and nods reassuringly and hands me my passport back.

Mmm, maybe, but… "No, I don't think so. Her laptop computer was still at her home – she wouldn't have gone off without it," I tell him, "I think I know her well enough to know that. It has all her work, all her data. She wouldn't leave it."

"Mmm," he says, waggling his head. He sees my point but is still not convinced. He reaches for a notepad. "*Endaxi,* give me your number. I will call you if I hear anything. Because you have a worry, even I will ask with the airport," he says grudgingly. "OK?"

I take the pad and scribble down my number. "What business did she have with you - with the police?" I ask.

"My friend," he says with exasperation, "I have already told you I cannot say."

"She was doing some work at the new resort, 'The Poseidon'," I say.

"I know already," he says. He gets up and offers his hand. The meeting is over.

"Was it something to do with that?" I ask.

The fat cop gets up and, smiling, points to the door behind me. As he has indicated already, the meeting is over. "You go now," he says.

****

I just know they will do nothing. But there *was* something. They know her and she clearly had dealings with them. I'm also sure it has something to do with the Poseidon. Maybe Michalis will have some news from his friend, the developer of the new resort, Papademos I think he said, somebody Papademos. (Or was it Papageorgios? Something like that anyway.) I must ask Michali when I get back. Maybe she's *at* the Poseidon – he could call and ask.

I suppose I *should* check at the harbour. Just in case. Don't want it to be embarrassing, even though I think it's very unlikely… But not impossible, I have to concede. I don't know Lucy that well. Maybe she *doesn't* take her laptop everywhere. That's what *I* do – I can't assume she's the same as me. Maybe she uses her Blackberry for sending stuff out - I don't have one, so I don't know what its limitations are. Perhaps she relies on a notebook and pencil - old-school. Could be. Lucy is pretty old school - virtuously lo-tech as I remember it. Still…

The young girl at the ticket office is probably just out of school or even *still at* school, and is, not like the cops, against my expectations, quite helpful. She looks pleased to have something to do. There is only one ferry a day, so not much to do, but probably the Union has organised for her to be there the whole day so she can earn a decent wage. Good for her, I think, why not? Her family are no doubt poor, and she is their hope – an educated girl, with a good job. She can help her family. Her mother is probably asthmatic and crippled by arthritis, her father is…

She looks up and interrupts my reverie. No Lucy or Discombe on the travel list in the last two weeks. She is disappointed, apologetic even.

But she says she only has the list of passengers who bought tickets *on the day*. My friend may have bought a ticket through a Travel Agent. I'd have to ask them. She tells me there are three travel agencies in the port. I thank her and leave. In my bones I feel it'll be a waste of time - Lucy is almost certainly still on the island. She is probably going to show up suddenly and laugh at her wimpy friends, worried by her taking off on an adventure. She'll gleefully tell me that the story she's got will make it all worthwhile. Then we'll fall into each other's arms… I put off the idea of checking the travel agencies. It would put me in a bad mood to find out that Lucy had fucked off and that I'd come here for nothing.

I find a coffee shop which offers "Internet Free" and order a sandwich and a regular coffee. I have to use the shop's own computer, which is a surprisingly modern Dell. The owner has an American accent and a Wall Street haircut. A recent returnee? I guess that with all the money coming in from the EU, a lot of Greeks who left for American jobs before, are coming back. I could check that out – *that* would make a good story. I'll pitch it to Marsha, see what she says. "The Returnees – Why Greece is Now Better than America."

I check my e-mails. Irini has responded. Lucy has still not contacted her and still no reply, and, under the circumstances, she agrees I should try to 'access her computer', as she puts it diplomatically. As for the password, she suggests I try the name of Lucy's cat – she'd doted on the cat in Amsterdam. Sophocles. The cat had died last year and Lucy had been bereft. Maybe she used it in her password to help keep the memory of her cat alive. She thought that a picture of Sophocles was her screensaver. Yeah, I could play around with that. Sounds promising. At least now I have Irini's agreement – permission – to hack into Lucy's computer, so I don't feel as guilty or voyeuristic. Purely professional.

I dash off my proposal to New World Order for a series of articles on island life.

I've got some time still, so after I've finished my coffee (American, weak) and sandwich (bland, too much bread), I walk around the harbour, the pleasure boats of the rich and the fishing boats of the poor democratically arranged on the dark green water. Grizzly old fishermen disentangle their nets with nimble fingers and mumble to each other, each battling manfully to talk with their unlit cigarette butt balanced at the corner of their mouth. Tiny black fish swirl in pockets, looking for scraps. The water is clear, all the way to the bottom.

There are *tavernas* all along the harbour road. At the least modern, and, it must be said, the least pretentious, at a table in the sun, I see Calliope, the Communist Party apparatchik, with the handsome older man she was with at the police station. She is watching me. I nod to show I recognise her. Then on an impulse, I go over and introduce myself. She takes my hand and grips it in hers firmly. She does not lose her stern expression.

"From London?" she says, "I lived in London for many years. Islington. I stayed in Islington. You know Islington?"

No way! What a coincidence! I tell her I *live* in Islington. She used to lecture at "the Poly", now a University – "Should have stayed a Poly," she opines. "Universities are for the elite. The Poly was a democratic structure." The man next to her nods. "My husband, Nektarios," she says. He offers his hand glumly.

"So what do you do on the island?" I ask.

"Now I write," she says, "and I make trouble!"

Her husband nods, and smiles. "For sure," he says.

"My husband would prefer to remain in his studio and make his sculptures," she says. Her tone is dismissive, but her eyes betray her warmth for the handsome man at her side. "And you? What do you do?"

I explain my job (Calliope is impressed that I write for a progressive journal – I can see her eyeing me up to see if she can get something published through me), and that I am on the island, looking for a friend who has gone missing.

"Who is your friend?" Calliope asks.

"Lucy Discombe," I say, "an environmental activist. You know her?"

"I never met her, but I know of her. Like me, she is a trouble-maker," Calliope says with an ironic dipping of her left eyebrow.

"Who was she making trouble for?" I ask.

"The developers, the Mayor, PASOK – the Socialists, *and* the workers," she says. "She was saying things, criticising the new resort and the roads, the new developments on the island. She was not understanding that on the island we need the jobs. There are a lot of poor people here, especially in winter, when the tourists go back to their comfortable homes in Germany, Austria and Sweden. The developers are a piece of shit, but we need their jobs." She takes out a packet of cigarettes, shakes one free and lights up. She offers me the packet. I tell her I don't smoke. She looks at me as if this confirms I am a soft liberal. "She does not understand the dialectical nature of development."

"But what about the environment?"

"Exactly what I am explaining. The Greens want us to put the environment before everything else, even before the wellbeing of the people. The environment is not before or after – it is side by side with the economic uplifting of the proletariat, and, in this country, of the peasant class too. It is in the *matrix of production*; it is not the *organising principle*," she asserts emphatically, daring me to disagree.

"I disagree," I say, accepting, with a grin, the invitation to be contrary. I sense this is what the old Marxist wants.

"Mmph," Calliope snorts, tipping the ash off her cigarette, "You are a privileged cosmopolitan. You have surplus capital. Have you ever been poor? Have you ever gone hungry?"

"Why are you arguing with the young man?" her husband asks benignly.

"We are not arguing - we are debating!" Calliope says. Now she grins. "It is nice to have an intellectual debate with someone from London. It takes me back!"

I suddenly have a picture in my mind of this firebrand, extolling the virtues of communism to lively young students in the bar at Middlesex Uni, berating complacent liberals, scorning Thatcher and her fawning acolytes, when I would still have been in nappies. She has dignity in her upright posture, in her high cheekbones and sunken cheeks, in her silvered hair – almost an aristocratic bearing. She must have been impressive in those days, even beautiful.

I change the subject and ask about the protest she led that morning.

"The Socialist, PASOK, the ruling party," (she says in italics) "play it safe. Can you imagine – for all the bravery of the Resistance – it was our party who fought the Germans, our party that fought for our freedom from imperialism after the War – there is not one statue to commemorate them? So many people on the old Left sold out – became Social

Democrats – capitalists, and they don't want to open old wounds, they say. Instead they will forget the brave men and women who gave up their lives for their country. Look at the body they found in the bridge. When the Colonels took power in the late 60s, who was it they persecuted? It was us. The Communists. It is our comrade in that old bridge. So many disappeared when the junta came," she says sadly. "The Struggle continues," she pronounces. "*A luta continua.*" She savours the texture of the old left-wing rallying cry, before continuing, ardently, "But the Mayor, who says he's socialist, doesn't want a statue of our fallen comrades, because he says it is not good for '*inward investment*' to honour communists. The Americans, especially the Greek Americans, will keep their money back, if they think this island is going too far to the Left. Fuck him! It's *our history!* The People will rule again. Capitalism will collapse under the weight of its own contradictions. Believe me, it will happen. Nektarios is already working on a *beautiful* statue. We will, we *must* remember *our Struggle!"*

I look at my watch. Christ, it's two thirty. I have to meet Yiannis at the van.

"I must go," I tell them. "My lift back to Agia Anna… It's been nice talking. We must meet again."

They nod at me in rhythm. Calliope raises a fist in solidarity and gives me a weary smile. Then her expression deepens, there is a dark shading to her concern, "Tell your Lucy to be careful. People are not happy with her."

6

Yianni's van has been pre-heated by the midday sun; it is sweltering on the way back. There is no air conditioning. Yiannis smokes all the way, steering around the hairpin bends with one hand on the wheel, singing along with the burr of the *rebetika* music from his old car radio. By the time we get back to Agia Anna I am ready to throw up and am slip-sliming in my own effortless perspiration. The cool ocean beckons. A swim, a beer, then down to work. I thank Yiannis, almost offer to help him unload but then think better of it and instead go straight to get my swimming trunks and towel and hurry down to the beach.

The water is mirror-like, unfurling lazily as it reaches the shore. I dive under; the coolness and silence is so what I want, that I put off coming up for air until there is only one second of air left in my lungs. I emerge, breathe and then submerge myself again. I open my eyes. The water is salty but doesn't sting my eyes, the visibility – the endless blue – is a mind-blast. I let myself swim a slow breast-stroke, then float on my back, crucified, refrigerated. Perfect. I plan a list of things-to-do.

1) Check Lucy's laptop – see if I can get in with the help of Sophocles (deceased).

2) Go to The Seaview – get online – check if Marsha has responded to my proposal yet.

3) See if Michalis has any news from his friend, the property developer. *Is Lucy there?*

4) Maybe get something written for New World Order – an essay? A report? – not sure which – maybe one of each – one on land ownership and it's ironies (maybe interview Yiannis again and maybe Michali's mother, or is that too provocative?); one on environmental protection and the "dialectics of development", as the formidable Calliope put it; there was one more – oh, yes, the Returnees and the American Dream.

That should keep me busy. Earn my keep. I hope Marsha agrees. This working in a sunny climate, swimming in the temperate sea, eating freshly cooked seafood isn't for everyone, but someone's got to do it. May as well be me.

I hope Lucy is okay and that she turns up soon. My worrying about Lucy comes in waves. Right now, floating gently in this warm salty water, I feel an upsurge in my spirits and a confidence, a certainty that she will turn up in time, and that the explanation for her absence will be a simple one, something I have not yet thought of.

I swim back to the shore with sure, aesthetically-pleasing strokes, feeling the power in my muscles, the possibility of a tragic turn dispelled.

****

I almost expect to find Lucy waiting for me at the cottage, but the house is empty and silent. I change into cotton trousers and a loose-fitting cheese-cloth shirt. I am ready to work.

I go to get out Lucy's laptop out the cupboard, but it is not where I thought I put it. I think back to when I used it last, where else I might have put it. I look everywhere, even on the back patio – did I have it there? Nothing. It's gone. There are no signs of a burglary. Nothing else seems to be missing. But, wait, wasn't her hoodie over the back of the chair. That's not here either.

Then the obvious sits up and slaps me in the face. *Lucy is back!* She has rushed in, collected her laptop and hoodie and gone out again. Excellent! What a relief! There I was, just about to succumb to Irini's life-is-a-drama version of life. Fuck, I realise as I exhale and feel a weight lift off me, I was on the verge of starting to think that Lucy may be *dead!* Mental note to myself: don't listen to your sister.

I wonder where Lucy's gone and what she's made of my stuff in her place. Does she even know it's *my* stuff? – maybe she thinks she has a *squatter!* Could she have gone down to the Sea View to get online? She could be mailing me right now. I could do a magic number on her and pop up in front of her, just as she presses "Send!" Like a genie out of a lamp. Grinning to myself like a crazy person, I grab my laptop and go to meet her.

But at the Sea View, no sign of Lucy. Nitsa, Michali's wife, says she hasn't seen Lucy. Michalis is having a nap, but Nitsa plugs me in and collects my five euros. I am deflated but reassure myself that I'll catch up with Lucy later, that the wait will only make the meeting even more tender and passionate. I am so relieved she's back. Excited with the possibilities. We'll have dinner together. We'll have a bottle of wine. Candles. Soft sea air. She'll look into my eyes, see my love for her, take my artfully placed hand in hers, we'll alight the boat, which will be the rest of our lives, and set afloat on the tranquil waters of contentment. No life jackets required.

But first – work. An e-mail from Marsha. She wants more details, more of a feel for what I would write. I sketch out the topics I had in mind and tell her about what I've been up to. I search more articles on environmental protection in Greece and download two of them to add to my research. I tell her of the body in the bridge and the Communists' campaign. Maybe there is a story in that for us.

I think about working on the veranda of the Sea View, but there are some noisy kids squabbling there, and the music (is this "The Best of Robbie Williams"?) will be a distraction. Maybe I'll go get a Greek coffee and a Metaxa at the run-down looking bar on the wing of the bay next to the low fishermen's houses at the other end of the beach, facing the mountains. Looks quiet.

The bar, "*Kafenion*", (literally "coffee bar", but they also serve brandy and ouzo) is on a long, shaded veranda built on to the water. A concrete jetty extends a short way and harbours one large and two small fishing boats. The grey and ochre mountains rise up suddenly across the small bay, clouds banking up on the windward side. Pine forests green the folds. In places, gigantic boulders and sandstone rock faces stand proud. From this side the sea is spread out in unfathomable shades of aquamarine and deeper greens. I sit at a table over the water and look at the view. The owner is at a table near the door to his establishment, smoking a cigarette, a peaceful tragic look in his eyes. He nods to acknowledge me and waits for me to get settled before he comes over and waits for my order. Evidently, he is a man drawn to silence. He's got the right spot for it. It is very peaceful here. I guess you get used to your own company. I order a coffee and a brandy.

I flip open my laptop and begin, putting in order, as best as I can remember it – there will be time to edit it later – what Yiannis told me last night about the ironies of matriarchal property rights on Mythos - how, since ancient times, the fertile land was passed down from mother to daughter and the men had to make do with the dusty, wind-swept land near the sea, at the mercy of marauding pirates; how, as they prospered, the islanders' mainly vegetarian diet started to include more meat and fish, and it was this, in Yianni's opinion, especially the consuming of razor clams, that caused mothers to produce male children, and how consequently, the bride price had become exorbitant; landless men had to leave the island to find lucrative employment enough to buy a bride, the less adventurous going to Piraeus, Thessaly and the mainland beyond, the more adventurous braving the hungry seas to make their fortune in America. Some got lost somewhere in between. All came back – the luckless with empty pockets and a foreign wife – Greek of course, but not from the village – the lucky ones with disposable income and electrical gadgets – phonograms, electric lights, fans which blew by themselves – the wonders of the modern age, waiting in a back room for electricity to come to the island.

I end with: "But now, with the growth of tourism since Greece entered the European Common Market, what was the best land – the most productive farming land - owned mainly by women, is now of much less value than the land next to the sea, land which used to be thought of as wasteland. As land values invert, the socio-economic hierarchies are reversed and old scores are settled. Change brings conflict."

I read it back. Not bad for a first draft. Good enough to send to Marsha anyway.

As I am looking for the owner to order another coffee, a taxi pulls up outside and a neatly dressed man in a suit gets out, pays the driver and with a briefcase in one hand and the other dragging his suitcase behind him, he comes towards me. The owner comes out of the *kafenion* when he hears the percussion of the suitcase wheels on the irregular concrete floor of the veranda, grins and opens his arms to the visitor. "Stelio!" the visitor says joyfully and they embrace. *"Ti kaneis? Kala?"*

"Nai," says the owner, who I guess is called Stelios. He takes the visitor's suitcase from him and goes inside. The visitor sees me regarding them.

He comes to me with his hand extended. "Hello," I say as I offer him my hand.

"Ah, English," he says. "Antonis Ionidis," he says, "Inspector of Police, Athens."

"Tom Pickering, journalist, London," I retort.

"Antoni, *ela*!" Stelios call to the visitor.

"My cousin, Stelios," The Police Inspector explains. "Wait, I am coming back," he says and goes inside hurriedly.

He doesn't take long unpacking. He returns without his jacket, now more relaxed. He is about my age, but shorter than me, although probably heavier – he is thick-set which gives him a muscular appearance now, but which, in middle age, will turn into a paunch and a fat back. His bulbous eyes and his smile which goes almost, but not quite, from ear-to-ear give him the appearance of a puppy keen to earn an affectionate pat. He carries a pack of cigarillos and a zippo lighter. He sits himself down at my table, assuming my invitation. He is keen to make the acquaintance of an English journalist, someone with whom he can have uplifting conversations, someone with a broad world view. He is a man of the world, a graduate of the University of Thessaly with a Masters in Political Science, he is quick to tell me. His accent is American inflected, no doubt from watching American crime movies. He has only recently been promoted to Inspector and this is his first case for the Political Crimes Unit which he has just joined.

"You heard they found a body in the bridge?" he asks me earnestly. I nod. "The communists are making a stink, o-boy! My superiors want this to be, what you might call, nip-ped in the butt," he says. He put himself forward for the job. He championed his cousin, Stelios, the owner of the Kafenion, as a man well-connected, who could smooth the way for him and give him valuable insider's knowledge of the island. In return for his superiors' confidence, he would save the Police Department the expense of housing him for the duration of his stay on the island by staying free of charge with Stelios in Agia Anna. Rumour had it that the son of the corpse under investigation lived in Agia Anna, so it was just as well.

He lights a cigarillo, then offers me one. I decline. I don't smoke, but I do like the aroma of a good cigar, so I don't mind. He smokes in an affected way, like he's a character in a movie and displays a confident social manner which only serves to accentuate his insecurity. I bet he is from a small town, probably the son of a grocer or a factory worker. But there is humour in his eyes. He doesn't take himself too seriously. I like him.

Stelios brings him an ouzo and puts one down for me too, but he does not join us. He goes back to sitting in his seat by the door and looks into the distance, immersed in his thoughts.

Antonis – he waves away my calling him "Inspector" – and I have a pleasant chat about literature – he is a fan of John le Carre – and football – a male bonding thing. He supports Iraklis, the team from Thessaloniki, who are not doing too well and are in need of a new manager. He wonders if Arsene Wenger could be tempted. He laughs with gusto at his outrageous suggestion. He asks me about London and the club scene – he'd love to visit and meet English girls. He has all the CDs of Coldplay including X+Y, which has only just become available in Athens, he tells me enthusiastically.

"Tonight I must be with my cousin, but maybe tomorrow we will dine together, no?" he says with hope in his voice. "It will be my pleasure," he says sweetly, hand on heart, to show me he is not just being polite. My "new best friend".

7

As I am approaching the Sea View, the same taxi which brought the Inspector (I recognise the driver) pulls up, and an excited young woman jumps out and into the onrushing open arms of Michalis. "Xanthe! *Kori mou!*" Michalis shouts, his eyes closed in rapture as he hugs her. Nitsa waits her turn with a benevolent smile, eventually Michalis gives up the new arrival into Nitsa's firm embrace.

An old woman, all in widow's black, effecting a dignified bearing, even though she leans heavily on her walking stick, emerges from the shadows cast by the awnings and the young woman grins at her and hugs her. "*Giagia,*" she sighs. *Giagia* – I know *giagia*, to my ears "yaya", means grandmother – the young woman must be Michali's daughter. The *giagia* must be the legendary, Stavroula, Michali's mother. Stavroula's coal black eyes smolder with pride as she holds her granddaughter away from her to see her properly. I feel a prick of a tear. I wonder whether my Greek grandmother would have bathed me in so much pride, so much love. I think I'll eat here tonight, be part of the warmth of Greek family life. I do so hope Lucy is back and we can come here together. This atmosphere will be just right for *our* reunion.

Michalis, frowning, counts out a few notes for the taxi driver and instructs him in an off-hand way to carry his daughter's suitcase and bags inside. He resumes his proud, beaming smile. His daughter returns to his embrace. He kisses her on the forehead, and with his arm around her shoulder, they go inside. Stavroula sees me watching them. She dismisses me contemptuously. There is something harsh in her eye, determined, malevolent. She shuffles round and takes herself inside. Funny old bat! My e-mail to New World Order can wait. Stavroula for one would not appreciate my intrusion.

I walk up the lane to my abode, grinning to myself, and suddenly I just *know* that Lucy is back (I'm intuitive like that), I begin to plan what I am going to say when I first see her and she gives me that ironic smile of hers. "I forgive you and absolve you of all the sins we're about to commit, honey child," I'll say and bless her pontifically with the sign of the cross. My smile broadens at my own wit.

The curious stare of the ancient lady leaning on the front gate of the decrepit house across the road makes me aware that my lips are moving.

"Geia sou," I say in greeting. She grunts and mumbles complaints to herself, then turns and shuffles back to her front door, still murmuring her disgruntlement.

I go to Lucy's front door, turn the handle silently and press – she's locked it. I insert the key, my smile still imprinted on my face, unlock the latch, turn the handle… and burst in. The stillness and emptiness of the room assaults me. The room is as I've left it. No sign of Lucy.

Oh, well. Intuition is not a science.

Not time for dinner yet, so I may as well read the articles I downloaded on the environmental shit that is going down on the Greek coastline – may as well get up to speed. Lucy will be impressed, and when she gives me the story she's brewing, I won't come over as a complete idiot. In fact, I intend to come over as well-informed and interested. But is there a link to the body in the bridge? If there is, I can't see it yet.

I open my laptop, find the articles and begin to read. It's the usual story of good spin and zero delivery. The "Natura 2000 Project" so-called, under the auspices of the Ministry of Production, Environment and Energy (I just know which of those three Directorates has the smallest offices) has demarcated coastal areas of environmental sensitivity as "Special Protected Areas" to bring Greece into line with the EU's Integrated Coastal Zone Management regulations (in order, no doubt, to qualify for generous EU environmental protection funding). But since then, there have been squabbles in parliament and between departments about zoning and boundaries, with the elaborately named Directorate of Biodiversity Protection, Soil and Waste Management coming off second and sometimes third best. The Deputy Minister in charge has more recently thrown in the towel (or should that be *trowel*) and devolved decision-making to local municipal level, that is to the Mayors of the contested areas, to resolve. This had led to some controversial reversals and "concessions", and an NGO (not named in the report I was reading) had taken action through the Council of State to have the ministerial decision over-ruled. (I make a note to try to find out which NGO that was.) Could this be what Lucy is on to? This sounds like her territory. There is more to read, but enough for now.

I close the laptop, take a shower and get dressed to go out for dinner. I am feeling pleasantly warm from my first light sunburn. I examine my image in the mirror. My skin has darkened. I see a pleasing resemblance to my father in the picture of him from his student days. Do I need to shave? – no, the stubble makes me look rugged. And more local. I want to look my best in case Lucy shows up. Which reminds me: I must leave a note to say I'm at the Seaview for dinner and ask her to join me. I find some note paper, scribble a Dearest Lucy message, deliberate on sticking it to the fridge or the front door, decide on the front door, and go out. I find I am whistling. I never whistle.

Michalis greets me warmly. "Come, my friend, come sit. Here, a good table for you," he ushers me to a beachfront table for two, dimly lit. He lights the candle in its blue glass holder on the table. "*Psomi*," he says to himself, "Bread... I will get and come," and he hurries off. The waitress with the copper blonde ringlets ambles over. "Something to drink?"

"*Pos se lene?*" I ask her name, trying out my phrasebook Greek.

"Agapi," she says, with a look of curious amusement. Buoyed by Lucy's return, I feel gregarious, magnanimous, lucky.

"Agapi?" I try it out, smiling to put her at ease.

"No, Agapi – chg, chg – Achgapi," she says with mock exasperation.

"Achgapi," I say tentatively, sounding the guttural "chg" (like "loch", I tell myself) like I am clearing my throat.

She chuckles. "No, Agapi," she says. When she says her name, it is with a soft elision, like a cat's purr. Her eyes close in an endearing muting of her pride that she has such a name, one that can conjure itself into a sound of intimacy, one she can use as a joke or a gift. When she opens her eyes, I see how emerald they shine. Her face is gently yellowed by the candlelight, her strong cheekbones and full lips accentuated.

"Agapi. What it means?" I ask in my best assimilated English for Greeks.

"It means 'Love'," she says and looks at me amusedly, ironically. "I did not give myself this name," she jokes. She wears her cynicism lightly. She knows the effect announcing her name has on most men, the ribald reposts that are sure to follow. But her humorous inflection suggests she regards me as different from those sort of men. I am gratified, collusive, and surprised to feel a flock of butterflies take flight in my chest.

"Hilarious," I say, to show her I get her jokiness. "Agapi," I try out her name again, and in spite of myself, I find I pronounce it with a seductive inflection.

She waggles her head, and grins back at me. "And you?"

"Oh, I'm Tom," I say and then don't know if I should offer my hand. No, better not. Not cool. I should be cool and English. But friendly. Should I get up and kiss her on both cheeks? Would she expect... No, better not. I keep my hands firmly on the table cloth and lift the apex of my eyebrows like Brad Pitt, as if to say, what do you think of that? Fuck, I am such an idiot!

"So, Tom, what you want to drink?" she says eventually, releasing us both from the awkward moment.

I order a beer and she goes off, a small smile curving her full lips at their corners in a quiet affirmation of her allure. Michalis comes back and places a menu and the basket of bread in front of me and adjusts the cutlery. "I spoke with Christos from The Poseidon. He hasn't seen your friend either. But you can go and see him. He is away for maybe three days, but after. He will show you The Poseidon – is nearly finish. *Nai?"*

"Oh," I tell him, "No worries. I think Lucy is back."

Before he can take this in, his daughter sidles up to him and puts her arms around his waist. *"Paterouli mou,"* she says.

"Ah, *asteri mou,"* Michalis says contentedly. He has missed his daughter. Turning to me and putting his arm around his daughter's shoulder, he says, "This is my daughter, my little lamb," he says, and kisses her on the side of her head. "Xanthe."

"Pleased to meet you," I say. "I'm Tom."

"Hello, Tom," Xanthe says with a hint of flirtation that confirms I am making a good impression on the local women. I hope Lucy will be as impressed. Xanthe and her father go off arm-in-arm. Nice.

Then I notice Yiannis from next door, looking at me with a look of hurt. I am supporting his competitor. I wave and nod a greeting. I will go to his place later I decide. I signal to him. He turns away.

At a table further into the *taverna* a family of a father, a mother and their two early teenage sons are sitting down. The father is flustered and organizing the seating arrangement in a loud authoritative voice and with extravagant hand gestures. His sons look unamused, his wife indifferent. She is bloated and rubicund. She and the husband are dressed smartly. Their boys have on short-sleeved checkered shirts with crisply ironed creases, probably bought cheaply by their mother from a supermarket. These are people from the village up in the mountain on a night out, people who were regarded as well-off before, who will now get left behind by progress. Michalis comes out and greets the father enthusiastically. They hug and slap each other on the back. The wife looks relieved and coy. Michalis chats easily to the boys as he hands out the menus. The older boy's responses are monosyllabic. The younger one says nothing but looks at Michalis suspiciously. Their father is magnified by the special attention of the *taverna* owner and he beams at his family indulgently. Michalis leaves them to consider their options.

I examine my menu. Lots of tempting looking starters. And fresh fish. But the prices are not cheap. They have been tailored to the European tourists with their euros and dollars. I glance over at the village family. The father is studying his menu intently. I can see the worry in his frown as he sees the prices, his self-importance deflates. He whispers something to his wife without looking up. She gives the merest glimmer of a grimace, which he just catches out of the corner of his eye. He glares at her, but the wrinkle in his brow implores her to be kind to him, to show solidarity. The older boy points to something on the menu to his younger brother and they laugh. The father is realizing that he cannot afford this restaurant. It was a bad idea. But he can't get up and walk out. Michalis comes back with two glasses of ouzo, which his gesture indicates is complimentary. The paterfamilias accepts his drink politely, his smile frozen. His wife silently refuses hers, Michalis returns inside with the glass. The father goes back to studying his menu. He leans over and talks quietly to his wife. He needs her cooperation and support. She turns to the sons and says something, which is either bland or dismissive. The older boy looks at his father with disdain, points at the menu and says something which his brother laughs at, and suddenly his father can't contain his anxiety, and to release himself, he slaps his older son and wags his finger at him. The wife sits stiffly back and avoids eye contact with anyone. The younger boy glares at his father accusingly – he was partly responsible for his father's rage. The older boy is at first shocked, then embarrassed, then hurt. He looks at his father incredulously, silent angry tears coming to his eyes.

Agapi has been watching them also. She goes inside and emerges moments later with a bottle of water and four glasses. She sets these down and regards the father coolly. The wife looks her up and down. Agapi says something to the father and by her sweeping gesture, I work out she is making a suggestion for their order. She says something to enthuse the boys, and they nod. I sense she is from a village too. She knows these people. She has found a way to make this okay. They will keep their dignity. The father looks grateful and relieved. "*Nai*," he says decisively, and puts his menu down. He glances at his family for their approval, but they all avoid his eye. He sips his *ouzo*, considers it, and pronounces it to his liking, "*Kala!*" He sits back and looks around him with a superior look, his status restored.

Both parties of German tourists at tables along the veranda studiously avoid looking at him. One group is dominated by expressions of disdain, the other with a patronizing sympathy. I realize I am tending to the latter and affect an analytic countenance, neither one thing nor another. But I don't want to appear to be rude or indifferent. I settle on feeling sad.

Agapi comes to take my order. I could afford culinary excellence at a price, but feel this will shame the village family. I order something modest. Agapi looks at me with one eyebrow raised. I sense she has noticed my change in mood. She doesn't press me to order more. She leaves it at that and goes off, and I am touched by her sensitivity to the family from the village, none of whom is looking at the other.

8

I leave straight after my main course. I would have liked something sweet, but the village family have pointedly not ordered a dessert or ice-cream and this reminds me that I promised myself I would go to Yianni's after. I leave Agapi a generous tip. Over my shoulder, as I am leaving, I see her collecting the coins. She looks puzzled at my sudden exit.

Yiannis has three tables of customers tonight – busy for him I surmise. There are two tables of families who are probably from the village. They are talking loudly. The younger children are running around in a game of catch-me-if-you-can and shrieking. Their mothers tell them off. Their fathers look on indulgently. A young hippy couple sits in the shadows, silently reviewing the pictures on their cameras. Probably students.

Yiannis is overjoyed to see me. I think he gave up on me and now wants to make it up. I tell him I would love an ice-cream. His face falls. "Oh, my friend, the outside refrigerator is not work. All my ice-cream is melt. Why you not have *rizogalo*? – Soulla is make. Is warm. Is taste…" he kisses his finger-tips to the heavens. "Or *baklava* and Greek coffee? Come, come," he orders me to the kitchen and shows me the rice pudding, puts it to my nose. Its fragrance of honey and rosewater is wonderful. Yiannis sees the effect his wife's pudding is having on me and laughs. "*Ena rizogalo, nai?*" His eyes shine with self-pride - he can please me; his establishment will not be humiliated by its affluent neighbour. "Go sit. I come," he says.

The rice pudding is sweet and creamy and warms me with its benevolence. I recognise it as something my father used to make. Only we just called it rice pudding, not rizogalo. But there is something decidedly Middle Eastern about it... honey, not sugar... cinnamon... and *cardamom* – that's it. I must remember that. I am pleased with the refinement of my palate, that I can taste these subtle undercurrents. My father would be pleased. I look around at the other customers, unaffected local people, as if for their acknowledgement of me as one of them, as a Greek. The village families who are eating here ignore me. But they are at ease and I can shake off the discomfort I felt at the Seaview. I just wish Lucy was here so I could share this with her.

These are young families. The oldest child is probably seven or eight. Two families I think. The two men, the fathers, chat to each other and smoke contemplatively. They must be brothers - they have the same mournful faces and squat builds. The women are animated, collecting their children together, holding an arm, checking under a chair. They are preparing to leave. Yiannis brings my coffee. "Wait," he says, "I will drink with you." He goes to say goodbye to his customers and walks with them, conversing amiably. Yiannis suddenly remembers something and rushes off, signaling for them to wait.

Just then, the mother from the beleaguered family I saw earlier at the Seaview comes in with her youngest in tow, and, ignoring the women, who scowl at her, she goes to the two brothers and admonishes them tearfully. They look nonplussed and say nothing. The shorter of the two brothers, shaking his head, takes out his wallet and dismissively gives the woman a ten euro note. She snatches it, mumbles a thank-you and turns to leave, head down, shamed, as Yiannis reappears brandishing lollipops for the children. He greets the woman from next door and offers her son a lollipop too. The boy looks to his mother to see it is okay. She nods sullenly. He takes it and smiles shyly. The other two mothers yell at their boys, who are giggling. I can tell from their insistent tones that they want them to say thank you to "*theo* Yianni". He laughs and ruffles their hair. One of the little boys does not like that, and scowling, reassembles his hairstyle. The mother from next door has skulked off.

Yiannis gets his coffee and cigarettes and the bottle of brandy and sits himself down at my table, legs splayed. "Metaxas," he says as he examines the label of the brandy bottle, "The General. Ioannis Metaxas. You know General Metaxas? *Patriotis* – you say?"

"Patriot."

"*Nai*. Patriot. And *fasistis*. Fascist – *nai*?"

I tell him I know a little from the book on Modern Greek history I read on the plane coming over. I know the ardently anti-communist General Metaxas was put in power by the King in the mid-30s, because the King wanted a strong man to oppose the rise of the increasingly popular Communists, who held the balance of power in the parliament.

Yiannis pours us each a generous shot from the General's bottle. "So what Metaxas he do? – he say no more political parties! Just like this." He snaps his fingers. "Like Mussolini. The Kommunistica peoples he put in the jails. No freedoms. Newspapers? - only the ones for him and for the King. Books? - they burn in the street! – even Plato! Even Aristophanes! Wil-liam Shakespeare! Unbelievable! But the army? - for them, everything. Nice uniforms, guns, everything they wunt.

"Metaxas and Mussolini, like two dogs with one bone. When comes War of the World Number Two, Mussolini and Metaxas they make a big fight. Mussolini send his men when it is winter in the mountains. Can you believe it? Macedonia. Albania. The Italians…" he shakes his head, "freeze in the snow. All of them die. Metaxas is a big hero. For few months only. Then he also die - in his bed! And the Germans come. In two weeks, in Athens."

"How was it on Mythos in the war?" I ask.

Yiannis slugs back his drink and pours himself another shot. I am still sipping slowly. He loosens a cigarette from his pack and lights up. "You see the Greek families was here before? Lambros. Brothers. Their *Baba*, grandfather, Aris Lambros - Kommunistica." He exhales and tips ash which isn't yet formed. "The woman who was come in after - Limoni, is their sister, married to grandson of Garidis. Konstantinos Garidis is *Fascistis*. The two families no speak for fifty years, only after Limoni marry to Fotis Garidis and she have a baby - at the Christening they speak. The young ones, what they care? What they know of the war? But now, when they find the body in the bridge, now they don' talk no more. The body in the bridge it makes people to remember."

He takes a puff of his cigarette. "I was just a zmall boy. Garidis, the grandfather, Konstantin - he was a young man, very handsome and lots of muscles. He like to show us his muscles and what he could lift up. The Italians they come here first, and a few Germans. Garidis was work for them. He was one who show who is a Jewish – two families in the port, in Agia Sofia. Finished. He show who is *Kommounistika*. The men - the *andartes* - went to the mountains. ELAS. But what guns they have? – to shoot rabbits only! Their families they suffer. No food. No can make work. Garidis have uniform, and boots... He walk up and down like famoos man."

"Was there much resistance on the island?" I ask.

"Later, after 1943 when Germans come – the Germans kill-ed some Italians, so Italians helps us. The Germans, some of them not so bad; they give us childrens sweets, respect the woman (not like the Italians) – but the Gestapo…" he can't find the English words to match his expression of disgust. I glance at the young hippy couple, still at their table in the shadows. Are they Germans? Yiannis sees my glance. "Dutch," he says, "Not Germans."

"It was worse in the big cities. In Athens 300,000 people they die of no food. The Greeks in the government – *trothotiz* – Rallis – he make Security Battalion – you hear Security Battalion?"

I have heard of the infamous Security Battalion and their excesses and mimicry of the Gestapo.

"They punish everybody who is not support Rallis and the Germans. Garidis, he make himself head of the Security Battalion in Mythos. After the war, Garidis in prison, but only few years. *Malakas.* The bastard – they should have shot him! But he is still have his business, his factory – he live in the village up there in the mountains," says Yiannis pointing to the faint pinpricks of light in a cleft in the dark hills. "Kasteli," he savours the name. "His grandson is marry with the grand-daughter of Aris Lambros who was with ELAS in the mountains. First they don' speak, then they speak, now again they don' speak. *Istoria* – history…" he gives a shrug, "like a drunk man. What you can do?"

9

When I get back to the cottage, the note I left for Lucy is still on the door. Lucy is not back yet. The night has not turned out like I hoped it would. I must be patient. Maybe she'll come back in the night.

She doesn't. When I wake, I go to her bedroom to see if she's returned, but her bed is still made. She has not been home. I guess she is on some urgent assignment. Still, she could have left a note. I presume her phone is still not working or lost, or she would have called me. At least I am now sure she's got her laptop with her, so I could e-mail her again.

On my way down to the Seaview for breakfast, I compose a message to Lucy in my head.

Dearest Lucy, Maybe you've worked out that the mess in your cottage is me. I'm here. So much for the surprise! Now that I am so close to you and see your things around me, I miss you ~~with the intensity of a volcano~~ *(... no, that has sexual connotations) ...* ~~I miss you with the intensity of...~~ *I miss you even more. Lucy, I am so happy we are going to be together. I think this was meant to be. I hope you feel the same. Please come back soon. With all my love, Tom.*

Yeah, that should do it.

Lucy, who I first glanced through a half-open door, sitting with her back to me on my sister's bed, a seventeen-year-old girl, clothed only in a Javanese wrap, her towel-ruffled red hair splayed over the smooth whiteness of her shoulders, poised, delicately tilted up, like small angel wings. A vision of beauty. I felt it indiscrete to gawp, but was transfixed, until she looked around, her jewel-blue Slavic eyes opening slightly in surprise, drawing me in to drown. I'd rushed away, embarrassed.

****

London. Five years earlier. March, 2000

Irini's friend is with her at the breakfast table, their heads close together, whispering conspiratorially. When they see me, they part and go silent, smiling knowingly. "Morning," I say, being cool and older-brotherly.

"This is Lucy," Irini says. The girl, Lucy, lifts her chin at me, defying me to make the first move. Her firmly drawn lips and deep tapering of her cheeks make her appear more handsome than pretty. But it is the luminescence of her cobalt blue eyes and the wildness of her luxuriant auburn hair that make me look away. So much beauty is dangerous. "Lucy is going to stay with us," Irini says with certainty.

This is the day after my mother's funeral, the day after Irini's panicked phone-call. All I heard between her sobs was "vomited blood" and "ambulance" and I dashed back from university, just as I was about to take my Finals, hoping against hope that there would still be time to say goodbye. I'd arrived too late. My mother had been ill for a long time, deteriorating slowly from cirrhosis of the liver, although she hid it well from me. She did not want her indisposition to affect my studies. The moment of her death came as a shock - I did not think she would die then, not before I'd got my degree. But now she is dead. And Lucy is here.

Irini tells me, when Lucy goes to the loo, that Lucy is now her best friend, she's had a tough time and can't live with her family anymore. Our mother had agreed for Lucy to stay, but had stipulated that Lucy should not have the use my bedroom. She and Irini were sharing a bed. She smirks when she says this. She can tell how turned on I am by her beautiful friend, but I will not give her the satisfaction of owning up to this. I am her older brother, the man of the house, the grown-up. Irini is, to me, still a kid. And so, by extension, is her friend. Therefore out of bounds. "Do you mind, Tom?" she asks provocatively. I grunt my assent.

For the next week, we are often inevitably in each other's company, casual everyday things - preparing meals, eating together, watching telly - but I keep to my resolve to be the dutiful older brother, so I do not make a move on Lucy. She and Irini go to movies, but I don't go with them. They don't invite me, and I don't impose myself. I tell myself that my sister's new best friend is at least five years too young for me. She looks up to me in a way I find touching. Still, I find myself tongue-tied in her presence.

A week after she arrives, I am sitting in my bedroom at my make-shift desk, revising for the re-takes of exams I hadn't taken, when, with an informal knock on the door, Lucy walks in. "I thought you might like some tea," she says, placing a steaming mug on the desk.

"I usually take it with one sugar and a drop of milk," I say.

"I know," she says, with a smile of accomplishment. She must have been watching me. She examines the cover of a reference book for my Politics course. "Primitive Rebels by Eric Hobsbawm. Is this any good?" she says.

"Yeah, well the guys a genius. Have you heard of Eric Hobsbawm?" I ask.

"No," she says, defensively, as if I'm testing her, which I am not. "What's it about?"

"Outlaws," I tell her, "Outlaw peasants who took a stand against the prevailing elites. The original class warriors. You can borrow it if you like," I say, hoping she will and that later this will be the portal to a lively discussion wherein I can display to her the fast bends of my analytic mind. Her face opens into a wide smile, even as the colour rises from her neck into her jawline.

"Really?" she says. She is evidently pleased that I am prepared to treat her as intelligent enough to read a book for 3rd year students. She turns the book this way and that. "Outlaws. I like that. It's only fair when there is so much unfairness in the world," she says. "We should make things fair." A hard look narrows her eyes. What has she had to deal with, I wonder. Irini said she'd had a bad time with her family. "Yeah, but then... like guns, in America. That's what *they* say - a gun makes things fair, so you can stand up to bullies and criminals. But then all those poor schoolchildren who were killed. How come those two boys even had guns?" She is talking about Colombine, the shooting last year in an American high school. Everybody outside of the US National Rifles Association is up in arms, as it were, against guns, but a year on, you can still buy a gun at a petrol station in some states.

"You know what I saw on Channel Four?" she asks, her eyes wide, her voice sharpened by outrage. "There's a bank somewhere in the States which, if you open an account with them, is giving customers *a free gun!* I hope they don't also give them the bullets! A gun? In a bank?" I grin at her fervour. "What?" she asks, grinning back at me. "Are you laughing at me?"

"Take the book," I say with a chuckle. She does. I don't see the book again. And we don't get to have that discussion.

What we do have is a row. A few days later. I am woken by the irresistible smell of fried bacon. I have studied deep into the night, trying to store dates and places in my mind for my History exam, and it has not been going well. My brain feels like wet clay. I put on a tee-shirt and jeans and, barefooted, go into the kitchen, knowing that what I want, what will put the world right, is a couple of BLT sandwiches. There's a double pack in the fridge - should be more than enough. But there isn't. Irini and Lucy are scoffing a pile of bacon, and I see the empty packet on the sink. "Fuck off!" I explode. "Have you two just eaten all the bacon?"

Lucy looks guilty, her fork poised near her mouth. Irini has her mouth full (overfull), and is trying to chew and swallow it down so she can defend herself. "You fucking pig!" I shout. She looks so ugly to me in that moment.

Lucy puts her fork down. "You can have some of mine," she offers. Irini glares at her.

"I don't want some of yours - I want mine!" I say churlishly (or could that be childishly), realizing I am being a pillock, but too far gone now to stop myself. "You realize I am paying for all of this with my grant. You two are paying *nothing* towards your upkeep."

Irini is chomping her food as fast as she can, but the effort is keeping her silent for the time being. Lucy is watching Irini's vigorous chewing with fascination. She is waiting for her to say something. But then she loses patience. "I don't have any money. I used up all the money the social worker gave me. I can try to get some more though," she says, the doubt in her voice poignant. I feel a pang of sympathy (and sorrow) for this girl who has been kicked out of her family. I want to tell her it's not her I'm angry with – it's my gluttonous sister I am angry with - but I don't.

"I suppose you've eaten all the eggs too?" I growl.

Irini has started crying. Lucy gets up to comfort her. I check the fridge - there are still eggs. I turn to see Irini fleeing the kitchen, with her best friend's arm over her shoulder. Lucy looks back at me at the doorway, her eyes smoldering. I think I also detect a look of disappointment in me - coming from a seventeen-year-old. I want it not to matter, but it does.

I fry myself two eggs but my anger doesn't dissipate. Irini and Lucy have left bacon on their plates, but I can't bring myself to eat their leftovers. I scrape their plates into the bin. I am filled with self-righteousness and I am digesting that last look of Lucy's. God, she's so beautiful. An intelligent mind too, I think. I want her to like me. I want *her*, but I can't let myself have her. I can't. Can I?

Then a few days later, I come home from the library to find that Irini has moved my mother's things out of my mother's room, stuffed my mother's clothes into prosaic black bags ready for the charity shop and has moved Lucy into my mother's bed. I am not ready for this. I am still acutely feeling the loss of my mother. I want to regain her. I want her scent in her bedroom, the familiarity of her possessions anchors on which to tie childhood memories, already fading. Irini is taking my mother away from me. I hate her in that moment. "You've always been ungrateful, Irini, always *contrary*. You *never* respected our mother, never tried to understand her. You just always wanted everything your way. You had no compassion for what she had to endure after Dad died. You still don't. None."

Irini glares at me. "You don't know half of it," she hisses at me.

I have been unfair I know, but I am seething and want to be right. "You're taking the piss," I snarl.

"You're not my parent!" Irini screams at me. "You can't tell me what to do!"

"Yes, I can! And I want your friend out of here!" I shout back and immediately regret it. I mean the bedroom, but I know, when I see Lucy's face, she has heard it as 'out of the house'. Lucy looks shocked, mortified, then goes to Irini to comfort her, as if Irini is the one who will suffer.

When I come back from sitting my retakes a week later, Lucy is gone.

10

I stride into The Seaview with my laptop. Nitsa doesn't wait to be asked. She gets up, goes into the office and puts the modem on. I give her my five euros without a word being exchanged. I click 'Get mail'. Nothing from Lucy yet.

But there is something from Marsha back at the office. She suggests I send her more brief essays as "Letters from Greece", but to make them "less dry" than my previous attempt. She likes the environmental angle, but it is the body in the bridge story which has piqued her interest. Do I have any contacts?

I do, as it happens, Marsha. Antonis Ionides, my new friend, the Inspector from the Athens Political Crimes Unit. I could ask him if I can tag along. Also, that communist woman, Calliope. I should get an interview with her.

First though I draft my e-mail to Lucy, get it sounding heartfelt but not too earnest and send it off. With this done, I shut my laptop and go to find the Inspector.

He is on the veranda at the *Kafenion*, finishing his coffee. "Ah, my friend," Antonis greets me enthusiastically. I tell him that my editor is keen to do a story on the body in the bridge and I would like to start with a profile of the lead detective. I sit myself down. Antonis smiles broadly, then he shuffles his features into the demeanor of a modest professional. "Yes," he says, "You can make a report to your newspaper. Why not, my friend? You will need a photograph of me?" Already he is imagining his fame, the subject of a newspaper report in London. "If the story is read outside of Greece, my Minister, the Minister of Public Order and Citizen Protection, will give us more money for the investigation." He offers his hand. We have a deal.

A car pulls up outside. "My car," the Inspector says, "Come. Today we go to the bridge."

We stop off at Lucy's house for me to get my camera and shades, then we take the winding road back to the bridge. At the bridge, the heavy building vehicles form a guard of honour, respectfully silent, digging arms lowered. There is a small group of people in discussion, who look up and nod a greeting when we get out the car. Antonis goes to shake hands with the Mayor and the Police Chief, both of whom I recognise from the police station. The Police Chief looks at me suspiciously and asks Antonis something. Antonis gestures at me and says something offhand. The fat cop says nothing, but he is not pleased to have me there. Together we go to a group of men and one woman in white overalls and masks. The woman takes off her mask and talks to Antonis. He nods. They go together to examine the hand protruding from the concrete – it has turned black and is putrefying. I see Antonis grimace and hold his nose discreetly. There is a police photographer, also in overalls, taking pictures. I take a few quick photos with my Canon. Not the best light – the hand is in the shade – but it will have to do for now. I take a shot of Antonis and the female forensic archeologist (which is what she turns out to be). The fat cop comes to me and puts his hand up. "No pictures. No pictures," he says curtly.

Antonis comes back and gives me a commentary. The archeological excavation team say the body is likely to be well-preserved in the concrete, but as soon as it is exposed to the air, it will deteriorate rapidly. So, the plan is to take out the entire block of concrete and fly it back to the laboratory in Athens, where they will excavate it under controlled temperature and humidity. But they will have to work fast. The construction company will have to cut the block carefully so that it does not crack open and expose the corpse. It will have to be packed to avoid vibrations when it is transported to the airport and then in the plane. The female forensic archeologist will supervise this. The foreman has assured her they have the right equipment. She is satisfied.

Antonis, serious and focused, speaks to the Mayor and the Police Chief. The Mayor hands over a wad of documents. The Inspector examines them carefully. He shuffles them and finds one he puts to the front. He comes over to me. "Okay," he says without looking at me, still preoccupied with the documents he has been given, "The construction company building the new road, Atreus Constructions…" he consults the documents "… belongs to Christos Papademos." (I register this is the same guy who is building The Poseidon. Could this be a link Lucy is pursuing?) "But it was a different company before that was building this bridge. If it was Papademos's company, maybe he would not want a body to be found." He chuckles and gives me a mischievous look. "But, okay, let's see." He examines the documents again. "The construction company that built *this* bridge, the old bridge, according to this document here, was owned by someone called… Konstantinos Garidis."

Konstantinos Garidis – the bully boy for the Gestapo on the island in the war. That fits. He could have taken it upon himself to do his patriot bit by burying old communists in concrete.

I see Antonis and the Police Chief talking earnestly. The chief scratches his head. Antonis nods and comes back to me. It seems the Chief has had the same idea as me. He also knows Garidis's reputation. He knows where the old man lives and has offered to drive Antonis to see him, not to formally interview him, but merely to root around – see what he knows, hear what he has to say. The Inspector wants to know if I want to go along for the ride. I notice that the Chief is not too pleased to have me along but seems to have deferred to his Athenian counterpart.

On the way to the patrol car, the Chief asks me if I've seen Lucy – the airport had no listing of her having flown out of the island. His tone has softened, I surmise he is trying to dissipate the tension there is between us, before we go on a long drive into the mountains and potentially spend the day together. I too feel conciliatory. Maybe I misjudged him. I tell him that Lucy seems to have popped in and popped out again, having collected her hoodie and her laptop. I'm sure she'll be back shortly or call or e-mail me if she is going to be away for any time. He nods thoughtfully.

"Forget about her," he says, "She a crazy woman!" and smiles ruefully. "You *yoornaleest?* – you write about this investigation, Antonis tells to me – is better. Peoples they must not forget their history," he says somberly. He offers me his hand. "*Parakalo,* you call me Panagiotis. And the second name: Valoudsakis" – he spells it for me – "for when you write about me," he says, smiling modestly. He hitches his trousers up so his belt circumscribes the widest girth of his tummy and rolls his shoulders back, with the briefest glance at my camera. Vanity? Camera-derie? (Ho-ho.)

"So who do you think the body belongs to?" I ask in the car as we make our way up into the hills.

Antonis talks over his shoulder to me in the back of the patrol car. He has to shout to be heard over the roar of the engine, which is struggling against the gradient. "The bridge was built in 1969. The time of the Colonels. Of the 'junta'. So maybe political. We don't know for sure. Maybe an accident? – someone working, fell in the concrete? But we do not have any reports of anyone going missing – does not mean to say it did not happen. We will check again. But if it is political... the Communists have given us the names of two of their comrades who were arrested by the junta and never seen again. One of them was the father of the man who owns the restaurant in Agia Anna."

"Michalis Epistemos," I say.

"Exactly," the Inspector says, "Gregorios Epistemos, also known as Mavros. In English, "Blackie". Very dark skin. Maybe from Africa in his family." The Chief nods.

"And the other one?"

"Aris Lambros, the leader of the United Democratic Left on the island until the Colonels banned the UDL as soon as they took power – the UDL was the only properly left-wing organization in Greece. The Communist Party of course was banned in the 30s by the Great Patriot, General Metaxas. Gregorios Epistemos, Mavros, was also in the UDL. We will try to get dental records, but, you know, not many Greeks went to a dentist in those days, certainly not on an island like this. If your teeth were bad, a bone-fixer would pull the bad teeth out your head," he chuckles. "But there are other ways," he says. "We will find out who the body is."

73

11

We get to Kasteli which sits precariously high up in a cleft in the mountain. At its highest point there is a small church with a blue roof. All that is left of the castle, after which the village is named (there is a hopeful sign pointing to it), are geometric fronds of inglorious rubble overcome by revanchist weeds. The village streets flow like rivulets finding their way from the church down to the square by gravity alone. The main street is cobbled – the other streets are a mixture of potholed concrete and dust. There is a *kafenion*, outside of which old men sit. An ancient oak has been preserved at the side of the square, its trunk whitened with lime to slow the industry of demolition ants. Two young boys kick a plastic football. Their heavy-set mothers, baskets of laundry on their hips, chat in high-pitched voices like pigeons.

As the Chief parks his car on the square, an old crone in black peeks out a half-closed door, scowls and goes back inside. The door closes. We walk a little uphill to one of only two double-storied houses in the village. The house has been extended over time, but in the main area it is a product of the 1960s with squat iron-framed windows and garish tiles. The Chief pushes open a wrought iron gate and climbs the stairs to the veranda and the front door. A small dog barks hysterically inside. "Garidis," the Chief calls, *"Kalimera!"* He waits, then shouts out again, *"Ela,* Konstantino!"

He turns to us and raises his eyebrows and shrugs. I'm not sure what this is meant to convey. The dog goes on yapping. The furniture on the veranda has seen better days and smells of witch-hazel. There is a jumble of pots with plants in them - geraniums, nasturtiums, an assortment of miniature succulents and a bedraggled sweet pea creeper. A low table has an ashtray filled with butts on it and a glass half-emptied of some dark brown liquid.

The front door opens cautiously and an old man peers out from under luxuriant white eyebrows. *"Ti thelete?"* he croaks. I think we may have woken him up. "*Geia sou, kirios* Garidis," the chief greets him. The old man peers at him, to catch in his fragile memory a glimpse of familiarity which will reveal the stranger's identity. The Chief introduces himself and from the sweep of his arm, us too. He asks if we can go inside. The old man doesn't reply, but, eyeing us suspiciously, lets us in. The interior is dark and cool. The old man shuffles to the far window and opens the curtains and squints at us, baffled, as if he'd imagined us and now finds we are real. A ginger and white cat is woken by the beam of light from the gap between the curtains. The cat is at first mystified, then displeased and haughtily jumps down from the couch it was sleeping on and sashays out the door, tail erect with disapprobation.

Konstantinos Garidis, one hand on the arm-rest, eases himself into his plump sitting chair and regards us quizzically. We have not been invited to sit. The Chief looks irritated and sits anyway. Antonis and I follow his lead. Antonis, in a measured voice, brimming with politeness, asks the old man questions, which the old man answers laconically. I hear him refuting something, "*Ochi, ochi!*" and sighing heavily, he gets up and goes to a portmanteau and scrabbles about in some papers. Shaking his head, he shuffles across the room to get his spectacles from the dining table, where they lie on an open newspaper. He makes his way back to his paperwork and tries once more to find what he is looking for.

"The original documents for the road and bridge," Antonis whispers to me.

"*Endaxi,*" old Mr. Garidis says and pulls a bunch of documents out and proffers them to the Inspector. Antonis thanks him and peruses the papers. He compares two documents, frowns and then nods. "He's right," he says, "Although he signed the contract for the bridge to be built in 1969, it seems from this" – he thrusts a document at the Chief – "that he sold the construction company two months later – before construction of the bridge had started."

Antonis asks the old man another question. The old man answers, "Hektor Papademos."

The Inspector takes this in. He turns to me. "He says that he sold the company to Hektor Papademos, the father of the man who has the contract for the *new* road and bridge." (Also The Poseidon, I want to tell him, but I hold back – I don't yet know if that's relevant.) "Interesting," he says.

"Doesn't make no sense," says the Chief, "The Papademos family are PASOK. When it was the time of the Colonels, they were against. They are democrats." He was clearly wishing for the old fascist collaborator to be the guilty party. That would have been neat and clean.

The Inspector is evidently asking if he can hold onto the documents. But Konstantinos Garidis is not having that – he snatches the papers out of the Inspector's hand and holds them to his chest defiantly. The Chief says quietly, "There will be copies at the Town Hall. Let's leave him alone." He gets up and we follow him out. *"Fascisti skata!"* the Chief murmurs under his breathe.

So, they will have to question Hektor Papademos. The Chief says he will set it up for Antonis, if possible for tomorrow. He knows the family. They will cooperate. Which reminds me, I have an appointment with *the* son next week. Doesn't seem relevant, now that Lucy is back. I should phone to cancel.

12

We head back to Agia Anna in a pensive mood. Antonis invites the Chief to stay for lunch and I am invited to join them. The Chief recommends The Seaview. Suits me. "Sure, Chief," I say jauntily – this is my home patch.

"Ah, but you must remember to call me Panagiotis," he says silkily. He wants the locals to see he is a friend of the journalist from London who is covering the story in which he will feature.

We get there in time to see the Chief's son pulling his 1000cc police bike onto its stand and unfingering his gloves. He is wearing wrap-round shades and heavy leather boots, which must be hell in this hot weather. Still, image is everything. Besides, Kostas Valoudsakis looks everything like the macho cop of his Hollywood fantasies.

Panagiotis (as I must remember now to call him) questions his son peremptorily and admonishes him in assertive hissing. Kostas looks suitably told off and slouches over to a side table and sits down glumly. But perks up with alacrity as Xanthe comes out onto the balcony. Panagiotis, the long-suffering father, rolls his eyes. Xanthe sees the Chief. "Hello, Uncle Pano," she says sweetly and comes to kiss him on both cheeks. Kostas licks his lips in expectation. But Xanthe just nods at him and then looks away pointedly. Kostas is deflated and fiddles with the saltcellar, examining it assiduously, before glancing up again at Xanthe, to see if she has changed her mind. She hasn't. She has seen Bobby at the tavern next door eyeing her with his lovely amber eyes and she makes a show of waving at him in a friendly way. Bobby half-waves back. He blushes and turns away. Kosta can barely hide his chagrin. She waves at Bobby, who is a kid, yet she can't give him the time of day? I can see him fuming. Agapi goes to take his order, he mumbles, "*Mia bira,*" before quickly looking at his father, his boss, and changing his mind, "*Ochi. Nero, mono, nero. Parakalo.*" He is on duty. Its water only for him.

Meanwhile, Antonis has found us a table and the Chief is levering his corpulent frame into a wicker chair. I sit opposite the Chief. Michalis hastens to us. "Welcome," he says in English. "*Geia sou*, Panagiotis," he greets the Chief. His smile is forced. Panagiotis offers his hand. He and Michalis clasp hands with powerful muscularity. The Chief introduces the Inspector. The Inspector offers his hand too. Antonis offers to introduce me, but Michalis tells him we've already met. He gives me a broad smile like I'm a regular. Then Antonis looks grave and takes Michalis aside. They talk softly and go inside. Antonis comes back after a few minutes. "I think it is right I tell him the body in the bridge may be his father. He had already heard this." He shrugs. "Poor man. I would not want to find this thing out about my father."

"He won't remember his father," the Chief says, "He was a zmall boy when they took his father away. What he will remember? He does not even want to remember that it was *my father* who brought his father to the island. My father that paid for him, helped him escape the authorities in Athens. Michalis he knows this, but he never came to me and say thank you. Always at this *taverna* I pay full price! His daughter, Xanthe, she calls me Uncle – you hear her say this, *nai?* The family they know what we did to help them. Stavroula she knows this. But Michalis... pah!" He juts his lower lip into an expression of resentful irony. "He won't even allow his daughter to go out at the invitation of Kosta, my son. Look at him, the poor boy. Look how he is look. Xanthe is studying to be a doctor – Michalis wants for her to find another doctor to marry. A professor. He doesn't want her to go with a policeman. What you can do?"

At that moment, Xanthe comes to our table and with a proprietorial hand on "Uncle" Panagiotis's shoulder, she introduces herself to Antonis. Antonis introduces himself formally and shoots out his hand to her. She flashes him a seductive smile. "Ah, you're from Athens," she says in English, "Thanks goodness, at last, civilization!" she says and chuckles flirtatiously. She asks where he lives and they find out, as Antonis translates for me quickly, they live not far from one another in the University district. Xanthe is clearly enamoured by the possibility of having a Police Inspector as a friend and protector in Athens. By her pout, she may be even more interested than that. Or is this just a show to rile Kosta? Certainly the policeman has her attention and he is having trouble suppressing his jealousy and rage. His father notices his challenging stare and glares at him, so Kostas goes back to examining the saltcellar.

Agapi brings menus and places one in front of each of us. She has to lean over to place Antonis' and as she does so, I see his eyes fix on her cleavage and then up to her face with a look of longing. She catches his gaze and does her Mona Lisa thing, a smile halfway between cynical and pleased. She probably thinks men are like children. Antonis gulps and then tries to affect a suave expression. He is from Athens after all.

Xanthe is taking all this in, she is not best pleased. "Agapi," she says in English, "Don't just stand there. Ask the gentlemen what they want to drink. Look, this fork is not clean. Go and wash it. Bring a new one please." She smiles benevolently at Antonis. Agapi looks skeptically at her and turns up a corner of her gracefully curved lips in a demi-grimace. But she demurs and goes off, with the culpable fork in hand. "The girl didn't even take your drinks order!" Xanthe says, astonished by Agapi's incompetence. She looks at Antonis, celebrating her small but easy victory. Agapi is merely an employee. Xanthe is the boss's daughter. Antonis's eyes are on Agapi's swaggering bottom as she walks away. Xanthe frowns. I can see she is a determined girl, used to getting her own way. She will not give up the pursuit easily. "Inspector Ionides... or can I call you Antonis?" she asks coquettishly. Antonis nods his assent. "Could I offer you a complimentary glass of white wine, seeing this is your first time in our restaurant?" Antonis nods and smiles politely. "And you, Uncle Panagiotis? What would like to drink?"

"I will have the complimentary wine also," Panagiotis says with guile. Xanthe chuckles at his wit. "No, that's just for the Inspector," she says. Did she just wink at Antonis? The Police Chief laughs too, but his smile is fixed and his expression has darkened. He is hurt by this casual putdown by a twenty-year-old girl.

I interrupt the tense moment by ordering a beer. Then we all study our menus. I notice Antonis's eyes straying to the door through which Agapi went inside. He is waiting for another glance to tell him if she is as beautiful as when he first looked at her. I contemplate whether to tell him that her name means "Love", but I don't. I am irritated to find that I feel territorial about Agapi. I feel more inclined to point out to Antonis that the boss's daughter is a far safer bet.

Once we have our drinks – the Chief also orders a bottle of sparkling water – and the heat of the 2 o'clock sun, even under the awnings, has dulled us into a pleasant torpor, Panagiotis Valoudsakis, with an initial glance to see that Michalis isn't within hearing distance, tells us the story of Michali's father, Gregorios Epistemos, aka Mavros. As he talks, I wish I had my tape recorder with me, or at least a notepad. I don't. So, I can't say the article I compose and submit to my journal later in the day is accurate in all its details. But with the help of my History of Modern Greece, I get something down which is mostly faithful to the Police Chief's telling. It is too long, and I know it will be heavily edited before it goes to print, but this is how it comes out.

The body in the bridge. *A report from the frontline by Tom Pickering.*

Uncovered in demolition to make way for a new road, in the crumbling concrete of a thirty-five-year-old bridge on the Greek island of Mythos, is an interred body. According to my informant, Panagiotis Valoudsakis, Chief of Police on the island, these are the remains of a left-wing activist from the era of the Colonels, the military junta, in charge of Greece in the late 60s/early 70s. His story encapsulates much of what the Left in Greece claims has never been properly addressed, and the finding of the body has fueled the campaign by the Communist Party to have erected statues to commemorate their fallen heroes of old. The body in the bridge has become emblematic of this struggle and the man in this inglorious concrete tomb has become lauded as a hero.

Gregorios 'Mavros' Epistemos was an eleven-year-old boy living with his mother in the Grammos mountains of Northern Greece when the German troops arrived in the summer of 1941. His father had died when Mavros was a small boy. He was his mother's only child. From the age of eight, to help to support his mother, he herded his uncle's goats, in the heat of summer and in the icy cold of winter, chasing his recalcitrant charges, who, without understanding why, tried, whenever the opportunity presented itself, to escape up into the high mountains. So, Mavros learned the terrain as a goat would. Later this saved his life.

The Germans treated the villager's worse than how the villagers treated their livestock. The invaders confiscated for their own use the grain and potatoes the village people had saved for the winter. They slaughtered the few animals the villagers still had so that German officers should not have to go without meat. They arrested and tortured local men and women for the names of the sympathizers providing intelligence or succour to the ELAS resistance fighter, the andartes, hidden in caves and mountain camps.

At the beginning of the war, ELAS, the Communist Partisan Army, started as small bands of poorly-organized fighters. But as the Germans' cruelty became relentless, more and more people joined the resistance. The Germans retaliation against any village seen to be supporting ELAS was punctilious and stark – anyone caught supporting the guerrillas was executed in the square in front of the assembled villagers and the home of their family burnt to the ground. Many old people and children (including Gregorio's grandmother and two of his cousins) starved to death in the next two winters.

When Gregorio's uncle (his mother's brother) was casually executed by the Germans for hiding his corn, Gregorio was so full of hate for the Germans, that without telling his mother that he was leaving (he knew she would try to stop him), he went to join the partisans. He was fifteen. It was his new comrades who gave him the name, the nom de guerre, Mavros ("Blackie"), the name he would keep for the rest of his life. It was for him a medal.

He was a brave fighter. His knowledge as a shepherd, was invaluable when it came to identifying the most propitious places to ambush German patrols. It turned out he was also good with the old Lee Enfield rifles, smuggled to the ELAS partisans by the British SOE, which had last seen action in the war against the Boers in South Africa at the turn of the century.

Mavros killed Germans dispassionately, but like his commander, General Markos, his special ire was reserved for the collaborators of Rallis's Security Battalions, his fascist countrymen. General Markos - Markos Vafiades - the leader of ELAS in the Grammos Mountains was fond of Mavros, this boy who could fight as fiercely as any man under his command. He kept Mavros close and took it upon himself to educate him. Although Mavros never learned to read or write, he could recite, with heartfelt passion, the tracts of Marx and Lenin that General Markos taught him.

By 1944 the Germans and nationalist army were in retreat and the units which Markos led was making a push towards Athens. In May of that year, General Scobie, commander of the British forces, landed from the sea and by October, Athens was liberated. He instructed ELAS to wait outside the city for the Greek Government-in-exile to arrive from Cairo. So, when the people of Athens shouted, "Laokratia!" "Freedom!", singing in praise and rapture for their liberators, it was the British and the Right-wing nationalist soldiers they lauded, not the ELAS fighters, the andartes, who had suffered so severely and fought so bravely.

This was not to be the only outrage. ELAS and the communists, the KKE, controlled most of the country outside the cities and they expected to be part of the new government. But this was not what the British and Americans had in mind. To decide the fate of the liberated lands, Churchill (or "Tsortsil" as he is better known in Greece) made a deal with Stalin over a leisurely lunch – Stalin got the East – Bulgaria, Romania; the British got Greece. The "plan" was drawn out on the back of a serviette. With such thin threads is history woven. So determining was Churchill's anti-communist and pro-Royalist doctrine, the British released fascist collaborators and incorporated them into the new army and police force and demanded that the ELAS disarm. ELAS fighters were prohibited from joining the new army. The Communist ministers, who had joined the government of national unity under George Papandreou, were incensed and resigned. Stalin was indifferent.

The communists called a General Strike. It took the government, with assistance from British tanks and Spitfires, thirty days to put down the popular uprising. George Papandreou, to his credit, resigned. Then the crackdown on the Communists in Athens and Thessalonika started in earnest. 12,000 men and women of the Greek Left were arrested and interned in the concentration camp on Macronissos. So, ELAS went back to where they had support, to the countryside, to the mountains and took up arms again, in what was to become the Greek Civil War.

Mavros ended up back in his village, where he was reunited with his mother. Made old and decrepit by the hardship she had suffered, she could do with his help. She found him a wife, a woman as young as Mavros, the cousin of her neighbour, also an ELAS combatant. There was no big wedding – they were poor people, they had nothing, they were at war - but still, for that night, there was dancing in the square.

Through the Civil War, until the ignominious end in 1949, Mavros and his wife fought side by side in the Grammos mountains. But in one of the last battles of the war, Mavros's wife was killed. It was a terrible time. The deadlock was broken by aeroplanes of the Greek Nationalist government whose pilots were trained by the Americans to drop napalm in vast quantities, the first time the Americans had experimented with this new weapon. Crops destroyed, water supplies poisoned, the peasants were starved into surrender.

So, when there was no more hope for ELAS, Mavros walked over the mountains in the east, first to Bulgaria, and then to Soviet Union.

But in 1960, his mother died in the same house Mavros had known as a child; Mavros came back to bury her, crossing the border on foot again under cover of darkness. The Greek government at that time still prohibited the ELAS exiles returning to Greece. In his village, of course people knew him to be an ELAS fighter of old, so it was not safe for him to settle there. After he buried his mother and put a stone on her grave, he went to Thessaloniki. He had comrades there. They could find him a job, get him papers.

The job he ended up with was as a driver for the Left-wing politician, Grigoris Lambrakis. The anti-Royalist Left, under George Papandreou, was gaining popularity. This alarmed the British and the Americans and the Greek fascist Right, the remnants of the Security Battalion the Allies had nurtured.

In 1963, Mavros's boss, Lambrakis, was gunned down. Mavros saw the gunmen and recognised one of the gunmen as an off-duty policeman. He was arrested and tortured, but he found a way to escape and fled to Athens, where he was taken in by sympathizers, one of whom was the father of my informant, who smuggled him out of the capital to the island of Mythos where he had relatives.

Mavros fell in love with a local woman, a refugee from Smyrna, Stavroula Vogiatsis, and within a month, using his falsified papers, Mavros married her and soon they had a child. Even after Papandreou was elected in 1966, Mavros still could not get legal documents (ELAS fighters were pardoned only in 1981, when the radical Andreas Papandreou, son of George, was elected) and could not leave the island.

Then in 1967, with NATO's covert support, the King and the Generals forced Papandreou out of power. But the new junta were not anti-communist enough for the far-Right and the Colonels – the remnant of the Security Battalion – with the collusion of the CIA, deposed them, the King and his conspiring German wife and the luckless Papandreou Senior, went into exile.

Then in 1970, Mavros disappeared.

Until now.

The body will be shipped to Athens where forensic analysis will confirm his identity. The Left's fight to have ELAS fighters memorialized gains pace. The Struggle continues.

Tom Pickering.

Mythos. September, 2005.

13

I wake the next morning, stiff from sleeping with my legs hunched up to accommodate my length on Lucy's couch. Lucy is still not back. I make myself an instant coffee with the stale powder I find in a drawer; I sit, drinking it, on the back porch, watching the haze lift off the mountains. Where are you, Lucy? Fuck it! This is a bit much, going off like that without even a note to say when you'll be back. I toss my coffee away - I can't drink this shit.

I can't just hang about doing nothing. If I am going to cover the body in the bridge story properly, I suppose I can't just rely on Antonis for transport. I need wheels of my own. I saw a sign on the main road as we came into the village, which said something like, "Zeus Autos". I remember thinking that sounded quite grand. I could try them.

I take my wallet, check I have my British driver's license and set off. I find Zeus Autos on the back road running parallel to the main road. Zeus Autos consists of a garage with a truck up on a ramp, its tyres off, and a side lot, on which stands three motor bikes, a 125cc scrambler, a 50cc Honda and a dilapidated Vespa. No cars. A bulky man in an oil-smothered blue overall is working under the truck, unlit cigarette perched at the corner of his mouth.

"*Kalimera,*" I say tentatively.

The mechanic is startled, then looks at me coolly. "*Nai?*" he asks.

"*Parakalo.* You make rent… car?" I ask in my English for Greeks.

"Speak English!" he instructs me, the cigarette wobbles as he speaks. He establishes I want to hire a vehicle and that I am presently on my own. "A motorbike is better," he tells me. He doesn't have any cars. He walks me to the lot and wiping his oily hands on an oily cloth, takes the scrambler off its stand. "This one," he says. "Ten euros for a day. Fifty euros if you take it for the whole week." That sounds very reasonable. I get on the bike and fiddle with the gears and brakes. "Is all fine," he says, "Brakes, mirrors, engine, everything. Petrol – full tank."

He doesn't ask to see my license. I don't tell him I haven't ridden a motorbike since I was a teenager. I think it will come back to me. I sign a book he produces. He tears out the under-slip as proof of our deal. He has not smiled once, nor moved the cigarette from the corner of his mouth.

I drive out the lot, unsteady on the rough road. But I am grinning like an idiot, a surging feeling of liberation, memories of my adolescence tickling me... my first girlfriend, us going to crap pubs in Hertfordshire next to the canal, which didn't bother to check our age. I ride out the village and out along the coast, the road north unfurling, at first through forest, then a harsh barren land of stone and desiccated bush. I have not been north from the village before. The bridge and beyond it, the main port town, Agia Sofia, lie to the south. I should have asked for a map, but then again the island is small – how lost can I get?

The road takes me up onto a promontory where an old block house lies abandoned, staring with blind eyes out to sea. From here the road seems to sweep south again, if my sense of direction is valid, across the ridge of the mountain, until I come to a ravine, at which point the road winds steeply down though a forested hillside and at the bottom, the enticing turquoise of the sea. The view is spectacular. Cliffs plummet into the sea. Mountains rise majestically out of the blue water, fringed with turquoise and aquamarine. I wish I had brought my camera. I brake, skid and shudder to a halt. The bike cuts out. I put it on its stand, I look over the land and out to the horizon, shimmering in the midday sun. My body is still vibrating from the unfamiliar thrum of the motorbike. Around me there is complete silence, such an abnormal sound to my city ears. I am all alone on this mountain top. This view is mine alone.

On the hillside, opposite in the distance, I see a steeply angled road, recently tarred judging by its stark blackness. Construction vehicles lie silent at the roadside. The entire hillside and the mountainside beyond for miles, is charred and barren. The blackened corpses of small trees stick their fingers into the air in an arthritic death dance; grey pines hang their head, downcast. My eyes track down and near the bottom of the gradient, just beyond the firebreak, I see a new development, a smart new hotel complex, three levels of balconies and buttresses in white and glass, with numerous neat out-houses and a swimming pool, pale blue and regular, cut into a lawn – surely not a lawn? In this climate? The Poseidon – this must be the Poseidon. Construction is still going on. I can see activity – vehicles, tiny figures - but from this distance this all takes place in silence, like a movie with the sound turned off.

Beyond the hotel and the outcrops of rock which divide the coast into pretty, white-sanded coves, there is a lagoon surrounded by reeds and low bushes. The lagoon is an iridescent green. I can see specks of birdlife on the surface. The sea, where the lagoon attempts to regurgitate itself – is it semi-tidal? – bears a dark maroon stain, with, at its centre, a dollop of pink and cream. The red-brown smudge tapers toward the hotel but stops well short. It is probably not visible from the hotel. Is it a natural formation or is it a sludge of algal growth, pollution? Is *that* what Lucy is investigating?

I kick-start the bike and it comes to life with an encouraging roar. That's-my-boy! Should I go down to the Poseidon and introduce myself? Maybe they will know where Lucy is. On the other hand, I don't want to blow her cover. I don't know what she has told them about her interest. Maybe I should wait. I turn the bike around and go back to Agia Anna, the way I came.

****

Back in the village, I go past Lucy's, but she's still not at home. I think to ask the old lady across the road whether she's seen her, but the effort in trying to make myself understood and then trying to understand her, is too much. I haven't had lunch either. I'll go to The Seaview, get a Greek salad or a small plate of calamari and go online. See if there are any messages.

I should have eaten first. I lose my appetite and my feeling of goodwill is instantly macerated when I open my Outlook and find a message from Lucy. Excitedly I click to open it.

"Dear Thomas, I am going away. Do not wait for me. I will write you. Lucy."

For a moment I don't believe what I am reading. I have to read it again. "Do not wait for me." Jesus, no sugaring the pill; no trying to be nice. I've come all this way and she's given me the brush off. Plus, her tone – so matter-of-fact. She should have put in a 'Yours sincerely' at the end too! Fuck her! She is so mercurial, so fucking fickle. I've come all this way…

I shouldn't have got my hopes up. I realise I have made a lot out of that "I miss you." I have been *so* presumptuous! But not *groundless* - there *was* something – *something* in her tone on the phone in that message in London that promised more. Could it be I just imagined it? – wished it into being? But then again Irini had said Lucy was fond of me. How well does Irini really know her friend? – or was Irini just being manipulative as I first suspected? Fuck, I should have listened to that nagging little voice of doubt that has served me so well over the years. I should not have listened to my fuck-up of a sister.

I sit in a dark silence, too angry to breathe, too hurt to cry. Eventually, the intensity of my disappointment dissipates. I breathe. I sigh. I unwind my shoulders.

Then I send Lucy a message back, telling her, as coolly as I can muster, that I'm covering the body in the bridge story, so I'll be around for a while yet and hope to see her still. Do I actually *want* to stay for the bridge story now? Well, if I *am* going to be working, may as well be on a Greek island in the sun. Then if Lucy comes back, maybe I can still change her mind. If I still want to. Now I'm not so sure. Do I want someone so unreliable in my life? Depressing.

14

One year before. The Netherlands. November, 2004.

A wet Holland with ponderous charcoal skies. It's the morning session of the third day of the international Greens' conference in the Hague, which I'm covering for New World Order. I am in an over-heated auditorium, gainfully struggling against the cozy seduction of light slumber, when I glimpse the next speaker, shuffling her papers into order and tapping the microphone. I recognise her. Alert now, I quickly check the programme notes. Lucy Discombe.

Lucy, the programme notes tell me, has recently completed her Masters in Human Geography and is working for an NGO in the Netherlands, and will give a seminar on the effects of mass tourism on coastlines in the Third World. I stare at her, trying to get her to conform to the memory of her I have as a seventeen-year-old at my mother's house in Islington four and a half years ago. The young woman at the podium is a confidant speaker. Her passion for the legal rights of the natural world is perhaps too strident, but then she is only twenty-three (by my rapid calculation). I quote two of her declamations in my report later: "The natural world can cope without Humanity, but Humanity cannot cope without the natural world. So, who has the power?" and "Don't treat the Earth as a dependent child, in need of care, when it is your mother, who cares for you. Show respect." She sounds older and wiser than her twenty-three years, and to my eyes, and I'm sure to most of the audience, she is astonishingly beautiful in the spotlight.

Afterwards, I seek her out. My pretext is that I want to do an interview for New World Order, but actually I just want to be close to her beauty; I want to apologise for what a shit I was when we last met. I stand at the back of a gaggle of earnest and fawning fresh-faced young people (students I presume), waiting my turn with her. Will she know who I am? Will she want to see me? She catches my eye, smiles and tilts her head, a question, a surprise. I start to introduce myself, but she stops me. "Jesus, Tom, of course I remember you! - you were the reason I majored in Human Geography." She steps towards me and gives me a kiss on the cheek. I feel myself blush. I pretend nonchalance as I bask in the warm glow of her adulation in front of the acolytes waiting to ask her learned questions designed to reveal how clever they are. When she's done, we stand about awkwardly, until I get up the courage to ask her if maybe we could go for a drink in a quiet bar where we could talk and be heard. "Good plan, Batman," she says, a soft fist playfully applied to my arm. A punch withheld? She is toying with the ambiguity, not ready yet to concede forgiveness, and I think she likes to see that I feel guilty.

Later, when I confess that I have no plans for the weekend, she invites me to stay at her place in Amsterdam. "I have a spare couch," she says. That beguiling smile of hers. I find it difficult to read her. Is she actually flirting with me? She operates on two levels, not quite a contradiction, Something else. But I'm prepared to make allowances - she is spectacularly beautiful.

We leave soon after and get back to Amsterdam by three. Her place is a war zone. With a flourish, she clears a space on the couch where I am to sleep, dislodging open magazines, an assortment of wrinkled clothes and a collection of wire connectors and a string of LED lights. In amongst the tangle of clothes, I notice a bra intertwined with a collection of highly-coloured G-string panties. My heart gives a lurch. She sees my uncensored perusal and grins. Then, we are out of the door and straight to a rally to protest a march of the far-Right LPF. Lucy is fired up, talking at double speed. We are late. She walks with rapid steps, red hair bobbing like a torch. Getting ahead of me, she stops to give her commentary, before racing ahead again. "Mad as a bag of rats, fucking fascists, and just as easy to bait!" she shouts over her shoulder at me gleefully at one point. What am I getting myself into? I don't care. I'm with Lucy and I feel exhilarated.

When we get to the protest, it's already hotted up, with lots of noise and pushing up against the police cordons. Lucy hustles her way to the front, dragging me into the crowd after her. She's yelling creative scatological epithets right into the brutish baby faces of the fascists, taunting them, eyes flashing. I hear in their chanting, their fear and fury;

I see the pride and shame in their faces, their need for revenge. I am chickenshit scared when it comes to violence and when I see Lucy goading the men of violence, I think, hey, you're clearly identifiable with all that flaming red hair – you're setting yourself up. But the danger of it is such a turn-on. Lucy is enjoying herself. Bravery or madness? Hero or fool?

That night, we go with some of her friends to the Melkweg to debrief and celebrate. It's Amsterdam. Inevitably there's a lot of dope on offer. I tell Lucy I don't smoke. Lucy lights up, and says, "Wait," as she inhales. "Open," she says, pointing at my mouth. I oblige. She takes a deeper drag, then slowly blows her smoke into me. I get high. I drink tequila shots with her garrulous friends who insist on buying a round each. I can hardly refuse. At two a.m., we stumbled into the night with Lucy clutching my arm. We giggle our way home and in the hallway outside her flat, as she rummages in her cloth bag for her key, I lunge at her and kiss her. She recoils in surprise, but then smiles, a twinkling smile, leans forward and puts her lips on mine, as her eyes close. Her tongue is slippery and inquisitive. We stumble inside, kick off our shoes and discard our clothes in a rush.

Her body is lit transversely by the slatted streetlight coming through the blinds, her small breasts, perfectly formed, her nipples taut and deep red against her ivory white skin, the smooth taper of her tummy plunging to her groin, her angel-toned shoulders and sensuous long neck, her lustrous auburn hair. Oh, such a picture of beauty. I just want to stand here and look at her, take her in, to be in the moment. She wants more than that - she grabs my hand and pulls me to her bedroom, and as she falls back onto the bed, she places my hand on the softness between her legs.

God, she is vigorous, her hips rising to meet mine, desperate even, *relentless*. I am so aroused - beautiful and sexy Lucy *wants me!* I want to be at my best for her, to pleasure her – oh, it is so pornographic, looking down and seeing my cock entering her, and... *I come!* I bloody well come!- in a blinding flash, a gush which fills my whole body with warm light. Oh, the pleasure of it. And oh, *so frustrating!* I have lasted less than a minute! I wanted to be her perfect lover, to attend to her every desire, I wanted her to come. She lets me finger-fuck her and tongue her clit, but my cock has gone to sleep and my efforts to pleasure her are clearly an apology for the real thing. Eventually she pushes me away and masturbates until, with a whimper and soft exhalation, she comes. Ordinarily that would be a huge turn-on, but, in the event, it is just humiliating.

The next day, when I wake, she is on one elbow next to me in the bed. She is grinning. "You snore," she says and laughs, as if that's the cutest thing! She says nothing about my failure, but the frustration of it, the shame, sits heavily with me, and settles into an unattractive gloominess. Apparently in good humour, she makes us tea and French toast for breakfast, and says we are off to the flea market. "I go every Sunday. It's surprizing what bits and pieces you can pick up," she says. At a haphazardly-organised stall run by a woman in an abundant turban, I buy Lucy (as an apology) an Ethiopian necklace with a large lapis lazuli stone at its centre. It matches her eyes. The African woman says the piece is silver, but I doubt it. But so what? - Lucy is inordinately pleased with it and plants a big fat kiss on my lips. Either I didn't need forgiveness or she gave it very lightly. It's good either way. My mood lifts. She lets me put my arm around her, but after a short while, it begins to feel awkward and she manages, without any sign of intention, to free herself.

After a plate of Indian street food eaten standing up, she informs me that she is taking me to shoplift. "I take stuff from multi-national chains, Tom – it's my way of getting the buggers to pay their taxes!" she says firmly, clearly persuaded by her nifty ethical recalibration. I'm from out of town, I'm with a beautiful young woman who lives here, we're having fun, I am forgiven... Who am I to refuse? So I go along with it.

We nearly get caught in Zara and have to outrun the burly and, it turns out, unfit, security guard at the mall. Enough distance away, we duck into an alley, and laugh and hug and kiss as we catch our breath. "Oh, God, I get so turned on by doing dangerous things!" she says. Her look says she wants me. She grabs my hand. "Come." She has a plan. We get the train to some smart suburb on the edge of the city. It's all trees and gardens and big houses when we emerge from the station, but if I think we are there for nice scenery, I am mistaken. Disguised only by the beanies we've stolen from Zara, we are there to smash up a BMW belonging to a rich lawyer she knows who'd got Shell off the hook in some exploration and spillage off the West coast of Africa. Hiding behind hedges, running away down a wide street, my photo will probably be held on CCTV footage of the crime scene down at police head-quarters in Amsterdam for the foreseeable future. Will I even get out of the country? Shit, I think, this is getting too complicated for me, even as I imagine the sex to come.

She is onto me as soon as we get home, peeling my jacket off me, her lips pressed to mine, she thrusts against me. She disengages only to get her clothes off in two or three movements, standing on one leg, then the other to get her tights off. Her pale skin is mottled in places by the cold, but the inside of her thigh and her tummy are pink with heat. Her nipples are erect. I could fuck her right away, but this time, I want to show her how considerate I am as a lover; I want to go slow.

She doesn't. I try to slow her down with gentle stoking, but I am too self-conscious, too timid. Lucy is impatient, eager - she pulls at me, she bites me, her nails dig into me, she folds my thigh between her legs and rubs her cunt against me. Okay, if she wants more passion... I throw her onto the bed and spread her legs and tongue her. I put a finger a little way into her anus and she goes wild, bucking, pressing her cunt onto my willing lips. But then I shift up through the gears too quickly. I am too rough. I pull at and twist her nipple, she slaps my hand and grimaces. I grab her tit again and she squirms under me. Then I'm inside her, her arse is so soft, I mustn't... I mustn't... Oh, God, I mustn't... I come. In spite of my best efforts, I come before her again. I am mortified. I have lasted less than three minutes!

This time she doesn't even bother to masturbate. I think from her sigh as she flops back over to her side of the bed, that she must have given up on me.

After a pause, she says, "When are you going back to London?"

****

Back in London, to counteract my shame, I tell myself that Lucy is a head-case; that I got off lightly. But I find it hard to get images of her out of my mind – her humorous, taunting eyes, the hollow under her clavicle, the soft bonelessness of her slim thighs. She had *wanted* me. She *had.* If only…

I almost contact her again, but my poor self-esteem comes to my aid and I rein myself in just in time – she's probably relieved to be rid of me. She needs a big reckless bloke with lots of muscles, not some pale North London journalist who's let his gym membership lapse and can't keep his powder dry. If she wants to get in touch, if she's had second thoughts, she knows where to reach me. I can wait. Experience tells me I should wait. So I wait.

Not that I have much experience to draw on. I had not been one of the 'popular' boys at school. I was, I suppose, a bit nerdy, often referred to as 'gay' – not as in homosexual, but as in uncool and pretentious. I read a lot. I thought about girls a considerable amount of my waking time and of my dreamtime, but in the presence of a girl who was even vaguely attractive, I was paralytically shy, my tongue a lugubrious frog in my mouth. Oh, yes, I found big words to hide my embarrassment, behind a screen of pomposity and erudition. My disability with girls was compounded by my alcoholic mother being intermittently over-indulgent and more often, completely unaware of my presence, and by the absence of my father who thought to die of a cerebral aneurysm just before I entered the cauldron of puberty.

I did get a scholarship to Warrick to read History and Politics, where my peculiarity was more favourably regarded by the opposite sex, especially, I found, by big girls who more-or-less literally took me under their wing. Gradually, through their tutelage, or perhaps in spite of it, I became more acceptable, even regarded as good-looking in a rakish sort of way (if the light was advantageously angled). I had my first sexual encounter – my first fuck – in second year. Not a work of art, but I was pleased to get it under my belt so-to-speak.

I got my first job as a journalist straight out of Uni, through a "friend" of my mother, who had been a colleague of my father's and fellow member of the Socialist Worker's Party. I turned other people's turgid prose into readable copy for a publication that went tits-up two months after I started. But I did meet Marsha Galpin, my editor, there, so I suppose I can say I was "headhunted" to work for New World Order, working until recently as an investigative journalist in the field (although, since the crisis in publication a few months back, I've returned to the same desk job I did when I started my career).

****

And working at New World Order *is* how I got to meet Lucy again. What were the chances? A gorgeous girl like her fancying a guy like me?! I should think not! She is beautiful, intelligent, although younger than me by several years, several steps up the ladder of sexual experience, therefore, well… it is difficult to just let her go. Both my shame and sober judgement urge me to move on, but my tenuous, testosterone-fuelled ambition whispers, "Wait… maybe… who knows?"

For my self-preservation I suppose, when I *do* think about Lucy (quite often and at surprising times), I have to suppress bubbles of ridiculous hope that effervesce to the surface by *forcing* myself to remember the things I *hadn't* liked about her, to the point of getting irritated, angry, self-righteous. Her impetuousness, her arrogance, her bluntness… And yet…

Then, gradually… well, life happens, and, like the zen master I am (sometimes… in my head), I let her go. I stop obsessing about her. Start dating the amorous Amanda, who, I convince myself, is more my type. We like the same movies, the same books… It lasts six weeks and ends abruptly when she overhears my supercharged drunken dinner-party rant against "those pretentious, entitled middle-class Earth-mother fascists" I think I called them, who think that people who don't want kids are lesser beings. Amanda, it turns out, is one of them. I was already far-gone, but I think her earnest rebuttal provoked me to overstate my case emphatically, and the reasons I put forward (having kids gets in the way of having fun, having a career and being politically relevant) were probably objectionable to an intelligent, fertile young woman I admit. It's not that I don't want kids ever, but the example my parents set (one dying, one going missing in action), made me think I would make a shit parent. I don't tell her that. Amanda returns only one call after that – to tell me I am immature and not what she is after. At least it gets me over Lucy.

Until Lucy calls. I have had to wait quite a bit longer than I'd anticipated – six months in fact, before business brings her to London. She's arranged to hook up with Irini and we agree to meet for a drink near Old Street. In spite of my *definitely* being over her, I change the sheets, air the bedroom, put out fresh towels, buy flowers for the dining table and a bottle of Sauvignon Blanc for the fridge. I try on three changes of clothing before I settle on what to wear to meet Lucy again. Definitely over her. Yeah, right! On the bus down to Shoreditch, I realise from people's looks that I have probably overdone it with the after-shave.

Lucy, who unusually for her, has make-up on and is looking even more beautiful than I remembered her, is at a table with Irini, sitting too close I think, with a dagger-thrust of jealousy, to the hunky Wim Mueller, a war reporter of some repute. I've met him briefly before and didn't like his smug balefulness at the state of the world. Lucy tells me straight-off, to remove any ambiguity, that she is staying at Irini's that night. (Damn, am I that obvious?) Shit, I have rehearsed her coming back to my place so meticulously that I've *assumed* her acquiescence – fuck it, she practically owes me! Why had she called me otherwise?

Three tequila shots in, her casual destruction of my preferred storyline for her and me still seems so numbingly heartless, that I do nothing to stop my slide into behaviour which is at best awkward, and at least, to use the description of the sainted Amanda, immature. I lay into the witless Wim Mueller. I call him self-indulgent and masochistic – all that death and degradation. Shit, I tell him, there's more to life than that. Lighten up, Wim! (I think I call him Wimp, supposedly inadvertently.) The world-weary award-winning documentarist takes it all in his melancholic brooding stride and I suppose that makes him more sexually appealing to Lucy. Lucy, for her part, laughs in a faux-conspiratorial way and is friendly and chatty, but clearly not desperate to go to bed with me. *Obviously.* Jesus, had sex with me been such a let-down?! Good move that I hadn't called her after all.

So much for my romantic notions about Lucy. But now we are back in touch, we keep in touch professionally. She sends me stories which she thinks will be of interest to New World Order and I get some of them published (with a bit of judicious editing, it must be said – she is a bit *loose* in her writing – too *conversational*); I keep track of the good work she is doing via her blog and facebook, and occasionally send her articles of mutual interest. Purely professional interest. Or is it?

Then, on a warm Saturday in the middle of July, she turns up on my doorstep at eight in the morning, pushes me inside, unpeels me from my towelling gown, finds my lips and my cock, and staggers me back into my bedroom. With no over-thinking, our love making – I call it that, because it is – is delicious, unhurried and luxurious. She comes, her thighs, clasped around my hips, quivering, her gasp of pleasure drawing into a low growl, her cunt pulsing like hungry tongues.

Afterwards, she lies on her back, eyes closed, smiling. I notice she is wearing the Ethiopian necklace I bought in Amsterdam. The silver has not tarnished. I trace the furrow in her taut belly with my finger. She is a thing of wonder.

"I've thought about you a lot," she says.

"Me too," I say.

"What? You've thought about yourself a lot?" She sits up and grins at me.

"That too," I say, laughing.

We get out of bed at midday and have breakfast at my local greasy spoon café, then go to my place, get back into bed and make love again. We order a take-away later, and, from the comfort of my bed, we watch a movie on the telly. "When Harry met Sally." I've seen it before - Lucy hasn't, and loves it. It is a fortuitous choice.

"Move in with me," I say. "You'll find a job in London."

Lucy looks straight ahead. She smiles and squeezes my hand. She doesn't say no.

The next day, a Sunday filled with light, we take the train to Broxbourne and walk along the canal, her hand in mine. We have lunch at a pub looking out onto the Lee. "This is nice," she says, "I do miss it." After lunch, Lucy takes pictures of the narrowboats and the reflections of the silvered clouds on the verdant water. "That's what Heaven looks like," she muses, one eye pressed to the view-finder. "I want a picture of us," she says suddenly, and importunes a passing couple with her request for a photo of us, her arm in mine, smiling, in heaven. The man (I think he is Japanese) obliges, getting down on one knee to get the perspective just right. A real pro.

Later, when we get back to Islington, we shop in Tesco for delicacies for supper, on condition she doesn't shoplift. She giggles. "I don't do that anymore," she says, and squeezes herself close to me, savouring the memory. Lucy loves cooking too, I'm surprised to find. She is a judicious shopper, choosing her vegetables carefully. Together we make a dinner of vichyssoise with fresh dill (her contribution) and poached cod with capers and wine (mine). The bottle of New Zealand Sauvignon Blanc lasts only as long as the evening. I light candles. It's all very domesticated. Very adult. Like we are man and wife. Later she sleeps in the fold of my embrace. It is all so perfect.

In the middle of the night, something rouses me from the soft cushion of a dream. Lucy is in the other room, speaking in a hushed voice to someone on her Blackberry. I drift back to sleep.

When I wake on the Monday morning, she is gone.

15

The sea shimmers, indifferent to my travails. I finish the feta salad I'd ordered half-heartedly - Agapi can sense there is something wrong but has the decency not to ask – and I drain the double vodka and tonic I'd felt I needed. The alcohol only intensified my gloom. Lucy's e-mail is on repeat in my brain. *"I am going away. Do not wait for me."* I can't very well stay at her place now.

On my way back to her place to collect my things, I spot Yianni. I ask if he knows of anyone with a room in Agia Anna. "No problem," he says, taking me by the arm, "We have room upstairs. Very nice. From there you see the mountains, the fields, the olive trees. Is nize," he says. "Cheap. Ten euros only." He is enthusiastic for me to stay and insists I view the room immediately. He shouts something at Soulla, she shrugs in her long-suffering way, smiles and leads me upstairs to the room, which is dark and cool, until she opens the shutters and light floods in. There is a double bed, with a bedside table, on which stands a jug and glasses, a wash basin and roughly constructed shelving. Soulla unlatches the French doors, which open onto a small balcony. The view to the mountains is interrupted by haphazard electricity and telephone wires, strung on blanched wooden poles.

On the balcony next to mine, a teenage girl in denim shorts, with gypsy black hair draped untidily over her face, her feet up on the railings, is painting her toenails. This must be Kat, their daughter. Soulla says something in a peremptory tone, the girl, snarls in frustration and goes inside in a huff. She is not pleased to have visitors. I shall have to make friends with her later. Soulla shakes her head. "What you can do?" she says, echoing the cries of mothers of teenage girls the world over. I remember Irini at that age – her and my mother, each absolutely convinced by their own irrefutable logic, which led them, like straight lines on a curved surface, to opposite extremes, implacably opposed and absolutely furious with the other's stupidity.

I take the room, offer Soulla the ten euros, which she waves away ("Later, later you give") and go off to get my stuff from Lucy's house. The old lady across the road from Lucy's place is at her front gate. When she sees me going in to Lucy's, she calls to me, and engages me in a lengthy one-sided conversation. *"Milate Anglica?"* I ask her, "Do you speak English?" She doesn't. She sighs. There is something she wants to tell me and tries to get this across by simplifying her sentence, then repeating it. But I don't understand. She puts her hands over her ears, grimaces and then wags her gnarled finger at me censoriously. *"Dhen kataleveno,"* I tell her, "I don't understand". She sighs again, her eyes moving sideways, thinking of what else she might do. But then she gives up, pats my arm, turns and shuffles back up the path to her front door, muttering to herself. It strikes me that perhaps the old lady is Lucy's landlady and is wanting her rent. Well, I think with what is reprehensible but gratifying spite, this is no longer my problem.

I pack up my laptop and go back to my new abode, open the door and windows for air, lie naked on the bed and fall into a deep and troubled sleep.

****

I am mending a paperback book whose pages have come unbound. The sticky tape I am using is getting twisted and stuck to itself. I apply glue, but the glue is now stuck to my fingers and my fingers are sticking to the paper. My mother is somewhere behind me out of my sight, saying, "Must you try to fix everything, Tom? Stop it now - it's not necessary. Just leave it." (The last in an exasperated tone.) I feel like giving up, but the book is now considerably worse than when I started my repairs, I can't just give up, but my fingers are stuck to each other and the pages, a scream of frustration is building in my chest…

I wake up. The feeling of frustration dulls but doesn't leave me. I get up, splash my face at the wash basin and decide I must get out – go for a walk to clear my head – I don't have the energy for a swim… but maybe if I did swim, it would revive me. I hedge my bets and take my swimming trunks and a towel with me just in case, and head out to the beach.

The sun is just above the horizon. I decide to make for the cove over the hill – where the wind blows, I have been told. The road out the village on the far side follows the ridge. There is a steep path to the beach. The sea on this side heaves strongly, waves crash to their demise on the white sand and unfurl in spumes of froth up the beach. Today there is no wind. The sun is red and full over the sea.

I see on the shoreline, a mother (I assume it's the mother) watching over a small child, who is running into the foam, then retreating hurriedly as the next wave crashes down. The woman turns, grinning at the child's adventure. Her copper curls and her full figure are unmistakable. Agapi.

I stroll down the beach, with an uncertain sense of expectation. Agapi sees me and waves. The child stops to inspect me from a distance, then she hugs Agapi's leg and hides.

"Hello," I say when I'm within earshot, "*Kalispera.*" Agapi smiles but doesn't reply. The little girl peaks out at me, frowning, curious. "Hello," I say to her in a child-friendly voice and bend towards her, to make myself more her height. "Who is this monkey?" I ask.

Agapi smiles proudly. "She is my daughter, Eleni." She says something to the child and the child whispers, "*Geia sou,*" and then hardly audibly, "*Hero polee.*"

I chuckle at the child's shyness. She is a beautiful child, with her mother's emerald eyes and the crimped bronze hair. Agapi prises the little girl's hand off her skirt and says something in a humorous tone. The girl runs off and then, looking to see if we are watching her, races into the onrushing foam with a determined look. The water eddies around her, she turns and stomps back effortfully against the rip of the retreating sea. She gets herself free and glares at us victoriously.

The water has turned golden in the setting sun. There are rainbows where the foam has atomised and scintillated. As the waves rear up, a deep blue, the blue of Indian ink, rises from the depths, and as the wave unburdens itself, tangerine and salmon pinks are released, and here and there, pale blue and silver, like dancing fish.

Eleni takes her mother's hand and says something emphatically. Agapi tucks her skirt into her panties, with a look to me which is not the embarrassment I would expect from an English girl, but one which *challenges* me to laugh at her, which *knows* I will be enchanted by the innocence of her gesture. She holds her daughter's hand tight, screaming, they both race into the wave's afterlife.

They come out, laughing together and Agapi folds Eleni into a towel, holding her in her arms, she turns to watch the sun sinking into the ocean. We watch in silence as the sun drowns slowly. Above it, a fierce orange melds into yellow. A faint green hue is discernible before it shades into gradients of blue, darkening towards the apex of the sky. The orange turns pink and mauve as we watch.

"I must go back to work soon," she says. "First I will feed my daughter. There," she points to the ridge at the far end of the beach. "That is my house."

"Your husband is at home?" I ask.

She hesitates. "He is dead. My mother is there. She looks after my child when I am work." She looks far out to sea. "My husband had his own boat. He was fisherman. I am married when I am sixteen. He died when I am carrying Eleni. He did not come back."

"I'm sorry," I say.

"It's nothing. I was too young to marry," she says. She doesn't want me to be sad on her account. She did not mean me to feel responsible for her adversity. But I see a great sadness in her eyes. She hugs the child in her arms for comfort. I feel a lurch of tenderness for her.

"I must go," she says. "I will see you later? At the restaurant?"

"Yes," I say, my voice husky and almost inaudible. "Yes... *nai,*" I say, more firmly, "I will come later". She smiles serenely, beatific in the gathering twilight.

16

For a while I watch Agapi ambling down the beach, her daughter skipping along the outskirts of the waves. The little girl had given me an endearing smile when I'd said good night. I turn and wander back to the village. Over the ridge, on the other side of the bay, the night gently darkens the sky, a blush of mauve on the horizon, bruising before blackening, as the stars come out. The air is cooling. Autumn is coming.

I have told Agapi I will come to the Seaview for dinner, but I could have done with a light meal at Yianni's and an early night. I am feeling melancholic, the fantasies I'd elaborated about a life with Lucy are disarticulating themselves in the glare of my new reality, her cold rejection of me tarnishing the mirror in which I take stock of myself, my usual irony now tinged with contempt. Perhaps I am tired.

I convince myself that I should work. Not only is this expedient, but also it will be a distraction. I must check the articles I downloaded on the environmental impact of tourism on the Greek coastline, in case I check out the Poseidon for myself. That rusty sediment along the coast did not look healthy. Also, I should be prepared and knowledgeable should Lucy return, so I could pitch a *collaboration*, rather than giving the impression I am stealing her story, if that is her gripe. Okay, a quick meal at the Seaview, just so as that I don't let Agapi down (as if she'd mind! – I am so presumptuous). Then back to my room. It is not warm enough tonight to warrant staying outside anyway.

As it happens, when I get to the Seaview later, Agapi is busy with a party of Norwegian tourists, excited young men, so young they must be just out of school. They have just arrived in Agia Anna – I have not seen them before - and they are loud and demanding, unlike the usual Scandinavians. I suspect they are rich kids celebrating the new freedoms of their nascent adulthood. They are drunk already. They make lewd remarks to Agapi in accented English – the *lingua franca*, if that is not a contradiction. (Why is it called *lingua franca* when most of the time the *lingua* is English?) Agapi smiles benignly and does not rise to their excited chatter.

Xanthe, who evidently has been roped into the family enterprise, serves me and is pleasant, but I am not in the mood for chatting. When my reply to her jaunty enquiry about my day is a cursory ("Fine"), Xanthe looks puzzled and mildly affronted, but she leaves me alone with my mussel soup. (Do they get mussels on the island or are these imported for the tourists? I think to ask Xanthe, but I don't want to get bogged down in conversation, so let it go.) I finish my soup, pay the bill, leave a tip and get up to go. Then I think, do I leave a tip *for the owner's daughter*? Is this an insult? What is the etiquette? I almost take the tip back, but think better of it and leave.

Back in my room, I open my laptop, find the articles I downloaded and start reading. Next door, Katerina's radio is tuned to a station playing the latest pop hits. The sound is thin and distracting. Occasionally I hear Katerina singing along. I recognise Eminem, James Blunt, Robbie Williams, Oasis… interspersed with rapid-fire Greek, delivered with that universally recognisable radio dj intonation. Fucking irritating. I look at my watch and am surprised to find it is only nine thirty. I can't very well ask her to turn the volume down. Christ, I'm getting old! I try to read, but only gets bits of what I'm reading.

The first article I read is on the scandal of re-zoning - redefining which land is deserving of protection and which is open to development - with money changing hands, in some district in the Peloponnese. The second is a *vox pop* with locals in a fishing village on what turns out to be Mythos's neighbouring island on the colonisation of their waters by what are referred to as "rabbit fish" – "They are foreign – they are eating all our fish. We have nothing to eat. The rabbit fish is not good to eat." Nothing on algal growth – I must remember to google this tomorrow when I get online.

Then there is an article on the social effects of tourism in rural communities – the younger generation, who invariably speak some English – it is taught in schools – are, accordingly, in the frontline of tourism and benefit disproportionally from jobs in the service industries (especially from tips) and are no longer deferential to their parents' generation. There is, in some places, according to the researcher, "an inversion of the family power hierarchy", which will have long term implications for traditional structures and the place of the Greek Orthodox Church in rural society. The Orthodox Church has been the cohesive force in these communities for centuries – 85% of Greeks identify themselves as Orthodox. But the young are now more tuned into the global culture and consumerism, and are turning away from the church. (An article relating "the dilution of superstition and ritual by American cultural imperialism" is cited. Should be a fun read!)

Segue to the music from Katerina's room. Madonna. American cultural imperialism. I am not going to get anything written tonight. I close my computer, turn off the light and fall asleep.

17

The next morning, from the vantage point of what has become already my "usual" table at *To Meltemi*, Yianni's place, I notice next door on the balcony of The Seaview, Antonis is breakfasting, and engaging in an enthusiastic exchange with Agapi. Xanthe is nowhere to be seen. I don't expect that she does the early shift. Just as well - she would not be impressed by Agapi flirting with the Inspector from Athens. Agapi laughs at something Antonis says. They chat so effortlessly in Greek. He has an unfair advantage, I catch myself thinking.

Then I chide myself. Why do I slip so easily into possessiveness of Agapi? I still feel an allegiance to Lucy – my possessiveness of Agapi feels like the slithering tendrils of treachery – but isn't my pursuit of Lucy over? Can I still be harbouring a hope of getting it together with Lucy? Don't be a fool, I tell myself irritably - move on. So I let myself – I *compel* myself – to regard Agapi with a discerning interest. What I notice is that compared with Lucy's brazen beauty, Agapi's beauty holds itself more easily. It is more contained in the tilt of her head, the shy curve of her belly. Agapi is more… yielding, more *dependable*. It must be said, she is more in my league. I don't feel in awe of her, I don't feel intimidated. She puts me at ease. Is it because she is a mother already? Am I looking for mothering? Is it because she is Greek? Could this be my hidden Greek soul looking for its mate? Or is this my unconscious doing its skulduggery to make Lucy jealous, even if this is, for now, only in my mind?

But I *do* need to check in with Antonis about my story, so I go over to the Seaview as soon as I've had my coffee, eggs and toast. Antonis is pleased to see me. He is in a good mood. I don't know him well enough, but I suspect he is often in a good mood. He has, what my mother would have called, a "sunny disposition".

"My friend!" he exclaims, opening his arms in a gesture of welcomes. "Come sit. Have coffee. I have news." He tells me that they have checked the paperwork at the Town Hall and Garidis was right – although the contract was signed in 1969, construction of the bridge was only started after the company changed hands. The new owner – Hektor Papademos. He and the Chief have arranged to have "a friendly chat" with Mr Papademos he says, evidently proud of his mastery of English police terminology. Do I want to come with?

"We must go to Agia Sofia this morning early also because I must put on the next aeroplane to Athens this" - he shows me a plastic tube – "a tissue sample, from the inside cheek, from Michalis, for DNA analysis to see if the body in the bridge is his father. It must go straight away, so it doesn't spoil." He looks serious but satisfied.

Agapi comes with his bill. "Ah," Antonis says, his face opening into a dazzling smile, "I have asked the lovely waitress, Agapi, if she would like to come with me for lunch *al fresco* tomorrow on the beach – it is Saint's Day – and she has said she would. Isn't that wonderful?" he asks me, not taking his eyes off Agapi.

Agapi smiles back at him, then she turns to me. "You can come too, if you like," she says sweetly. I catch the discombobulation of Antonis's features, as he wonders in an instant whether to oppose this and risk being seen as churlish and small-minded, undoing the good work he has done to make himself attractive to the young lady of his fancy. Or to grin and bear it. Which is what he settles for, grinning fixedly, determined not to let himself down. I am his friend after all. He is hoping, nevertheless, that I decline her invitation. I should. But I don't. She wants me to be there – otherwise why did she invite me? She didn't have to? It was cheeky of her. She must want me there for a reason. Safety in numbers? A chaperone? I affirm. "Sure," I say, "I've got nothing better to do."

She turns and swaggers off. I turn quickly to Antonis as soon as she is out of earshot. "Don't worry, mate," I assure him, "I won't get in your way. I could even help your cause," I tell him.

He looks relieved. "Bless you," he says earnestly, "This girl, I like."

****

The driver arrives in a silver Merc. All the other taxi-drivers drive white Mercs. This must be for VIPs. We get taken into Agia Sofia, where we meet the amiable Chief of Police ("Please, you call me Panagiotis"). The Chief asks if I've heard from Lucy. I tell him about the e-mail. He shares my disappointment, then shrugs with his women-what–you-can-do? shrug. We drive to the edge of town, where there are congregations of flat warehouses, fenced off into plots. We drive in the gates of one site which seems to specialise in building materials. Bricks, timber, heavy moving equipment. "Altreus Construction", a sign says in English (or American?) and below it in Cyrillic script, a bold font for the title, and a less emphatic one for the small print down to the bottom. We drive up to a door at the far end of the building. The door is reinforced with flattened steel. We go in.

There is a long counter, with shelves behind it, stacked with nails, bolts, brushes and industrial-sized tins of paint. A man is busy doing inventory with a clipboard. The Chief addresses him curtly. The man straightens and is flustered – he didn't mean to give offense. The Chief is not interested. He asks to see the Boss. Antonis translated the man saying that the Boss is at the Poseidon. Panagiotis revises his request. "*Hektor… Hektor* Papademos," he says menacingly. He does not like to be corrected. The man smirks and goes down a short corridor to an office at the back. He opens a door, asks someone something, then comes back and still smirking, leads us to the office of Hektor Papademos.

The Chief leads us in. He is avuncular now and greets Papademos the Older warmly. Hektor Papademos, for a man in his eighties, is upright and elegant. He is dressed in a grey suit and tie – old school. His wavy white hair is still decently thick and carefully maintained. The moustache over his wide, flat lips is precisely trimmed – a man who takes care of his appearance. To good effect. He is a handsome man, a man of stature. Only the hollowing of his cheeks and the dulling of a cataract in one eye suggest his true age. His full lips widen slowly into a smile which is *considered* – not bestowed without good reason and to good effect. He extends his hand. I half expect the Chief to kiss it. He doesn't. He shakes it vigorously and turns to introduce us. The *padrone* regards me curiously, takes my hand is his meaty grip, his good eyes boring into me, before he releases me, and nods to us, indicating the chairs in front of this desk. Antonis is watching him carefully.

The Chief hands over to Antonis. Antonis waits, pursing his lips as he considers his opening line of questioning. Then he begins, careful to maintain a respectful tone, enough to indicate that this is a conversation, an enquiry only. I read their body language. The old man remains patrician, his hands on his knees. Antonis straightens so as not to lean in, as the replies become more controlled, more carefully crafted. I hear the Inspector casually drop in "CIA". I notice the Chief shift uncomfortably in his seat. Papademos Senior's eyebrows lift. He eyes the Inspector coolly, then he smiles a benign smile and waves the question off with a contemptuous, "Pah!" and gives a reply, steeped in sarcasm. His eyes have not changed their expression.

The Inspector lets this go and proceeds, his voice patient, modulated. Another question. The old man frowns with an air of erudition as he tries to remember a detail. He gets up, pushing on the armrests of his chair, grunting with the effort and goes to a filing cabinet, peers at the labels on each drawer, until he finds what he is looking for and calls Antonis over. He gives Antonis instructions and the Inspector sorts through files until he pulls out a folder, opens it and reads it through. Antonis nods. "Garidis," he says to us.

There follows a brief, business-like exchange with the old man, who looks pleased with the outcome, the Inspector and the Chief shake his meaty proffered hand and then we leave.

We are just emerging into the sunlight, when I remember that I had a camera with me when we arrived. I have left it in Hektor Papademos's office. I excuse myself and hasten back to the office to retrieve it. Just as I am approaching the door, I overhear the old man's voice, a hoarse whisper, an angry menace. I get to the door and see he is on the phone, his back to me. His tone changes to placatory: "Stavroula... Stavroula...!" I knock discretely. He spins around, wide-eyed, then scowling, his hand over the receiver. "Yes?" he asks peremptorily.

"I left my camera. Sorry," I say, hastily collect the camera and leave. He takes his hand off the receiver and the conversation resumes with a long sigh of exasperation and a whispered exhortation.

I return to where the Inspector and the Chief of Police wait for me near the air-conditioning vent. "Okay," Antonis tells me, "He *did* own the construction company by the time the bridge was built. I asked him whether he'd ever worked for the CIA. He laughed. He said he was on the side of the people who were taken. Anyone will tell me that." The Inspector shrugs. "My colleague in Athens had him down as working for the Americans. Maybe they are wrong." I can tell he thinks they are not. "*And*, he tells me, the *cement* all came from *Garidis*. Garidis sold the construction company, *but he kept the cement factory*. It was Garidis and his men who poured the concrete for the bridge. He said if we want to know how the body got into the bridge, we should ask Konstantin Garidis. *Endaxi*," he says with some satisfaction, "We will have to go back and speak again with Mr Garidis."

18

Garidis sits squat in his well-cushioned chair, his fingers interlaced and his bulbous eyes mocking the Inspector. The Inspector is courteous, almost apologetic, as he sets out the reason for our return visit. I hear Hektor Papademos's name more than once. Garidis scoffs. Then the Inspector subtly shifts into second gear. He produces a notebook and folds back the pages, until he gets to the questions he has prepared. Garidis watches him, a brief glint of alarm, then the blinds come down. Antonis, in a measured tone which coddles a threat, enumerates the questions he has formulated, a pen poised, ready to capture the old man's reply.

Garidis leans back into the plush folds of his chair. He takes his time, surveying the big city cop with disdain. His tone when he deigns to answer the Inspector's questions is perfunctory, dismissive and rich with sarcasm. The Inspector persists, the tilt of his head deferential. Garidis explains something to the Inspector with long-suffering pedantry, condescension, but when Antonis does not demure, the old man's voice rises with indignation. He is a man who is affronted by the insinuations, an innocent man he will have us believe. But Antonis has spotted something, some incongruity I intuit, and his next set of questions are delivered with a sharper point. Garidis starts to sweat, his eyes shifting to seek the support of the Chief of Police who knows him, who will not bully an old man. Panagiotis turns his mouth down to save himself a shrug. The old man attempts a smile, but without the affirmation from Antonis it calls for, it is stillborn; Garidis returns to squawking and blustering. Antonis folds his notebook away with a look of quiet satisfaction. Garidis offers something, at first with urgency, then, when Antonis accepts his offer, his offer becomes steeped in reluctance. He wants to regain his pride and his protestations of innocence. Panagiotis looks at him with a mixture of contempt and disappointment.

In all the time we are there, Garidis has not offered us refreshment. On the way back to our car, the Chief tells us this was a definite affront – it is unheard of in the villages, if not the towns, not to offer guests at least a glass of water and dry biscuits or bread with salt. Garidis had signalled that he did not consider us his guests; we were intruders.

The Chief and the Inspector discuss the interview on the way back to Agia Anna in the car. Antonis explains to me that Garidis has of course denied any knowledge about how a body came to be hidden in the cement of the bridge. He acknowledged it was his cement and blamed the memory of an old man for not having specified this at our earlier interview. But he said he knew all his men personally – not one of them would have dreamt of doing anything criminal, like disposing of a dead body. He acknowledged that he had supported the military coup, insisted that it had brought stability to the country and that the crimes of the Colonels had been vastly exaggerated at what he had considered to be "show trials" worthy of Josef Stalin. According to him, the Communist had got what they deserved. If the Colonels hadn't taken over, the country would have gone to the dogs. "We would all be Albanians!" he said – Antonis mimics his gruff voice and chuckles. "The man does not know his history," he says.

Importantly, Garidis said that all the Communists who had been arrested had been sent to the political prison on Macronissos. There had been no executions on the island. He would have known. "He says we should check the records," the Chief says, "The bastard even smiled. He knows all the records were destroyed before the Colonels were toppled. He probably burned the records for the island himself. We won't find anything. He's not going to talk. *Malakas!*"

Antonis nods in agreement. He turns to me. "Anyway, we asked him to give us all the names of the men who worked on the bridge. Maybe one of *them* will talk, if any of them are still alive. It was a long time ago. I suppose we must get the names of all the construction company workers also. Or else Garidis will say we targeted him. Panagiotis, you will do this?" The Chief nods. "So now we will wait. Tomorrow is the naming day for Agia Sofia. Tomorrow we don't work," says the Inspector with a wistful look.

Antonis is thinking of Agapi.

19

I turn down Antoni''s invitation to dine with him – I feel a pressure to get something written to send off to Marsha and fear I will surely be distracted by Antoni''s anticipation of the picnic with Agapi tomorrow. Which reminds me, I need to get something from the store in the village to contribute - a bottle of wine maybe.

On my way to the shop, I think to go past Lucy's, just in case she has changed her mind and has returned. The old lady opposite is at her gate, as soon as she sees me, she jabbers away, gesticulating I think to indicate her head hurts. The rent – she is wanting the rent and hoping to get my sympathy. I go to her and take out my wallet and show her I don't have much on me. She looks at me like I am crazy, she is insulted, turns and walks back up her path. Two cats scuttle into the house ahead of her.

No-one at Lucy's. No signs of life.

The shop is busy – the young woman behind the cash register tells me they are closed tomorrow for the Saint's Day and everyone is getting their last-minute additions – most will have done their main shopping in the port, in Agia Sofia. The shop has beach paraphernalia, two fridges with fizzy drinks, water and juice, an almost empty rack of vegetables and fruit – what is left is certainly not worth buying - shelves of tinned foods and at the back, a surprisingly well-stocked rack of wine and spirits. I know nothing about Greek wines, but select a bottle based on its price (reasonable) and its stylish label. I buy a tin of *dolmades*, stuffed vine leaves and for good measure (why not) a packet of fig biscuits. A pale cheese. A bottle of black olives from Kalamata. I don't want to look like a cheapskate. Then again, I don't know what Antonis will be bringing. I didn't think to ask. How lavish will he be in his wooing?

Back in my room, I go onto the balcony to take in the last of the light. Katerina is on her balcony next to mine. "Hey," I say. "*Geia sou.*"

"Hey", she says, her eyebrows crinkling with curiosity in spite of her teenage torpor.

"I'm Tom," I say.

"Kat," she says, "I'm Kat."

"Hey, Kat," I say, "I'm a friend of Lucy's – the Australian?"

"The crazy one," Kat says in matter-of-fact voice.

I grin complicitly. "Yeah, I guess you could say so."

Kat nods. "You want breakfast tomorrow?"

When I say I do, she tells me her parents, Yiannis and Soulla, will be going to the church in the big village in the mountain for the service of thanksgiving to St. Sofia and she will be left behind to see to any tourists who come into the *taverna*. She doesn't "*do*" religion, she tells me, so she doesn't mind. Boring. Her father wanted Bobby to stay, but he insisted on going with them to the church. He never used to go, but this year, Xanthe will be there with her parents, and Bobby, she tells me gleefully, will want to look his best. She speaks fluent English with an American twang that comes straight from MTV. The devilish look is entirely of her own making.

****

Something startles me out of my sleep in the night. I am suddenly wide awake. Something about that e-mail from Lucy wasn't right. That wasn't Lucy. I don't know how I know that, but I know I'm right. I can't hear her saying *those* words in *that* order. Or what is it?

I consider waiting for the morning, but now I feel certain I won't sleep until I've worked it out. I open my laptop and check back in Outlook for Lucy's e-mail. "Dear Thomas, I am going away. Do not wait for me. I will write you. Lucy." What is it that doesn't sound like her voice? Her calling me Thomas rather than Tom? – that could be just a jokiness. No, there is something else. The Americanisation of "I will write you"? – do Australians also do that? – leave out the preposition? They don't, do they? - they're like the English... Commonwealth, colonials. But it's not that. I scroll back through my inbox and search for other e-mails from Lucy. There is something else...

I re-read some of her old e-mails, and I see what the stylistic difference is. It is very clear.

I'll have to wait until I can get online before I can check it out. How early will Michalis open up at The Seaview? – it is Saint's Day – he won't want to be getting up too early. I may as well try to get back to sleep.

20

I wake at nine and go straight down to the Seaview with my laptop. Michalis is in a dark suit and tie, his hair slicked down, carefully parted. His wife, Nitsa, is in a fashionable two-piece, with a pill-box hat and carrying a small bag that bears the logo DKNY. Not cheap. Not bad for the daughter-in-law of a communist guerrilla. She does not look pleased when I ask to use the internet, but she unlocks the office and switches the modem on. She goes out and I hear her calling Xanthe in an assertive voice, some of the irritation I'm sure, emanating from having to indulge my untimely request. I hear Xanthe's frustrated reply from somewhere inside, with the English-American "*Oh my God!* What do you want from me?!" added on.

I send the e-mail I've composed to Lucy. No time for anything else. I don't want to hold Michalis up. Right, let's see what comes. With a mixture of excitement and foreboding, I press send. It's gone.

On my way out, I thank Nitsa and hand over my five euros, but she waves this away. Maybe you're not supposed to exchange money on a Saint's naming day. Or maybe she doesn't want to be bothered. Michalis is helping his mother into the front passenger seat of his Mercedes. Stavroula sees me watching and gives me a steely look with her dark eyes. She does not like her infirmity to be on public display. Surely not the Stavroula the aristocratic Hektor Papademos was cajoling on the phone in his office yesterday? I presume there are lots of Stavroulas on the island, but they *are* of the same generation and I presume they know each other. It's a small island. Is there a connection?

The old lady turns away with a look of disdain, as Xanthe emerges, flounces past her mother and sashays to her father's limousine. Bobby will not be disappointed. Xanthe looks like she stepped out of Vogue.

****

I string out my breakfast to pass the time. Kat is not a bad little cook, I get sausages with my eggs and fried tomatoes sprinkled with wild thyme. After my third coffee, I go down to the beach which is occupied only by me and the Scandinavian party – the boys are slumped in their deck chairs, litre bottles of water at hand, their exuberance pulped by the ouzo and brandy they no doubt have over-consumed. I wait until I see the first of the church-goers returning in their family-full car, before I go up to my room for a shower and get ready to go to the picnic. My mind turns sporadically to the e-mail I've sent to Lucy and waves of excitement and trepidation ebb and flow.

I take the bottle of wine and the provisions and set off. I see Antonis from a distance, coming from his cousin's *kafenion,* head down, shoulders slumped. When he gets to me, he apologises even before he greets me. He has only drinks and crisps, he tells me, which he got at the last minute from his cousin's bar. He left it too late to get provisions from the store, it was closed when he got there – so none of the extravagant delicacies he was counting on buying to impress Agapi. He looks forlorn.

I hand him the dolmades, olives, cheese and biscuits I have bought. "Here," I tell him, "You can say these are from you." He looks at me in disbelieve, then gratitude. "Take it," I say. He takes the bag from me. He looks deeply into my eyes. "For this, I owe you, *file mou*," he says earnestly. He puts the bags down to give me a fulsome hug which goes on longer than I am comfortable with.

We go over the ridge towards Agapi's house, beyond the beach where the waves swell and break. She is standing, waiting. She waves when she sees us. She calls out, and first her daughter, then her mother, come out to stand with her to welcome us. They are dressed in their dresses for church, black and severe for the *Giagia*, green and simply-cut for Agapi (to match her eyes) and denim for Eleni. Their clothes are probably bought in a supermarket, from a rack of identical dresses, simple and inexpensive. They do not have excess. I had thought to buy sweets for Eleni, but my middle-class London values deterred me from buying sweets for a kid without the mother's permission.

Antonis hands the bag of meagre provisions to Agapi, with a brief apology. She hands the bag to her mother and invites us into her home. The cottage is simply furnished. The table and chairs are old and bleached. Photos of the family compete for wall space, with copies of paintings of icons and saints. A large black and white wedding photo of two people from an earlier generation, stiffly upright in wedding attire, takes central stage. Agapi's parents. I briefly compare the young woman in the photo with the old lady, now putting glasses on the table. She has made freshly-squeezed lemonade and there is, beside it, a bowl of breadsticks covered with sesame. A smaller photo, not on the wall, but in a standing frame, shows a younger Agapi in her wedding dress, her childlike features luminous, with a young and handsome man – her husband for such a short time. Agapi sees me looking at the picture and is amused but touched by my sympathetic regard. I hand my bottle of wine to her, she accepts it with a look of concealed pleasure. She touches my arm, her hand lingering, a simple act of intimacy which is not lost on me. Antonis is making formal conversation with Agapi's mother, who stifles her grin and covers her mouth with her hand – she has no teeth and this embarrasses her in such company.

"My mother has made lemon chicken and *skordalya* – potatoes salad with garlic and lemon," Agapi says, "And we have a round loaf of aniseed bread, special from the festival. Come, let us go down to the beach further around. There is shade there, for my mother."

From the look on Antonis's face, I can tell he wasn't expecting Agapi's mother to join us. But he quickly recovers and then is over-zealous in his hospitality to the old lady, taking her arm solicitously as we set off. Agapi and I are left carrying the provisions. Eleni carries a blanket and an old and scruffy hand-knitted doll. Agapi sneaks an amused look at me, as she watches Antonis shouting in the old lady's ear, telling her to be careful at each step, she who knows this path better than any of us. She looks at him like he is a mental patient, but she lets him steer her. Perhaps it is indeed a long time since she had the arm of a man.

At our designated spot, under an overhang of beautifully contoured and coloured sandstone, we set up the picnic. Antonis seats himself on a rock which is shaped like a throne. He likes the regal authority this gives him, but his seat places him a little away from the rest of us, where the blanket has been placed on flat dry sand. He considers getting up and joining us, but will wait until his grand presence is acknowledged and he can comment on it, before jokingly relinquishing his throne and coming down to our level. When he does sit on the sand, I see he is afflicted with the common male problem of tight hips and has to position himself on his side, leaning as casually as he can on one elbow. Eleni wants me to join her. She takes my hand and leads me to a shallow rocky inlet where barnacles cling and crabs scurry. Agapi looks with pleasure to her daughters' forwardness with me. She has only met me once, but she trusts me. Antonis meanwhile has her mother's attention, and in his anxiety to impress, is being garrulous. The old lady is polite, but when he looks away, she regards him curiously. She is not sure what he is about or what this educated man wants from her.

After a while Agapi gets up and joins Eleni and me at the rock pools. Antonis considers getting up too, but doesn't want to seem needy, so instead he rolls over and lies on his back, examining intently the patterns in the rock face above his head. Then, with alacrity, he sits up, uncorks the wine and pours a glass for himself and one for the old lady. She declines, but he insists, he clinks her glass and shouts "*Yammas!*" with forced exuberance, before pouring the dark red liquid down his eager throat. The day is not going as he wished, but there is still time.

Later, when we have finished the delicious chicken (if I'm correct, flavoured with coriander, fennel and oregano), Antonis brings out his cousin's bottle of Metaxa brandy – a fourteen-year-old – and insists we all drink a toast to Agia Sofia, the island's saint. "My cousin explained to me, Saint Sofia, Agia Sofia, is the saint for this island because of the way the island looks – with the big mountain in the middle and the three smaller mountains towards the sea, is like St. Sofia (Wisdom) with her three daughters, Pistis, Elpis and Agapi – Pistis: Faith, Elpis: Hope, and her youngest, Agapi: Love. So today, on this beautiful day, with these beautiful women" – he raises his glass to first the old lady, who giggles girlishly even though she probably doesn't understand the English in which Antonis has chosen to make his speech for my benefit – and then with a wink, to Eleni, who looks at him suspiciously - "we drink to Agia Sofia, to Wisdom, but also to her daughter, Agapi. To Love," he says, lifts his glass to Agapi and then downs his brandy. Agapi murmurs "To Love", but she does not make eye contact with him. Instead she turns her gaze to me.

21

Because I'm using the internet service so much, often briefly, Nitsa now doesn't charge me every time – she gives me a book with hand-drawn columns and says to put down the minutes I use and pay her 5 euros when I get up to an hour. Very decent of her. Her mother-in-law does not approve. Stavroula continues to eye me with haughty suspicion. But then she's like that with everybody, except Xanthe, whom she lets fuss over her.

I check my e-mails before going to bed. There is no reply yet from my e-mail to Lucy. I must be patient. There could be any number of explanations. At least two of these are alarming, but I must wait it out. I compel myself to consider the benign, banal possibilities and let them float me like lifebuoys.

The *is* an e-mail from my editor. Marsha is encouraging about my last posting on the body in the bridge story – Mavros's story - but she says, as I expected she would, that it is too long and that I have time to shorten it myself – it won't go to print until the story comes together more. She is equivocal on the environmental story – she says it's too tentative, speculative and has been done before.

I ponder Marsha's response to the environmental story – she's right of course. But what is the story Lucy was chasing? She wouldn't have contacted me if it hadn't been something hot. What exactly is going on on this island? I think I will keep my appointment with Christos Papademos after all.

****

This time I go to the Poseidon via the main town. I want to see the lagoon and get a closer look at the sludge. The road from Agia Sofia is all new tar with precipitous edges, dropping a good six inches onto the gravel in the culverts. The route is mountainous and serpentine, lined by pines of varying ages, some old and twisted, others young and vibrant. Cicadas are in full voice and the sky is deep blue. The road out of the town ascends to a non-descript small town on the ridge. A small all-purpose store, a chapel on a ridge, a *kafenion* and a hand-painted sign saying "B+B. Nice. Cheap." Once through the town, the road follows the coast and on my right the cliffs plunge into the sea far below. I must drive carefully, I think, as I accelerate and feel the wind in my hair. The views are spectacular, the mountains magnificent and silver, the forests dense and undulating, the ravines terrifying and muscular, the beaches at their feet inviting and tranquil. Finally, after about a thirty-minute ride, I get to a crest from which I can see the lagoon shining below, beyond it, in the distance, on a promontory, tastefully decorous, the Poseidon, all steel and glass, all smoke and mirrors.

On my left, as I descend, the forest becomes a fire-ravaged ghost of itself. Dark grey ash lies thick on the ground. Blackened skeletons of trees and bushes claw at the sky. Here and there, green shoots burst out defiantly. Half way down, men are at work repairing a section of the road, they have to stop what they are doing to let me ease past. They look at me, some curious, some impatient. I greet them cheerfully. Not one responds.

At the bottom of the decline, the road flattens and follows the sea. A concrete pipe juts from the hillside nearest the Poseidon, disappears under the road, emerges again on the beach and then continues resolutely into the sea. I pull my bike over and set it on its stand. The hum of the motor lingers in my bones, but the only sound is the sea. The beach is pebbled and there is a high-water mark of foliage and debris from a storm surge. The water at the sea edge froths brown, and beyond, the surface glistens a sickly rust and maroon, flecked with nauseating pink and yolk yellow excrescence. The tang from the sea is inflected with sulphur and ammonia. Not healthy. The slick extends, perhaps a hundred metres into the sea, maybe more, and is about two hundred metres wide. I notice some seabirds have made it home, bobbing easily on this discoloured surface, occasionally dipping their beaks in and then shaking their heads vigorously to swallow. It may look like shit, but to them it's tasty. Don't know how much good it's doing them.

I go back to my bike and set off, looking for a road which will take me to the lagoon. I have to go only a few hundred metres before a dirt road on the left takes off into low bushes and reeds. This must be it. I go carefully on the rutted road. A lizard scuttles across the road in front of me, stops looks around, then scuttles back again. Probably forgotten something at home. The road becomes a track and I decide to go the rest of the way on foot.

I don't have far to walk. Soon I am at the water's edge. The water is dark and finely rippled by the sea breeze. I make out at least four different species of bird floating on the water and nipping the ground at water's edge for bugs and worms. A pair of pelicans stand proud and cranky in the shallows towards the far shore. A cluster of ducks (or are they geese?) squabble amiably amongst themselves. In the sand, an imprint of something reptilian which has slithered into the reed bed. Are there snakes here? A rat, nose twitching, back hunched ready for flight, sneaks towards the water and licks a drink, before scuttling back into the bushes. I have seen enough.

The Poseidon is further along the main road. The tar sweeps in between two heraldic gates, emblazoned with gilt-tinted sea gods, tridents at the ready. A watering system hisses over the iridescent lawns, neatly trimmed and edged. A rosemary hedge is in its infancy. On a terrace to my left, men are at work constructing a wall. A digger crunches and groans, and darts into reverse, before depositing its load. A gardener is at work in a flower-bed, planting succulents. The road opens into a wide turning at the entrance to the hotel. Over the elaborate front entrance, "Poseidon Luxury Spa and Eco-Resort" announces itself in bold confident lettering. The doors glide open as I reach the portico. The reception area is empty and as yet unfurnished. My footsteps echo on the granite flooring as I approach the front desk.

A hirsute man with a prodigious moustache pops up from behind the counter, pliers in hand. On his knees, only his head visible over the counter, he looks like a dwarf. His dust-imprinted attire and body odour suggest he is a construction worker. "*Nai?*" he asks peremptorily. He must suppose I am here to deliver something.

"Christos Papademos?" I ask, "*Pou ine?*" Is it my syntax or my accent that gives me away?

"Wait," he says in English. He walks off, fiddling with some sort of electrical thing with wires attached. His pungent body odour is at odds with the silence and the sharply defined edges of marble and chrome. Plaster busts relax in the shade of impressively realistic ginger flowers perched like cranes in long vases. Accommodation here will not come cheap. The hairy guy ambles back a while later, still fiddling with his connection box. "Come," he says, jerking his head over his shoulder without meeting my eye. He turns and I follow.

Christos Papademos gets up to greet me as I am led in. "Christos Papademos," he says, extending his hand. "Chris," he says, smiling. He must be in his early forties, lean and fit-looking, his head shaven into a stylish trim of blonde stubble and his lavender shirt is newly-pressed. "Tom Pickering," I say and place my hand in his. His grip is comfortable, his hand large and meaty. His eyes examine me curiously from behind blue-framed designer spectacles. He smiles beguilingly. He is used to being sociable. "What can I do you for, Mr Pickering?" he says. His American accent is immediately apparent. "Ah, wait… Tom…? Tom… Michalis sent you? Yeah? You the journalist looking for our mutual friend, Lucy? Crazy chick. What's happened to her?"

Christos's office looks out onto an unnaturally green lawn, encircling two four-foot palm trees, recently planted and edged with crisp hedging, beyond which the pale blue of the pool beckons. Maybe the man's pretentions will mean peacocks in the garden at some stage.

"Last saw her a few weeks ago. She came and stayed over. But I haven't heard from her since. I was getting a bit worried myself. But you know, chicks, eh? And our Lucy was far out," he says with a chuckle. "Say, you want something to drink?" Why not? I accept his offer of a Scotch on ice. He goes over to a cabinet and pulls out a bottle of fifteen year-old Laffroaig. "This okay for you?" he asks. He smiles. He wasn't really expecting an answer. He tinkles ice into a tumbler and pours us each two fingers.

"I'd love you to write something about our resort for the London papers," he says as he hands me my glass. "Its eco-friendly," he says, "I think our Lucy was quite taken with it." He sits himself back down behind his walnut desk. His plump leather chair sighs contentedly as if it has missed his presence. "It's all my own money, or my father's money actually. We made our money in New Jersey."

"I met your father briefly," I tell him. "He is… urbane," I say.

He chuckles. "Urbane - I love that. He'd love it too. Urbane," he chuckles some more. "I love the way you English people speak." He toasts me and sips his single malt. "We emigrated to the States in the early 70s. My dad had just started his construction company, but, you know, the new government, under old Karamanlis, was tidying things up so we could join the EU (the Common Market as it was then) and well, some people got scapegoated – they had to make an example of some people, some businesses, to impress the suits in Brussels. My dad had business interests with the States…"

I can't stop myself. "CIA?" I say with a complicit grin.

Christos's eyes narrow momentarily and then he affects a look of astonishment. "CIA? Where did you get that crock of shit from? He was on the other side, dude!"

I want to tell him I've known lots of cases where the undercover operative goes to extraordinary lengths to prove they are loyal to "the other side", but I desist.

"No, he'd worked in the States before, in the 50s, he knew people in Jersey, he did business with people who became… unpopular… 'undesirable'. Italians. You know what I'm saying? Anyways, after the junta fell, there were strong anti-American feelings over here in Greece. So my dad suffered for his American connections. I don't blame the government – they had to do what they had to do – I would have done the same. Luckily for us, our American contacts helped us get set up in Queens. That's where I grew up, where I went to school, where I met my first wife. Where I *left* my first wife. And the kids. Lucky me." He chuckles, his eyes going to slits with his amusement. "Don't print that," he says. I realise he is giving me an interview for an article on the Poseidon I haven't agreed to.

"Also not for printing, we came back to Mythos in the late 90s when our Italian partners got greedy, the IRS got too nosey and the EU was offering tasty incentives for businesses in underdeveloped economic zones. You know, in Greece, taxes are optional," he says straight-faced, then laughs with hilarity when I look nonplussed. "Only joking, man," he says. "What a hoot!" he laughs. "But, and here I am being serious, the EU were keen on eco-friendly tourism – the Green lobby, political correctness, all that – so getting an eco-friendly design for this resort was win-win – we got the grants and tax allowances, they got low carbon and zero pollution - well, we *all* want that, right?"

"Well," I say, "What is the slick on the water in the sea near the lagoon? I couldn't help noticing it as I rode in."

"Oh, that – that is… temporary. Got it covered. Just something from the effluent that's built up from the construction process. We've had the local municipality take a look at it – all fine, all in hand. The Mayor has signed off on it. You should go and see him. Nikos Angelopolis – great guy. Yeah, it's all there – Lucy and that NGO she was working for, came for me, guns blazing – but's it's all A-ok. Check it out: the re-zoning, the environmental impact report – it's not a walk in the park with all the paperwork the fucking EU want, man! – the approval for the new road – it's all there. Lucy was bowled over by how thorough we'd been and she was charmed, I think, by the technology we got working for us here. We are carbon neutral and we have subsidised a recycling centre in St. Sofia. The ducks on the lagoon have never been happier. We want them to be. It's a huge draw card for us – bird watching. There is a huge variety, all year round. We are constructing bird hides, in keeping of course with the local flora, all around the lagoon for the guests we hope will flock here, like the birds, from next season. Win-win. We don't *do* losing." His smile is pure PR confidence, pure Americana.

"You want another finger?" he asks, holding his glass to the light. "Mmm, this is good stuff, the best thing to come out of England since the Beatles!" My Scottish friends would bristle, but I restrain myself. "Lucy and I became good friends," he says. "You're not her boyfriend, are you?" he asks, dipping his head forward.

"No, just friends, colleagues," I tell him.

"Phew," he says, "That's okay then, 'cause I fucked her. Or should I say, *she* fucked *me!* Crazy chick!" I try to hide my chagrin. He doesn't seem to notice. "Jeez, like the second time she came here, she wanted to suck my dick. I'd offered her a decent amount to write a favourable report on the Poseidon, to get that NGO she was with off our backs – they had no justification, but those batshit crazy NGOs have some clout in

Germany and we didn't need bad publicity. What I was prepared to pay her was what she'd have earned in a year she told me. She was so happy she wanted to blow me right here in this office! Said she it would pay the deposit on a house in the country in Holland she was keen on. She stayed here for four days – couldn't get enough of me and the lifestyle I guess. A bit more luxurious than she was used to. But she got stick from her NGO when they found out she had switched sides."

"What NGO was it?" I ask.

He looks at me and frowns. "You know, I don't think she ever said. If she did, I don't remember. Just the woman she was working for had a grand-sounding German name – von Something – that's like royalty, right?"

I shrug. No aristos in the German Green movement as far as I know. Must be a small self-financed operation, probably some rich kid's plaything.

"They didn't like it one bit. I think they threatened legal action of some kind. Breach of contract or something. I heard Lucy on the phone, telling the woman to go and get fucked. But she wasn't sleeping and getting a bit... I don't know... *wired*, shouting crazy shit, broke some crockery. I took her into town to see a friend of mine, Phil Trepanis, one of the local medics. No shrinks on the island. He gave her some meds, she said she was going to fetch some stuff in Agia Anna and I haven't seen her since. It surprised me – I thought she was keen on the job I offered. I tried to phone, but I got nothing. So I thought she'd changed her mind and had left the island. But you think not?" he asks me, his forehead crinkling. "Maybe you should speak to Dr. Trepanis. Maybe he knows more. Let me give him a call," he says and reaches for his phone.

I'm struggling with two things. One, could it be that Lucy would have written a favourable report for money? Was she that desperate? She seemed so principled. And two, Christos Papademos is suggesting she was having some sort of breakdown. Could this be true? It's not the first I've heard of Lucy being referred to as "crazy", but I didn't think this meant *actually* mentally ill. But was she?

Christos puts his phone down. "His secretary will call you with a time. You should go and see Phil Trepanis," Christos says again and nods. "He wouldn't tell me anything – confidentiality clause – you know, doctor-patient thing. But maybe he'll tell you – you've come all the way from England, looking for her and you're practically family, know what I mean?" I nod. "Let me know, will ya? She was crazy, but a hell of a fuck, I hope you don't mind me saying. Wouldn't mind getting her into my bed again." He gets up. "Now, do you want a tour of the property? I'll make it worth your while – have the kitchen staff prepare us something – the kitchen is just about up and running."

After the tour (he is especially keen for me to see the banks of photovoltaic cells out the back), we eat (alone) in an expansive dining room which overlooks the sea. For all his Americanism, Christos Papademos is engaging company and a generous host. He tells amusing stories about the Italian mobsters he and his father worked with in New York. He is clearly fond of his father. "He is supposed to be retired, but he still has his office and wants to micro-manage the family business. Watches every cent. Heh," he laughs, "If it had been up to him, they would never have found that body in the bridge. For him, it was like, 'Why spend money on demolishing the old bridge? The new road goes around it.' But for me, it is an eyesore. I have my aesthetic standards," he says with a self-effacing smile. "Our backers want what the tourists will admire and that's what I give them." In spite of his zealous entrepreneurship, he and his family are ardent supporters of PASOK, the social democrats, Greece's version of the Labour Party. "The big earners, ship owners, all have their companies registered in tax havens. Our economy now depends on tourism – for the good of the people, we must do what we can."

We dine on swordfish, lightly grilled and drink a delicious Sauvignon Blanc from a South African vineyard. I can see what Lucy must have seen in him. When I take my leave of him, he clasps me to him and I, for all my earlier scepticism, return his warm embrace. He is an okay guy – rich, but okay. As I make my way back to my motorbike, I am grinning for no reason and my legs feel light. With all the Scotch and the wine I've drunk, I must ride extra-carefully. I must not ruminate on the images in my mind of Lucy being fucked by Christos. Will there be a reply to my e-mail?

22

I intend to check my e-mails when I get back to Agia Anna, but I am so
drowsy that instead I go straight to my room and collapse on the bed. I
wake when it is already darkening and confuse this for the light of dawn.
Only the sound of activity from the *taverna* – Yiannis shouting, Soulla
shouting back, *rebetika*, the clatter of dishes - re-orientate me. I shower
and go downstairs for something to eat, even though I'm not hungry.
Force of habit. I remember that I should go to the Seaview and check my
mail, but something holds me back, makes me put it off.

As I'm walking down stairs, the dream I had of Lucy resurfaces.
Naked and forceful, she'd wanted to be on top and for some reason I had
not wanted her to be. We'd struggled. She'd overpowered me and rubbed
her cunt vigorously on my thigh with a look of determination. I swear I
could even smell her sex. "Get off me!" I'd shouted, even as my cock
had rebelled and gone rock hard. I pushed her and she'd landed on the
floor, astonished, strung... I had been left with the still undecipherable
taste of feelings, swirling together, not blending. But the remembering of
the dream had rekindled my erection and I turn and go back upstairs, and
consider taking myself in hand. But, back in my room, my arousal
dissipates, I'm left with the entirely irrational feeling that I've cheated
on *Agapi*. Agapi! Why? I don't have any claims on Agapi and she doesn't
have any claim on me. Ridiculous. Anyway, Jesus, it was just *a dream*.
Curiously, though, I feel a sense of propriety with Agapi that I never
quite managed with Lucy. I should have been angry that Lucy had
cheated on me by fucking Christos, having practically invited me to the
island. I should have felt jealous. But I hadn't. I'd only felt deflated. So
why the dream?

Anyway, I don't feel like to going to the Seaview now. They're
probably busy anyway. I'll get my e-mails first thing in the morning.
Instead, I go downstairs again and find that my usual table at Yianni's
occupied by a German couple staring into one another's eyes with

adoration, holding hands across the table. Annoying. Yiannis must attribute my expression of irritation to not having my preferred seat, he shuffles to me solicitously and whispers, "Soon they will leave. Come, sit here. When they go, you go there." He ushers me to a small table near the kitchen door, to reinforce the temporary nature of my positioning to the tardy canoodling Germans. He marches over to them and pointedly places the bill in front of the man. "*Logariasmo.* The bill," he says curtly, his smile a grimace of hospitality, before he turns and walks back to me, stands next to me and watches the woman take the bill from the man, put on her spectacles and then read the itemised bill carefully. It's all in Greek I know. I don't know what she is examining. I see Yianni's fingers drumming. He turns to me, "They come here before. They no leave a tip. Nothing." He does his each-hand-wiping-the-other-clean gesture of finality. The German couple call him over and question something on the bill. He crosses it off. They give him money and wait while he counts out the change. They get up smiling. The man thanks him and slaps Yiannis on the back in a show of brotherliness and no hard feelings. Yiannis lets him, but turns his face to me and shakes his head in a show of what he has to put up with. "Please come again," he says unconvincingly. The lovebirds leave with stiff backs. I imagine them back in their air-conditioned room, fucking to a metronome. Click-clack, click-clack.

I get up and move to my table and wait as Yiannis clears their debris, before sitting down. I tell him I've been to the Poseidon and that I've met Christos. "*Kapitaleest,*" he says by way of insult. I tell him that Christos supported PASOK. "Is like Blair in your country," he says, "New Labour. New PASOK. Andreas, the son of Papandreou, he came from America a professor, a revolutionary. And what he became? – a rich man... *kapitaleest.*"

"Socialism is not everyone being equally poor," I quote Deng, the Chinese leader.

"But do the poor peoples get rich? Or the rich get more rich?" he says. "Later we talk, my friend," he says.

After my simple meal – I settle for *spanakopita* – spinach and feta pie – Yiannis leaves the last table still going for Bobby to attend to and sits down with me, his cigarettes and brandy as accompaniment. "Bobby, *dio kafedes – metrio,*" he shouts to his son to bring us Greek coffee.

Bobby, silent as ever, nods with the slightest of frowns. His father could have asked nicely, said please. The absence of the *"parakalo"* is a signal of the hierarchy between father and son, which the son resents. I am sure Kat wouldn't have let her father get away with it.

"So, you met Christos Papademos? The *Amerikano*. Did he tell you about his father? Hektor."

I tell him I met the older Papademos and that his son told me some very amusing stories about their dealings in New York with the mafia.

"CIA." Yiannis says. "Even before the Colonels, Hektor Papademos was work for the CIA. He was President of the American Friendship Club on the island. The CIA was at the backside of the Colonels. Many peoples – *sosialistes* - they not like the United States – because of the war. Hektor, he say he support PASOK, but Hektor only support what make money for him. The Americans, the CIA, give him lots of money and they make him in charge of the money they send for to build a hall for the peoples in Agia Sofia, for to make better the harbour. If you want a jobs in America for you or for your sons, you go to Papademos – he fix it." Each hand wipes the other clean. "For America Independence Day, big party in Agia Sofia for everybuddy - flags for wave in the street – the Stars and Stipe-pes. When the junta was finished up, the CIA was pay for Hektor and his family all to go to America. They come back rich… more rich than when they was here before. But now is Christos, the son, in charge. Christos he is clever – he make big donation to PASOK, he make a party for all the peoples so they will vote for Nikos Angelopolis to be the Mayor. How you think they let him build there? That land – all the beaches, the forests – it was protected. But no protected from Christos Papademos. His father walk around like he is the King. Ha!" Yiannis barks a derisive laugh. "He is like what-is-name, Don Corleone! Ha!"

Our coffee arrives and Yiannis accepts his cup with a mild distraction. I make a point of thanking Bobby, Bobby smiles and raises an eyebrow. He sees I've noticed his father's dismissal of his son as not requiring the formality of a thank you. "Go tell your mother I will come to help her when I have had my *kafe,"* Yiannis says in English for my benefit. "That woman she is work hard."

I ponder what he has told me about the Papademos family. Their allegiances have soured my feelings – I had admired the older

Papademos as patrician and had quite liked Christos. I don't know what weight to give Yianni's cynicism. Is what he said true, or does he resent them because they have done better than him in history's fickle flow?

23

As it happens I over-sleep and get woken by a call to tell me Dr Trepanis can see me briefly after he has finished his morning clinic. I have thirty minutes to get into Agia Sofia. I shall have to check for that e-mail later. When I get to the hospital, I am directed to Dr. Trepanis's clinic and told to wait. I get to wait thirty minutes. I could have got my e-mails, I think irritably. Then I hear my name (mispronounced), and see the good doctor advancing on me. He thrusts his hand out, introduces himself cursorily and then rushes in front of me into his office and goes behind his desk to grab his sandwiches and bottle of water. "You don't mind," he says, as he unwraps what is either a late breakfast or a very early lunch. He has had a frustrating morning and is irritated that he has agreed to fit me in. He practically growls when a nurse walks in without knocking and hands him a stack of folders and waits while he initials prescriptions. They don't speak. I know from the receptionist to whom I chatted while I waited for him, that after this, he has minor surgery, and then an antenatal clinic this afternoon and home visits later. He is one of only two doctors at the hospital, in fact on the island. People who need major surgery and even mothers delivering babies have to go to the big island by the single propeller plane that makes the thirty-minute journey twice a day.

Dr Trepanis must be in his mid-forties, although his world-weary, deeply-riven frown, hollowed cheeks and thinning hair suggest he may be younger than he looks. The medical certificate on his wall is from Manchester University Medical School. "You want to know about Miss Discombe?" he asks. I explain the nature of my enquiry. I tell him that Christos Papademos sent me. "Christos, how is he?" he asks. He is not really interested. He is giving himself time to think. "I saw your friend, Miss Discombe, but you understand I am bound by confidentiality." I tell him why I am worried – she has not been seen for nearly a month. He hesitates. He takes a big bite of his sandwich and chews it pensively. I tell him what I already know from Christos. He nods and purses his lips.

"Okay. I prescribed Valium. But maybe she needed something stronger. I am not a psychiatrist you understand, but from what I have seen before, maybe she needed something more... a mood stabiliser perhaps. Perhaps I should have... I gave her an appointment to see me again, but she never came back. I thought she'd gone back to... where was she from? Australia?"

"What do you think is wrong with her?"

He inspects me - a risk assessment. He wants to ascertain how much he can trust me. "Okay," he sighs, "If she is missing, then I must tell you. I think she might be at risk. In my opinion, Miss Discombe was hypomanic when I last saw her. I think she may have a bipolar affective disorder." He pronounces the diagnosis carefully. "If she is missing, it could be because of this."

Fuck, could Lucy have had a serious mental health problem all along? That would fit, I think, feeling, fleetingly, a stupid smug glow of vindication, before I remind myself that the harsh, rejecting e-mail may be fake and my concern for her reasserts itself. Jesus, where can she be? In what sort of state? What has she been getting up to? What has she got herself into? Fuck, what have I got myself into? "So..." I begin tentatively.

"If her hypomania progressed to full manic, she may have become delusional, acting irrationally, without restraint, disinhibited..." says the doctor, who is looking grim. "On the other hand, it would not be uncommon for someone with bipolar to make a mood switch and become severely depressed very quickly. Has your friend ever been suicidal, do you know?"

I tell him I don't know, but I shall try to find out. I must get hold of Irini – perhaps she knows more. I offer to text Irini from his office, but apologetically he tells me he won't have the time to wait – he has to prepare a report for a mother in premature labour who is due to fly to the big island within the hour. I thank him for his time.

I stand in the street and text Irini straight away. I think I should probably let the Chief of Police know – now there is definitely good reason to be looking for Lucy urgently.

Panagiotis receives this news circumspectly. "What I can do, Dhomas?" He sees that I am floundering and throws me a float. "Okay,

I will speak with Dr. Trepanis," he says with a sigh, "I will phone the airport and the harbour authorities. Maybe we will find her." He places a fat encouraging hand on my shoulder, and tells me, "Don' worry, my friend." This does not convince me. I ride back to Agia Anna reconstructing all of Lucy's cries for help and feeling like a real prick for being so self-centred, cynical and shallow. I promise in future to be more diligent and serious-minded and compassionate.

Irini replies before I get back. "We need to talk. Skype later?"

So I go straight to the Seaview and get online and skype Irini. Suddenly there she is, blurred but real, tangibly apologetic, shame-faced. She is probably looking at me scowling full-screen at her. Yes, she tells me, Lucy did have "mental health issues". In fact that was how they met – in an adolescent mental health unit. Irini and my mother had not wanted me to be troubled in what was my final year at university, so they had kept this from me. Maybe also, Irini confessed, both she and my mother felt ashamed, felt I'd judge them as my father would have done. Irini had developed an eating disorder – bulimia. Lucy's problems were more acute – she'd tried to kill herself soon after she'd moved to the UK. Her mother in Australia had been institutionalised and her estranged step-father in England had offered to pay for private schooling at a prestigious school if Lucy came to live with him. Within weeks, under cover of a drunken state, he had raped her. But, Irini is quick to add, Lucy had been a fighter, a "survivor". She'd recovered with the help of the therapy team and she had been the one who'd helped all the other girls in the unit, been the big sister, especially to Irini. She'd moved in with Irini and our mother after they'd both been discharged, even though the unit had not been in favour of this. Lucy had been her "rock" and protector. "Sorry I didn't tell you all this, Tom. I kind of felt it was private, you know...? I didn't want it to put you off."

"Fuck it, Irini, I've come all this way and Lucy could be anywhere. Jesus, Irini!"

"I know. I'm sorry. What can I say?"

"You've still not heard anything from her?

"No, nothing," says Irini, her voice muted apologetically.

"Was she bipolar?"

"Not that I know of..." Irini offers hesitantly.

Just then, the ping of a new message and when I check New Mail, it's from Lucy. It's the e-mail I have been waiting for. "Just hang on!" I instruct Irini firmly. I must read the reply to the message I sent.

There it is. I feel my blood drain, my feet go icy cold, the goose bumps rising on my arms. Lucy remembers *very well* the time we spent together in Prague. "Please send to me the photos." I read it again to be sure.

I was right. Lucy and I never were in Prague. *Whoever wrote this reply is not Lucy.*

The e-mail I'd sent to Lucy's e-mail address, telling how much I'd enjoyed Prague with her and that I had pictures of her in Prague Castle which I treasured. If it had been Lucy, she would probably have mailed back, "WTF?" or something like that. She would have assumed I was being weirdly cryptic or very drunk. But what I have instead is confirmation that someone has Lucy's laptop and is trying to put me off the trail. Someone is pretending to be Lucy. The hairs on my neck prickle.

I'd worked out what in that previous e-mail hadn't sounded like Lucy's voice. Not just the Thomas instead of Tom, and the Americanised "write you", it was the absence of the *apostrophised verbs* – the "do not" rather than "don't", the "I am" rather than the "I'm". I'd checked her e-mails from before which had always sounded so conversational and casual. I'd had to correct this stylistic quirk so many times when sub-editing the reports she sent to New World Order. She always used apostrophised verbs.

Suddenly I know, with a feeling of certainty, what I have tried to keep at bay - Lucy is dead. *Or is she?* Maybe (I clutch at it) ... maybe she is out of her mind, and someone is covering for her. Or (it is a possibility) someone is *holding her prisoner.*

"Oh, God, Irini," I say back to my sister's image on my screen, "This not good."

As I say this, I know I will have to find her, to find out what's happened to her. I pray she's still alive.

24

I should let Panagiotis know. What will he say? "Don' worry, Dhomas." Dhomas… he calls me Thomas – everyone else calls me Tom – he got my name off my passport when I first saw him; everyone else has my name from me – Tom. Is that just a Greek thing, or is it significant? Do the cops have Lucy's laptop? If so, why? What would she have on her computer they want kept silent? Who else might be involved? Who can I trust?

Across the bay I see Antonis sitting on the balcony of his cousin's *kafenion*, taking in the last of the afternoon's rays. I could ask him what to do. Maybe *he* can investigate. I trudge around the arc of white sand of the beach, my steps in the soft sand fast and determined, then alight the gravel path to the *kafenion*. Antonis is looking perturbed, reading some papers intently. He does not greet me in his usual friendly way – he just gives a tip of his head and a grunt. Is he annoyed that the afternoon with Agapi hadn't worked out the way he'd wanted. She'd remained polite to him, while giving me the amused affectionate glances he'd craved. Even the little girl, Agapi's daughter, had rebuffed him and had sought me out instead, intuiting her mother's preference in the way only small children can.

But I can't let this deter me. I sit down opposite Antonis. "I've got a problem, Antonis," I tell him. "This is serious."

"*You* have a problem? I too have a problem," he says still perusing his documents. For a moment I think he is going to tell me what a cunt I am for stealing the girl of his dreams. "The body in the bridge… it is not Mavros Epistemos," he says, frowning. He looks up, and waits for me to take this in.

"And it's not Lambros, the communist leader either. He was even more old. The body is the body of a young man, or a teenager. They can tell this from the bones. The Pathologist is very sure of this. The body has all his teeth – rotten, but all present. We checked with the families –

Mavros and Aris, they both have some teeth missing. So who was this in the bridge we cannot say. The Police Chief has checked the records – no missing teenagers from those times. And why the badge in the hand?" He shakes his head. "Maybe not political. But the badge…?" He looks downcast. "Maybe we don' find who this body is. This I don' like." He pauses. "You will still write about my investigation for your newspaper in London?"

What can I say? Probably not. Shame, the poor guy is not going to get the fame he was hoping for. I prevaricate, not wanting to bring him down too quickly. He looks grateful.

"So, you have problems too?" he asks

I tell him I am worried about Lucy. I explain to him the conundrum about Lucy's missing computer and the incongruous and almost definitely bogus e-mails. I tell him about my conversations with the doctor and before that with Christos Papademos. He ponders this. "Maybe if she is not well in her mind, this changes her writing. Maybe she was confused when she was writing the reply to you. Maybe she cannot remember and is embarrassed. So she says she *can* remember this. What you say in English?"

"Suggestible?" I offer.

"Yes, maybe she is suggestible?"

Could it be? Have I convinced myself that the respondent isn't Lucy to prove how clever I am? But if she has my e-mails, she will have had Irini's too. Why has she not got in touch with Irini? – especially if she is having a breakdown. She'd know Irini would help her. But manic people don't think they need help, isn't that right? Is she perhaps worried that Irini will find out that she isn't as robust as Irini needs her to be to continue to hero-worship her? Fuck, I'd almost convinced myself she was dead. Now I don't know.

"You should talk to Panagiotis," Antonis says.

I tell him I can't trust his colleagues – until I have evidence to the contrary, the "Thomas" suggests they might be involved in Lucy's disappearance, or at least are trying to fool me into leaving. It's all I've got. I can't assume Lucy was confused. It doesn't add up. I can see Antonis thinks I am being paranoid. "My friend, this is not in my jurisdiction" (he pronounces it 'jurisdi*shiyon*'). He shrugs. "So what I can do?"

I look out at the vanishing light on the distant mountains. I am on my own. Lucy, where are you? Please be alive.

25

The Mayor. I shall have to see the Mayor. What did Christos say? – the Mayor will know the name of the NGO Lucy was involved with. Does the NGO know where she is? Or are they, Christos and the Mayor, somehow connected to her disappearance? Convenient for them if she is now out of the picture, if Christos *fabricated* the story of her offering to write a favourable report on the resort development. That doesn't sound like Lucy. If Christos and the Mayor *did* want her out of the picture, how far were they prepared to go? But what if she *did* change her tune, if she *was* manic, how would her commissioning NGO have reacted to that?

I get into town by ten a.m. The town is busy with Greek women with stocky legs and shopping bags, getting in their supplies for the week, handfuls of onions casually tossed into their carriers, each tomato turned to the light for any blemishes. The women seem to be of two types – jowly and taciturn, or garrulous, loudly chattering like geese. Delivery vans park in traffic and set off a chain reaction of indignant hooting from the cars behind. Drivers lean out their windows and shout and gesticulate, but know the way of the world and the delivery men offload without undue haste. I am now used to my motorbike and weave like a local.

I get to the Town Hall just as Calliope, with her husband, the world-weary Nektarios, emerge. She recognises me immediately. "Mr. Journalist," she says. "You have heard? – they say the body in the bridge is not political. The fucking Mayor has now the opinion that now is not the right time for a statue to our heroes. Fucking neo-liberal stooges! No balls! We will not stand for this. You will see. The people will rise up!" She raises her fist and her husband half-heartedly does the same. Then she pats me on the shoulder, smiles and walks off.

The Mayor's secretary tells me the Mayor only sees people by appointment, but when I tell her that I have been sent by Christos Papademos, she takes my card and goes to ask the Mayor whether he will make an exception. Moments later she shows me into his office. Nikos

Angelopolis gets up to greet me, hand outstretched. "Come in, come in, Mr Pickering," he says, his voice booming, the kind of deep bass that has grown up on brandy and cigarettes. He is a broad-shouldered man with a very firm bony hand grip and a wide well-practiced smile. Popular no doubt with women voters and their inferior husbands. He exudes patrimony.

"You have come about your friend, Miss Discombe? Christos told me you had been to see him. An exceptional woman," he says, "Yes, an exceptional woman. We agreed on all matters concerning the environment. She was interested in the wildlife of the lagoon with the building of the Christos's hotel. But I assured her everything was in order. We did the environmental impact report ourselves – we have to; since last year we are responsible for administering the EU regulations – devolved to Municipalities, you see. It's not the central government any more that takes care of our protected areas. We are in a better position. We know the land, we know the people and what the people want. What they want most of all on the islands is jobs, not only jobs in the summer, but all through the year. So, infrastructure – roads, bridges, water supply, harbours. Environmental tourism – tourists who will come not just in the summer but come for the migrating birds in the winter. So, it is important for us to protect our wildlife," he says, smiling benevolently. He gets up and takes a framed picture off the wall behind and hands it to me. "Konstantinos Simitis. He was our Prime Minister until last year. PASOK. A very good man. He brought in all new protection for the environment. Natura 2000. Simitis did very well in negotiations with the EU. We got lots of money for developing the island. All friendly to the environment. With EU behind us, the banks have been very generous. We are a good investment," he says proudly. Then he looks more sombre. "Last year unfortunately we lost the elections and I'm not so sure about the new Prime Minister, Karamanlis – also Konstantinos. From one Konstantinos to another Konstantinos – they should change the name of Athens to Konstantinople!" He laughs heartily at his joke which is fraying at the edges from over-use.

I don't want to piss on his parade, but I mention the slick out to sea near the lagoon. "Temporary," he says emphatically. "This is only while they are still building at the Poseidon. It is of no danger to the birds. I showed all the documents to your Miss Discombe. She will tell you." He sits back and waits for my response, fingers entwined on his lap.

"Who was she working for? Do you know? Christos may have told you that Miss Discombe has gone missing. We are quite worried about her," I tell him.

"Yes, I heard this. I hope you will find her in good health," the Mayor says sincerely.

"She was working for an NGO?"

"Yes, but not one of the usual ones." He presses a button on his desk and the secretary comes in. A button on his desk – old-school. He says something to her and she goes out. He sits back and regards me. "So, how do you like our island?"

I am about to reply when the secretary comes back in and hands him a document. He puts on his designer-framed glasses, has a brief look at it and then hands it to me. The letterhead says in bold type, "Radagast Environmental Action". It is a letter from Lucy, handwritten, introducing herself and her NGO, dated some months previous. Printed in small lettering at the bottom are the contact details of the organisation – their website, e-mail address, and address in Lower Saxony, and a German telephone number.

"Can I have a copy of this?" I ask.

"That *is* a copy," the Mayor says with satisfaction that he had anticipated my needs. He is a politician after all. "Call them. But I don't know how helpful they will be. Your Miss Discombe had come to see things our way. I think her boss was not pleased with this. I imagined, from what Miss Discombe told me, that her boss was one of those women who prefer to oppose than to accept change. Someone who enjoys to fight. Maybe someone also who prefers the company of other women." He smirks as he looks to see that I have understood his typology.

"Do you have a name?"

"Yes. Of course. I did my research. The CEO is a woman called Erika von Strondheim. She is an heiress – very rich. She likes to get what she wants. Good luck!" he says and chuckles. Then as he gets up to see me out he says, "But I recommend you are careful. She works with a man called Jurgen Preissler. He is what the Americans call the Enforcer. He was here with your friend. He is not a nice man. If you meet him, you will see what I mean."

26

I google Radagast online when I get back. I get numerous references to Radagast, the Brown Wizard, from The Lord of the Rings, friend of the animals and the birds. That must be the origin. Not one of the wizards I am familiar with, but the job description fits. After further impatient scrolling, I get an article referencing Radagast Environmental Action. It's about the trial of members of the organisation and their direct-action campaign against vivisection in some German medical school, the freeing of imprisoned animals and the blowing up of the laboratory wing, with the consequent fatal wounding of a technician working late and a cleaner. The ring leader, Jurgen Preissler, was found guilty of manslaughter and sentenced to seven years in prison. The report is from 1994. So, he's been out for at least four years. I search Jurgen Preissler and get the same article. I search Erika von Strondheim and get a publicity shot of a handsome, well-coifed woman wearing a cravat, looking just like the German aristocrat she is. Her age is not mentioned but she looks to be about fifty, although if the photo is touched up, which it looks to be, she could be as old as seventy. There is a haughty tightness at the corners of her thin lips and an elevation to the chin which allows a better view of her nostrils. I bet she loves her horses. Her money comes from her mother's family – they cornered the market in plastic containers and vacuum packing. The article underneath the picture, in what I assume is the German equivalent of Tatler's from the look of it, says craftily that all she got from her father was his aristocratic name. The implication is that he was penniless.

There are articles further down the search which reference Erika von Strondheim's more recent environmental activity and her involvement with Radagast. She has been the CEO for four years. She is quoted as saying that the organisation is a "lean" organisation, which is well-funded and achieves, due to the devotion of its staff and members, much more than its relatively small size would predict. There is no mention of illegal activity, nor the jailing of its members in the past. Maybe that's history. Maybe now they are legit. I should call Erika.

****

Erika has a PA. The PA's name is Gunhilda. Gunhilda politely and definitely tells me that Frau von Strondheim will call me back presently but she cannot tell me when this will be. Gunhilda cannot tell me anything about Lucy because she does not work for the organisation – she works for the Baroness, sorry, please excuse me, *Frau* von Strondheim exclusively.

As it happens I don't have to wait long. German efficiency. Have no doubts - it's hardwired.

Erika von Strondheim's voice is well-crafted, the syllables punctilious, precise, the tone measured, the Germanic accent almost imperceptible. "So, you are a friend of Lucy Discombe." This is a statement, not a question. "She is no longer contracted to our organisation. We had an irreconcilable difference of… perspective," (she chooses her words carefully) "and we terminated our agreement a few weeks ago. What has happened to her? Not that that is any concern of mine."

I tell her Lucy is missing. She may be unwell.

"As I said, Mr. Pickering, that is not my concern. Lucy Discombe is no longer associated with our organisation, and as such we bear no responsibility for her actions or whatever she writes. This is the legal position. We have disowned her."

Her coldness inflames me. "Well, maybe she got it right. Did you consider that? Or did you want her to write only what benefitted you and your '*organisation*'?" I spit out.

"Who, may I ask, have you been talking to, Mr Pickering?" Her tone is imperious and disdainful.

I tell her I have spoken to both the Mayor and to Christos Papademos.

"Ah," she says, "Did the Mayor tell you he was a… what do you call it? - a sleeping partner with the Papademos' construction company?" She can tell from my silence that they did not.

A barely discernible, "Hmph" before she goes on. "The EU only releases regional development funds if the region is environmentally compliant. The Mayor signs off on the compliance report and the money flows like magic into the Papademos coffers. Did they tell you about the re-zoning of the National park? - about how they burned down pristine forest on the mountain next to the lagoon, so the land would show up as barren, so that they could move the boundary of the protected area to the other side of the hotel? It used to be a nature reserve. The fire was accidental of course." The sarcasm in her voice is corrosive. "Those fires always are. Your Mr. Papademos will tell you there are lots of wild fires on the island. But somehow, very conveniently, this one occurred immediately before the determination of the boundaries for the re-zoning.

"No? They didn't tell you this? And did they tell you how they have diverted the run-off of mountain water for use by the hotel instead of feeding the lagoon? No? How the salts in the lagoon are becoming more concentrated and that in ten years' time or maybe less, the lagoon will dry up? Already the population of fresh water fish in the lagoon is degraded. The fire they set killed off the wild boar population that had taken *decades* to re-establish on the island? You know how long it took us to re-establish the native boar population on the island? And now, not one boar alive. And did they tell you how the fires they set drove the rats down to the lagoon edge and increased the rat population there catastrophically for the birds? - the rats eat the eggs of bird species which have used the lagoon as their breeding ground for centuries. Both the Audouin's gull and the Yelkouan Shearwater are approaching extinction. But I suppose they didn't tell you that." I feel myself reddening.

"And the overgrowth of algae from their effluent system? Have you seen the colour of the sea off shore of the lagoon? All it will take will be one storm surge at the right time and that poisonous water will flow into the lagoon and the birds will die.

"And the rabbit fish? You know about rabbit fish? They come from the Red Sea. But their eggs are also in the bilge of the boats which deliver the fine Egyptian sand for the plaster on the walls of the glorious Poseidon. It gives the plaster a pink hue. Very popular. Very tasteful, *ja*?" She is getting angry now and in trying to suppress this, her German accent is escaping its lair. "The rabbit fish eat all the coral, so all the indigenous fish which live off the coral can't survive. The rabbit fish grow and grow. It can't be eaten – it is bitter, not nize.

"But somehow your friend could not see all zis. Your friend, Mr Papademos, is very persuasive is he not? Mr Papademos was good enough to warn us that Lucy, whom I used to respect enormously, would be writing instead about the benefits of tourism to the local economy."

"You heard that from Lucy herself?" I ask.

"No, but we wrote to her and she did not bother to get back to us. She did not pick up her phone. So we terminated her... contract. Our lawyer wrote to warn her not to write anything adverse about us or we would take the necessary action to prevent zis. Radagast is my life's work, Mr Pickering. *I vill allow nussing vich vill jeopardise zis.*"

I don't know how to counter this. She has told me lots of stuff I didn't know and I feel I have been naïve and gullible. But still I need to find Lucy.

"Okay, but have you heard from Lucy? Do you know where she is?"

"Lucy Discombe is no longer my affair, Mr Pickering. Thank you for your time." She hangs up.

27

I swim to clear my head and wash away my annoyance at Frau von Strondheim and her shadowy, pretentious NGO. I am annoyed at myself for being gullible, not checking facts, getting caught up in a rich businessman's PR seduction. Fuck, I'm getting flabby. Not like me. I'm usually more on the ball, more incisive and critical, trust me. I swim harder and let my frustration out in hard decisive strokes. Dip, pull… dip, pull… glide…. The water opens up to me, let's me pass, easing a furrow of silver in the blue. Kick, kick. Dip, pull… dip, pull…

I lie back on my deckchair, breathing hard and let the heat of the sun dry me. I close my eyes. My mind goes clear for about ten seconds. Then I hear the click as the entitled Teutonic noble woman cuts me off. I hear, "Lucy Discombe is no longer my affair" in that clipped, mannered tone. The harshness of it. *She will not have the last word.* I compose a retort – what I should have said next, what I will write instead.

"You want something to drink?" It is Agapi, come down to where I am lying. She has her tray and an amused smile. The sun flames her golden hair.

"Oh, you will bring it?" I ask in my English for Greeks.

"Yes, of course," she says.

I order a bottle of *retsina* and a plate of olives. She looks pleased. "How is Eleni?" I ask.

"She is well. She is with my mother. But tonight maybe they come for the concert. You must come tonight, to the restaurant. *Famoos zinger!* Theodoros Chrysanthymos. From Kreta. His popular name *"Psaroxilos"* Chrysanthymos – is mean Lips of the Fish, because his lips go…" She pouts delightfully and giggles. "Every womans is love him!" She laughs, turning away in her embarrassment, at her daring. She goes off quickly to get my order.

A bald man is swimming to the shore as if he is fighting the water at every stroke. Ripples roll out in a crenulated V around him. He gets to the shallows and strides out, proud of his strength, his belly hanging corpulently over the waist band of his flamboyant baggies. He high-steps over the searing hot sand, quickening his steps to get to the beach chair where his wife lies reading a magazine. It's too hot for his pale feet. He shouts at his wife and runs back to the sea and flings himself in belly first in a gigantic indelicate splash. His wife puts down her magazine and releases herself from the comfort of the chair, collects his beach slippers and walks them down to the water's edge where she places them. He waves to her. She does not acknowledge him. The fat guy emerges presently and this time carefully slides his feet into the slippers, steadies himself, then shuffles back up the sand to the chair next to his wife's, his grimace now a smile. He grins at his wife who has resumed her place on her chair. She tightens one corner of her mouth in response. She goes back to reading her magazine. Undaunted, he grabs his towel and dries himself vigorously.

I close my eyes. Lucy, where the fuck are you?

****

I arrive early at the Seaview. A small bandstand has been set up at the far end of the balcony, the end nearest Yianni's *taverna*. I see Yiannis examining it with baleful eyes. Then he waggles his head, sees potential advantage and goes off with what may have been a little dance move.

Agapi has reserved a two-person table for me near the bandstand. She is excited and pleased I have come. She points out her mother, with Eleni on her lap, sitting against the wall on the side. They don't need a table – they won't be eating. Stavroula, the matriarch, shuffles onto the balcony leaning heavily on her stick. She sees Agapi's mother and the two old women nod in greeting, but there is no warmth. Stavroula turns away quickly. It strikes me the old ladies probably knew each other as young girls, both poor, but Agapi's mother was a local, while Stavroula would have been an outsider, an immigrant with affluent antecedents, come down in the world. Now *Stavroula* is rich, her son, a man of influence, Agapi's boss.

Antonis arrives a while later, with his cousin, Stelios, who has closed the *kafenion* for the duration of the performance – no one would have come anyway – everyone will be here. Antonis sees me and comes over and greets me joyfully. He too is excited that Fishlips will be singing here soon. Stelios moves another chair in. It is a squeeze and at a table for two, one of three will have their back to the performers. The singer is obviously of more importance to Antonis and his cousin, so I volunteer to take the backseat, so to speak. As I move my chair and sit myself down, Agapi comes over, frowning and barking at Stelios. The table is for me and for my comfort. There are tables at the back, Stelios has not reserved a table – he must go to the back. Stelios, shrugs and goes off. Antonis has been discomforted, but Agapi looks satisfied. She straightens the tablecloth and takes our drinks order, smiling at me, but not looking at Antonis.

I notice Kat and two teenage girls giggling at the back. I wonder where Bobby is and look over to Yianni's, and sure enough, Bobby is there, looking coolly envious of his sister, who has no responsibilities for maintaining the family business. He straightens up as Xanthe, radiant in a light strapless summer dress, emerges to take Stavroula to her seat at the table reserved for family and esteemed friends. Xanthe seats her tight-lipped grandmother solicitously. Her grandmother doesn't thank her for her consideration.

At the far end of the table and slightly back is Hektor Papademos, immaculately dressed in a pale blue suit and a silk scarf, his silvered hair slicked back. He sits upright, his chin lifted, shifting this way and that on his seat, checking his view of the stage, which is evidently impeded by the stiff hairdo of the woman in front of him, the wife of the mayor, I surmise. Hektor is not happy with his seat. I see Stavroula glancing at him with her dark, hooded eyes, but he looks everywhere other than at her. Is he strenuously avoiding her gaze her? With her black widow's dress and hair in a tight bun, she is clearly not his type. He is sophisticated, she (at least in his eyes) is plebeian. The older Papademos is not at ease. He looks to where his son and Michalis are in jovial conversation. A look of pain crosses the old man's face and then one of muted pride. He will not ask to be moved, but he does not appreciate being in the back seat so to speak, as if he was only an afterthought.

Just then, there is a commotion at the entrance of the restaurant. The musicians have arrived. Michalis, with Christos and the Mayor in tow, goes to greet them. There is a lot of effusive salutation and back-slapping, then a parting of the group as the singer enters and the assembled audience gets their first sight of him. Psaroxilos Chrysanthymos is a towering figure of a man, slightly hunched to accentuate his world-weariness and humility, his lower lip down-turned in a cascade of pallid fleshiness, his upper lip as curly as an oyster, his full head of black hair slicked back like a Cretan Elvis. He surveys his audience who return his gaze with hushed respectful silence and nodding acknowledgements.

Michalis is reverent, clutching the singer's hand – this is a big deal for him – the famous singer has come all the way to tiny Agia Anna to grace *his restaurant.* No doubt the photo of the singer and Michalis, which Michalis will insist on later, will be framed and hang behind the bar of The Seaview for many years to come.

After the singer has been shown to the table for VIPs, there is a second wave of activity as the band bustle through and begins setting up. Presently the band leader, who has the sober appearance of a bank manager, tells us (Antonis translates) that the band will play a few numbers with their two regular singers from the Agia Sofia hotel where they are contracted for the summer. Then Theodoros Chrysanthymos (he does not call him Psaroxilos to his face) will come on. They will back him – they know his songs. The audience cheer and heckle. *Of course* they know his songs – who doesn't? Antonis finds this very funny. He confides to me in a reverent whisper that Psaroxilos is very famous in all of Greece.

The band starts up. The leader stands to play his synthesiser. The guitarist next to the *bouzouki* player takes a puff of his cigarette and then places the still-lit cigarette upright between his ring and baby finger as he strikes up the first chord dramatically. The woman singer's voice is light and quavers playfully. She moves seductively, practiced over the years in bars and hotels, not taking herself too seriously, her tight-fitting dress shimmering like a fish; her elaborate hairdo does not move. For the second number, she is joined by her partner, a portly man in his forties, in waistcoat and tight black trousers, who makes his entrance from the back for effect, stepping briskly, pressing his heels to the ground, the bulk of his inner thighs impeding his forward movement into a waddle. His determination quickens his pace. He holds a bottle of sparkling wine aloft, as he gets to the bandstand, he peels the foil off the top and pops the cork with a gush and a flurry. His face is expressionlessness and his unblinking eyes the only clues to his fear that he will get something wrong, sing a note off colour and embarrass himself in front of his hero, the prodigiously-lipped singer from Crete. The duet between the two local singers is a saccharine, popular song evidently and the audience greets this with affectionate derision. The singers are not put out and accept this gracefully – they are professionals. They sing another song which is apparently quite risqué and the audience laugh and applaud. A ballad is delivered confidently and with feeling. The woman singer bows and goes off to her coterie of male admirers at a table, already festooned with bottles of wine and beer. Her portly partner accepts his applause with modesty and retires with relief to the order of backing singer in the band. He lights up a cigarette as a reward, well-deserved, in his humble opinion.

Then Fishlips comes to the stage. There is wild applause. He takes the microphone and thanks everyone sincerely. Then he pauses and the audience goes quiet. He waits until the only sound is the sound of the sea and the clatter of dishes from the kitchen inside. Then he nods his head to the band's leader and bows his head.

Psaroxilos Chrysanthymos, the man with the lips of the fish, sings with eyes closed, his eyebrows lifted into an inverted V of exquisite sadness, his voice, deep and resonant, pleading, giving way delicately in the chorus to an angelic unwavering falsetto soaked in the love of a child for an elderly mother. Without understanding the words, I feel the depth of history the lyrics convey. O Greece, the birthplace of tragedy. My father's land. I glance at the VIP's table. The Mayor and Christos are beaming, proud that their island is hosting the great singer. Stavroula, although her face is set to grim, has tears coursing down her cheeks. I feel myself welling up. What has this woman been through in her life time?

Then the great singer releases them from the depth of their despair into a song of survival, of resistance. All the people seem to know the chorus and sing it out with gusto, as if to repel their tears. They clap the off-beat. They are one. Antonis shouts to me out the corner of his mouth between choruses, "A song of the *andantes*, the partisans. Famous," before hastily re-joining the singing. The audience is now in a joyful mood and with the next song, men are up and forming a circle for dancing, arms across shoulders, nimble feet side-skipping back and forth. Shouting, "*Oppa!*" at each change of direction. Michalis and helpers move tables to give more room for dancing. The *bazouki* is building to a pitch of quick-fingered exultation, the guitarist thrumming bass notes to underpin the rhythm. Now, finally, Fishlips looks up. He is smiling philosophically.

I notice, among the men dancing, Kosta, the Police Chief's cop son, short sleeves rolled to show off his steroid biceps, throwing himself about and whooping. He is drunk. In a group of men gathered at the edge of the circling dancers, his father, Panagiotis, watches indulgently. Kosta sees Xanthe passing and makes a grab for her, to get her into the dancing circle. She shrugs him off irritably and glares at him. He grins, embarrassed and renews his whooping with greater vigour to hide this affront to what in his own mind is his irresistible sexual attractiveness. He grabs at one of the teenagers who is with Katerina and she obliges, thrilled to be chosen. Kat gives her a sceptical look, as in "Really?" and then laughs with her other friend, throwing her head back, scandalised.

Xanthe makes her way over to our table and holds a hand out to Antonis. He is her chosen partner. With a quick glance at Agapi, he accepts and reaches out for Xanthe's hand. He cannot do otherwise. Agapi, I am surprised to see, looks a little annoyed, but turns smiling and goes on clearing the table she is at, of the empty bottles and plates. When she is done, she comes over to me and says sadly, by way of apology, "*I* have to work. *I* cannot dance." The emphasis also makes clear that this is also a reference to Xanthe's advantage as the daughter of the boss. I wonder if she is jealous – of course she must be - and whether, actually, she is playing hard to get with Antonis. Am I the bait? I examine her face, but she is giving nothing away.

Xanthe and Antonis dance to one side, hands linked in the air. Antonis is light on his feet and Xanthe is well-practiced. They make an attractive couple. As the circle comes around, Kosta barges Antonis, who stumbles into Xanthe and they sprawl into a family group at a table, who shout with alarm and protest. Kosta laughs and shouts over his shoulder, "*Signomi!*" ("Sorry") He doesn't mean it. Xanthe straightens herself up

151

and makes a show of brushing off Antonis's shirtfront, glares at Kosta and when she sees he is watching her, she pulls Antonis close and kisses him on the mouth. Antonis looks surprised, but he doesn't resist.

28

The sun is coming through a chink in the curtain. My phone is buzzing. I close my eyes against the harsh light and reach for my phone on the floor next to the bed. Fuck, who is phoning me this early? Shit, I only got to bed at three a.m.

"Yeah," I growl into the phone. My throat feels like it's lined with pigeon feathers.

"Mr Pickering? Dhomas?"

"Yes. Who is it?"

"It's Panagiotis Valoudsakis, Mr. Pickering... Dhomas. The Chief of Police."

I prop myself up on an elbow and rub my eyes with the back of my hand. What could be so urgent? "Hey, Panagiotis," I say, "What's up?"

"Mr. Pickering... Dhomas, I think you should come to the Police Station," he says gravely. A pause like the cold silence of a tomb. "I am sorry to tell to you this, my friend. Miss Discombe, her body has been found. She has kill-ed herself."

Am I dreaming this? Am I still asleep? I sit up straight. No, I am awake. But this is a nightmare. Lucy has been found. My worst fear, the fear I wouldn't allow myself, is confirmed. Lucy is dead. Beautiful, clever, full-of-life Lucy is *dead*. Can that be? She is still so *young*.

"What?" I exclaim. "When? How?"

"She was found by an American tourist woman making snorkelling at the old harbour at Vassilaki. Is an old fishing village. No persons living there no more." He hears my silence, my disbelief. "I am sorry."

"Okay, I am coming," I say as I hastily get out of my crumpled bed. My legs feel weak under me. "I'm coming."

****

"I want to see her," I tell the Chief of Police.

Panagiotis looks me in the eye and then he looks down. "I don't think you want this," he says.

"Yes, I do! She is my *responsibility!*" I shout at him. Who the fuck is he to tell me what I want and what I don't?

He looks at me calmly with a look in which I discern compassion. "Okay," he says, after a pause. He shrugs almost imperceptibly. "I suppose someone who is not police should identify the body." He gets up. "We must go to the hospital. The mortuary is there." He collects his policeman's cap and pockets his sunglasses. He puts a hand on my shoulder. "But, my friend, I must tell to you, she is now not look how she was look. If is not for the note and her clothes, I myself would not so easy know this is Miss Discombe. My friend, the crabs they have... they eat first the most soft parts – the lips, the tongue, the eyes."

Oh God, what is he telling me? Her beautiful face bursts bright into my mind – her, smiling with mischief, her eyes, their intelligence set in an iridescence of deepest blue, her lips... her delicate lips, lips I kissed, that kissed me, wanting more. How has she been transfigured in death? Can such beauty have been ravaged, disarticulated in such a cruel way? She couldn't have intended to be found like that. Oh, God, how awful! What a fucking horrible thing. How she must have been suffering terribly to do something like that. Did the Police Chief say she left a note?

"She left a note?" I ask.

"Yes, it was with her shoes next to an old petrol drum," he says. "The sea it is deep at the end of the jetty. Is where the fishermens was go to fish – but no more – no more fish there – so no more fishermens. If the American tourist not go to make snorkel there, we never find," Panagiotis says.

As we walk in the not-yet-hot sunshine, he tells me the American woman was swimming with her husband, looking for shells at the bottom of the sea, when she saw something shining. So she dived down and then what she first saw was Lucy's red hair flowering out of her head, then the contours of her head, then her body beyond at unnatural angle, so that at first it was difficult to tell it was a human body. As the woman got closer, the holes of the eyes and the mouth showed up for what they were. The terrified woman had finned her way to the surface as fast as she could and screamed for her husband. When she gave her statement to the police, she was horrified that she had almost touched the body and that the flesh may have come away under her fingers. She was very preoccupied by that. By revulsion, not by compassion. I don't judge her. It sounds like your worst nightmare, even second-hand in the Police Chief's imperfect English. I steel myself.

The air in the mortuary is cold and grey; the smell is sweet, pungent and chemical. The room is below ground and lit by dull neon lights. An attendant looks to the Chief for guidance, after the Chief checks with me, he nods and the attendant rolls the sheet off the corpse on the concrete bench.

It is worse than I'd imagined. Lucy's flesh is bloated shades of green and purple. I try not to look at the face, but I am drawn to it, to its grotesque caricature of a face, a badly painted Edvard Munch's scream, impossible to relate to the beauty which had previously inhabited her features. What a *travesty!* I think, furious with Fate, that she should end up like this, furious with *Lucy* for doing this to herself. Then I see, around her neck, the Ethiopian necklace I'd bought her in the Amsterdam flea market. The shine from this is, I realise, what had attracted the American woman. If it hadn't been for this gift I had given her as an apology almost a year ago, Lucy's body may never have been found. I would never have had to see her like this. I feel the hot tears in my eyes. It would have been better if she'd just vanished.

But then she'd left a note. She'd wanted to be found.

I nod and turn and walk out. Panagiotis puts a comforting hand on my shoulder. "I am sorry, my friend," he says sincerely. When we get outside, he offers me a cigarette. I haven't smoked since I was at university, but I accept. To still my shaking hand. To evict the smell of death from my nostrils.

"The note she left. I want to see it," I say. Panagiotis nods. I inhale deeply. The nicotine hits my system. My head swims and for a moment I think I am going to faint. I steady myself. Panagiotis ushers me to a wooden bench under a small palm. He goes off to get a bottle of water for me from a street vendor nearby in a small cabin. By the time he gets back, all my weeks of suppressed worry, trying not to think the worst, has burst through me and I have given up to the tears that flow freely now. He hands me the bottle. I thank him and gulp the ice cold water down, gasping, drowning,. Panagiotis hugs me to him. I bury my head in his prodigious chest. I smell his perspiration and cheap deodorant. I draw myself away. I take a deep breath and let it out slowly. Okay, okay, I tell myself, you can do this. You *must* do this.

Then I vomit.

We go back to Panagiotis's office. Panagiotis respects my silence and I am thankful to him for this consideration. He shows me to the only chair other than his in his office and hands me a stained piece of A4 paper. Scrawled on it is, "Sorry. I can not go on. Lucy Discombe." That's all the note says.

And there it is again – the absence of the elision – the "can not" rather than the "can't" I would have expected. Not even "cannot", but "can not". Is this even Lucy's handwriting?

Panagiotis is speaking. "Dr Trepanis said it is what he was worry, that she would go depress-ed and kill herself. Is very sad." I am still studying the note for any familiarity. When have I seen Lucy's handwriting? – we have always corresponded in electronically-processed letters. But I *have* seen her writing – the Radagast headed letter of introduction from Lucy that Nikos Angelopoulos, the Mayor, had copied for me. That was handwritten. Something makes me hold back from telling this to the Police Chief, sitting opposite me with a look of abject compassion on his fat features. "She was tie a rope around her and then around a big concrete – there is a lot of old brick and concrete on the old harbour from when was break down, when it was finished. She was strong woman to carry to the end of the jetty and then throw herself in the water, poor woman." He watches me for my reaction. I shake my head sadly for something to do. "Is maybe why she tell you to go away?"

I remember the e-mail. Should I tell him the e-mail was almost certainly a fiction, a decoy? But did I tell him she told me to go away? How does he know that? *Did* I tell him? I don't remember telling him. Was he the author I was supposed to think was Lucy? He is the one who calls me Thomas *("Dhomas.")* I study him for any tell-tale signs of dissembling, of deceptiveness, of cunning. But all I see is his concern for me, then gradually his puzzlement as he perceives my suspicion-fuelled examination of him. I sit up, straighten my face and murmur my agreement. He looks relieved.

He asks me about Lucy's next of kin and I tell him what I know. Shit, I am going to have to tell Irini. She's going to go nuts. I start planning what I am going to say. Panagiotis is telling me he will arrange for the Australian Consul to make arrangements for the body.

"Will there be an autopsy?" I ask.

"The police on the big island will decide this. But I think no, they will say she is kill herself."

Fuck, what should I do? What if she's been murdered? They *must* do an autopsy. Fuck, they don't even know how long she's been in the water – the e-mail was recent. To me it looks like Lucy's body had been underwater for much longer. But what do I know? Someone should do an autopsy. But the police here? – will they whitewash it? Already they're treating it as a foregone conclusion. But the e-mail - the deception - someone was trying to put me off. It *must* be murder. Surely?

I'll wait and talk to Antonis. He's from Homicide in Athens – he'll know what to do.

29

It is only when I come over the rise before the village, that I realise I have ridden all the way from Agia Sofia without taking in any of my surroundings. I have been in my head. My legs are a long way down and numb. I have been thinking of Lucy, trying to call up all the nice memories of her I have stored, but it is difficult to eradicate from my mind the image I have of her on the slab in the mortuary, her eye-sockets hollow, her mouth a rictus like a perpetual scream. With her lips eaten off, her teeth and gums were exposed. Her teeth are far longer than I had expected. Her long teeth are a shock. Her gums were a blue beyond purple.

Beautiful, brave, crazy Lucy. Why had I asked to see her dead body? Why did I agree to identify her? What did I expect? Now I will live with that image of her in death to obstruct all the other memories of her I have. She won't rest in peace. In my head anyway.

I detour past her house, the house she lived in on the island. I stop outside. I find myself revving the engine, my anger thrumming, burning petrol, wanting to leave, not able to go. The old crone opposite comes to her gate and remonstrates in her creaking goose-like clatter of consonants. What does she want of me? Is it about Lucy's unpaid rent? I think of trying to tell her that Lucy is dead, but can't face the tortuousness of the untranslatables, so I put the bike in first and wobble down the corrugated lane to the waterfront.

I go to my lodgings. I find the handwritten letter the Mayor had given me, ostensibly written by Lucy. I compare the handwriting with the suicide note. As I expected. The handwriting bears no similarity. Either the letter the Mayor had given me was not written by Lucy, or the suicide note was not hers. Why would the letter of introduction be phoney? That wouldn't make any sense.

I must go to find Antonis.

He is on the balcony at the *kafenion*, drinking his coffee and smoking a cigarillo meditatively. "You're lucky I am still here. I must go to the main town, but only after lunch," he says, as he indicates for me to sit.

"She's dead," I say flatly.

"Oh, no, my friend!" he says, shocked. His face, when I tell him about her disfigurement contorts with horror and disgust. "Oh, no! Oh, my friend, I am so sorry," he says, putting a hand on my shoulder.

Then I tell him about the bogus e-mail and my suspicion of the police's involvement. "Don't you think it suspicious that the laptop went missing hours after I told Panagiotis I'd found it in Lucy's cupboard? Plus, the first e-mail to me from her computer – addressing me as "Thomas" – that's what Panagiotis would have thought was my name from my passport. Lucy knew me as Tom. It didn't sound like her – "Do not" rather than "don't", "cannot" rather than "can't" – it wasn't her style – I can show you old e-mails." Then I show him the two handwritten documents. He examines them and then he concedes that they could not have been written by the same hand. He returns them to me. "So what you want from me? This is not my jurisdiction."

"They will cover it up. Panagiotis says they may not even do an autopsy. Can you at least get the body sent to Athens for autopsy, get a pathologist's independent report? Say it's because she is foreign and with the coverage of the body in the bridge, the foreign correspondents will be all over it and wanting answers. Say you must be sure there is no linkage to your case. I can back you up. I can write something to suggest a connection. You are an Inspector. Can an Inspector over-rule a Chief of Police?" I ask.

He grimaces irritably. "Panagiotis is a *Sergeant*. He is Chief because he is the most senior on the island - he supervises the other three. He calls *himself* this: 'Chief of Police'. Hmph!" He shakes his head derisively and then settles back to thinking about my proposition. He takes a drag on his cigarillo, exhales ponderously, takes a slow sip of his coffee, places the cup carefully back on the saucer and then nods. "Okay, I think I can do that. But we have to tell Panagiotis that you suspect what you call 'foul play', no? We have to tell him about the e-mails, yes?"

"If we have to," I say. "Do we have to?"

"Yes," he says, "I cannot go behind his back side. If this comes out later, it will not be good."

He waits to see that I agree. Then he continues. "Maybe I should go with you to look around her house, see what a policeman can see," he says, with the smug insinuation that I have missed something obvious.

He jumps on the back of my bike behind me and we ride over to Lucy's house, or what used to be her house. The old lady is at her front gate as usual, when we pull up, she shouts at us and gesticulates. "What is she saying?" I ask.

Antonis smiles. "She says you make too much noise with your bike." The old lady is still jabbering away. "She says ever since Lucy came here, all her nights have been disturbed by your big motorbike. Every night Lucy was there." The old lady's grumbling is petering out. "Now, not so much, not since Lucy is not there."

But I wasn't here when Lucy was here. It wasn't *my* bike that woke her. Who was her visitor? The only one I can think of with a big bike is Kosta, the Police Chief's son, the macho cop, with his police bike. What would Kosta have been doing visiting Lucy late at night? As we walk up to the front door, I voice my suspicions to Antonis. He looks dubious, like maybe now I'm making it up, getting paranoid. Maybe I am. Who else has a big bike? What about that German guy, the Enforcer, what was his name? Jurgen Something. Did he have a bike? Kind of goes with my image of him. Come to think of it, how did Lucy get around? Did *she* have a motorbike? "Good question," Antonis says, and asks the old lady. Lucy had a scooter. So where is it? Panagiotis made no mention of a scooter where she was found – that would have been obvious to the American divers surely? He'd have mentioned it. It will be part of the investigation, Antonis assures me, as I collect the key from under the flowerpot where I last left it.

Antonis looks around the house. He is looking at it very differently from me. He is clinical. I am imagining Lucy here, her objects and her clothes evincing fantasies of her living, being here, in this room, at the chopping board with vegetables, at the cooker, stirring the large steel pot, choosing what to wear from her drawer, in the shower, naked. In my mind, her skin turns blue. I shut out the image. Antonis uses a pen from his pocket to move things, to uncover things, the habit of not disturbing evidence at a crime scene. But if he thinks there is anything suspicious, he is not telling me.

He takes out his phone and calls a number. I hear him greeting Panagiotis. They exchange friendly banter, and then Antonis gets serious, and I hear *despeeneedha* Discombe mentioned. I see Antonis listening with a patient look and he raises his eyebrows to me, as if to say, "I told you he wouldn't like it." He says, "*Nai, nai,*" a few times, then the conversation is over. He puts his phone away. "He says he will need authorisation from his superiors at Regional Head Quarters on the big island. I said I will phone them. It's okay. The Commander there used to work in Athens. I know him a little bit."

"That's good," I say. I feel relieved and gratified that I am doing something to put right this injustice, this travesty.

Antonis looks at me thoughtfully. "But he says, if she was killed, he knows who may have done it." He doesn't keep me waiting long. "The NGO you were asking about, the man who is called The Enforcer – Jurgen Preissler – he didn't leave when his boss did. He is still on the island."

30

My phone is in my hand. I have to call Irini. To tell her that Lucy, her friend, *our* friend, is dead. That she has probably been murdered. That the killer may have been sent by the NGO she was working for. That he is still lurking. That Lucy's face in death was a horror show that haunts me every minute of the day. What do I tell her? What do I leave out?

I sigh and make myself punch in her number. She answers instantaneously. "Hey Tom, what's up?"

I tell her. I tell her Lucy has been found. I leave a pause. "It's not good news." I hear her intake of breath (or imagine it into being). "She's dead, Irini. They found her body."

"Oh, God, no!"

"They thought she'd killed herself, but I think she may have been murdered," I say. The "murdered" sounds so melodramatic. Should I have just said, "killed"? "The NGO she was working with may be involved," I say, sounding, to my own ear, dispassionate, professional.

"Oh, God, Tom, how are *you*?" Her concern for me suddenly chokes me up and I can't speak. "Tom?"

Eventually I say, "Bearing up," a trite phase that I've heard people using in these situations to imply fortitude. I feel disembodied.

Then her tone changes. "Fuck, fuck, fuck, why didn't we do something straight away? You kept saying not to worry. I knew something was wrong. I fucking *knew* it! Why didn't you fucking listen to me? Fuck it, if you'd gone straight away she'd still be alive! *Jesus, Tom!*"

I hear her anger and it enlivens mine, to myself. She is saying what I didn't want to think. All she is saying is true. Why did I doubt her? Was I so caught up in my petty romanticism, my hubris? I am too fucking shallow. I am immature. I am a fucking…

"Tom? You still there?" Irini is sounding contrite.

"Yeah, yeah," I say, involuntarily sounding sorry for myself, hurt. What a cunt. I agree with her and now I'm trying to make *her* feel guilty.

"Sorry," she says, "That was unfair. I'm sure you did what you could."

I absorb her patronising me. I could say, Why the fuck didn't you drop everything and come to Greece yourself? But I don't. I just think it, with some self-gratification. Instead, I say, "This is not over."

"What are you going to do?" she asks.

I tell her about the autopsy that I've organised, and that I'll be in touch with the Australian Embassy and that I'll stay here until the killer has been caught.

"Be careful," she says. "Don't do anything crazy."

"Like what?" I ask tersely, aggressively. She doesn't respond. How would she know what I could do if came down to it? "Can you contact Lucy's relatives? Or do you want the Embassy to do that? They'll have to decide what to do with the… *her* body."

After a pause, she whispers, "Okay. Okay, I'll do that. I don't know if I can get anyone… Maybe it's best if the Embassy do it."

Yeah, yeah, pass the buck. Quick to criticise, but when it comes to doing the hard stuff… Fuck it, let it go, I tell myself. "I'll let the Embassy know. Maybe you should at least let me have any contact details you have. You think you can do *that*?" This last bit comes out more acerbically than I'd intended. Or did I?

"Oh, Tom," she says, "Poor Tom." Her forte is sympathy and concern. Fuck her. She's useless. I'll do this on my own.

"Bye, Irini," I say and click off just as I hear her going, "Oh, Tom," one last time.

I put my phone back in my pocket. I know what I must do. I will go with Lucy's body to Athens. I will take her. I will not let her do her last journey alone.

****

I open my laptop and begin to write. The world needs to know what is going on here. I write and write. I let my anger infuse the sentences which flow out my fingers like Russian vine, the tendrils - my hatred of political manipulation, of short-sightedness, of self-interest, of the egos of small NGOs around whom the world-as -they-know-it rotates, the degradation of the environment for short term gain, the fabrications of eco-tourism. I let rip. "Radagast" gets roasted. Fuck it, I don't care if The Enforcer is still on the island. I name him. Jurgen Pressler, I am coming for you. Erica von Strondheim, don't fucking put the phone down on me again, you rich bitch *fuck*! I name The Poseidon and its developer, Christos Papademos. Don't fuck with my friends, you lying cunt, you silver tongued Judas! I outline the political machinations of the Mayor, his pragmatism and his opportunism. New PASOK. New Labour. Sell-outs, all of them. In thrall to capitalism, to making a buck. I have a go at the ineptitude of the local police. Anything for a quiet life. Jumping to false conclusions, accommodating the local players. Is there even more to come? I sit back and ponder this and realise I'm done. I'm emptied out. My anger is on the page. This is how I fight.

I read what I've written. A bit strident in places, a bit more determined and categorical than my usual measured style, but what the fuck, it reads well. I want it to be powerful. I write, to finish the piece, a precis of Lucy's shortened life – her struggle with the demons of a fucked-up childhood, her clawing an education, becoming a brave and tireless campaigner and journalist, a hero of the struggle for a better planet.

I stride over to the Seaview, cursorily accept Michali's and Nitsa's condolences, plug into the modem and press "Send".

31

The next day, I wake early, swim, shower, drink my bitter coffee and eat the sweet biscuits, which are courtesy of Yiannis and Soulla, as a token of their sympathy (they look grief-stricken themselves) and go to find Antonis. Stelios, his cousin, tells me Antonis has already left for Agia Sofia – some colleagues from Athens have arrived and he is going to meet them. Perhaps, I think to myself, this is the team that will take Lucy's body to the capital for a post-mortem. In my head I thank Antonis for his diligence but feel a little let down – I could have gone with him. Maybe he didn't want to trouble me. Maybe that's his way – get things done quietly and without a fuss.

I call him on his phone. I tell him I will accompany the body to Athens. He hears in my voice that I will not take no for an answer. He tells me he will arrange this. The plane will take her body tomorrow.

I walk. I need to clear my head, regain my equanimity, my oneness with the world. I head off around the point, this time heading up, to get to the summit of the headland. It's only three or four hundred metres up, and the path, if you can call it that (probably furrowed by the hooves of goats over the centuries), is forgiving, although the gravel is loose in places and I shall have to be careful when I descend. The air is rich with wild oregano and the tang of the sea. As I ascend, the breeze picks up and is bracing. I need that. I stride purposefully and can feel my mood lightening as the muscles in my thighs begin to strain. Then I am in a gully and the wind is above me, all around is silence and wilderness. I breathe the air in deep... and let it out slowly. I detect that animals have used this place for shelter and defaecation, but the smell of dried animal dung is liberating. This is not the world of people. This is 'away from it all'. Peace. I close my eyes.

Something rustles in the bush near me. I jump and think 'snake'. I scan for something slithering, but what I see is a mouse nervously emerging onto a rock from out under a grey bush. It sees me and scuttles away. My tranquillity having been disturbed, I proceed to the summit, clambering up the last part, up a natural sculpture of sandstone rock. I survey the land and sea below me. The village to my left is, I see, only two rows of buildings. Between gusts, I hear the sound of a tractor and in a field behind the village I see one farmer ploughing more or less straight lines first this way, then that. Further along, land has been cleared and levelled for what will probably be a hotel for all the tourists who will invade when the new road reaches the village. The sea, far out beyond the reach of the bay's promontory, is specked with tufts of white surf. Right below me is a cove and an isolated homestead. Is that Agapi's house? On the beach I see two small figures. Could that be Agapi and Eleni? Perhaps I will go and see.

As I descend, the oppression of my grief rises to meet me, like a fog responding to inverted pressure. I get down onto the beach and see Agapi and her daughter playing at the waters' edge and wonder if I should disturb their good humour with my darkening mood. But then Agapi looks up and sees me. She comes towards me and I plod down the sand to meet her. She walks straight up to me and enfolds me in her arms. "I am so sorry," she whispers. I put my arms around her and feel between us, her soft breasts yielding. I hold her tight. "I'm so sorry," she says again hoarsely, the closeness of her tears brings tears to my eyes. I sob. She holds me closer. I don't want to let go of her. Eleni comes up the beach to us. She looks at us, worried by our distress and our intimacy. I let go of Agapi and we stand apart, I, with her hands in mine.

"Come," Agapi says, "I will take you to my mother. She will know to help with your... sad feeling." She pats her heart. "The old people, they know what it is sad; they sad many times in their life. They know also from their parents," she says, her voice now more certain. We walk to her house hand in hand. Her hand in mine feels comfortable. A good fit. No suggestiveness, no promises, just there. Eleni skips behind us, reassured.

"Ma-*ma*," Agapi calls out as she opens the gate to her yard and we go to her front door, a door built for short people. This is an old house. Her mother is peeling vegetables at the sink. "Ma*ma*," Agapi says and holds my hand in hers out for her mother to see. She talks to her mother in a gentle tone which captures my sadness, I see in her mother's

166

expressions she understands that I am bereft and in need of restoration. She nods and purses her lips, then goes to a shelf and takes down a jar with some sort of grain and pours this into a pot, covers it with water and puts it on the flame. "This is *kolyva*, boil-ed wheat," Agapi tells me, "It is…" she shows me, with her hand, something connecting, "Life and Death." Her mother sprinkles in a herb which looks like wild parsley. "I don't know what is that," Agapi says, frowning. "Is good," she says, "From the old peoples. Maybe, I think, it forgive all the sins." Her mother goes to the window and opens it wide, then takes a cloth and covers the mirror on the wall. "Must let out the soul of the dead person. You must not think of yourself, only of the one who is gone," she commentates, nodding, pleased with herself for understanding these rituals which she has known since childhood. In which she must have participated when her husband died, I think, feeling a bit guilty for the pleasure of her soft hand in mine. "The *mnemosyno*," she says, "Is what we do."

Her mother puts a pot of coffee on the stove to heat up, sets on a plate the same sweet biscuits Yiannis and Soulla offered me and takes down a dusty bottle of brandy from a high shelf. The brandy is not often used it seems. "*Nai*," she says to herself. Then she gets a glass and fills it with water and comes to me and takes my hand (Agapi relinquishes it to her mother's ministrations) and she leads me outside. The wind has risen and howls in sympathy. The old woman looks at me through her wrinkles, looks right into me, then, with alacrity, pours the water out at my feet and smashes the glass on the stony ground. She begins to sing a lament as sad as any I've heard. Her voice is thin and strained and evokes from the melody all the tragedy of existence. Agapi joins in the chorus, her voice mellifluous and tuneful. Then silence, as the dirge ends and the wind is respectfully and eerily silent.

"*Endaxi*," Agapi's mother says, turns and leads me inside. She pours the coffee and the *metaxa*. We knock back the brandy, the old lady shouts, "*Sti zoi!*" "To life!" Agapi translates. We drink our coffee and eat our biscuits, then, when it has boiled for a good twenty minutes, we all eat from the pot of wheat and herbs to bring us close to the dead and to bring them to us.

The mother gives me further instructions. Agapi tells me I must grow my beard and not eat any meat for forty days, then I must return on the *Psychosavato* (which is, it seems, All Souls Day in Greece) in the Spring: "When the soul of your friend will be freed from the Underworld." Agapi looks at me gravely and takes my hand. "You will come back in the Springtime. Yes?"

I hold her gaze. Her eyes are luminous, a deep green. Deep enough for the drowning.

32

Five a.m. First light. Two men load the coffin on the twin engine plane which will fly us to the capital. The one man, the shorter one, is sombre, the other man is business-like, brisk – he does not want to be infected by the tragedies of people he doesn't know. I have packed a spare shirt, underpants, my laptop and my toothbrush into a small bag. I don't intend to stay in Athens long – just as long as it needs for me to see that Lucy is treated with respect; that she will be taken care of. I need more time to say goodbye. I have left my razor behind. I shall grow my beard as directed by Agapi's mother – then my grief will be there for the local people to see; they will be able to share my grief if they are moved to.

In the plane I sit staring straight ahead. The coffin with Lucy's body is on the floor at the back. I had to step over it to get to my seat. Her body is so close. I do not look back.

When we land in Athens, a police van is on the tarmac and the coffin is transferred with minimal perturbation. I am allowed to sit in the back of the van on a side bench. An expressionless police woman sits with me. The body is transported to the mortuary, a grimy building in a narrow cul de sac near Syntagma Square. They wheel the coffin through thick plastic curtains into the neon beyond. I am allowed to go no further. The officer in charge is respectful, but firm on this.

Suddenly she is gone. The finality sucks something out of me, as if I am stuck in a gasp. I feel cold, a sense of derealisation, as if I am watching myself in a movie about a man who has lost his love and with this, his future has suddenly and irrevocably shifted.

I go off and find a hotel and check in. I get a cup of coffee sent up to my room and phone the Australian Embassy, where eventually I get put through to a cheery sounding woman, whose voice drops when she hears what I tell her. We arrange to meet at eleven. Of course, they will do what is necessary. I pass on the information from Irini about Lucy's relatives.

I look out at the street below. People going about their business, unaware of my misfortune. The people on the pavements divide into those who bustle and those who move with practiced slothfulness. Athens. Where my father was born, where no doubt some of his family still live. Poor Lucy, no family to be with her, no one to collect her body. If I died, who would come *for me*? There is only Irini. Like Lucy, I have lost the trace of my family.

I wonder if I have family still living in Athens. I remember my father had a sister. If she is still alive, she would be in her sixties, or even older – she was his *older* sister I seem to remember. I doubt whether either of his parents are alive, although it is possible. Suddenly – perhaps it is the surge of my grief – I want to connect to the family I have never met. I want them to know me. I want to find out about my father – what he was like as a child, as a student, as a son or brother – to bring him close, to understand why I have never met this family in Greece, why my father left, why there was the rift, the casting off, the rupture that ruined my mother. I want restitution for my losses.

The Receptionist of my *pension* is very helpful. I give her my father's surname, Xanakis and she sets about making calls as if finding my long-lost Greek relatives is the most important duty of her day. She will help to reclaim me for Greece. She finds three Xanakises listed – Spiros Xanakis, Fotini Xanakis (both at the same address – probably married) and Anastasia Xanakis – am I making it up, or do I remember my father joking about having a sister called Stacey? It could be her. The Receptionist calls her number. No reply. She tries the other numbers – no reply from either of them too. I tell the Receptionist my father's full name and when he left Athens, she agrees to call the numbers again and make the necessary enquiries. I thank her and go to meet the woman from the Australian Embassy.

Who is as tall and athletic as the stereotype will allow, another version of handsome. I explain that we can't find Lucy's passport. "It doesn't matter," the official says, "We know she was in the EU. As long as she was positively identified…" (I nod)… "that's good enough. We have to deal with these kinds of situations sometimes. It's tragic." She is, I feel, over-solicitous, the sympathetic tilt of her head exaggerated and *wrong* on her muscular neck and body. But I am happy to have someone who will now take care of the practical details of, what the lady from the Embassy terms the "disposal of the body". She cannot be buried in Greece legally, she tells me. Once the autopsy is completed, the "deceased" will have to be transported back to Australia, paid for by the Embassy, so I have no need to worry (with a light touching of my arm to console me). As I hand over the paper on which I have written the details I know of Lucy (mostly from Irini), I feel a lightening, a letting go – and with it, another surge of grief. "Don't worry, don't worry," the woman from the embassy says, as she sees me welling up. I fight back my tears and grit my teeth.

"You'll make sure they do the autopsy properly?" I ask the official sternly. "They may try to cover up that she was killed. She didn't commit suicide."

"Of course we will. We'll get the report and have one of our doctors back home check it over. No worries. We'll get to the bottom of it," she reassures me.

But will they? One thing is for certain: even if it takes me forever, the person or people who did that to Lucy, who took such beauty from the world, will not escape justice. I will make them pay.

I get back to the hotel in a grim mood. But as I enter, the Receptionist beams at me and comes out from behind her counter to announce that she has found my aunt, because it turns out that my memory served me well – Anastasia *is* my father's sister, a spinster who lives by herself just the other side of the new stadium – in Pangrati - on Markou Massourou, a beautiful street, the Receptionist tells me with breathless enthusiasm. She too has a relative who lives on that very street! It is not far, but I will need a taxi which she can call for me. My aunt has said I can visit, but that I should come before three p.m. which is when she has her sleep. "She is retired lady, who has certain illnesses," the Receptionist tells me as if confidentially – it seems she had a long conversation with my aunt (as I must now think of this phantom of a Greek lady). "She speak very nice. Educated," the Receptionist pronounces reverently and nods, as if letting me in on a secret.

The taxi takes me to a neighbourhood which is more old-Greece than new, although I notice some trendy coffee bars and galleries too. Markou Massourou is a steep tree-lined street, with three and four storied buildings clamouring for space, the upper stories visible above the flowering bougainvillea. The smell of jasmine is piercing and fresh. My aunt's home is older than its neighbours, the paint on its outer wall flaking decorously, the newer yellow revealing its earlier progenitor, a pale cornflower blue, like a lady come down in the world, her dress torn, her slip showing. The house has evidently been sub-divided, and I have been told to ring the bell marked 36C.

I hesitate before stabbing the black button tentatively, then I press again more vigorously – if she is old, she is probably deaf. I hear beyond the green door muttering and complaining (at my impatience?), then a vent in the door at eye level opens, curious dark eyes glare at me, the vent closes, there is the clatter of locks and bolts being undone and finally the door opens, and then suddenly there she is. The portal to my Greek heritage.

My aunt is, to my surprise, tall. She must be nearly six foot, as tall as me at least. With a proudly thrusting breast and a square jaw - a woman of substance. Her hair, pulled back off her face, is still black but with streaks of silver. Prodigious nose, generous lips pursed in expectation of judgement. Her ears are large but well-shaped. Her eyes are like mine. Like my father's. It is startling. She is my family, clearly my father's sister - my aunt.

She examines my face and evidently satisfied, she ushers me into the dark hallway and closes the door behind me, first glancing at the street outside, to see to whom she will have to explain my arrival, who of her neighbours will be curious. Then she navigates the stairs to her apartment. I see now she is using two walking sticks and her progress is slow and uneven. It did not take her long to answer the door – she must have been waiting for me. (Perhaps the Receptionist at my hotel let her know I was on the way. I must remember to thank her for that consideration.)

My aunt's apartment is as cluttered as a second-hand furniture shop in Bethnel Green and as eclectically appointed. The bookcase is overflowing and on a venerable table in the centre is a display cabinet with the outcome of an encounter between a taxidermist and a fox, the animal's teeth bared in an ironic grimace. My aunt clears a space for me on a sumptuously stuffed couch. The room is pervaded by the smell of cooked onions and camphor. There is a small yellow bird in a cage against the far wall. It tweets, flusters, tweets again and then goes silent. My aunt sits herself down in a well-worn armchair in the light and breeze of the French doors to the balcony on which I glimpse a forest of pot-plants. She retains her sticks. Her knuckles reveal disfiguring arthritis, which I suddenly worry may be a family affliction that my father died too young to reveal. My aunt is nodding her head contemplatively.

"So," she says, "You are Petros's boy." Her voice is steeped in brandy and cigarettes.

"Yes, Petros Xanakis was my father," I say.

"*Milate Ellinika?* You speak Greek?"

"No, I'm afraid not," I apologize.

"Mmm," she says, weighing me up. "What do you know of us - your Greek family? What did he tell you?"

I explain that my father told my sister and I next to nothing about his family, or why he left Greece.

"You have a sister? Petros had a daughter?"

I tell her about Irini.

"Irina was our grandmother," she says. "Wait," she says and gets up with effort and goes to the heavy, dark-wooded sideboard. I see her reflected in its facetted mirrors. She rifles in a drawer and comes back armed with a bunch of photographs, places them on the table and sorts through them until she finds what she is looking for. She hands me the yellowed photograph – two elderly people, the man grim-faced, the woman smiling gently. My aunt taps the face of the smiling woman. "Your great-grandmother, Irina," she says curtly. I stare at the picture, looking for resemblance. The wide forehead of the man? – he must be my great-grandfather. The rounded cheeks of the woman? – my great-grandmother.

I feel a cloud of sadness rising up to cover me like a blanket. Then I feel anger welling up. How come my father never showed me pictures of my Greek family? How come they, his family, did not try to contact us, especially after my father's death, when they knew our address? My aunt, it seems, did not know about the existence of my sister – or is it that she has she forgotten? Or that she wasn't interested?

I get up uninvited and go to the table and examine the other photos of my family – the family I have not known, who have not known me.

"Dhomas - you - you are named for your father's great-uncle, a friend of Venezelos," my aunt says, coming to stand at my side. Her tone has softened. She recognises my distress. She shuffles the photos. "Here," she says, pointing to one of three middle-aged men in black suits. "The brothers. The one in the middle is your great-grandfather. The one on the right is Dhomas." The black and white photograph is remarkably preserved, precise. Dhomas Xanakis, my namesake, looks back at me, his thin face condescending, learned. The eyes are unmistakably mine. My great-grandfather is severe. The youngest brother is almost cherubic, smiling ruefully. "Come, you sit down. I will tell you about our family." She calls out a name peremptorily and a teenage girl appears out of what must be the kitchen, carrying a tray, with a teapot, biscuits and plates. The girl smiles shyly at me as she places the tray down. "The daughter of next-door," my aunt says, "She helps me and I give her lessons."

My aunt, it turns out, was, before her retirement, a senior manager in the Department of Works and Pensions, an accountant by training and is helping the neighbour's daughter to pass her bookkeeping entry exam. The girl pours our tea and loads our side plates with biscuits. "Xanakis, our family, was well-known in Greece before the war. Not so much now. Only the composer – you have heard of him? That family Xanakis, we do not know them. Must be different Xanakis."

A breeze stirs the curtains and light spills onto the floor. My aunt tells me that she was my father's only sibling. So it was hard on her parents when he left – their only son, on whom so much of their hopes for another glorious chapter in the history of the Xanakis family depended, gone. She had surpassed her parents' expectations, in part to make up for my father's absence, by working steadfastly, long hours, no respite – which is why she never married. "I had no time for men, for social activity," she says pointedly.

"Why did he leave?" I ask.

She sips her tea, considering how to respond to my question and then she replaces the cup carefully. "He was at the university, a junior lecturer. Politics, that was his subject. He had long hair in those days. Nice looking. He had a girl. Anna Moustraki. She was one of his students. She came from a good family with many connections in the government. They should have married," she says, eyeing me, lifting her chin. "They lived together. That was a new thing then, a man and a woman living together without being husband and wife. The old people did not like this – not her parents or ours. Your grandparents wanted him to marry her. But it was a time of revolution. The Sixties. The Colonels were in power. Your father led protests at the university – he was part of the Progressive Students' Council. So the police came for him. He was taken for questioning. Her family, Moustraki, they could have helped. But they did nothing. They were on the Right. They did not like that their daughter was living with a communist. Eventually he was released. The ESA, the Military Police, had tortured him. He was thin and what they did to him made the grey come into his hair, into his beard. He did not sleep. He ate little. My parents wanted him to marry the girl so her family would protect him. But he refused. He wanted nothing to do with her family. Then, when he heard the police were coming for him again, he fled." She sips her tea again. She looks to where the afternoon light is filtering through the half-open curtains. Fine dust floats on the beams. She turns to me and her eyes narrow. "Anna Moustraki was pregnant with his child."

She waits to see my reaction. I give none. She goes on. "It was something of great shame for the families, ours and hers. He could have sent for her. I don't know if she would have gone to England, if her family would have let her go. But nothing from him. My parents wrote to him, begging him to come back, to marry her, to take away the shame there was for them. But he was cold. He refused. So they cut him off." She does the Greek thing of one hand wiping the other clean, each in turn - a gesture of ineluctable finality. "From him, no regret. He started a new life. He met your mother then I think."

I think about my father's first love, the baby he refused to acknowledge… My aunt intuits my apprehension. "The baby died. Well, by then he – it was a boy - was two or three I think. Meningitis. That is what we heard. I don't know if Petros, your father, knew this or not. I think so. He still had friends here on the Left, but they too complained he never wrote to them. One of them saw him at a conference in London some years later. It was after you were born, so we knew he had a son.

We did not hear this from him. Anna, we did not see her again, until the funeral we had for your father here in Athens. She was there. I don't know how she knew he died. She was not beautiful anymore, but rich. She married an old man, a friend of her father. She was a woman who had a child out of marriage – she took what she could get. But at least he was rich."

"Is she still alive?" I ask.

"She will not want to see you," my aunt says, her eyes questioning my intentions.

"My... brother... half-brother... what was his name?"

"Angelos," my aunt says sadly. "Angelos. It was prophetic."

"Where is he buried?"

She hesitates. "The Proto Nekrotafeio. The First Cemetery. Behind the Temple of Olympian Zeus, behind the Panathiniakos Stadium. But I do not know where in the cemetery. We were not invited to the burial," she says tersely.

"Is it where my father is buried?" I ask.

"You want to see his grave?" she says. I detect a note of hopefulness, as if this will expiate the family who did not allow his children to see him interred. "I understand this... inclination," she says grandly. "I will come with you," she says, already getting up unsteadily. "I will call the taxi."

The taxi arrives promptly. On the way to the cemetery, I sit in air-conditioned silence, my thoughts filled with snatched memories of my father, like watching old DVDs. My aunt chats to the driver. She asks questions in an imperious voice which he diverts with laconic replies. He holds his cigarette out the driver's window so as not to offend his passengers and blows his smoke out the corner of his mouth. The smoke may be preferable to his body odour which wafts into my range from time to time. When we get to the entrance to the cemetery, he gets out with alacrity and comes around to my aunt's door to help her out. There is something about her manner which demands respect. I pay him and wave away my aunt's feeble protest.

She leads the way, surprisingly nimble with her two sticks on the level ground. We pass impressive mausoleums and heroic statues, festooned with heraldic angels, tributes to the famous and wealthy dead people buried here. There are groups of tourists with their guides, cameras at the ready. We go down an avenue of ancient cypress trees and come to a part of the graveyard which is more mundane, the gravestones pressed closer together, the angels less flambouyant, until we come to rows of simple stones and carved crosses, with, on them, old black-and-white or, on the more recent ones, tinted photos of the deceased loved ones: tributes of plastic flowers and lamps to be lit on memorial occasions. We turn down a narrow path and go about fifty metres before she stops at a grave on which is a photo I recognise of my father as a young man. His family would not have had any photos of him as he'd looked in middle-age, when he died. The poignancy of this discrepancy catches me in the throat.

We stand in respectful silence. Then my aunt takes my hand. I glance at her. Her face is hard, but her clutch is gentle.

The writing on the tombstone is in Greek. "What does it say?" I ask.

"Petros Xanakis – his name. Under it 1933 – 1987. Then it says, 'Never forgotten by God.'"

My father may have forgotten his God and may even have offended Him, but in the family's eyes, He did not turn his back on His child – as if to appease themselves for casting him out, as if to say "Never forgotten by his *family*". There I am, an atheist, son of an atheist, weeping with the comfort of God's grace - my father's family have not forgotten him and therefore they have not forgotten *me*. I am part of them – they are part of me. I feel an upwelling of... what is it? – pride? – identification? – belonging? I feel I have returned to this place I have never been.

We try to find my half-brother's grave, but without anyone to help us, it is hopeless and we give up. My aunt is tiring, visibly wilting. We sit on a bench in the shade and watch pigeons feeding on scraps left by the bird-loving bereaved, who see these creatures as emissaries from the world beyond, who carry the souls of their loved ones back to Earth to visit.

My thoughts drift to my Lucy lying on a cold slab in a mortuary. I am mourning her, my father and the brother I never knew I had. It is a lot to bear, but having wept at my father's grave, I feel less heavy, like something has lifted.

When I take leave of my aunt later, she kisses me on the cheek and gives me, to take with me, a bag of almond biscuits and the faded photo of my namesake and his brothers. Lost and found. Lost and found.

33

When I get back to the island, I find, when I log on, that Marsha has been busy on my behalf. She'd like the piece I'd posted. "Sorry about Lucy, Tom, but you write well when you are angry," she'd written. She'd offered my piece around and sure enough had got takers, including certain tabloids in Greece, which is how my article has found its way to the island while I was in Athens. Good for me, my career, my bank balance, but my in-your-face coverage has made me unpopular with the locals I bad-mouthed (understandably) and some that feel bad-mouthed by association. As I find out more-or-less straight away.

When I go over to the Seaview to get online, Michalis comes at me waving a newspaper. "This is *you*?" he jabs at an article on page three of the Greek tabloid in his hand. I don't read Cyrillic, so I don't know if it is me or not. "No, my friend," he says, his head tilted in disappointment, "No, is not good. What you say. No, no. Tourist, they read this, they decide not Mythos. May they go Italy or Spain. You don't know what you write; is just *suspicion*. But you make it that this is the way *it is*. That it is *fact*. Christos is…" he makes a circular movement with his hand over his stomach, "*sick* with his anger for this. For what you say, about him; for what you say about The Poseidon. Already he is expecting cancellations, for not people to book with him… And Nikos, our Mayor? Panagiotis? All these people, they have been kind, they have helped you." He puts the newspaper down in front of me and walks off, disconsolately. I have let him down. I am no longer welcome.

Fuck off, this is my job, is my first reaction, although I don't speak this aloud. But his hurt, his turned back, the sad shaking of his head as he goes back inside, temper my self-righteousness. I have to admit that my report was not grounded in well-corroborated evidence. I wrote it when I was deeply grieving. I was… I *am* angry, I want justice for Lucy. But perhaps I did over-step the mark. Did I? Maybe I should have posed questions rather than making assertions. Have I slandered people? It got

179

by Marsha and I'm fairly sure she would have got legal advice. Could Christos sue? - what I've got on him is speculative. We haven't yet heard from Radagast, from the sure-to-be litigious Baroness von Strondheim. They are not going to be happy with me either. *And* Jurgen Preissler is still on the island somewhere. The Enforcer.

I leave without going online. I jump my motorbike into life. The roar, as I wind the throttle, is satisfying. I am angry and righteous. I'm not going to back down. It hurts me that I will no longer be trusted, that I will lose the goodwill of some of the people I have met and grown to like. Some of them I *don't* like - their goodwill, their patronage, I don't need and I don't want. It's *them* I'm going after. I rev the engine into a higher register, feel the vibrations course through me. Take off, in search of the clean air up in the mountains to clear my head, to ground me.

I bend low at the corners, totally in control, as I snake my way up the hairpins on the way to the summit overlooking The Poseidon. The sea stretches out on my left all the way to the top, then it reverses around the cape and sweeps towards The Poseidon. I stop at the top, take off my helmet and breathe. I fill my lungs. I expand myself. I let myself free.

The variegation between the dark green conifers and the turquoise sea below is as delicious as ever. The vastness of the panorama is awesome (as in *inspiring awe*, not the 'awesome' which is followed by 'dude'). Even the dense blackness of the burned forest on the mountain opposite lends grandeur – drama – to the setting, a sculptural dimension. The unadorned mountain is shown in its true relief, angular, Herculean, the flat limestone cliffs near its peak, muscular, self-confident. They have been there forever… Well, actually that's not true – they were thrown up by a tremendous seismic force millions of years ago, tumbling granite and sandstone upward, before they came to rest, lifting their heads to the sky. Now they look so nonchalant, like they *have* been there forever. Nothing has been here forever. Everything changes.

Was the forest burned to justify the rezoning? Or is that a conspiracy theory, dreamt up by a sensation-seeking rich bitch with too much time on her hands? The land is very dry – surely they have forest fires here regularly. Although I must admit the pattern of the burning is very precise, too neat. The Poseidon was never threatened. The water supply? – will the lagoon dry up? I notice the stain on the sea beyond the sandbar is still there. But Michalis' criticism still stings – he was right – I have proceeded with little evidence. I will have to be more diligent, read more stuff, do properly recorded interviews, be able to quote them. That's what I'll do.

In a clearing on the side of the road a hundred metres from me, I notice a gleaming 4x4 backed into the shade. A tourist's car – no local's car would be so clean. Someone going for a walk up the mountain no doubt. I should do that some time – get some real elevation. The higher I go, the more easily I breathe.

I kick my bike into gear and set off down the mountain back to Agia Anna. I have work to do.

I am rounding a bend about halfway down, when I realise the 4x4 (is it the same one?) is very close on my tail. Fucking tourists! – don't know the rules of the road. Probably a German wanting the road to himself. A German - fuck! - The Enforcer! *Fuck!* Is it? I peer into my rear-view mirror, but I can't make out the driver. The mirror is too dusty. He is getting even closer, at speed. He flashes his lights and begins to overtake me – on a bend – forcing me to the edge. But he doesn't overtake – he slows to be next to me, leaning me onto the verge. The 4x4 is huge and so high above me, I can see only, even as I glance panicked sideways, a vague shape in the driver's seat. The drop-off from the tar to the gravel is a good 6 inches. I can't just drive onto it – my wheel will buckle. The next hair pin is coming up. The sea sparkles far below, a dizzying drop down and the road is uncurling and beginning to curl again, the cunt next to me is forcing me… I grip the handlebars with all my power and hit the brakes hard. The back of the SUV passes within inches of my head. The bike bucks and I go into a wild accelerating skid, to my right, towards the edge. I frantically twist the handlebar and the bike jack-knifes to the left and across the road, bucks onto the gravel and crashes into a bush beyond, into a ditch. The 4x4 swerves in front of me, horn blaring, emergency lights flashing disparagingly. He takes the bend at speed, his tyres protesting, then he guns the 4 litre engine and is gone around the next rise. Fuck! *Fuck! Jesus!* Shit, that was close! Fuck, I should have got the registration number.

My impulse is to go after him, I am that angry. But then I start to feel the dull throb in my left thigh and see the blood beginning to stain my jeans, then the burning, searing pain all down my leg. Shit! I examine my leg tentatively. I bend my knee with trepidation, expecting to feel the sudden agony of a broken bone. But I can bend my leg. Good. Next the hip. That seems okay too. I can try to get up. It hurts when I put pressure on my left leg. The ankle – I think I have sprained my ankle. The blood is already beginning to cake – good, it is not still bleeding. I must have taken the skin off the side of my thigh as I skidded across the tar. Anyway, better than falling 300 feet to my certain death on the rock below or into the sea. At least I am alive. "It'll take more than that to kill me, you fuck!" I think, like I'm in Diehard 4 or something. Jesus, that was close!

Then I start shaking. The light gets intense. I pass out.

I come to with the sun in my eyes, a big moustached Greek guy with solid breath breathing all over me. I start and sit up. Alarmed. Then the pain in my leg hits the surface again. The Greek guy jumps back, his face terrified. I think he thought I was dead. I groan to reassure him I'm still alive. I see his delivery van in the road, the driver's door open.

"Agia Anna…. you – take – me – Agia Anna? Please?" I say in my English for Greeks.

"You stay in Agia Anna?" he says in passable English.

"Yes," I say weakly.

"You want me to take you to the hospital in Agia Sofia? Maybe is better," he says.

"No, it's fine. Just a graze and some bruising," I say bravely, quite pleased with my fortitude. "I've got some stuff. I can manage. It's alright. *Endaxi,*" I say.

He looks sceptical, but helps me up and around to the passenger door, which he opens for me and pours me into the passenger's seat. His dog makes way for me, looking apologetic and disgruntled. There is a year's worth of sweet wrappers and empty cans on the floor. The cab smells of nicotine and stale sweat. It is somehow reassuring.

The motorbike lies crumpled in the ditch, the front fender is hopelessly bent. The Zeus Motors guy will have to fetch it later. Shit, did the bike come with insurance? Another reason to find the driver of the 4x4 – and make him pay.

But then again, maybe the driver of the 4x4 will come looking for *me.*

34

I tell my saviour that I am staying at the *taverna*. He drives right past Yianni's and stops outside The Seaview – clearly he assumes tourists will stay at The Seaview. He runs around to let me out, helping me stand somewhat unsteadily. Agapi sees us and rushes over. My bloodied trousers must be impressive – she gasps, hand to mouth, eyes wide in alarm. "What is happen?" she shouts accusingly at the man who has saved me. I put her right and tell her I am not badly hurt. "Look all the blood!" she says, as if I am a recalcitrant child. She puts an arm around my waist to support me. "Come, we take you inside."

"No," I say, "I want to go to my room. Next door."

Agapi looks at me sceptically. Then she waggles her head and acquiesces. With my two helpers, I make it (gingerly) to Yianni's. When he sees me, he calls out to Soulla and they both come running to me. I am touched by their solicitude. With Soulla going ahead to open my room, the other three manage me upstairs. "Give me your jeans – I wash," Soulla instructs me. I sit on my chair and very carefully Agapi extricates me from my trousers. Soulla eyes Agapi suspiciously, then looks to me for my response to a young lady undressing me, sees my trust and relents. Agapi gives my bloodied jeans to Soulla, who holds them at arm's length with a look of mild disgust. "Maybe you need new," she says, turns and walks out.

The van driver stands awkwardly, not knowing whether he is required further. "Thank you for your help," I say. "*Efcharisto poli.*" "*Parakalo,*" he mumbles diffidently. Yianni makes his enquiries of him in Greek, when he gets a reply, he smiles broadly and slaps the van driver on the back and embraces him.

"I take him downstairs," Yianni says to me. "I fix him something to drink and eat. He is good man. You want something also?" I could do with a bottle of cold water. He says he will send Bobby up with it straight away. He sees me examining my leg. "You need to go hospital?" he asks.

183

Agapi asks me, "You have something to make clean?" pointing at my wound, which is a long and wide graze down the side of my left thigh, nothing more, luckily. I have a small First Aid kit which I take by habit on all my travels abroad. Agapi gets it from my bag.

Yiannis snatches it from her, looks inside and decides he has a better one, for the restaurant... "bandages, creams, everything..." He goes off, quite excited now by the drama and the reassurance that I am going to be ok. The van driver follows him out like a puppy – I can almost see their tails wagging.

Agapi takes my hand. "It is sore?" she says, eyebrows furrowed with concern.

"No, it's okay," I say, being the man, but wincing sharply as I extract a piece of cotton from the wound. Her hand tightens on mine.

"Wait," she says, "I will clean properly, when Yiannis comes back." She looks around, sees the pitcher next to the basin, goes over, turns the hot tap on and waits. When it is the desired temperature, she fills the pitcher and comes back to squat on the floor next to me. I offer my hand again, she takes it and is pleased with my gesture of gratitude.

Yiannis come in and hands over his First Aid kit, which looks like an ex-Army issue one. Inside are rolls of bandages and dressing, gauze for burns, I notice. That should do the trick. Agapi examines the contents. "Before I was marry, I was, one year, a nurse," she tells me. She has a look of shy pride, and I intuit, a nostalgia for the future she once had.

"You will help him, Agapi?" Yiannis asks. She nods. He nods back, then leaves her to it. I thank him as he goes out.

Agapi, frowning seriously, pours something strong smelling into the pitcher of hot water, then from this onto a patch of gauze and she very gently begins to wipe the blood off my leg. She glances at me for my reaction and interprets my silent grimacing as permission to proceed. She is focused and precise, only exerting the smallest pressure needed to get the wound clean. Her left hand, placed further up my thigh to keep my leg still, is comforting and sure. She bends close to my thigh to see she has the wound perfectly clean. I see the top of her head and her glorious hair spreading out, and I involuntarily imagine her going down on me, and... I tell my male-brain to shut the fuck up and focus on the pain. My look of exaggerated distress alarms Agapi. "What?" she asks. "Is sore?"

"It's okay, but maybe I should lie down," I say and get up, with Agapi's help, to my bed.

"Wait," she says and gets an impregnated dressing and a roll of bandage to finish the job. I mustn't stain the sheets. She finishes the dressing with Elastoplast to keep it all together. The pressure of the covering is soothing. Agapi plumps my pillows, smooths the sheet and helps me get my tee-shirt off.

Then she locks the door, climbs out of her dress, unhooks her bra and gets into bed with me, cuddling me like a wounded child into her delicious soft warmth.

35

When I wake up, she is gone. I can still feel her glow in the bed next to me. The satin touch of her skin and the curve of her breasts are still with me. She was so careful with me, so careful not to hurt me as she stroked me and covered me with light kisses, healing me. Then she'd turned on her side with her back to me and pulled my hand to her breast and with her other hand, guided me into the sumptuous heat of her wetness. Her hair smelt of honey.

My erection is back. I long for her, for the comfort of her body. I ease my legs over the side of the bed and sit up and become aware of the throbbing in my leg and in my left shoulder. I get up, wash my face and take a couple of paracetamols. My erection recedes. I get myself dressed. Luckily, I have a pair of loose cotton pants. Just the thing. I slip on sandals and go out. I must thank Agapi for her kindness, and reassure her that I have no claim on her.

But first I go to thank Yianni and Soulla. They sit me down and insist that I eat something before I go any further. Soulla delivers a bowl of broad bean soup with what looks like arborio rice. To be honest, I would have preferred a salad; soup is a bit too warming in the middle of the day, but I cannot refuse their hospitality. The soup is certainly nourishing and actually very tasty. Yiannis insists I drink a glass of wine also. He hovers solicitously. He is conscientious about taking care of his guests. "Its okay, Yiannis," I say, "It's good. *Efcharisto.*"

"I can't help," he shrugs, "Is *philoxenia. To welcome in strangers.*" He opens his arms wide to show his commitment to brotherliness and social responsibility. I reciprocate by drumming with my hand on my heart. He nods. "*Nai,*" he says. "*Philoxenia!*"

After I've eaten, they are prepared to let me go, but not before Yiannis has offered me a walking stick, which he looks for and finds in the kitchen. I try it out and, actually, he's right – the walking stick helps. So off I go, limping, but mobile on my stick, to break the news to the proprietor of Zeus Motors that I have wrecked his bike and he'll have to go and collect it half way up the mountain road. Mr. Zeus (I establish his name is Yiorgos) is not best pleased. I eye the wrench in his black-oiled hand with trepidation as I see his knuckles whiten. He growls and stamps his foot. Then he notices I am leaning on a walking stick and he regains his composure and asks if I am okay. Maybe he's worried the accident was caused by some fault on the bike and I will sue him. I don't know. He tells me the insurance will pay – I mustn't worry. But there is paperwork and I must report the accident to the police – to the Sergeant. He takes me to his make-shift office and eventually locates his phone under a pile of car manuals and unopened letters. He dials the number for me and hands me the phone.

Kosta answers. I recognise his off-hand manner. I ask to speak to Sergeant Valoudsakis. Panagiotis comes on the line.

"*Kalimera,* Panagiotis, its Tom," I say.

"Hello, Dhomas," he says coolly. I assume his tone is a rebuke to me for my recent syndicated article which no doubt he has now read. I tell him what happened. "Oh, my friend, this is not good. You must be *carful,*" he says. I notice the apposite mispronunciation with a wry smile.

I ask if he knows what car Jurgen Preissler drives. "This I do not know," he says. "We have checked all the car rentals, but nobody has rented a car or a motorbike to him by this name. Maybe he has use a different name. I will check now all jeeps – all the '4 times 4' cars on the island. If we find one paid with German card, maybe is him. This is how we catch him. Yes?"

"Thanks, Panagiotis," I tell him. Before he hangs up, he reminds me to keep safe. A bit late for that.

I've forgotten again to ask about Lucy's scooter. I turn to the mechanic and owner of Zeus Motors. "Did you, by any chance, rent a motorbike, a scooter, to my friend, Lucy Discombe?" I ask. Maybe if he has, he would have been and collected it from the harbour.

He looks at me nonplussed and shakes his head. "She said I rented to her?"

"No," I say, "It doesn't matter. *Dhen peirazei.*"

But it does matter. Where is Lucy's scooter? Perhaps I should go and look around the harbour myself.

36

I am aching, even from the mild exertion, so I go back to my room, lie on the bed and promptly fall asleep. Probably a self-protective response. I've heard our bodies heal themselves while we sleep. I will see Agapi later.

I am woken by a restrained knock on the door. It is dark. I must have slept for hours. I put on the bedside light, ease myself upright and then limp over to the door. It is Antonis. He has heard of my accident (word travels fast in the village; it's a small village) and has come to find out how I am and to invite me to dine with him at the Seaview. I feel I owe it to Yianni to dine here tonight, but Antonis is keen on the Seaview ("So we can be served by the beautiful Agapi") and won't be dissuaded.

As soon as we are seated at a table for dinner he tells me that the autopsy on "Miss Discombe" (he won't use her first name out of respect; he is professional) will take place in two days' time ("Then we will know *when* she died, and if she suicided or something else was happen"). Agapi brings us each a menu, as she puts mine down, she strokes the back of my arm and gives me the briefest look of intense longing before walking away. Antonis of course notices this straight away: the intimacy of her gesture and look. His eyes narrow, his jaw clenches and his Adam's apple takes a ride – up, pause and then down. He studies his menu. Did he think he still had a chance with her? Xanthe and he were certainly loving it up at the concert. What has happened while I have been away? Local intrigue.

As if to change the subject, he starts to tell me about his progress with the body in the bridge case. His voice is terse, official and his speech is directed somewhere over my left shoulder. He and Panagiotis have been through the list of all the employees from Hektor Papademos's construction company and Konstantin Garidis' concrete factory and have cross-checked against any right-wing political affiliations. They identified three people of interest, but two had died and the other one was now living in America. It'll take time to trace him. He has a cousin still living right in the south of the island; she may know where he is living. They still don't know the identity of the body – there were no recorded missing teenagers on Mythos, nor on the big island at that time. It's a mystery.

The deep-throated roar of a motorbike drowns out his speech for a moment, as the bike comes to a stop and revs boastfully to announce its presence. Then it cuts out and Kosta dismounts, undoes his helmet with one hand and strides, wide-based and manly, into the restaurant. Xanthe comes to greet him and allows him to kiss her lightly on both cheeks. She sneaks a look at Antonis as she submits to Kosta's familiar greeting. Antonis affects a look of supreme disinterest, which shows he must have some interest.

Agapi comes to take our order. I order the lamb chops and Antonis chooses the meatballs in tomato sauce - the *soutzoukakia.* Antonis turns away as Agapi gives me a meaningful, amused look, pressing her lips together and lifting her breast as she straightens. Antonis pretends to be enraptured by the after-sunset sky, which admittedly is spectacular in a quiet way – deep purples and mauves. The first stars are emerging. Once Agapi has left, he turns his attention back to me and I can see he is hurt and even accusatory. I feel I may have been treacherous, but through no fault of my own – Agapi has clearly made the running. I don't know if I should apologise, but that would be patronising, so I don't.

Antonis sees Xanthe standing at Kosta's table, talking to him without smiling. "Xanthe," he calls to her, "Xanthe, *ise poli oraia!*" with a gesture indicating that she is very beautiful, from her elaborately coiffured hair to her gold strapped platform sandals. He kisses the tips of his fingers at her. "Come and say hello us, you special young lady." He is, in his own mind at least, exuding ostentatious charm with his caramel voice and a grand chivalric sweep of his hand. Xanthe smiles at his attention and saunters over.

"Hello, boys," she says, "You alright?"

"Oh, yes, but we would *love* your company," Antonis says with what I am sure he thinks of as a seductive dipping of his head and raising of one eyebrow only.

189

Xanthe does the love-chuckle. "Oh, but I am working," she says drily. "I have other customers to serve."

"But not ones who will offer to take you dining in Athens," he says. "You will come on a date with me in Athens when you go back to university?" (They speak in English for my benefit - I am the audience. Is Antonis wooing her to show me that to him there are other pretty fish in the sea? Is he doing it to make Agapi jealous?)

Xanthe frowns. "Mmm, I'm not certain. Maybe you have missed the boat, Inspector. There is someone else who has reserved me," she says and chuckles again. She is not a girl who will settle for being second best.

I see the disappointment flit across Antonis's face, before he quickly restores his benign countenance. I notice, also across the balcony, Kosta, has been observing the interaction and he is smirking.

"But maybe," Xanthe says and swaggers back to her post, hips moving sensually. Saucy minx! She is playing hard-to-get! As she goes past Kosta, he grabs her arm and says something. She says something back and he responds, she looks over her shoulder at us, amused by what he has said evidently. Kosta grins sardonically and challenges Antonis with a mocking stare. Antonis stiffens, but his face is expressionless. He turns away, as if unaffected. But I can see he is fuming. When our food arrives, we eat in silence.

"Excuse me," Antonis says, as he pats his lips with a serviette, neatly places his cutlery on his now empty plate, gets up, and goes over to Kosta and says something quietly in his ear. There is menace in this. Kosta gets up and follows him out of the restaurant. Kosta is cocky and makes a mocking sign to Xanthe. She, for her part, looks concerned to see her two suitors leaving together.

I follow. Antonis leads Kosta around the corner into the shadows, then - he must be some sort of martial arts expert - Antonis has Kosta on the ground and Kosta's arm is twisted behind his back, his face is pressing concrete and Antonis has a knee in his back. Antonis growls at him. Kosta winces, but is too embarrassed, I guess, to call out. "I will speak to you in English for the convenience of my friend," Antonis says. "You will address me as Inspector, you mother-fucker. You understand?" Kosta grunts. "You understand, motherfucker?" (Antonis has been watching "The Wire" or some other American cop show.)

Kosta whispers urgently, "*Nai, nai.* Yes." Antonis twists his arm, an impressively vengeful look on his face. I've clearly under-estimated him. So has Kosta.

Antonis extends Kosta's arm into an even more painful hold. "Yes who?" Antonis seethes.

"Yes, *Inspector*," Kosta hastily concedes. Antonis lets go of his hold on Kosta, slowly. Kosta gets to on to all-fours and shakes his head clear. Antonis steps back, alert, ready to act again if Kosta tries anything.

"Okay, now you will come with us to Miss Discombe's house. I have some questions for you," Antonis says.

Kosta looks up, frightened. "*Ti?* What questions?"

Antonis tells him, "Bring your motor bike. You will ride in front of us there. Slowly."

The fight has gone out of Kosta and he obeys, like a small boy, his head hung in shame. He starts his bike and we follow him up the lane to the house where Lucy used to live. The old lady across the road is watering her plants with a watering can. As soon as she sees Kosta, she bumbles over to her front gate as fast as her arthritic legs will carry her and she shouts at him as he comes to a stop.

Antonis calls out to the old woman and she responds, "*Nai, Nai!*" pointing with a belligerent prodding finger at the downcast Kosta. Antonis taps Kosta on the shoulder and Kosta turns fearfully. "You visited Miss Discombe late at night? What for?" Antonis asks him.

The old lady is still having a go. Kosta turns to her and growls and then shouts a command at her. She backs off and shuts up. "*Endaxi! Endaxi! Nai, nai!*" he shouts almost in tears and babbles away. Antonis doesn't compel him to talk in English now. He lets him loose and Kostas spills the beans, his voice desperate, pleading, imploring. Antonis lets him dribble to a standstill, then he turns to me and translates.

"He says he did come here to see the 'deceased'… 'deceased' is right?" he asks.

"Yes," I say, "Lucy."

Antonis nods. "Miss Discombe. Correct. He says it was *she* that *wanted* him to come. For sex only." Antonis asks Kosta something and Kosta replies in a dull tone. He mumbles like a teenager caught shoplifting. "Yes, he says. She wanted just sex. He wanted too. He says he didn't kill her."

"Ask him about the computer and the e-mails," I say.

Antonis asks him. They talk in Greek, rapid-fire questions and answers. Antonis says Kosta doesn't know anything about her computer. Kosta says something jocular which includes what I take to be a lewd reference to "laptop". Antonis shouts at him and the smile shrinks into his face, he goes mournful.

Antonis considers the options. Then he seems to conclude that there is nothing further to gain, he dismisses Kosta, who looks mightily relieved and rides off at a respectful speed, until he gets to the main road, at which point he guns the engine and his tail-lights disappear in seconds. Antonis looks to see if I am critical of his actions. I am disappointed he has not got more out of Kosta, but I can see it his way. Some rules you have got to stick by. Kosta was too shit-scared to be fabricating, his story *was* kind of plausible and there is actually, as yet anyway, no evidence to the contrary. So, on balance, it's likely he was telling the truth – *a* truth anyway.

Antonis has shown himself in a different light. He is a man of purpose.

But we are still no closer to finding out what happened to Lucy and how she ended up at the bottom of the sea.

37

Yiannis puts down the plate with the eggs Soulla has fried for my breakfast, next to it, a basket of cut bread and thick-cut butter. "Wait, I will get the coffee," he says and goes back inside.

In the distance, walking down the hill into the village, dragging a suitcase on wheels behind him, an elderly man with a face so dark I cannot see his features against the shock of white hair. He has on a black suit, his white shirt open at the neck. The suitcase clatters on the uneven surface. Soon this will be smooth tar. There will be no clatter, just glide.

Yiannis returns with my coffee. He glances cursorily at the man approaching, but just to see what I am looking at. One look and then he pays the man no further attention. Perhaps he knows him. Maybe it is not unusual. Perhaps it's none of his business who chooses to walk into the village in a suit with his suitcase behind him when the day has hardly begun. Yiannis busies himself arranging tables. I watch the man in the suit as I eat my breakfast. He is unhurried. I notice him stop a short distance out and survey the village and the bay. He wipes his forehead with a handkerchief, folding it carefully before replacing it in his pocket. Then he proceeds again and soon rounds the bend where the road curves behind the "To Meltemi" and is out of my view.

He reappears at the entrance to the *taverna*. He stands and watches Yiannis laying the tables. Yiannis looks up and nods a greeting, goes back to replacing the salt... then he does a double-take and stares open-mouthed at the stranger. "*Mavros!*" he gasps. "Mavros Epistimos!" The stranger nods slowly, pleased to be recognised, sad to have been missed. He comes forward and he and Yiannis fall into an embrace.

Mavros has returned from the dead.

Yiannis remembers my interest in Mavros's story and rushes over to me. "Unbelievable! Un-be-*lieve*-able! It's *Mavros!* Come to meet him. Unbelievable!" He ushers me over to Mavros. "Mavros, this is Tom from London. Yoornaleest. *Demosiografos.* He make big newspaper story about you!" Then he says this in Greek for his old friend. He pushes me forward and I shake the old man's hand. He has a firm grip and steely eyes, still handsome in his 70s, although his face is lined and his cheeks hollow. Yiannis chats excitedly to him in Greek. I hear them mention Stavroula and Michalis and intuit that Yiannis is filling the old man in on news of his family.

"*Milate Anglika, Mavros?*" I ask when Yiannis pauses for breath. "Do you speak English perhaps?"

"Yes," affirms the old man ruefully, "I learned. I spent five years in the kitchen of the Russian Embassy in London in the 1950s."

"Wow, can I interview you for my journal?" I ask, excited by what I am sure will be an intriguing story. Where has he been? Why is he back? "I work for New World Order, a weekly in London. Very Left-wing," I add, hoping my socialist credentials will get his interest.

He gives me a non-committal head-waggle. Soulla comes to him and kisses him three times on both cheeks. "*Kalosirthes,*" she says her voice choked with emotion.

"Welcome home," Yiannis says in English, for my benefit. Yiannis steers Mavros to a table and we sit, other than Soulla who is delegated to fetch the coffee and *loukamadhes*. "You know everybody is look for you?" Yiannis tells Mavros. "We thought you was dead, in the bridge! You know what is happen here?"

"That's why I came back," Mavros says. "I know who it was in the bridge."

He sighs deeply and frowns. It is obviously painful for him. He gathers himself. He has come back for this moment.

He looks from my face to Yianni's. Then he says gravely, "The body in the bridge is my son. It is Eleftherios."

"*Eleftherios?*" says Yiannis, surprised, incredulous.

"Yes," Mavros says, "I gave him the badge that was in the hand of the body they found. From Cuba. It was given to me in London by a comrade from the struggle in Latin America."

"*Eleftherios!*" Yiannis exclaims and smacks his forehead with the heel of his hand. "*Fiisiika!* Of course! Why I not remember?"

"You don't remember because it was easier to forget," Mavros says.

Yiannis is transfixed by Mavros's steady gaze. His expression moves from pity to shame and then apology. "I am sorry we don' help you with the boy," Yiannis says. "I know you suffer with him."

"When I was on Macronissos with the other political prisoners, 1970 sometime," Mavros says, "a few months later, after I was taken, someone tells me Eleftherios was missing from Agia Anna. I thought the army had done with him what they said they would do. Then, when I saw, three weeks ago, in the newspaper about the body in the bridge, every day I look for someone to say this could be Eleftherios. But nobody came forward. No one remembered Eleftherios went missing. Like he never was in the village."

"I'm sorry," I say, "Who is Eleftherios?"

Yiannis turns to me. "It was his son, his first son, the one he came to the island with."

"He had another son? How come nobody mentioned him?" I ask.

Yiannis steals a guilty glance at his old friend. Mavros looks at me sadly. "My son was ..." (he points to his head) ... "he had mental problems. From the War. He was like a small child. The Greek people here on the island are superstitious about people with problems of the mind. Nobody wanted to know our problems. Even our neighbours," he looks pointedly at Yiannis, "made like he wasn't there, to spare us the embarrassment."

Yiannis looks down glumly. "Maybe we are ashamed to remember, so we forget," he says, then he has a thought. "When you first was come Agia Anna, he was okay. Good boy. You remember?" Mavros nods. "Only later, he was taking his clothes off in front of the young womens, and... It was no good, *nai,* Mavro?"

"It wasn't his fault," Mavros says, "He had the longings of a young man, but the mind of a child. Some of the villagers attacked him. He became frightened. We couldn't control him. Stavfroula... she...." Mavros shakes his head. "It was better we kept him in his room," Mavros says disconsolately, "Better for everyone that he should be kept where no-one could see, where he could be forgotten," he says bitterly.

"But the police said there were no missing teenagers from then?" I say.

"We had no papers for him. The police would not have had records," Mavros says.

"And his mother?" I want to ask, but it seems insensitive, so I keep this to myself.

Yiannis says emphatically, "You must go to Stavroula. To Michalis. You have another son. You have *grand-daughter*. Xanthe. Very beautiful girl." He tries to sound upbeat.

Mavros looks down. "I don't know if I can see them. I never wrote to tell them I was alive. I didn't enquire about Eleftherio. I am to blame for his death." His head slumps.

"Why you not come back before?" Yiannis asks.

Eventually Mavros answers. "I was ashamed. I thought everyone would know it was me who gave away Aris Lambros, my comrade, my leader." He pauses, examining his memories. He addresses *me*, as if I, a foreigner not a compatriot, will understand and forgive him. "Aris Lambros was our ELAS commander on the island during the War. A brave man. A good man. After the War, he stayed true to his beliefs. We were friends. We opposed the military takeover. I was arrested first. I gave him away." He looks anguished, disbelieving of his treachery, his cowardice. "I knew where he was hiding."

His head goes down again as he goes on, his words coming in a torrent. "When they first took me in, they put me in a cell with a young man, one of our fighters - I did not know him - they had already tortured him for days. He knew he would die long before they killed him." He looks at us pleadingly, asking us to judge him, asking our forgiveness. He clears his throat and then goes on, his tone bitter. "After they had burned the soles off his feet, gouged out his eyes, all he could see, he told me, were his sons' faces when they told them their father was dead, his youngest not understanding why his father had gone forever, his wife moaning and trembling, her hands over her face. He gave no names – he would never give up his comrades to them – I could have told them that. But once the torture started, it would only finish when the torturers had had enough, when they'd shown the American how ruthless Greeks could be in eradicating the filth of Communism." He spits this out. He narrows his eyes, his bitterness and sadness smoldering.

"Once the torture had gone that far, then it was certain the man would die. He knew that. But when they took him from the car, his mouth was numb. He wet himself, the stain spreading and with it his shame, which he tried vainly to hide from the men he knew were watching and judging. I don't know for certain he knew that I was there, but I believe he did. They made me watch so I would know what they would do to me."

Mavros does not make eye contact with us now. He is immersed in his memory, in his need to tell us of his horror. He goes on. "His legs could not bear his weight and his shoes, loose without the laces they'd taken from him so he would not hang himself in his cell, made a trail in the dust as they dragged him to his place of execution on the wasteland behind the town's dump, beyond the first ridge of hills. As they pushed him to the ground, he tried to scramble away, slithering on his belly, his fingers clawing the sand. He knew it was no use of course, but I understood his wish to go to his death resisting them, not giving in. A boot on his back forced him down. All of this in silence. The American grinned, his eyes under his dark glasses, hidden. The man, his face pressed to the earth, would have felt the metal of the gun in his neck. The air went out of him. I thought I heard him groan, '*Eleftheria*', but this may have been what I wished, my prayer for him. Then the explosion, brief, discreet. His body went tense... *ena lepto*... and then he relaxed."

Mavros sighs. "The American shook a packet of cigarettes loose, placed one on his thin lips and offered the pack around. The executioner rolled out the tension from his neck and shoulders, (he executes the movement as he tells us this, his face severe) and took one. His men murmured, each accepted the gift. The American flicked his lighter open and a flame sprang up, the faces of the defenders of Greek purity were lit, as they leaned forward, like a Caravaggio, proud and mean. Then the American, exhaling a thick cloud of fragrant tobacco in my face, offered the pack to me. I am ashamed of it now as I tell you this, but although my hand was shaking, I took a cigarette and allowed him to light it for me." He looks searchingly, then pleadingly, first at me, then at Yianni.

"I have carried the ghost of that man on my back for nearly forty years. He never leaves me and I must not desert him. To do this, I must be a wandering spirit. This is how my debt is paid. Greeks, in all their wars, have said *Eleftheria i Thanatos*. Freedom or Death. There have been many wars. Many people died. Who is free? Am I free? You tell me."

He looks at us to receive our judgement. He goes on. "They said if I didn't tell them where Aris was, they would torture my son, Eleftherio. The boy was a child. I couldn't let that happen. I tried to kill myself in prison, but they would not allow me to die, they tortured me for the fun of it. Then they brought Eleftherio to me. I had to save him." There are tears in his eyes. "I *had* to."

Soulla brings the coffee and doughnuts. We sit in respectful silence. "Drink," Yiannis says softly, shifting a cup closer to Mavros.

Mavros picks up the cup and takes a sip. He puts the cup down carefully. "I found him. Eleftherios. I found him in the Soviet Union. Many years later, long after the Civil War was over. He was in an institution, a place for orphans. It was a terrible place. He didn't know me. He didn't know he had a father who was alive. I found him." He takes another sip of his coffee. Yiannis offers him a cigarette, but he waves this away.

"Eleftherios was born in the last year of the War in the Grammos Mountains. 1949. His mother was a soldier like me. Eleni. She gave birth in the snow. That was a terrible winter. We could hardly keep ourselves warm. But she kept him alive. He was so precious. We had lost so much. We knew we were defeated. The Government forces had the support of the Americans and the English. Stalin gave in. We got nothing. Our leaders took pity on the children. We had to send all our children out of the war zone – to the Soviet Union, some to Yugoslavia. Eleni was heartbroken. When she gave the child over to the authorities, it was like something already died in her. She was killed in battle two weeks later.

"I was one of the last in our battalion. Eventually we retreated. The government forces had closed off our escape route to Yugoslavia over the mountains. So we went the other way, to Bulgaria. We nearly died. We had no food. I had to tie my boots together with cloth. It was so cold. Eventually, we got across the border and were helped by the Bulgarian Army. From there we went to the Soviet Union. To Tashkent. That was where they sent us, the ones from Greece. The refugees.

"I tried to find news of Eleftherio, but nothing. They said he was probably in Yugoslavia. I worked hard and they found out I could cook. I learned from my mother. We made a Greek meal for a visiting General and he liked my cooking so much, he requested my transfer to the Soviet Embassy in London when he was posted there. I spent five years in London. I liked it there. Highgate, Hampstead Heath. But I never forgot my son. Eventually I got word that he was in Odessa, in an orphanage.

"So I gave up my job and went to fetch him. When I found him he was dirty and thin. Because he couldn't do what the other children of his age could do, they treated him badly. Like he was an animal. My boy. His face was like his mother – the shape, the nose and lips. But the eyes - they were my dark eyes. He was dark like me. They sent us back to Tashkent. A doctor friend helped us and Eleftherios started at a special school. He liked it there. I was working in a factory kitchen. As supervisor. It was a good job. We were taken care of.

"Then I heard through others that my mother was dying. 1960. I wasn't allowed back into Greece – there was still no amnesty for ELAS fighters. The Communist Party was still prohibited. But I had to see my mother. I had put her out of my mind. But being away so long, now having my son, being a father – I *had* to see her. So I crossed the border, with Eleftherio, back into Greece, ten years after I had been forced to leave. Of course I had no papers, not for myself and not for Eleftherio – we were illegal aliens. In my own country." His anger and affront still smolders.

"I did not know who in my village were supporters and who were traitors, so as soon as my mother died, I left. I went to Thessaloniki. I had names of people there who would help me, help us. I worked for Lambrakis. He was a good man. A politician, but for the people, not for himself. He got me papers, but for Eleftherio, this was not possible. Then Lambrakis got shot. I saw the men who killed my boss. The police came after me. We fled. We ended up on Mythos. My son and I. So much we went through.

"After the arrest and the torture, after they found Aris, my commander, and executed him too, they sent me to Macronissos – an island for all the 'political' prisoners, the ones who were the enemies of the Colonels. Maybe it would have been better if they'd killed me, like poor Aris. I was released from there when the Colonels fell in 1972. I should have come back for Eleftherio. But I was so ashamed. I thought Stavroula could look after him. Better for him not to have a father who was a coward. Now he is dead. How can I face my family now?" He looks distraught.

"I will come with you," Yiannis says. "You explain, like you explain now. They will forgive you, believe me." Yiannis pats Mavros on the shoulder. "They are your family. They show you only love, believe me." He goes on talking to his old friend reassuringly in Greek. Mavros nods sadly.

"I'd like to come with, if I may," I say to Yiannis.

"No," Yiannis says, "let him first say hello to his family. Later I will tell you what is happen."

He's right. This first greeting will be a particularly sensitive and emotional event. They won't want strangers. I'll go find Antonis and tell him the tumultuous news. Then I should write up Mavros's story for New World Order. What a story. A Homeric tragedy. "Revolutionary fighter returns from the dead to reclaim his son." Wonderful for his family. Or is it? But for me, a story like this dropping into my lap, especially if Marsha can get it syndicated, is a godsend.

It will buy me time to get to the bottom of what happened to Lucy.

38

Antonis is a bit disappointed that it was not advanced detective work that revealed the identity of the body in the bridge. Well, it's not confirmed yet, as Antonis points out grudgingly.

Together we go over to The Seaview. Agapi is serving a couple on the balcony. Antonis asks her, in a tone which is over-polite and self-important, to direct us to where the family is gathered. Agapi looks askance at the Inspector and makes a point of smiling at me, before taking us up to Michalis' residence above the restaurant.

Mavros is seated on a couch, looking downcast, with Stavroula at his side but a little apart, her back turned to him. The old lady is crying silently, the hardness in her face cracked open. What must she be feeling, seeing her husband returned from the dead? Michalis hovers, uncertain what to do and how to respond to a father he knew only as a toddler. The old man on his couch is a stranger. Only Xanthe is open with her affection. She strokes her Baba's hand and looks sympathetically at his handsome face. Mavros's eyes are empty. Yiannis stands with hands together over his crotch, uncomfortable, embarrassed even.

Antonis takes it all in and observes a moment's respectful silence. Then he catches Michalis' eye, clears his throat and strides forward to introduce himself to the old man. Mavros shakes the Inspector's hand without enthusiasm. Antonis uses his official tone to explain his presence. Mavros nods. Michalis announces that he and Nitsa will go and procure refreshments for all. Yiannis signals to me with his eyebrows and we go out together.

"Unbelievable," he says, "They were not even happy to see the old man. After all this time. Only the grand-daughter was excited. Poor Mavros." He shakes his head sadly.

We go next door to his establishment and Yiannis takes two bottles of beer out the cold cabinet. He pops them and hands me one. "I need a drink," he says and pours half the bottle down his throat in one go.

"Stavroula say she think Eleftherios was run away. After the Security Police take away Mavros, Eleftherios disappear. She say she think maybe they also take Eleftherios to Macronissos, to his father. But I know she lies. Must I tell to Mavro this? She did not care for the boy. He was scared from her. He was live in an old hut up in the hills there – for the one who looks after the goats. What is called?"

"Shepherd?" I offer.

"*Nai,*" he says, "Hut for the shepherd. I was take him food sometimes there. He was live like a wild animal. Dirty. He was not right in the head. I feel sorry. *And* Soulla. *We* feed him, me and Soulla. (Is he saying this to exonerate himself?) Stavroula, she no care. Only she care for Michali." He takes another swig of his beer. "Then one day, Eleftherios he was gone from the hut. We do not know what happen." He shrugs. "What to do? He was not my relation." He slaps his forehead. "But how I'm forget altogether Eleftherio? The poor boy."

So, what *did* happen to Eleftherio?

An hour later, I am sitting at my usual table, a second beer at hand, typing up a report to send to Marsha, when Antonis appears. He did not press Mavro to give him the whole story, but Mavros did say, straight out, that when Eleftherios was brought to him in the makeshift prison he was held in in Agia Sofia, where he was tortured, amongst the gang restraining Eleftherio and humiliating and frightening him to the extent that he wet himself, was Konstantin Garidis. Garidis will know what happened to the boy. Garidis will be brought in for questioning.

39

After I send off my report, I wait for Agapi with a cup of coffee for company. We will talk when she has finished the lunchtime shift. Michalis and his family have not come down. There is a waiter I have not seen before doing a shift. He is all sinew and bones, with a prominent Adam's apple and the kind of protuberant front teeth which suggests bad breath. But he is attentive and diligent. He takes his job seriously.

The heat of the day has gathered and there is electricity in the air. Towers of greying cloud on the horizon promise rain. "Rain later?" I say to the waiter as he collects my cup.

"Only for the sea. The rain will not come here. You can zwim later," he says without humour.

I watch the sea lapping lazily, giving itself up to the beach as if it's bored with its own fluidity, then relenting, withdrawing and coming in again, as full and as bored as it was before, the loss of water to the sand an illusion. Oh, Lucy, so much you had to give. What would we have been like together? Never to be. A wave of grief washes over me, an immense sadness, a pool of blackness, swirling turgidly, smoking grey, condensing into a blinding red and I am angry, frustrated - with myself for not saving her, with *her* for not being more careful, for the arbitrariness of Death. But Lucy's death was not arbitrary – someone was to blame. Someone has taken Lucy from me, robbed me of my time with her. Someone is going to pay.

Just after two p.m., Agapi collects her bag and we leave the restaurant together. She sees I am agitated and takes my hand as soon as we are outside. She looks at me, concerned. "Come back to my flat with me," I say hoarsely, urgently. I want to fuck her. I want to expel the fury I feel, the impotent rage burning in me.

She gives her Mona Lisa smile, amused by what she must see only as the urgency of my sexual arousal. "I have only little time to see my daughter and I must sleep. Tonight I work," she says, giving my hand a little squeeze of condolence.

"Please," I say, pleadingly, "Sleep with me. See Eleni, then come and sleep with me. Or come with me now and sleep later," I babble pathetically.

Agapi chuckles. "Okay, quickly," she says and leads me hurriedly next door and up to my flat, where I'm out of my clothes in a flash and she has her panties off, I don't even let her get her top off before I'm up inside her, she's so wet, I fuck her hard, I pull her hair, her back arches. In minutes it's over. She puts her panties back on with a small self-satisfied smile, pleased that she could rouse my passion to that degree; that she could make me come like a schoolboy. I flop onto the bed and let my perspiration evaporate pleasingly. Oh, God, the release... I whisper, "Thanks," as she leaves and as the door closes, "I love you. I think I love you," before drifting into a slowly undulating drowse. Oh, Lucy!

I dream of the swim I will have later, the water's surface smooth and wan, the only sound will be the lapping of the ripples my strokes make as I pull myself effortlessly forward. I am surrounded by soft, white clouds, reflected on the water and above me in the sky. I am alone, at peace. I do a languorous duck-dive and see the light through the water, before going further down into the grey-blue depths. Then, suddenly, I am being dragged down into a vortex. I kick and try to get back to the surface, but the harder I pull towards the light, the more *urgent* the force, which is dragging me down. Then I see her face, her red hair billowing. I am being sucked into Lucy's gaping mouth. The hollows of her eyes are being eaten at by crabs. My lungs are exploding. I can't hold my breath any longer. I have to breathe. The foetid water is in my mouth. I breathe it in.

40

The interview with Konstantin Garidis is arranged for ten the next morning. I get a ride into town with Antonis and his driver in the silver Merc. There is no news about Lucy yet, but the autopsy has been scheduled for later in the day. The Australian Ambassador has given his consent.

The interview with Garidis will happen in a back room, which is accessed through a locked door between the two cubicles in the Charge Office. Panagiotis's office is too small to fit us all in. The "interview room" is an antechamber to the holding cell behind. A small table has been set up in the middle of the room with four folding chairs arranged in front of and behind it. Garidis hasn't yet arrived. Panagiotis eyes me suspiciously, his concern for me after the attempt on my life (or was it just an accident?) now supplanted again by his resentment towards me for the report in the Greek tabloid. I have hurt him and his standing in the community, and he wants me to know it. Antonis and Panagiotis have a brief exchange, glancing at me, each in turn holding up a hand to dismiss the other's objections. I surmise that the Chief doesn't want me there and Antonis is saying, in effect, "He is with me. I am in charge." Antonis prevails, Panagiotis gives in by turning his head away from me and examining the graffiti left on the far wall by drunk or disgruntled citizens detained against their will.

The door behind us opens and Kosta announces the arrival of what our cops at home would term "the man who is helping the police with their enquiries". Konstantinos Garidis shuffles in, leaning heavily on his stick. He will want sympathy and an easy ride. He is followed in by a harried looking man in a badly-cut suit and crumpled tie. Is he the lawyer or a relative? From the formal manner towards him and the briefcase he carries, I presume he is the lawyer. His nervousness probably indicates he is not used to cases of this importance, with the national press involved and ready to take him down for any misstep. Panagiotis signals to Kosta, and moments later Kosta returns, transporting an ancient folding chair. He sneers at me as he plonks it down still folded and leaves me to unravel it. It hasn't been opened in years and I wonder if the intention is for me to fall flat on my arse. The smell of mould is effulgent as I open the canvas supports. I sit down tentatively.

The lawyer has placed his briefcase on the table and has extracted a ring-bound notebook from it. He wipes his face with a yellowed handkerchief, before writing a heading on his pad, underlining his writing twice and inserting a full-stop with alacrity. Antonis's measured, almost bored tone indicates he is telling Garidis his rights. This is the preamble. Garidis makes out he is having difficulty understanding (or is it hearing?) what he is being told. He looks to his lawyer, who gives him a non-committal response. Garidis shakes his head sadly, as if to say, "Why are you putting an old innocent man through this?" He wets his lips and fiddles with the head of his walking stick.

As the interview progresses, the old Fascist becomes more agitated, his voice rising an octave in protest, his fist drumming on the table to emphasise his mortification at the insult to his good name, his eyes wild with anger, flickering with fear, no vestige of his swagger of old. Antonis proceeds calmly. He is being systematic, logical, formal, but his politeness carries a whiplash, its sting unexpected and the more painful for it. Garidis' hapless lawyer makes notes and intervenes only once, appearing to concede the point to Antonis, who responds with patience and exactitude. Garidis' eyes fill with tears, his expression disbelieving, exasperated. He sits back in his chair and shrugs. There are a few more questions, to which he responds tersely. Then he and his lawyer get up and leave, the old man bent double over his stick, holding his hip and groaning pitifully at the pain he has been caused. We should, he thinks, be ashamed.

Antonis completes his notes and then looks to Panagiotis, who has sat, arms folded and impassive, throughout, for his response. Panagiotis says, "He knows more than he is say." Antonis nods. "But he said enough for now," Antonis says, before turning to me. "Okay, so this is what we have. He was present during the interrogation of Mavros Epistemos. But he says he knew nothing about the killing of Aris Lambros or the other ELAS prisoner. He reminded us that he said already Marvos was not executed. But he says he does not know what happen-ed to the boy, to Eleftherios. He thought he was return-ed to his mother, but maybe he was also sent to Macronissos – he would not know this – what happen-ed to the 'politicals' *after questioning* was above him. He just helped bring them in. He claims he knows nothing about how the body got into the bridge."

"Do you believe him?" I ask.

Antonis waggles his head. "Maybe."

Panagiotis chuckles. "No way," the Chief says, "How you believe a man like that?"

I agree with the Chief.

As we are leaving, I turn to the Chief. "Oh, can I ask you, did you find Lucy's scooter at the old harbour?"

Panagiotis looks bemused. "What is scooter?"

"A Vespa maybe?"

"She have?"

"Yes. I mean if she killed herself, she would have had to have driven to the old harbour, yeah?"

He gives this some thought. "We no find."

41

Unintended consequences. What can tangle, will tangle.

My article on the body in the bridge is taken up by the Greek media in a flash. It's even on the national television news. The tabloids mangle my story into a shape of their fancy. The headline in *Eleftherotypia*, the most widely circulated newspaper in Greece, translates as "Island of Shame".

Antonis is furious. He shakes the newspaper at me and prods his finger at a picture of himself on page three. He lets me know in no uncertain terms he is finished with me. He has helped me, he has given me access to every interview, he has been my friend. Now I have stabbed him in the back. "Inspector Antonis Ionides solved the case when the deceased handed himself in!" he translates angrily. "You say I wasted everybody's money, that I am a *stupid flatfoot*! Why am I on the island? Why was I sent here by my Department? – now also I am in trouble with my superiors. Why is this not a job for the *local* police? The newspapers ask, like it is a scandal that money is spent on finding the guilty parties from crimes of long ago."

I try to stop him, to explain that *my* report was not critical of him at all, that I didn't write anything about his investigation being a waste of public money. Not even close. But he is so angry, he does not hear me. He storms out. Damn, I was counting on *him* to help investigate Lucy's death. Doesn't sound like he is in the mood to do me any favours now or in the near future. I'm guessing I won't be getting privileged access to his investigation from now on. But, Jesus, it's a bit of an over-reaction – not even letting me explain. Is his anger also to do with Agapi, that she likes me more than him?

Okay, so now I'm on my own in ensuring the police draw the right conclusion in their investigation of Lucy's murder, that they investigate it properly. Well, fuck it! I've been on my own in the field before. Maybe it's better. This way, I don't owe anyone anything. I'm free to do what I like, to write what I like. That's actually *better*.

But I notice even Yiannis is cool towards me now. Kat finds it amusing – "You've stirred the shitpot, dude!" she laughs when she sees me. It seems I am being blamed for the bad feelings that has arisen between neighbours all over the island – between people who were on the Left against those who supported the Right, between those who wish to forget and those (I suppose like Calliope and her ilk) who say we must remember. As if I am to blame for it all. Talk about shooting the messenger…

Later in the day, I see what I'm up against if I'm to go on covering the body in the bridge story. The Greek press arrive in numbers, even a television crew arrives. I see from a distance a smartly dressed young woman with an oversized microphone interviewing Antonis. I'm not going to get a look in.

Among the horde, I notice Calliope and Nektarios. Nektarios is being his usual glum self. Calliope is expostulating to any journalist who will listen about the injustices the Left have had to suffer and why are there no statues to the Communist Party's fallen heroes? They have come on behalf of the Communist Party to welcome back one such of their fallen heroes, the esteemed Gregorios Epistemos, also known as Mavros. When Calliope sees me at my table at Yianni's later, she comes over to shake my hand. "You understand nothing, but you have put the story of our heroic struggle in the light. For that I thank you," she says grandly.

I invite them to sit with me. Bobby comes over and the venerable lady orders a beer for herself and for her husband, water – he is driving. Nektarios looks aggrieved, but says nothing.

"You know Mavros is ashamed of having given away his comrade? It's why he didn't return." I say tentatively.

"My young friend," she says, "what people give away under torture is not their fault. We don't judge him. He is still one of us. He suffered. He should also be rewarded," Calliope says. I am impressed by her humanity. Not a Stalinist then. "We told him this. He is welcome among us."

When her beer arrives, we clink our bottles and she agrees to an interview, for me to write a profile of her and her campaign to have a statue built to honour the Communist heroes of the struggle against fascism. "We will not forget," she says.

42

The next morning, early, I get a ride to the old harbour with Bobby. Yiannis heard I wanted to see where Lucy died and asked his son to take me. He will persuade Kat to cover for two hours. Breakfast is not a busy time. He and his family wish they could do more for me. He doesn't like what I've written about the island, but they can't help it - they are good people - they feel bad for me losing my friend.

After about twenty minutes on the road going north, we turn down a pot-holed road, which is more of a track - basically two furrows and a Mohican of weeds. The harbour has two jetties of cracked concrete, its sides protected by tractor tyres, grey with age and decorated with brushstrokes of green algae. The only building is, what was once a warehouse, now a rusted shell, the doors half-off their hinges. Concrete blocks and broken bricks lie in dissolute heaps, next to upturned oil drums, empty, now except for their echoes. The only sign of life is a single seabird, which flies off as soon as we park.

No scooter. I check the warehouse. A shaft of light beams hazily through a miraculously intact but dust-encrusted pane of glass in a high window. It illuminates an assortment of decrepit machinery and rotten planks of wood. The weeds have colonised the floor-space, paying little heed to the concrete which was meant to keep them at bay. No scooter here either. A rat scurries across the surface and into a dark corner and is gone.

Bobby and I scout around, but there is definitely no scooter to be found. Either she came here with the person who killed her, or she was killed elsewhere and her body deposited here by her killer.

I walk onto the jetty. With a heavy heart I look out at the water where Lucy was found. What happened here? There are no clues.

The surface of the water is smooth and at this early hour, silvered. The precise reflections of fat-bellied clouds could be a Renaissance painting, a religious epiphany. I remember what Lucy said about just such a reflection when we'd walked along the Lee - and feel for my beautiful and troubled Lucy: she'd found her way to Heaven.

43

After breakfast, Antonis seeks me out. He is contrite. He apologises for having judged me too severely. He has read my original article online and realises he was too hasty. Pride does not allow him to make a full apology and I don't press for one. I suspect the coverage he is now getting in the Greek press and on television has helped. He is famous. But it also means he no longer needs me for his publicity.

But what has he come to see me about really is to give me news about Lucy. He has the autopsy report. Because of the immersion, they can't accurately say when she died. But from the accretion of dust on the clothes she left behind, this was probably at least three weeks before she was found. But this was a very rough estimate. What the pathologist has said with more certainly is that Lucy had extensive bruising to her neck and face. The marks on her neck suggest she was held from behind with some force and the scatter of the bruises suggest she would have struggled with her assailant. She also had abrasions and bruising on both knees. It could be she was hit in the face to subdue her, forced onto her knees and then held under water and drowned. Her lungs contained a high concentration of a rust red algae (they are still waiting for further analysis on this) and of rabbit fish spores, neither found in the water of the disused harbour where she was found. The conclusion is that she was killed elsewhere and her body tied to a concrete block and dumped in the disused harbour. So I was right. "They are still examining under her nails for human tissue for DNA, from her struggle. Maybe…" He trails off. Then quickly, "I'm sorry," he says, "this is a terrible death."

Red algae and rabbit fish spores – the Poseidon. Has to be. In my mind I see the red slick in the sea off the lagoon; I see the windswept rocky beach - was that where she was murdered? I blurt this out to Antonis. He holds up a hand to slow me in my tracks. "You must discuss this only with Panagiotis. I am now only busy with the case of the body in the bridge. This is now a big story in Greece and to get me back my good name I must solve this case. You understand? We have the list of workers from the cement factory and the construction companies – I have to make interview with lots of peoples. Panagiotis is now dealing with your friend's murder."

I see he will brook no argument. But can't he see this should be investigated by someone *independent*? Maybe Radagast and Jurgen Preissler are still the chief suspects, but if Lucy was killed on the beach at the Poseidon, then the politicians, the police or the developers could all be involved. Christos must know more. Surely. Well, let's see what Panagiotis says. Maybe he'll surprise me.

But the Chief doesn't surprise me. "My friend, why should I trouble Christos Papademos? He is important man on this island. Maybe she was kill-ed where you say. How can we know this? And so? I am looking still for Jurgen Preissler. Maybe he kill-ed her on the beach. Preissler is Suspect Number One. Until he will show me he is not the guilty one, it is him I am look for. Christos? – no. Why he kill her? She was help him."

"We only have his word for that," I say, knowing already I won't persuade him.

"For me, his word is enough. You want me to question the Mayor, Nikos?" he snorts derisively. "Our Mayor is good man. What I ask him? Nikos, you kill Miss Discombe? Ha!"

"No, but…" What's the point? I have no evidence. I, myself, am not even sure what or who to believe. But is it right to believe without evidence, other than Christos's word, that Lucy agreed to do his bidding for money? What if he's lying? What if she *said* she agreed, but was double bluffing, playing him, to get information from him? Is it right for the police to have only the *one* suspect? Would Erica von Strondheim really have had Lucy murdered just to stop her publishing a report favourable to the Poseidon, if indeed that was what Lucy was going to do? Why would it have meant so much? Hubris? That's a bit much, isn't it? At least they should question Christos Papademos, shouldn't they? Maybe one of his construction workers saw something?

"Panagiotis," I say, trying to sound my most reasonable and patient best, "surely the police should at least check if the red algae in her lungs are anywhere else on the island, and if so, whether there is a high concentration of rabbit fish spores there too? Are there any other construction sites which use the Egyptian cement, for example?" I ask.

I hear Panagiotis's deep sigh on the other end. He too is trying to sound reasonable. "My friend, perhaps the Municipality can tell you this. It is only me and three other policemen for the whole island. Two big investigations. Journalists. What we can do? We don' give parking tickets no more. We too busy!" I can see his ironic smile. "If you want, you ask the Municipality. I don't have the time for this. I'm look for Jurgen Preissler. For me, he will tell us who kill your friend. No need for me to waste my time with fish." I can hear he is itching to terminate the call.

"Mmm, okay," I say, after a pause. "I will do my own enquiries."

"Good," he says. "Have a nice day to you." He puts the phone down.

Fuck you too, Panagiotis, I think, as I disconnect.

44

Okay, I'm an investigative journalist – I can do this. First, let me see what I can get on the algae and the rabbit fish on this coastline. Maybe the Municipality *can* help. I presume, somehow, that they will be inefficient and unhelpful. But let's see if they can confound my expectations. I shouldn't be too hard on the Chief. Panagiotis *is* working with very few resources and little back-up.

I get a ride into Agia Sofia with Bobby. He's a cool kid. I like him. We listen to Guns and Roses on the ancient cassette player. His taste, not mine.

"How's it going with Xanthe?" I ask, being a bit snide, I know.

He gives me a quick sideways glance before going back to concentrating on the winding road. "Okay," he says, without conviction. "What has my sister been saying?"

"Nothing," I say, but my grin gives me away.

"She's just jealous of Xanthe," he says and turns the volume on the cassette player up. "This conversation is over, bro," he says over the music.

The Municipal offices are dark and gloomy, but the coolness is welcome. I explain as best as I can to a woman at Customer Services that I need information about the coastal water around the island. I try to sound as neutral and academic as I can, so as not to alarm her into resistance. She nods, writes something in her log and goes off to speak to a colleague who may be able to help me. She comes back a short time later with a serious-looking young man, mid-twenties I guess, dressed in an open-necked white Polyester shirt and black trousers, creased to precision like a knife-edge.

"Yes, can I help you? I am the Environment Officer. Tsammis Grissos," he offers me his hand. His accent has a North American inflection. "Sam, if you can't manage Tsammis," he says with a sly smile.

I shake his hand. "Canadian?" I ask.

He grins broadly. "How did you know? Most people say 'American'. I hate that. Thanks for noticing," he says pleasantly.

I explain what I am after. I don't tell him about the autopsy and he doesn't ask. He takes me into his office, which is no bigger than an average stationary cupboard and taps some keys on his computer. "I'm trying to go paperless," he says, looking at the screen which has lighted up with maps and diagrams. "You're not the first journalist to be interested in environmental degradation on Mythos," he says.

Shit, why didn't I think to enquire here before? Of course Lucy would have thought to check out the local Environmental Officer. I didn't even think there would be one. "You met Lucy Discombe?" I ask cautiously.

"Sure," he says, not taking his eyes of the screen. "We were partners in crime," he says and sneaks me a naughty look. "Well, not *actual* crime. But we saw things the same way."

"Christos Papademos at the Poseidon said she'd changed her tune, that she was going to write a report favourable to them," I tell him.

Tsammis scoffs. "No way! Lucy? No way," he says. "She had all this stuff on rabbit fish breeding and algal overgrowth and unsustainable water supply to the lagoon. No way."

I feel my goose-bumps rising, and it wasn't just from the coldness of this office. "Do you by any chance know Jurgen Preissler?" I think to ask.

"Jurgen's a friend. He stayed with me recently," Tsammis says nonchalantly.

I swallow. "Do you know the police are looking for him in connection with Lucy's murder?"

He looks at me sharply. "Lucy is dead?"

Fuck, I'd assumed he would know. But maybe a geek like him doesn't follow the news. "She was overpowered and drowned. The police think Jurgen did it."

"No ways!" he says incredulously. "Lucy dead? Jurgen loved Lucy – well, not romantically – Jurgen is gay. But as a friend, a fellow eco-warrior. No way could he have overpowered Lucy. She was much bigger and stronger than him. Jurgen is puny!"

"He is called the Enforcer," I point out.

"That's because he knows so much about environmental law. He's German – you know, pedantic. A 'letter of the law' kind of guy. He ties officials in knots. They're terrified of him!"

"He's killed before," I remind him.

"The poor guy had to have *years* of psychoanalysis to get over his guilt at those workers dying in the fire. He never *meant* to kill anybody. Trust me, the guy is harmless," Tsammis says.

Yeah, well, you are his friend, I think, so you are biased. Is Tsammis gay? Was Jurgen his lover? I search his face for clues, but I don't even know what I'm looking for. What if he is right? I have never seen a photo of The Enforcer. Have I just fanaticised a burly square-headed juggernaut killer because he's German and called The Enforcer? Am I biased against Radagast because I have a deep-seated prejudice against aristocrats and women with fake accents? Does Panagiotis know what Jurgen looks like, that he is "puny"? Has he been leading me on?

"I'm so sorry about Lucy," Tsammis says. "She was great. I liked her very much."

"Thanks," I say, needlessly. "I'm trying to find out what happened. What have you got on the algal growths and the rabbit fish distribution along the coast?"

He looks back at the screen and taps some more keys. "Okay, so look here. A satellite photo. Infra-red. The only place with any density of the algal growth is off the lagoon. And," he taps another key and the picture changes, "the only place where the rabbit fish are congregating are at the Poseidon beach and on the very southern tip of the island." He taps the keys again and sits back. "But the only place they co-occur is near the lagoon, near the Poseidon."

As I thought. I could kiss him, but I don't. In case he *is* gay and gets the wrong idea. "Thank you so much, Tsammis. I'm going to have to buy you a drink," I say, offering him my hand.

"We'll drink to Lucy," he says.

45

I ride back with Bobby to Agia Anna in a better mood than I've been in since Lucy's body was found. I feel as if I'm doing something for her; I'm getting somewhere. I feel... *effective*. I feel less guilty. I ponder whether to reveal my new information to Panagiotis. The evidence is inferential and Panagiotis will be sure to rubbish it – he is fixated on getting his German arch-villain. I need something more. If only we knew who had, or could find, Lucy's laptop. And where is Lucy's scooter? I should check all the rental agencies in Agia Sofia. Maybe Panagiotis has thought of this already – I should check with him.

My phone goes. I am surprised to see it is Marsha calling from London. That's unusual – normally she is rigorous about cost saving and would e-mail me. Must be urgent. "Hello, Marsha," I say in a debonair voice, "to what do I owe this pleasant surprise?"

As soon as I hear her desperate tone, I wish I'd not answered the call and let it go to voicemail. "Oh, Tom, you *have* to come back! I'm at the end of my rope. Eric has gone off sick." She almost says the inverted commas aloud. Then she corrects her tone. "Well, he has appendicitis – he's in the Royal Free. Apparently it was touch and go. But now he's going to be off for *a month*! I'm all alone in the office and I can't keep up. You only had two weeks leave. You've used that up now, as of today, right? I can't extend your leave. You *have* to come back. I'm up to my eyeballs with the Labour leadership election and the IRA decommissioning and I need you to cover the international stories – two big ones – the Israelis pulling their settlers out of Gaza and here's one close to your heart, the very first gas and oil exploration in the Arctic – the Norwegians are about to start drilling in their Snohwit (I think that means Snow White) field north of Hammerfest in the Arctic Circle. Greenpeace are going in. Maybe you could go in with them? Use your contacts." A pause. "Or on second thought, scrub that – I need you here. Maybe just use interviews with your contacts, you know live-and-direct," she says, trying to talk up what will probably be following someone else's story from a distance.

"But I haven't finished my work here," I say, deflated. Marsha is pig-headed and self-serving when she wants to be, which is, like, *usually*. *She* likes to call it "single-minded".

"The body in the bridge story has gone viral. You did well to break it. But now the big news agencies are on to it. They'll cover it better that we can. They have the resources and the contacts. They have people who speak Greek, for Christ's sake. We're a small outfit. I don't need you to be on the ground there. I need you here," she says, trying to make it sound like that's a *good* thing.

"There have been developments in the Lucy Discombe case too," I say.

"Oh, yeah. What?"

When I try to formulate this in words, I realise that nothing much has changed – not substantially. All I've got to go on is inferential. "It's a big story," I squeal. "Circumventing environmental regulation, degrading coastlines, threatened species…"

"It's old news," Marsha says tartly.

"It's happening now!"

"It's been said before. Its stuff people know about. It doesn't have traction. It doesn't have *leverage*. It's *boring!"*

"Marsha, once an environment is ruined, it stays that way. When a species is eradicated, it doesn't come back," I say in as level a tone as I can manage.

"Fuck, Tom, who do you think you're talking to? It's not *the issue* – it's the *story*. It's nothing new."

"Killing environmental activists isn't newsworthy? Not a good enough story?"

"Tom, you've got nothing that conclusively proves your friend didn't just go crazy and kill herself. That's not a story. At least it's not a story that should keep you there, not here."

"She didn't kill herself. She had bruises on her face and neck. Her body was moved!"

"You don't know that for sure…"

"Yes, I do! It could be a rival environmental outfit. It could be a conspiracy."

"Tom…" I can almost hear her sigh.

"Just give me a few more days… a week," I say. I know I am losing the argument. But I need to be here to get Lucy's murder solved.

"You have until after the weekend. Three days. Book your flight. I expect you at your desk on Monday morning," my editor says with finality. She, who must be obeyed.

"Yeah, okay," I concede, hoping my dispirited tone will make her feel guilty.

"Right," she says, not guilty at all, "I thought you would see it my way."

46

There is also Agapi. I recognise that she is one of the reasons I don't want to leave the island yet. I feel so attracted to her, and almost... am I imagining it? - a *spiritual* bond? What do I want? Am I just using her as a salve to the open wound of my grief? Or is it my *destiny* to meet a Greek woman, to find the Greek in me through her? Is she *the one*? I have three days to decide.

As soon as we get back I go looking for her. She is not at the Seaview. It is after two p.m. The humourless stand-in waiter tells me Agapi has gone home to sleep. I walk quickly over to her house. Short, assertive strides, my sandals snagging in the pebbled road not once, but three times, and I get a thorn in my foot! This does nothing for my mood.

Agapi is not asleep. She is helping her mother hang up washing on a line. She smiles when she sees me approaching and comes to meet me. Her mother watches her with narrowed eyes. Agapi holds out her hands to me and we kiss, discretely, on both cheeks. She picks up on my serious mood. "Come," she says and we walk down to the beach below her house.

"Please sleep with me tonight, in my bed, the whole night. I want to wake with you next to me in the morning. Your mother can look after Eleni," I say.

She looks at me quizzically. "Why?"

"I have to go back to London soon. My work..."

She nods. A little frown clouds her face. "What is happen with us?" she says and then looks out to sea. A wave crashes and foams. "Yesterday, when you fuck me so quick, you was think of her, the one who was killed. *Nai*?" Agapi says.

Is she right? In my subconscious, was it Lucy I was fucking so violently?

She takes the absence of a response as affirmation. She nods sympathetically. "And also, you didn't have on..." She shows me with a hand over an extended finger. I was so turned on, I didn't use a condom. Stupid.

"I'm sorry," I say regretfully.

She waves away my apology. "It was nice feeling. I like-ed. But after, I worry. I think, you not going to stay on the island. You will go back to your home and to your family. If I get… with child…" She trails off. "I don' want to look after two children without a father for them." She folds her arms across her chest like a shield against the cold. "If you stay, is different." She turns to look at me sympathetically. She is also sad for herself. "You would stay for me?"

I look to the churning water. Would I stay? What do I really know about her? She is a poor waitress from a small Island in Greece, with a limited education and experience of the world which for her extends as far as the next bigger island. She has a child. She has a mother she looks after. What do we have in common? On paper, this relationship has nothing going for it. But I know my heart. Or do I? I *feel* love for her. I am *in* love. Am I being blinded? Am I vulnerable because I have lost my dream of Lucy? I have lost Lucy – is Agapi just a convenient replacement, a transitional girlfriend? - because she cares, because she is a comfort?

"I don't know," I say softly and the wind carries away my words. We stand in silence. Then I blurt out, "Come to London with me."

Agapi snorts. "What I do in London?" she scoffs. "I have here my mother and my child. Mythos is place I know, is *all* what I know. Why I must leave?" She smiles wistfully. "My mother she say to me, 'Take shoes from your own place, even if they need mending.' Is mean is better to take a man from your village. *Me katalavenis?* If you stay, maybe is different." She looks at me intently, her squiggled frown ironic? Playful?

I have to look away. I am in danger of falling, I am so taken with this woman's casual beauty.

When I do look back at her, she still has her eyes on me. Agapi nods, seriously. "It is for you to decide." She lifts herself on tiptoes to gives me a kiss on the cheek, then turns and walks slowly back to her mother, who is watching her all the way.

47

The sun has gone down. I play with the *stifado* Yiannis has put in front of me. He is very proud of his wife's pork and bean stew and I'm probably hurting their feeling by not tucking in with relish. But I haven't the heart for it right now.

What should I do about Agapi? I know the answer I will reach eventually when I've played with my feelings enough, churned myself through the washing machine. Washing cycle set to Fragile item. I am such a coward. I am so stuck in my ways, like I'm middle-aged already. Is it the security of the known I can't give up? Do I fear uncertainty so acutely? Yet I know I can be more than I am. I *want to be* more than I am. Has Agapi been sent to me by my father's spirit to help me find my Greek self? Would he want me to marry a Greek woman, to bring him home, to keep alive the name of Xanakis?

But changing who I am also means giving stuff up – to live here on this island, I would have to give up my flat, my neighbourhood (as smelly as it's become), my local, BBC Radio Four, Sadler's Wells, the Tate Modern, the view of the Thames embankment from Waterloo Bridge, the friends I have (although most of them are wankers), the familiarity of places I went to as a child... Fuck, I am so sentimental! Or is it risk-averse? Self-protective? If only I were brave, more *adventurous*.

I suppose coming *here* was adventurous, although I didn't know it then. But what have I *achieved?* I came to find Lucy, but I wasn't the one who found her. I didn't rescue her. I didn't *save* her. I have made enemies of people on the island I would like to have had as friends. I've stirred up a hornet's nest. I've made their lives more fraught. And for what? Where will it lead? Okay, I found Agapi, but if I'm honest, I've probably infused my image of her with naïve and self-serving fantasies. Anyway, what have we got together? - what *will* it come to? - probably nothing. As usual. I'm such a loser. And with Lucy's murder? - I haven't been much help. I suppose I *did* press for the autopsy, I think I've pinned down the murder scene to the beach at the Poseidon and I've probably got an innocent man, Jurgen Preissler and the dubious NGO he works for, off the hook. But what does this add up to? - practically *fuck all!*

And what make me so sure that I *have* got Jurgen Preissler a reprieve from a miscarriage of justice? Fuck, I don't even know for sure that Jurgen Preissler *isn't* involved. I should have asked the Environmental Officer if he had a photo of Jurgen Preissler – is he as puny as the Canadian Greek guy described? What was his name? – Tsammis. What if Tsammis is his lover and is protecting him? He could be in on it also? Even if he is not, he wouldn't be the first person to be taken in by a charming psychopath.

My phone rings with strident presumptuousness and startles me out of my self-hating reverie. It's Panagiotis. His officers have just arrested Jurgen Preissler.

They found him holed up in a disused farmhouse on the south of the island. They have taken him to the police station to be questioned. The Chief is very pleased with his catch and I can hear him waiting for my congratulations.

He is not pleased with my saying, with fierce sarcasm, "Oh, so this gangster killer you've been chasing, he's a huge muscle-bound guy who *could possibly* have overpowered Lucy Discombe, is he?" Fuck his feelings – I'm in a bad mood.

There is a pause, before he comes back at me, "Who you talk to? Who gives you this informations? Maybe is zmall, but is very strong. It was take three policemens to hold him down when we arrest him," he says with a calmness which is a slick over his anger at my grudging response.

"I have evidence that Lucy was killed on the beach at the Poseidon," I say, not to be defeated so easily. "You should at least interview Christos Papademos. The water in her lungs in the autopsy matches the contents of the water in the sea off the Poseidon – the algae are the same, the rabbit fish spores…"

He cuts me off, openly angry now. "Mr Pickering, don' tell me how I must do my job. I have found the man who was kill your friend. You no thank me for this? This Jurgen is a friend for you? When we find him, he say he won't come with us, he run away, he *fight* us – this is the behaviour of an innocent man? Leave Christos Papademos out of this. Also, don't make trouble with the Mayor. You have already, with your reporting, made our island look like a bad place for tourists. You have point your finger at innocent peoples. You think we will say thank you? Maybe, Mr Pickering, it is time for you to leave the island." He puts the phone down. The after-burn of his anger crackles and hisses in my ear.

48

Maybe he is right and maybe he is wrong. But I do know that the Chief of Police will protect his friends, like the Mayor and men of influence, like Christos Papademos. What's more, if there is one thing people who know me will know, it is that *I don't like being told what to do*, and as a journalist, I certainly don't like being told what to write and what not to write. I'm practically allergic. I'm *contrary*. If someone tells me where *not* to look, that's the first place I am going to look. As an investigative journalist, that's in my DNA. Especially when I am in bad mood. This year, 2005, has been a record-breaker for hurricanes. Global warming kicking in. My mood is building into a category five shit-storm. I feel like doing damage, something for people to remember me by. My own carbon footprint.

So, of course, the first thing I do after the call from the Police Chief, is to get on the phone to Christos Papademos. "Christos Papademos," comes his smooth voice.

"It's Tom Pickering," I say evenly.

"Oh, Tom, I've been meaning to phone you. Sorry to hear about Lucy," he says, sounding sorry.

I don't get suckered into mutual condolences. I go straight in. "I've been doing some digging, Christos, and from what I've found and with the autopsy report, it seems to me highly likely that Lucy was killed on the beach near the Poseidon."

"No ways!" he comes straight back at me. "I keep a close eye on whatever goes on around here. I'd heard something. Somebody would have seen something."

"That's why I'd like to interview your construction workers. Maybe jog their memories," I say. (Maybe my hostility is making me involuntarily threatening. I should rein myself in a little.)

"Maybe you should leave any enquiries to the police. I don't want you bothering my workmen, especially after what you've written about us so far. Fuck it, Tom, that wasn't on. I was nice to you. I was helpful. You chose to rubbish everything I said. Made me out to be some sort of an *uber*-capitalist scumbag! That was not cool, dude."

"I write it how I see it," I say.

He picks up the self-righteousness in my tone. "Who the *fuck* do you think you are? You fucking journalists! You're so *arrogant!* You don't take any responsibility for the shit you write. I have responsibilities. People's livelihoods depend on me and me making a go of this place. Lots of people. You only think of yourself. You English – you still think you're the centre of the world, like you've still got all your colonies. You treat us Greeks like we're a Third World banana republic. It's fucking insulting, dude. It's not like you've got a Pulitzer Prize. I looked up the rag you write for. Got a circulation of a few hundred?"

"A *regular* subscription of nearly *eight* hundred," I correct him. "We sell more than that." I could tell him about our online readership - but fuck him! Why should I have to justify myself?

"Call me a liar…" he says sarcastically. "You're small fry! You don't even register!" I hear his heavy breathing. "Look, it's not like I don't care about what happened to Lucy. I cared about her too. I'm upset about her death too. But you're on a mission to fuck things up for everyone else, to have someone *else* to blame, because *you* didn't look after her like a friend should. Tell me if I'm wrong, you wanted to fuck her too. You're jealous because *I* fucked her and *you* didn't. Right?"

He notices my hesitation. "I'm right, aren't I? Well, don't fuck up my business because of *your* sexual… *inadequacies*. Go back to London. See a shrink," he snarls, "Or get your cock enlarged."

"Fuck off, you… you… toe-rag!" is the best I can manage. ("Toe-rag"? I haven't used that phrase since I was fourteen!)

He is quite within his rights to put the phone down on me and that is what he does. I wanted to put the phone down on *him*, the prick! What makes me especially cross is that he was right about everything he said. But why should I let that stop me? I can be right about things too.

He definitely wants to keep me away from his workers. I don't buy this, "I don't want them bothered" shit. There is something he doesn't want me to find out. He protested too hard and too long. He is trying to scare me off. So what's he hiding? I can't rely on the local constabulary to find out. I'm going to have to go to the Poseidon myself.

49

I manage to persuade Bobby to lend me his car. Well, I hire it from him. He pockets the twenty euros with a smile. I don't tell him where I am going. I'm not in the mood to trust anyone and I don't want Christos to get a warning that I am on my way. Stealth is the key.

There is an almost full moon up in the zenith, which is just as well, because I shall have to go the last kilometre or so downhill on a winding road with a sheer drop to the sea, with my headlights off. If I crash Bobby's car, I won't have any insurance. This could be a very expensive fun-fair ride.

But when I get to the crest, with the lights of the Poseidon in the valley, the moonlight is more than enough. I shut of the engine off and freewheel all the way down, very slowly. My foot is on the brake most of the time and I worry Christos might see the brake light. But I reassure myself, from the side all he'll see is just a single red light – he'll probably think it's a bike or a conscientious walker. I roll the car into a siding just before the entrance to the resort. I shut the door quietly. The only sound is the sea, the waves rolling in and crashing gently with a whoosh and the crackle of pebbles as the water shifts them up the beach… and then back, as the sea recedes. The cicadas click insistently at the moon.

I keep to the shadows. There are lights on in the entrance and around the back in the kitchen area. Are there staff who live in there yet? I'd better keep my eyes alert for some chef having a crafty smoke out the back. I don't see any security guards. I creep around the side and try to work out which is Christos's office. There are no lights on here. I presume Christos has a place in town. Is the place alarmed? I look around for tell-tale CCTV cameras. I see one perched on a pole, but there are wires running out of it into thin air – not connected yet. They must think there isn't enough to steal. Besides, there can't be much petty crime in this area anyway. There are only four cops on the whole island.

I try a side door cautiously. I turn the handle and gently push. It opens. I slip into a short passage. White neon comes from a corridor leading off this one at the top of a short T. I wait and listen. Nothing. I tiptoe to the corner and peak around. The corridor is empty. Unless I am mistaken, this is the corridor that Christos's office is on. I advance. I'm right. This is his office. I try the door. It's open. Luckily, they're a trusting lot! I enter and close the door silently behind me.

I use the flashlight on my phone to see my way. The moonlight coming in through the far window helps. The bookshelves are still empty. The drinks cabinet is well-stocked - eccentric bottles, tumblers and wine glasses glint as the beam from my torch touches them. To one side of the office, leather chairs, a low coffee table with magazines tastefully scattered and behind that, the imposing desk. I walk quickly to the desk – let me try that first. I slide into Christos's swivel-chair and gently ease out the left top drawer. Papers – receipts mainly it seems. I can tell by the numbers – I realise this is going to be hard, given that I can't decipher the Greek letters. The next drawer is just pens and clips and shit. The bottom drawer is locked. Do I force it? Let me first examine the drawers on the other side of the desk. The top drawer is empty. As is the middle drawer. I'm expecting the bottom drawer to be locked, but it slides open.

There, lying quietly, is a thirteen-inch MacBook Pro. On its front is a Greenpeace sticker. It's Lucy's laptop.

I can hear my heart thudding in my chest. I place the laptop very carefully on the desk. I open the lid and press Power. A slight hesitation, then the Apple icon… and the blare of the opening clarion! Fuck! I instinctively shield the computer with my body. Fat lot of good that will do to cushion the sound. My heart is racing. I wait to hear footsteps. Nothing. All is quiet. The screen opens.

There it is: the confirmation, if I needed any. The Users' boxes: 'Lucy' and 'Guest'. I click on 'Lucy', hopefully. A box appears, asking for a password. What the fuck was the cat's name? What does it matter? This is Lucy's computer and it's in Christos's desk. I think I've found Lucy's killer.

Then, suddenly, the glare of harsh white office lighting. My heart tumbles in my chest as I look up and there is Christos, looking startled, his hand still on the light switch. He's caught me in the act. My mind immediately races to excuses, apologies, before I realise that he's seen that I have Lucy's laptop open and he's probably shitting himself. *I'm the one who is in the right here.*

Christos's expression has changed from surprise to fear, then it shifts again – now he is enraged, a cold malevolence. I have the evidence. He will be desperate to keep me quiet. I look around for a weapon, something to protect myself if he comes for me. The drinks trolley. I dart from the desk to the trolley in a flash and I grab the first bottle I see. A Talisker Dark Storm. Expensive. The right shape for a weapon. I grab the bottle by the neck and hold it like a club.

Christos crouches into a battle pose, arms out. "You've got this wrong, Tom," he says in a low voice. "Don't make me hurt you," he says, as he angles off crab-wise to one side, keeping his distance, his eyes fixed on me. Is he a martial arts expert? I suddenly wonder. His father was CIA. I've seen this in a movie before – a bar-room brawl, the protagonist suddenly vulnerable, the antagonist leering. What did he do? Harrison Ford, was it? I smash the bottle against the rim of the desk and I'm left with the neck of the bottle in my hand, a shard of razor-sharp glass extending out from it. I see Christos's face drop and he looks frightened, then he tries to bluff. But I'm one step ahead and I step boldly towards him. The look of fear reappears and he backs off, hands in front of him to protect himself. From me. Power surges into me, and with it, a cold anger. "You *cunt!* You've got Lucy's computer. You killed her, didn't you, you cunt?!" It's my turn to snarl.

"No, no," he protests. "Tom, listen to me. Kosta brought the laptop here. I didn't know what to do with it." He has backed himself up against the wall. He can see I mean business. "Kosta, the young cop. You know which one – Panagiotis's son. Yeah?" he squeals, imploring me. "I wouldn't have hurt her. I was *in love* with her. I've never had better sex with anybody. I swear it. We were having a great time. She was going to write up our eco-tourism angle. Why would I want her dead?" he implores me. "Believe me," he pleads. He is shit-scared I'm going to cut him, to ruin his handsome features. He isn't going to bullshit me and get me riled up, is he?

"Why did Kosta bring the laptop to you then?" I ask him.

"Okay, I'll admit it. My father was worried about what she was up to. He's still head of the company. He won't let anything get in the way of the family business. I run this project, but it's for the family, for the company. He has put up all the money, leaned on the politicians, got straight things to bend. He employed Kosta to keep an eye on her. Okay, I was in on it too, I don't deny it. But just *to keep an eye on her*! When she first came. Before I'd even met her. We'd heard she was investigating the Poseidon. We didn't know what she would find, what she would say. We wanted to be one step ahead. But then I met her and I was knocked out by her. She's... she *was*..." he says with a catch to his voice, "... my *type*, you know – athletic, sassy... and God, she was so beautiful! And so young!" His voice cracks. "Then she fell for me too. When she left and I didn't hear from her, I was so let down. I was torn apart." I know what that feels like, I want to tell him, but don't. "Then a few days ago, Kosta arrived with her laptop. Said he'd taken it – to try get into it, see if there were any incriminating photos – of him, of me! What the fuck was he thinking? He said we could see what she was writing about the Poseidon, if she'd changed her mind again. He'd watched her with her computer before - he knew her password. But the files on the Poseidon were encrypted. Then when her body was found, he didn't want to keep it at his place anymore – worried his father would ask questions – he lives with his dad still. So he brought it to me. Said maybe I'd want to keep hold of it. I don't know why he didn't just get *rid* of it. I don't know why *I* didn't." He lets out a sob. "Oh, fuck!" he says.

"Why did he take Lucy's *hoodie*? Did he know where she was?" I ask.

"The hoodie wasn't hers. It was his. He'd left it there. He'd thought someone would trace it back to him."

How would Christos have known that? "How do you know that?"

"He told me. He was like seriously anxious, you know... like when he brought the laptop to me. Lucy's body had just been found and he was worried people would think it was him."

Then a thought strikes me. "So, who e-mailed me? Did you?" I ask Christos.

"E-mail? No," he says, "What e-mail?"

Mmm, Christos would have been smarter, more flamboyant. The e-mails have Kosta's scent. He can see I am starting to believe him. His voice becomes more measured. "I think Kostas knows who killed her," he says quietly.

"Who?"

"I don't know. He didn't say. I just got the feeling he knew more and wasn't saying."

"Why didn't you report this?"

"Well, because I could have been implicated myself. I didn't know what to do. Put yourself in my position, Tom."

I can see that.

"We should talk to him, you and me together," Christos says. "Don't go to the cops – to his father – he'll just clam up – he'll deny everything. Let's get him here and see what he says."

I suddenly feel weary. It's the adrenaline going out my body. I just want this thing over now. "Okay," I say, "Phone him. But keep it simple. Don't give him a warning, I know enough Greek to know if you are warning him off," I bluff. I keep the broken bottle, my weapon, pointed towards him and signal for him to go to the desk, to the phone.

"I want this sorted out too," he says, moving slowly to the desk, his hands held out where I can see them. He reaches for the phone.

I watch his expression as he gets Kosta on the phone and speaks to him in a serious tone. He keeps his eyes on me. His voice is what I would expect it to be – urgent, commanding and persuasive. He keeps it brief. He puts the phone down. "He's coming," he says.

I exhale. I am relieved. Christos is looking at the weapon in my hand. "That was very expensive bottle of Scotch," he says wistfully.

"Sorry," I mumble.

"I think we both need a drink," he says and walks past me to the row of bottles, examines them, chooses a squat bottle and pours us each two fingers. I take the glass he offers me, but I don't let go of my weapon. Just in case he changes his mind. He goes behind his desk and sits in his usual chair and looks at Lucy's screen. "So, do you how to get past the encryption?" he asks with a faint smile.

"I don't even know her password," I tell him.

"There weren't even any photos of her," he says sadly. "She was amazing."

I sit down and sip my whiskey. It is full and smoky with peat, a dark earthy taste that burns and then explodes into an effulgent warmth. A hint of vanilla in the afterglow. I nod my appreciation and lift my glass. "To Lucy," I pronounce.

"To Lucy," Christos intones.

After that, we drink in contemplative silence. We wait.

50

About twenty minutes later, I hear the growl of a motorbike coming down into the valley. Christos hears it too, and abruptly there is a change in him - a quickening of his movements, a gleam that suddenly appears in his eye that catapults me out of my torpor into a state of hyper-alertness. Fuck, this is a trap! "What?" Christos asks, opening a smile which is meant to be reassuring. But it is too pat. I see it for what it is – the smile is *sardonic*.

I jump up. "You fuck! You've set me up!" I shout. And I suddenly see it all. Kosta will have a gun. They'll kill me and say Christos heard an intruder and called Kosta.

Christos puts on a look of surprise, a hurt look. "No," he says, "You've got it wrong."

No, I haven't. Why was I so stupid? I make for the door. "Wait!" Christos shouts after me. But I don't wait. I stumble down the corridor and left again, then I'm out the door and running across the lawn and into the shadows of the dark trees beyond. I must get back to my car, but I will have to go the long way around. I am going in the opposite direction.

I climb a bank, slipping on the pine needles under my feet and then collapse behind a ridge and look back at the hotel. I see Kosta pull up, dismount and put his bike on its stand. He takes off his helmet and loops it around the handlebars. Christos rushes out to meet him. I can just make out their frantic exchange. Christos points across the lawn to the forest, where I am hidden. They walk towards me, with determination. Kosta unfastens the holster on his waist and takes out his handgun. The light is behind them – they are in silhouette as they advance towards me, their shadows spreading across the lawn ahead of them.

I suddenly realise that with the light behind them, they will see me better than I can see them. I scurry off to my left, scrambling down a bank, trying to be as quiet as I can. But twigs crack as I rush from shadow to shadow. Trees suddenly loom right in my face. I swerve, keeping my head down, swearing under my breath. Fuck, which way now? I have to keep left, keep going down. But then I find myself in a hollow and I am disorientated. Do I go straight up the other side and risk being seen? Or left again? No, that feels like I would be looping back on myself. I hear their voices approaching and hide behind a big boulder, my shoulder pressed up against the cold stone. I see their forms appear over the ridge, stop, look around and then they come down into the hollow. They are feet away from me.

They are arguing. I hear Lucy's name mentioned. Christos' voice sounds accusatory. Kosta is defending himself, his voice weaselling and high-pitched. Christos is shouting at him, furious now. Kosta's response is stammering, whimpering almost.

Keeping my head low to the ground, I sneak a look. I see Christos push Kosta in the chest, hissing at him. Kosta backs off and then protests, and as Christos shoves him again, Kosta roars and hits Christos over the head with his gun, with the full force of his impotent rage. Christos topples forward, collapses onto his knees and then falls face down at Kosta's feet.

I am stunned. Kosta looks around furtively and then his eyes lock on me. I am surprised to find that I am on my feet. Kosta's eyes pinion me. We are trapped by each other's gaze. Then his expression changes. Something dawns on him. Without taking his eyes off me, he points the gun at his erstwhile employer and pulls the trigger. The gunshot is deafening. In a patch of moon-light, Christos's body twitches. I see it straight away – Kosta killed Lucy. He will shoot me and say I wrestled the gun off him, shot Christos, then he bravely got the gun back off me and he had to shoot me to subdue me – I was out of control. With Christos out of the way, I am the only one who can pin Lucy's killing on Kosta. If he kills me, Kosta will get away with all three murders. I turn and run.

The gun goes off again and I hear the bullet thud into the tree just next to my head. I get over the ridge and scramble through the dense undergrowth. I brush branches out of my way. I can feel my face is being scratched. The moonlight makes harsh shadows. Bushes look like figures crouching. I run blind, bumping into trees, readjusting, stumbling. I run into a clearing. Which way now?

Then Kosta strides out of the shadows into the clearing, his gun pointing straight at me. He must have come around my flank. He aims, his eyes narrow, he sneers.

Then there is a rustling in the undergrowth and a huge wild boar, not in the least extinct, clatters out the thicket, jack-knifing its body awkwardly and at speed, then, head down, with guttural trumpeting, runs straight at Kosta. Kosta squeals like a girl and then shouts his surprise as the pig smashes into him and sends him tumbling backwards. The gun spins out of this hand. I rush forward to grab it, but Kosta has me by the ankle and suddenly I'm tumbling and down on the forest floor, the pine needles rough on my face, my hand inches from the gun. The boar stops, its face inches from mine, its eyes glinting, frightened, vicious. I scream and the animal jumps back in alarm, rapidly jack-knifes again and scurries into the bushes.

Kosta's gun is just out of my grasp. Kosta's grip on my ankle tightens. He pulls me towards him. I kick out with my other foot. I miss. I kick again in blind panic. I hit something this time. I hear Kosta yell. I kick again, harder and hear him grunt. His grip loosens momentarily. I free my leg from his grip and scramble to my feet. But now he is closer to the gun than me. He realises this. We both go for the gun at the same time. He gets his hand to it before me, but I am on top of him, one arm around his neck, my other hand on his wrist. He wriggles violently to get me off him. I lock on. His ear is near my mouth. I take his fleshy ear in my teeth and bite as hard as I can. I fell my teeth go into the cartilage. Kosta screams and struggles. He is bigger and stronger than me. He rolls over onto his back and suddenly I am underneath him. His full weight is on top of me. I struggle to catch my breath. I twist my arm around his neck and squeeze with all my might. But he is too strong for me. He shakes my grip free. I clutch at his face. I feel along his cheek to his eye socket. I feel the soft roundness of his eyeball and dig my fingers in. Kosta yells, grunts, then screams as I feel something tear, something give. I've torn into his eye. I wriggle out from under him. Scramble into the shadows. The gun goes off and a bullet whistles into the trees above my head. He is firing blind.

I slide down another bank of pine-needles into a gully. I crawl on my knees down the gully and then slip into the blackness of a crevice between two boulders. Kosta is screaming insults. He is in pain. How much can he see? His muttering is getting closer. He is on the move. I hear him pass by me, a little above me and then off to my left. I see his shadow cross the gully, then stop. He is scanning for me. He must be able to see something still. I hear him swearing to himself in a low whisper. Then he moves off up the gully and over the ridge. I move tentatively, keeping low, creeping from shadow to shadow. My best bet is to keep him in sight at a distance until I can work out which is the way to Bobby's car.

We are at the bottom of the incline. I see his silhouette at the edge of the treeline. The white pebbles on the beach are illuminated in the moonlight. The sea shimmers beyond. He turns to look back into the forest. Then he trips on something, stumbles and falls, before picking himself up quickly, his gun hand raking the shadows, his eyes frightened. From the vantage of my dark hiding place under a shark-shaped rock, I watch him, his gun pointed into the forest, his face, anguished, looking at the obstacle which made him trip. I think I can make out handlebars. A bike of some sort. Then he is frantically kicking leaves and broken branches over it. I realise what it must be - Lucy's scooter.

This must be the beach where Lucy was killed. This is where her bike has been hidden. Kosta is crying now, frustrated. The tide has washed the bike into view. With a furtive look into the dark shadowed trees, he stops to listen for any sound from me, his quarry. Nothing. He puts the gun in his belt and starts digging energetically with his hands around the bike. He must bury it deeper. I can hear his heavy breathing from where I am.

I leopard crawl around to his right where I see it is more sandy. I see a fallen branch, about a hand-grip wide and two-foot long – a cudgel. I take it carefully, in case it is still attached to something that will rustle or snap and give me away. It is loose. I grip it tightly. Crawl again. When Kosta looks over his shoulder to check if he can see me anywhere, he is looking away from me now. Now I am near the beach and to his right. I must take care to keep out of the moonlight. Kosta has dug his hole. Grunting and wheezing, he lifts up the scooter – he has to put all his effort into it – and drops it into the hole he has just enlarged. He stands upright gasping and puts one hand to his eye – the eye I have damaged. He moans. He takes a handkerchief out of his pocket and wraps it around his eye. Then gets down onto all fours and he starts to bury the bike.

I creep slowly towards his hunched figure, praying I don't stand on any twigs or dry leaves. Kosta is piling whatever he can find on top of the bike. His noise covers any sounds I am making as I approach him, my stick in hand. I get within three feet of him, before he sees my moonlight shadow approaching. He spins around, but not fast enough. I lunge at him and with the roar of a wild animal, I bring the stick down on the side of his head with all my strength. He falls onto his side, his arm raised protectively, his other hand going for his gun. I hit him again. And again. He exhales through his nose and his good eye roll into his head. His hand with the gun comes up and points straight at me. I duck to one side as it goes off. I swipe at his hand with my cudgel. The gun goes off again, this time into the undergrowth. I hit him again. His hand goes down. I stamp on it and feel his arm spasm. I stamp again and his fingers splay… and then relax. His face is squashed to the ground. He is drooling. I stamp on his face. When he groans, I hit him again with the stick. I don't want him getting up. I grab the gun and step back.

Silence. Kosta lies still. I am breathing heavily. My teeth are clenched tight. I have to use all my effort to open my jaws. And breathe. I train the gun on Kosta's prostrate figure.

Kosta starts to groan and pushes himself up onto his extended arms, his good eye unfocused. "Stay still!" I shout. "Don't move! Don't try to get up!" I point the gun at him. I don't know if there are any more bullets. Kosta holds a hand protectively across his face. *He* thinks there are more bullets. That's good. Carefully holding my aim, I reach for my phone in my jeans pocket. Who should I call? If I call the police, will they not protect their own? Cautiously, with one eye still on Kosta, I scroll through my contacts, until I find Antonis's number.

51

Antonis arrives with Panagiotis, two of his officers and two paramedics. I tell them about Christos and one of the policemen goes off with the two paramedics to try to locate him. The other officer bandages Kosta's head. Fuck you, Kosta, you cunt! I think, I hope you have serious pain and that your bruises swell your head to twice its size! His eye, where I clawed him, is a mess. I may have blinded him. I feel no remorse. I feel high. Vindicated. Righteous. He shot Christos. He tried to kill me. He killed Lucy - he must be the one.

Kosta is sobbing and saying something through his tears and snot. His father, Panagiotis, is shouting at him. I tell Antonis what I know. Antonis goes over to Kosta, holds Panagiotis off and tries to calm Kosta down. When Kosta's sobs become a whimper, Antonis questions him. Kosta could claim I shot Christos and then overpowered him, but he keeps his head down and no-one looks at me, so I guess he hasn't done that.

What he *has* done, I find out a short time later, is confess that he killed Lucy.

Perhaps he thought I knew more than I did know. Perhaps he thought Christos had something on him and we'd find it sooner or later. Perhaps he just gave up – couldn't live anymore with the terrible truth.

When the cop who'd gone off to look for Christos returns, without the paramedics and with a sombre look and a shaking of his head, Kosta admits, gulping back his tears, to killing Christos too. He wails, head in hands, rocking himself back and forward, crossing himself, moaning.

What Antonis recounts to me later is that Kosta, having seduced Lucy in the line of duty so to speak, had fallen for her and had become intensely jealous of Christos Papademos, the rich kid, the American, who had taken Kosta's object of desire into his bed. When Lucy had been away for four days and Kosta had worked out she was with Christos, he had come to the Poseidon to have it out with her. He'd found her on the beach, in a manic state, tearing around like a mad person, excitedly shouting in his face her grandiose paranoid delusions, which were *unfair*, according to Kosta and she had humiliated his manhood, taunting him with all the sex games she and her new rich and handsome suitor had been getting up to. He'd slapped her, she attacked him, enraged, he'd first punched her in the face, then when she was on her knees at the water's edge, he had dragged her into the sea, at first just to get her to come to her senses, but as she'd struggled, he held her under, held her until she gave up and he found he'd drowned her.

The workers had all left by then, but he couldn't take any chances. He'd hidden her body further up the beach and covered her with branches and rocks. He waited until Christos had driven off to town later, before searching for Lucy's scooter – he knew it must be there somewhere. He'd found it round the back and had decided to hide it at the edge of the forest where no one would find it, so if anyone investigated, there'd be no clue that Lucy had been at the Poseidon, it would look like she'd driven off of her own volition. He'd meant to get rid of it properly later when the heat was off. But he'd forgotten it there, or had been too frightened or ashamed by what he had done, it had remained there undetected in its shallow grave near the sea.

Later he'd come back in a van he borrowed from a friend, uncovered Lucy's body and had taken it, under the cover of darkness, to the old disused harbour, tied the concrete block to her and thrown her in. Only later did he think of writing a fake suicide note. When I'd started snooping around, he'd thought to take her laptop in case there was anything on it that linked him to her. Then he got spooked and tried to sell the laptop to Christo for the files on the Poseidon - to be sure she hadn't double-crossed them. But even the rich American couldn't break the encryption, and reluctantly, it seemed to Kosta, complaining bitterly, he had parted with one thousand euros, merely for possession of the computer. One thousand euros! - that undid him - that was all Lucy's life had been worth. Then he'd been there when they'd brought Lucy's body out of the sea and he'd seen her disfigured face, he hadn't slept for days, exhausted and haunted, he couldn't go on. He'd loved her, the fool.

Her murder was nothing to do with her job, nothing to do with saving the planet. She was killed for love, the oldest story in the book.

52

The ambulance eventually arrives and the paramedics take Christos's body away under a red rubber sheet. What an ignominious end. All his scheming and manipulation, all his charm and deceit, all for nothing. He will not see The Poseidon open.

We travel back to Agia Sofia, Antonis and I in Bobby's car, the Chief, his two officers and his son, now their prisoner, in the police car. Antonis insists on driving – just as well – the adrenaline has left my body and my hands are shaking and cannot be still. Antonis has agreed, at Panagiotis's request, to be seconded, for the time being, to the Mythos force so he can take statements from Kosta and from me regarding the killing of Christos, the wounding of a police officer (Kosta – my doing) and, before that, the killing of Lucy Discombe. The Chief will let his superiors on the big island know of the events here and will request they send a team to take over in the morning. He cannot interview his own son. But he will take the news of Christos's death to his father, the venerable, Hektor Papademos. That is his duty and he will not evade it. He, the father of the killer, will ask the old man for his forgiveness on behalf of his son. It is a Modern Greek tragedy.

"What a terrible thing for Panagiotis," I say to Antonis as we get into the car. "Not only does have to tell Hektor Papademos of his son's death, but he will also have to break the news to Kosta's mother, his wife. Poor guy."

"Kosta's mother is dead. She died when Kosta was a small boy. Panagiotis brought Kosta up by himself," Antonis tells me. That makes it even more poignant. I feel for the Chief, I even have a twinge of sympathy for the son who grew up without his mother.

We travel in silence with the windows rolled down – Antonis wishes to smoke. The night-time trees float by, ghosts of their daytime selves. The moon drifts behind a thin cloud, with the face of an old man with sunken cheeks and gaunt eyes. Behind us, the lights of the police car follow, disappearing then reappearing as the road unfurls. As we go over the last ridge and see the lights of the town in the valley, Antonis remembers something. "Ah," he says, tapping his ash, "We got back the results of the DNA analysis. The body in the bridge, and Michalis Epistemos – there is no correspondence. There should be at least *some*. So the body in the bridge we can say is *not* Eleftherios Epistemos." He shrugs and we return to our contemplative silence. "So, who it is in the bridge? It is still a mystery."

Antonis parks Bobby's car opposite the police station. The square is empty and our footsteps clatter across the space into the shadows of the awnings at the sides. The police car comes to a respectful stop outside the door to the station and the officers get out, supporting Kosta, who has trouble staying on his legs, so wilted by his shame. His father turns his face away. I suspect he, too, is ashamed, but he must also be torn apart by anguish at the fate that awaits his only son and by his foreknowledge of the life he himself will now lead alone.

We go through to the single holding cell at the back. Jurgen Preissler has heard the commotion and is standing peering out expectantly. One of the officers unlocks his cell and signals for Jurgen to come out. Jurgen Preissler is indeed short and wiry as described, with a shifty belligerent look, as if he is not pleased to have been woken up. Kosta is hustled into the now vacant cell, while the German activist looks on nonplussed. The officer throws Jurgen's holdall out of the cell and it collapses onto the floor outside. "Hey!" Jurgen exclaims indignantly, "Don't do ziss! You break my electric *toosbrush*, you numbskull!"

"You are free to go," Panagiotis tells him in a lifeless voice.

"Go vere? It is the mittel of ze night!" Jurgen complains.

"Go anywhere you like. Just not here. Go. We are very busy now," the Chief says, pushing the activist out the door.

"No apology, no explanations, no *nussing*!" Jurgen whines. "*Ziss* is not *ze* end. Ze Ambassador *vill haf* your guts for garters!" he shouts defiantly as he slouches out into the unexpected night.

I go over to the basin and turn the tap on. I have a strong urge to wash, to cleanse myself. "No!" Antonis shouts, "Don't wash your hand. We must test you for cordite, to see if you fired the gun. Wait," he says and speaks in Greek to the Chief, who gives one of his officers (who I think is Vassilis) an instruction. After a rummage, he finds a kit and sets about swabbing the skin of my hands while Antonis looks on. Job done, I am instructed to wait while the one I think is Vassilis compiles the blank documents they will need to record my statement.

Panagiotis, glancing at the cell where his son is now held prisoner, whispers something to the officer guarding him and then goes out. He cannot further delay the job he has designated to himself, that of breaking the bad news to the relative of a deceased. He must look Hektor in the eye and tell him his son, Christos, his golden boy, is dead. The officer (the one who is not Vassilis) looks in on Kosta and shakes his head sadly. Hours ago, Kosta was his colleague, his boss's son.

Antonis pulls the table into the middle of the floor and arranges two seats on either side. He motions for me to sit. I will write a statement of the events of the night as fully as possible. I will write in English and this will be translated later. I set about doing this, my brain like caked mud, dark and lumpen. I plough into this, relentlessly methodical, straight lines, my words emerging mechanically, precise, without the intense emotions which will throw me off course. Reported speech, no quotations, as if once removed, disembodied. The night's events encapsulated in formal prose, as if I were an observer only and not a participant.

The officer (the one who isn't Vassilis) makes instant coffee for all of us. I notice in the mug for Kosta he puts in three sugars and stirs the dark liquid assiduously, like he wants to be sure to get the warming drink to the right pitch of sweetness for his erstwhile friend and colleague - an act of comforting. As I review what I have written, I hear Kosta gulping down the coffee and then pant with the effort. Then he gags and throws up all he has eaten and drunk for the last day. It spews out and between evacuations, he howls with his despair, until he has nothing left, save for his whimpering. The officer who isn't Vassilis brings a mop and bucket and cleans the cell, then he shuts the door behind him, carefully, like he doesn't want to disturb a sleeping child.

Antonis says I can go, but if I want to, I can wait for him and he will drive me back to Agia Anna when he has finished interviewing Kosta. I don't trust myself to drive Bobby's car, so I tell him I'll wait. I go out into the quiet night of Agia Sofia and amble down to the water's edge, interrupted only by the occasional shadow of a surreptitious cat. The boats in the harbour roll gently on the hint of a breeze. There is the faintest rim of dawn light emerging over the distant mountains. The sea is still silvered by the moon, now sinking lower towards the distant horizon. At the end of the jetty, a fishing boat has its lights on and two grizzled fishermen are offloading their catch of calamari and small fish, murmuring inconsequentially as they work, their cigarette glued to their lower lips, the rich aroma of the nicotine mingling with the tang of the fish and of the open sea. They don't acknowledge me.

I feel, more than ever, an outsider, an interloper. They will not know I have been here nor that I am gone. Perhaps when the light comes up, it will all seem real again. For the moment, I exist in a penumbra of something awful that has happened to someone else.

53

I wake up late the next day. My sleep has been dreamless, but when I wake, my bedclothes are tangled and damp. I let the water from the shower run cold over me as I stand motionless. I dry myself listlessly, brush my teeth, drink down a glass of water, put on a tee-shirt and shorts and go to look for Antonis. It is as though my mind is emptied out, a hollow echo-less chamber. I feel the sun on my skin. It feels good.

I find Antonis coming along the beach towards me. He too has just risen. His face looks slept in, his eyes bloodshot and heavily hooded. He steers me wordlessly back the way I have come. He hesitates at The Seaview, but then decides against it. There are complications there and he needs his coffee first. We go to Yianni's and sit at my usual table.

I can see in Yianni's face that word has travelled fast. He is solemn and respects the silence there is between Antonis and me. He hands us each a menu – it is already lunchtime, I notice with surprise. We order coffee to start and I also have freshly squeezed orange juice – my tongue is like a potato crisp. We study the menu. I try to imagine myself into hunger, but without success. Maybe I should have Soulla's bean soup – easy on the stomach and nutritious. I suggest this to Antonis and I can see his predicament has been the same as mine and he is relieved I have found an easy solution. He puts the menu down flat and sighs deeply.

"Hektor Papademos is in the hospital. When Panagiotis told him the news about his son, he had a heart attack," he says, his hand clasping at his chest. "The poor man. How terrible it must be to lose your only child. Tomorrow they will fly him to the hospital on the big island." He leans forward. "He has called the mother of Michali," (he signals with his thumb over his shoulder to the Seaview) "to come to his bedside. Why, I don't know." He leans back. "But it is strange, is it not? Stavroula Epistemos is not his relative. A married woman, whose husband has just returned to her. The tongues will flap in the mouths of the old women for sure!"

I glance over to the restaurant next door, just as Michalis and Mavros emerge onto the balcony. Michalis claps his father on the back, but it is a gesture more fitting for a friend than a father. Mavros gives a slim smile, hardly a smile at all, but he appreciates that his son is making an effort. It couldn't have been easy for them – Mavros back from the dead, when he wasn't dead at all, to reclaim his dead son (or so he thought) - he had never come back to be with his living one. Michalis must be hurt by that. To find out that there had been a son before him – Michalis didn't remember his older brother and his mother had never spoken of him. For Mavros, to see the son he had left behind, whom he had last seen as an infant. And to find he had a grand-daughter.

Xanthe joins them. She goes to sit on her *Baba's* knee and runs her fingers through his still thick white hair, neatening him up. He smiles at her warmly, folding his arm around her and she talks to him with an amused lilt in her voice that I can just make out. Michalis looks proud of her and how she can make his father fond, how relaxed they are with each other.

The body language between the father and the son, on the other hand, is formal, polite, forced. They are trying to be nice to each other. I wonder what they make of Hektor Papademos's request for Stavroula to come to him – what was there between them?

Yiannis returns with our coffee. "Yiannis," I ask him, "You know about Christos Papademos?"

"*Nai,*" he says. "And now his father is in the hospital."

"He has asked for Stavroula to come to him. Why Stavroula? What's *that* about?" I ask.

He shrugs. "Everybody know Hektor had the eye for Stavroula when she was still a young woman, but he was married man. Hektor's wife very rich woman. He take her money to start his business. What they could do? I think he tell her she must wait so he can divorce from his wife. But then came Mavros and straight away Stavroula marry him. Maybe Hektor is always love her and he wants now to tell her this."

"Hektor's wife is still alive?" I ask.

"*Ochi.* No. She die long ago."

"So why did he not tell Stavroula before?"

Yiannis shrugs once more. "After he return from America, he not speaking with Stavroula. Why?" He shrugs again. "In the church, they not even look to each other. Maybe to do with Mavros? Maybe something was happen. Maybe this is why he call her now."

"Unfinished business," I say with an uncharitable smirk.

"*Nai,*" says Yiannis. "Maybe I find out. Soulla's cousin is work in the hospital," he says as he taps his nose and winks at me, a conspiratorial gleam in his eye.

"You do that, Yiannis," I chuckle. I am now curious about this late intrigue in the lives of these two octogenarians. The spice of local gossip. Maybe I can find a place for it in my last report. I leave in two days' time.

54

Antonis has yet to tell Mavros the results of the DNA test, that the body in the bridge was not his son, Eleftherios. So, after our meal (Soulla's soup, after the first tentative mouthful, is quite delicious – flavoured with cumin and served with thick-cut stone-ground bread), we head over to The Seaview. As we get there, Michalis is rushing out. Stavroula, his mother, has called from the hospital and told him he must come straight away. He searches in jerky glances for something to anchor his worry and puzzlement and then suddenly turns, murmuring to himself, "Ai, ai, ai!" he walks with short urgent steps to his car, where Xanthe waits, frowning, leaning forward in the driver's seat, hands on the steering-wheel, ready to drive him into town.

Mavros watches him go with a look of foreboding. We approach him and Antonis greets him pleasantly. *"Geia sou, kirie Epistimos. Ti kaneis?"*

Mavros gives a non-committal head waggle and murmurs, *"Kala,"* without enthusiasm.

Antonis sits down uninvited opposite Mavros and considers how to begin. Mavros looks apprehensive. He can see something is up. In English (for my benefit?) Antonis tells Mavros that the body in the bridge is not Eleftherios. There was no match with Michali's DNA.

Mavros considers this. His eyes sadden. He purses his lips. Then he says gravely, "Michalis is not my son."

He waits for us to take this in. Antonis explains the result to him again in Greek this time, to be sure there is not a problem of translation. But Mavros shakes his head. "Stavroula was pregnant when I agreed to marry her. The father of the child was a married man. She would not say who." Again he waits for Antonis to comprehend him, before he goes on, "I accepted this arrangement. She agreed to take me in with my son. She gave me everything she owned, which wasn't much, but it gave me a chance to start again. She did this so she wouldn't live in shame." His sad eyes smoulder. "I think the man who made her with child is Hektor Papademos. I think it was Hektor who gave me away to the Military Police, so he could be with Stavroula."

The startling revelation is interrupted by a smoky, "*Kalispera, sintrofe* Mavre!" I look around. I know that voice. It is Calliope, with her husband, Nektarios, in tow, slouching behind her.

Mavros stands to receive her and is rewarded with a kiss on both cheeks. She is full of bonhomie and greets Antonis and me with expansive generosity. She sits down and leaves Nektarios to find a chair to draw up at our table. Then she notices the sombre mood and her face flinches into a respectful curiosity. Mavros's stillness has quiet dignity. Calliope looks from Antonis to me. "Have I...?"

"Calliope knows this story well," Mavros says. "Maybe she is the only one." He looks to Calliope, who in turn looks enquiringly at Antonis and then at me.

"Is this about Stavroula and Eleftherio?" she asks us. When we nod, she looks to Mavros. With a look of resignation, he waves an open hand of invitation for her to tell us what she knows.

"*Endaxi.* I came to this island in 1962. I had only just qualified as a social worker at the National Royal Foundation in Athens, which in those days was the only place in Greece where you could train as a social worker. Social work had only been made a profession the previous year and cautiously so. We were prohibited from any political activity or applying ourselves in a way which may have been thought to give people the idea that they deserved more from the State. There was a strong anti-communist agenda in those days. I was by that stage already in the communist underground.

"When Comrade Mavros came to the island of course I offered to help him settle, not for him only, but for the boy also, for Eleftherio. He had what now we call 'special needs', 'learning difficulties' – he was autistic. He was born in the Civil War in the mountains – the cold and the poor nutrition affected his brain maybe. He grew up without his mother. That too made a difference. But it was not easy. To get help from the State in those days you had to have a 'Certificate of national probity' – I think this is the correct translation. It was to prevent Left-wing people benefiting. It was harsh. And, of course, Mavros and Eleftherios didn't have papers. So I had to pull strings – lie for them – to get assistance for Eleftherio – to get him education – well, it was more sheltered work, training of a kind.

"Then when there was the military coup and Mavros feared he would be arrested, he came to me to ask me to make sure that Eleftherios would be taken care of. He didn't trust Stavroula. Before Michalis came – before she had her own child, she accepted Eleftherio. But after she mothered her own child, she wanted nothing to do with Eleftherio. She said he frightened her, he was not right in the head – that he was cursed by the evil eye and she didn't want the curse to affect Michali. That is right, *nai,* Mavro?"

Mavros nods sadly, remembering. Calliope continues. "After Mavros was taken, Stavroula came straight to me with Eleftherio. 'Take him,' she said, 'he is not my child.' She said she was a poor woman, probably now also a widow and she couldn't manage to look after Eleftherio. The poor boy – he was so ashamed and frightened. What could I do? – we didn't have papers for him. I could get him a small job, but nothing more. He ran away. I heard he was living rough."

"I heard about that," I interpose softly, "From next door – from Yianni." Calliope fixes me with a look that tells me I shouldn't interrupt her flow.

"It was after they brought him to see me in the prison," Mavros says. "I don't know what they did to him or what they told him. This is why he ran away – to hide from them."

"And from Stavroula," Calliope says firmly. "You must believe this, Mavro. The boy was frightened of her. Maybe she told him she would hand him over to the police, I don't know."

Mavros puts his head down to hide his remorse and his bitter anger. Antonis puts a comforting hand on his shoulder. Mavros lets it rest there.

"This made me so angry," Calliope goes on. "I decided I should find out what Eleftherios was owed by Stavroula. She had married his father and had signed over all she'd owned to him. *Nai, Mavro?*" Mavros nods sorrowfully. "I told her if anything happened to her husband, Eleftherios would inherit from him all that was hers. If she'd had a girl, she could have argued that the matrilineal inheritance tradition on the island would have entitled her daughter to her property. But she had a son. So, as it stood, Michalis was the second-born – he would have inherited nothing. I threw the 1959 United Nations Rights of the Child at her. She came from a wealthy family in Smyrna, but she herself was not well-educated. She was terrified of having nothing – she had suffered when her family had lost everything in the ashes of Smyrna. She still thought of herself as a lady, an aristocrat. She'd been humiliated by her father's poverty for so long. She did not want to lose everything. She was desperate. Then she got lucky: Eleftherios disappeared. I looked for him. I couldn't find him. I thought maybe the authorities sent him to Macronissos."

Mavros lifts his head and gives a sigh that is more of a shudder. "I must go to Stavroula. I have been a coward. I have left it all these years. Stavroula will know what happened to my boy. I must do this for his mother, for my Eleni, who is buried in an unmarked grave in the mountains. My son must be buried in a grave with his name on it." He gets up, his movements jumbled by his emotions.

"I will come with you," Calliope says decisively. "I did not do my job as a social worker. It has also been on *my* conscience."

"We will come too," says Antonis.

"And you, Nektario," Calliope says, pointing an exhorting finger at her husband, "You tell for Mavro - one day you will make a fine statue for his boy's grave."

55

Hektor lies propped up on a mound of pillows, his hands folded on top of the bed-clothes, his eyes closed. Even though the window is wide open, there is the cloying smell of old poor people that inhabits the room like a phantom. When we enter, Stavroula is sitting by Hektor's bed, one hand tentatively resting on the covering. She withdraws her hand when she sees Mavros. Michalis is standing at the foot of the bed, his arm protectively around Xanthe, his face scribbled with uncertain emotion. Hektor opens his eyes and looks alarmed to see us, then he shuts his eyes and sighs, and murmurs a resigned, "*Kala. Teleiose.*"

Antonis turns to me and whispers, "He says, good, it is over." We wait respectfully for him to continue.

He opens his eyes again and his impassioned look is directed at Mavros. "Mavro," he croaks and signals for him to come closer. Tears appear in his eyes. "*Signomi, signomi,*" he splutters. "*Sinxorese me. Parakalo.Parakalo.*"

(Later, Antonis will help me understand what happened. I shall record it as best as I can, fitting the words I will have translated later, to the drama I witnessed in that room.)

Hektor is asking forgiveness from Mavros. Stavroula looks alarmed. "Don't say nothing, Hektor!" she hisses at the old man in the bed, his face now drenched in silent tears as he clings to the hand of his old adversary.

"I must, Stavroula. I cannot go to my grave with this knowledge. It has been burning away at my insides for so many years," Hektor says pleadingly. He tries to make her accede, but she turns her head away. Hektor's look is pained, tender. "I must," he says. He wets his lips with a pale tongue. "Mavro... Mavro, Michalis is my son. I am sorry I could not tell you this when you married Stavroula. She was pregnant with my child. Please forgive me. Please understand. I thought it was for the best. Michali, I am so sorry I could not name you as my son before. It could not be done. It would have brought shame to your mother. You should have shared what I had. You would have been a good brother for Christo. But now Christos, my Christos, is…" He trails off into silent weeping. Then he forces himself to go on. "Ai! He is gone. He will never know you as a brother. My poor boy. But now, Michalis, all the family's companies will come to you. I give it to you. The Poseidon, the construction company, all for you. You are my son. Take it, take it." He sweeps all this to his reclaimed son with a tired gesture. His watery eyes try to draw Michalis in. Michalis, dumbstruck, clutches Xanthe tightly.

Hektor waits for some response from Michali, his forehead wrinkling, begging for some small sign of appreciation, some gratitude… some recognition at least. He wants somebody to carry his name forward, someone to benefit from all he has built in his life. Christos is dead. Michalis is now all he has. Michalis, who will now be a very rich man indeed, is paralysed by incredulity. He is only just beginning to come to terms with having a father, come back from the dead. Now he is gaining another. At the expense of his best friend's death, the friend he now finds was his brother. He will bury him as family.

Hektor turns away, dispirited. He looks to Mavros, imploringly and then to Stavroula. "Stavroula, you must tell then about the other one," he says, offering her his hand, his palm upturned - a supplication.

The old lady reaches for his hand. Her face clouds over. "I don't know what you are talking about," she says calmly. "You are ill. You don't know what you are saying."

He lets go of her hand and closes his eyes again, his expression one of deep sorrow. "Please, Stavroula, I cannot go to Heaven, I *will not get to Heaven*, with this on my conscience."

"Poor man, his mind is now confused," Stavroula says, turning to Michalis. Her look is meant to convey her sympathy, but her voice is poisoned with harsh dismissal.

Michalis scans her face and sees her dissimulation as thin as gauze. "Ma, please," Michalis implores her.

"What? You want me to make up some crazy story just to please him?" Stavroula shouts, her pitch rising with disdain. An edge of fear.

"Tell him, Stavroula. For God's sake tell the boy what we did!" Hektor's voice cracks with pain; he is wild eyed with agitation. "Tell him, or I will, Stavroula," Hektor says.

Michalis lets go of Xanthe and goes to stand right in front of her. "Ma? What else are you hiding? All my life you have hidden this from me – that this man is my father. Now you must tell me everything. If you want me to forgive you, you must tell me everything. What is it he wants us to know? What is it he wants *me* to know?"

"Tell him, Stavroula!" Hector croaks weakly.

"Tell me!" Michalis shouts desperately. "No more lies!"

Stavroula looks from her son to her erstwhile lover, and back again, her chin lifted imperiously, her back rigidly erect, holding her poise. Only her dark eyes flit, from one to the other. She is weighing up the odds. She contemplates the lined face of the old man who had loved her as a girl. Hektor's eyes blaze with anguish. Her son, whom she had had done everything to protect, for whom she had given all, is glaring at her as if he is seeing her properly for the first time – the horror in his eyes, the accusation... She cannot hold his fierce stare. She looks away. She sees Mavros, eyes narrowed, a calmness, a sense of inevitability about him. She looks again at her son, at his unrelenting fury.

And then it's all over. Her shoulders slump. She suddenly looks much older, tired. She affects a look of patient sympathy for the old man in the bed... an expression of compassion and irony, which morphs into disdain and then hardens like molten metal cooling into contempt. She shakes her head.

Her voice, when it comes, is chillingly measured. "The other one," she says, "he wasn't right in the head. He was an imbecile. Why should he have had what was mine? - we had so little." She turns on Mavros. "Why did you want my money, my land? You called yourself a communist, but you were as greedy as all the others. Pigs, all of you. I wanted my son, my Michalis, to have what was mine – to have what was ours. But that *bitch*," she hisses venomously at Calliope, "said it would all go to Eleftherio. What would he have done with it? We would all have been poor." She looks at Mavros, defiant again. "How did I know you would come back? I thought you had been executed. That is what your comrades told us."

Mavros holds her glare. "What happened to the boy?" he asks in a level voice, even though it must be taking enormous effort to hold back his rage.

Stavroula looks at him enquiringly, tightening her lips. Xanthe is watching her fearfully. Hektor whispers, "Tell him, for God's sake, Stavroula."

Stavroula scans our faces. She finds no succour. She braces her shoulders back – she thinks about continuing with her defiance… and then she is too tired of it all. The secret she has carried with her for thirty-five years is too heavy to carry any longer. And what for, now? "I poisoned him," she says. "I wanted Eleftherios to be dead and gone. It was better that way."

Xanthe gasps and buries her face in her father's chest.

Mavros just nods. I think he knew all along what had happened to his son.

Hektor's voice is thin but insistent. "I helped her with the body. Because I loved her. I felt I owed her. I had promised to divorce my wife and I didn't. I took the boy's body to the construction site." The old man's voice tumbles from him. "The supports for the bridge, they were hollow steel mesh columns, cages for the cement. I turned on the cement mixer, mixed the cement myself and I poured some into the mould. Then I threw the boy's body down the shaft and poured more cement on top. His body disappeared," he wails, his fist thumping the bed. "May God forgive me!"

Hektor's body rocks in anguish and then his face contracts in on itself, contorted with pain and horror. He clutches at his chest. "Oh, God," he rasps, his face drained of blood, his lips turning blue.

"Get the doctor!" Antonis shouts urgently to no-one in particular. When no one responds, he rushes out to get assistance. Hektor stays upright, holding his chest, eyes tightly shut against the pain. Stavroula looks at him dispassionately. For her, it is as well that he should die for what he has made her disclose. Their secret should have gone with him to his grave.

Mavros steps forward and places a consoling hand on the shoulder of the dying man. Hektor opens his eyes and he looks at Mavros with an expression which could pass as love. He and Mavros hold each other's gaze. I see the forgiveness that Mavros gifts his adversary of old, that Hector drinks in like sweet water on desert dried lips; I see the soft shadow of compassion between the two old men, two fathers who have lost much-loved sons.

****

We are standing outside the hospital later, Antonis and I, having a cigarette, as the night settles. Antonis has formally arrested Stavroula and she has been taken to the police station to give a statement, after which Antonis has instructed that she is to be allowed home on police bail. Mavros has gone off with Calliope. He will stay with her and Nektarios for the time being – he will not be under that same roof as the woman who killed his son.

Before she was taken away, Stavroula decreed that her right to the land on which The Seaview was built, which had reverted to her ownership after Mavros had been absent for five years, was to be for Xanthe. She did not want her son to be afflicted by the bad fortune of having obtained the property by the death of another. She said haughtily, that she wanted the tradition of land being passed from one woman to another down the generations to be continued. She said it as if this had been a good and fitting resolution, that something good had come from something bad. (Or perhaps that had been my charitable imagining of her offering.)

Mavros did not oppose this. He had no wish to have anything further to do with Stavroula and her family. He had got what he had come for.

56

One thing to do before I return to Agia Anna. Antonis will be stuck in Agia Sofia with paperwork. For him, the body in the bridge case is now solved. Soon he will return to Athens. I head off to the pedestrianised street behind the restaurants on the waterfront where all the shops and bars for tourists jostle for small margins. I leave tomorrow on the last flight. In the morning I will see Agapi and let her know my decision.

It is seven a.m. and all the shops are open the traditional hours – they close for the heat of the afternoon and re-open at six. I want something for Eleni, Agapi's mother and of course something for Agapi. The little girl I am sure would love something pretty to wear – she seems to have so little and her clothes are functional and cheaply bought. But I am not sure of her size and don't want any disappointment on her part to mar my last hours with her mother. The children's shop is the first one on my way – they sell toys as well as clothes. Maybe a doll – don't all little girls like dolls? But then what kind of doll? – I am ideologically opposed to Barbie – I'm sure she votes Republican – but the other dolls on sale are seriously retro – and quite fierce looking and unlovable. A soft toy? – cuddlesome, but a bit lame. A child mannequin, with blonde curls and exquisite blue eyes, so lifelike it is faintly macabre, grabs my attention. The dummy is wearing a spectacular silver and gold fairy dress. Eleni would look enchanting in that. If it fits. Maybe a dress after all – she can change it if it's not right. I size it up and it looks about right. It's very reasonably priced. I take it.

What for Agapi's mother? I go into a narrow shop selling hand-embroidered cloths and shawls, lacework, votive candles and badly painted vases and ashtrays depicting mythological events. I pick out a tablecloth which is in a basket of sale items, reduced now because it is the end of the tourist season and the owner wants to get rid of her excess stock. I am to be the beneficiary and in turn can afford to be beneficent to the old lady. The owner asks me who the gift is for – the tablecloth is a popular gift for a bride, she tells me. When I tell her it is for a dear old lady, she chuckles lasciviously and says the old lady will be charmed – it will make her feel young again! She insists on wrapping it in tissue paper and fastens onto it a stick of cinnamon and a sprig of wild flowers "to bring her luck and good health".

Now something for Agapi. I find a jewellery shop two doors down. The window is filled with garish gold and silver and diamante pieces, but inside at the back, in a glass cabinet, are necklaces, ear-rings and bracelets which are more to my unsophisticated Camden Market taste. The first to attract my attention is a spectacular pendant in turquoise and ornate silver, but also contending is a more subdued but equally stylish amber necklace with matching ear-rings. But what I see in my mind's eye as I imagine my lover's face are her green eyes. I know I will want something that will glorify that aspect of her beauty, something in green. Then off to one side I see the large green garnet, cut into an ovoid, held in a filigree of silver vines, on a chain of delicate silver. Perfect. Not cheap, but so right, I splash out. I want my gift to her to be splendid.

I must restrain my excitement and anticipation of their responses and put off dispensing the gifts until tomorrow. I'll see Agapi later tonight and tell her I'll come to her home in the morning. My plane leaves at four.

57

Tonight is my last dinner at Yianni's tavern. I could go to The Seaview, but this would be an imposition I feel – they should not be made to serve after what has happened today. Stavroula will not be at her post at the kitchen entrance keeping guard. Perhaps I'll have coffee there later, so I can see Agapi.

As I take my place at my usual table, (how I'll miss having a "usual table"), Yiannis sidles over, plonks down the bread basket and cutlery and utters his catchphrase, "Unbe-*lieve*-able!" with aplomb. He has had the news from Soulla's cousin in the hospital. "A terrible thing for their family. A tragedy. In Greek, in *Ellenica, 'tra-go-dia'*. You think the old lady she will go to prison? She very old. Soulla say 'Yes, she must'. Soulla was like for Eleftherio. Me, I say maybe." He shrugs. "Michalis is a rich man now. For me, I would not like this money. Good lucks to him. I am happy also for Xanthe. She is new owner next door." He sighs. "But for you, something to drink? For to eat, we have today very good, very fresh red snapper – to grill, with fried potatoes and maybe some *tzatziki* – I make today with lots of garlic – you like garlic?" he asks. I tell him I do. "Okay and maybe a Greek salad. *Psomi. Arketa.* Enough," he says, wiping one hand over the other, to denote "end of". Sounds fabulous. I realise I am now inducted into a love of Greek cousine. I like that. I will now, in my home, cook the food of my father's homeland. I feel my father in me. I feel my father coming home.

"Tomorrow I leave," I tell him.

He looks devastated. "Oh, my friend, why so quick you leave?"

I tell him I have to go back to my job in London. "Okay," he says, "Then for you, from me, I bring for you a bottle of very good wine from Kypros. Beautiful," he says, smacking his lips. "I will drink with you a glass." He goes off at pace, calling out to his wife and signalling to Bobby to bring two wine glasses.

I will miss this family. They have become like family to me. I love their casual generosity, their unaffected warmth and humanity. I will miss Soulla's cooking, for when the red snapper comes, it is cooked to perfection, skins crisp and flavoursome, the flesh moist and yielding, served on a bed of greens, inflected with aniseed and strands of seaweed, perfectly complemented by the excellent white wine Yiannis has gifted me, with which we toast the wonders of Greece.

58

The next morning, I am up early. I swim and shower before setting out for Agapi's house. The day is blue and warm, the sea tranquil, impervious to the dramas of the day before, as if such tragedies are only as significant as one tide. High tides and low tides, the sea is eternal. I carry my bundle of presents under my arm, feeling a lightness of being, a munificence. The time has come.

Agapi is waiting on the path for me. She steps towards me and opens her arms. I take her in my arms and feel her soft body yielding, smell her scent. We walk in silence to her home. I have told her I have presents for her mother and for her child.

Her mother is fussing over the stove when I enter the house. She turns to me and mutters away in Greek, something which Agapi finds scandalous. I smile in return and hand her the gift wrapped in fine tissue paper. The old lady looks shocked that I am offering her a gift. She points at herself, to make sure the gift is for her and when I smile and proffer the package to her, she wipes her hands off on her apron and licks her lips, her eyes gleaming. Eleni comes out of her room to see what her grandmother is so excited about. She watches as her grandmother fastidiously unwraps the tissue paper (Agapi tells me her mother will save the paper as something precious) and finds inside the embroidered table cloth. She holds it open and her eyes shine, she shakes her head in wonder. Then she comes to me and has me bend down so she can kiss me three times.

"Three kisses," I say, amused by her excess.

"This is the tradition," Agapi says. "French and Italians, two kisses, Mythos, three kisses!"

I hold out the package for Eleni. "For you," I say. The little girl wriggles with shyness, then approaches cautiously. Once the package is in her hands, she unwraps it with all the delicacy of a dog attacking a rabbit. She can't wait to see what she has got! Then she goes still when she sees the gold and silver cloth. Carefully, she unfurls the dress and holds it up, her brow wrinkled. She looks to her mother, who smiles and signals for her to go and put it on. She needs no encouragement – she races into the room she shares with her mother, hastily sheds her pyjamas and watching herself in the mirror, climbs into her new dress. She checks herself, front on, then side on, smooths down the folds and then comes back into the room where we are her audience, her face a picture of studious attention. She is worried that if the dress is not seen to be right, it will be removed from her and returned to the shop. Perhaps she thinks it is just to try on, not to keep. But as soon as we cheer and her *Giagia* has chirped, "*Poli oraia, Elenaki!*" her face widens into a glorious grin and she does a swirl which causes the dress to sparkle in the morning light. Her joy, that she has never owned anything as glorious, pricks my eyes. I want to sweep her up into my arms, but she keeps her distance, now with a serious look, a germ of vanity denied. She is, I sense, worrying now that she has something which, if it is damaged or taken, will devastate her. Ah, well…

Then, with a degree of bashfulness, I hand Agapi the felt-covered presentation box which the nice assistant at the jewellery had found for me. Agapi hesitates, then kisses me lightly on the cheek (she must not be intimate in front of her mother) and with eyes bright with expectation, opens the lid. She gasps and extracts the necklace, without raising her eyes to me, ties the chain around her neck. The plump pendant hangs at the apex of her exulted cleavage, the light of the green perfectly matching her enchanting eyes. Mother or no mother, she comes to me and kisses me on the mouth.

The she looks at me seriously. "You are leaving today?" she asks.

"I must," I say. "I have to go back to work."

"You will come back?"

I hesitate. "I will want to, but I don't know if it will be right," I say softly. I look deep into Agapi's sea green eyes. Is she the one? Can it be? If there is anyone who can help me inhabit my Greek soul, it is this gentle woman. "I must have time to think about it," I say, as I take her hand in mine. "I hope it will be."

Agapi's mother senses the conversation (or knows more English than she has let on). She says something to Agapi, who turns to her and then back to me. "My mother says you must remember to come back for the *Psychosavato*, the All Souls' Day, when it is the Springtime – to free the spirit of your friend. You must come back because before then, the spirits will not rest," she says with a wan smile.

I know she is talking not only of Lucy's spirit, but also her own. She is also speaking of mine.

59

Antonis has come to join me for lunch and to say goodbye. For one last time I take my usual table at To Meltemi, with its tamarisk-shaded view of the turquoise sea. The *retsina* is chilled, its scent of mountain pine evokes so immediately this Greece, shade from the harsh sun. We order grilled octopus, which, when it comes, is glistening with lemon juice and coarse pepper and is almost obscenely succulent.

Antonis tells me that last night, after he had done the paperwork for Stavroula's and Hektor's indictments and signed the order for police bail for Stavroula, Calliope had called on him, together they had gone to the harbour. Mavros had decided to catch the late-night ferry back to Athens. He would not say where he was headed. He did not wish to be found. He had done what he needed to do. There was no point in staying. He had left with the quiet dignity that seemed to be his nature. Already Nektarios was working on the drawings for the statue to be placed on the grave of Eleftherio, when the body was returned to the island. Mavros indicated that one day in the future he would return to visit his son's grave, but for now he entrusted his son's entombment to his old comrades.

Word had come from the Mayor this morning that he and the Municipal Council had agreed that it would be fitting, under the circumstances (and politically expedient for the Mayor it must be said), for a statue to be commissioned for the fallen heroes of the Civil War and wars there had been in the island's history, for justice and liberation from oppression. The statue would be called *"Eleftheria i Thanatos"*. Freedom or Death. Eleftherios would be doubly honoured. Nektarios Gavras had been invited to submit a proposal.

He tells me a Forensic specialist had looked at Lucy's computer. All the files had been wiped clean. Did Christos crack the encryption after all? If so, why scrub the files if they were favourable to the Poseidon? Had Lucy been playing a double bluff all along? Had she led Christos along, maybe even sending a misleading e-mail to Radagast to persuade him of her sincerity? Is that why she wanted me to come? – so she could get me to publicise the true story? Will we ever know? The hard-drive is being sent to Athens for further analysis. Something may yet turn up.

Poor Lucy. Her astonishing beauty barricaded from my mind by the insistent intrusion, when I think of her, of my last sight of her, dead and disfigured, cold in a morgue. Will I ever be able to remember her again, as she was - sleeping next to me, that weekend in my flat in London; in Amsterdam, dancing at the Melkweg; beautiful in the spotlight at that fortuitous conference, her life just beginning? Such a tragic life, lived bravely, vibrantly. I had come to Mythos looking for the love of my life. Would things have worked out between me and Lucy? How can I know?

Yet, I found Agapi. Is this love, this feeling of *belonging* she evokes in me? As I left her, she held me to her and made me promise that I would come back in the Spring. We shall see what happens then.

The Inspector and I look out over the settled sea. I turn to study his face, this man, Antonis Ionides, who has become my friend. His eyes are hooded by his deep lids, but he looks content, philosophical. He sips his wine meditatively. We have, both of us, come from far away, to converge on Mythos; soon we will go our own ways. He sees me regarding him and raises his glass to me silently to respect the depth of our bond. He will miss me as I will miss him. It was Antonis who declared to me in the car on the night of Kosta's arrest, "Now you are Greek!" I had drawn blood, I had joined the Struggle. He was acknowledging the mark I had made on the island - I have become a part of the story of this island, part of its history, unspooling into the torturous history of the country, my country now, my Greece. The eternal waves land themselves gently on the shoreline and are gone forever. New waves come.

Some way along the beach, where the surf arcs languorously, I see, at the water's edge, two young people, bare-footed and browned by the sun. The boy doesn't seem to mind that the water dampens the ends of his blue jeans. He does not give way to the tide. The boy says something to the girl and she laughs and moves in closer. She links her arm in his. Her blonde hair catches the light. They move on further down the beach, carefree, in love. Even at this distance, I recognise them by their manner, by their shapes. Bobby and Xanthe. They walk together, hand in hand, as if this is the way it was meant to be and always will be.

GLOSSARY.

andantes	partisans
archaiologoi	archeologist
arketa	enough
asteri mou	my star
baba	grandpa
baklava	dessert made with pastry, leaves, nuts and honey
demosiografos	journalist
dhen kataleveno	I don't understand
dhen peirazei	It doesn't matter
dhespeneedha	miss
dio kafedes – metrio	two Greek coffees- medium sweet
dolmades	stuffed vine leaves
efcharisto poli	thank you very much
ela	come here
eleftheria	freedom
eleftheria i thanatos.	freedom or death.

Ellinika	Greek (language)
ena	one
ena lepto	one moment
endaxi	okay
fascistis	a fascist
fascisti skata!	fascist shit!
file mou	my friend
fiisiika!	of course!
geia sou	hello
giagia	grandma/nan
hero polee	pleased to meet you
ise poli oraia	she is very beautiful
istoria	history
kafenion	coffee bar
kala	well/good
kalimera	good morning
kali orexi	bon appetit
Kalispera	good afternoon/evening

kapitalistes	capitalists
kirios	Mr
loukoumades	doughnuts
kommounistika	communist
kori mou	my daughter (affectionate)
logariasmo.	the bill
malakas	wanker
mia bira	one beer
milate Anglika?	do you speak English?
milate Ellinika?	*do you speak Greek?*
mnemosyno	memorial
mono	only
nai	yes
nero	water
ochi	no
parakalo	please (also: 'with pleasure')
paterouli mou	my daddy darling
patriotis	patriot

pio arga	very slowly
philoxenia	a love of strangers; hospitality
poli oraia	very beautiful
Pos se lene?"	what is your name?
proika	dowry
psomi	bread
Psychosavato	All Souls Day
rebetika	sad folk songs, described as the Greek 'blues'
retsina	a fragrant white wine infused with pine needles
riso	rice
rousfeti	bribes
se parakalo	if you please
sigga-sigga	in time
solo	by itself
souvlaki	grilled meat served with flatbread and salad
signomi	sorry
sintrofe	comrade
Sinxorese me	forgive me

sosialistes	socialists
Sti zoi!	to life!
taverna	*restaurant*
teleiose	it's over
ti?	what?
ti kaneis?	how are you?
ti thelete?	who is it?
theo	uncle
trothotiz	traitor/quizzling
yammas!	cheers!